A
BOOK
OF
ENDINGS

by Deborah Biancotti

First published in Australia in August 2009
by Twelfth Planet Press
www.twelfthplanetpress.com

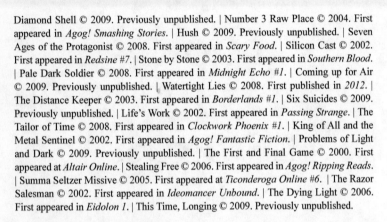

Edited by Alisa Krasnostein and Ben Payne
This collection © Deborah Biancotti,
              Alisa Krasnostein and Ben Payne
Cover by Nick Stathopoulos
Design and layout by Dianne Bateup
Typeset in Myriad Pro, Times New Roman and Garamond Premier Pro

All stories copyright © Deborah Biancotti

National Library of Australia Cataloguing-in-Publication entry

Author: Biancotti, Deborah.
Title: A book of endings / Deborah Biancotti ;
                     editors, Alisa Krasnostein, Ben Payne.
Edition: 1st ed.
ISBN: 9780980484151 (pbk.)
Notes: Bibliography.
Other Authors/Contributors:
                     Krasnostein, Alisa.
                     Payne, Ben.
Dewey Number: A823.4

The editors would like to thank Dianne Bateup, Nick Stathopoulos, Tehani Wessely, Joanna Anderton, Kate Williams, Amanda Rainey and Cat Sparks for their assistance in producing this book.

ACKNOWLEDGEMENTS

It seems fitting for a book with this title to start backwards.

So to you, the readers: thank you. Same again to the retailers, printers and the smart, hawkeyed proofers. To Dianne, for clean, careful, patient layout. To Graham and Rob for taking the time to not only blurb this book but to actually read the stories inside (my promise of several beers wasn't quite enough to convince them to add their names to this cover!). To Nick, for the cover: it's wonderful, beautiful, perfect. To Lauren, for helping me articulate what I wanted the book to look like. To Justine, for the warm and witty introduction (heck, you make me want to read me). To editors Ben and Alisa for thinking these stories through again and again (and in a couple cases, again!) and making them better than they had a right to be. And to Alisa for having the crazy, insane idea to publish this book in the first place. To the people who encouraged me early and often in my career, and the people who still remember to do it now when I need it (and sometimes when I don't, but I just want to hear it). To the international Spec Fic community and the Australian local writing scene for making me feel welcome then and now. To my family, for knowing when to push, when to celebrate and when to shut up.

And to Chris, for everything else that everyone else hasn't been able to do for me.

Thank you.

Contents

Introduction

I don't know about you but I always skip introductions. You should skip this one. Because what I've written here is a lot less interesting than Deborah Biancotti's stories themselves.

In fact, if you're smart enough to pick up a book of Biancotti's stories, then you're way too smart to be told how to read them. So off you go! Go read them and then come back.

I'm pretty certain that's what you did in the first place, because *everyone* skips introductions. And you're only here so you can disagree with all the rubbish your humble introducer has spouted and mock her misreadings.

Well, I have news for you. There are too many ways to read Biancotti's stories to mock me properly. That's what I love about them. They're spare, uncertain, unresolved, leaving themselves open to a dozen explanations. But all the while managing to be full of pathos and angst and wry humour.

Not as much humour as Biancotti herself, though. She's someone who can see the wry and absurd in everything. She's pretty much always laughing. Yes, sometimes at us. (Well, okay, mostly at me.) But always with reason. She's one of those people who enjoys the absurd and can extrapolate from it. The worlds Biancotti sees are not the same ones most of us see. Lucky she writes, eh? That way we can get glimpses at her many and varied worlds.

As you've already noticed while reading ahead, some of what she sees is not wonderful. Worlds with hardly any water (wait, don't we already live in that one?), where the rich and overly cosmetically–altered determine the lives of their carers (ditto), with human brains that outlive their bodies, housed in animals and obliterating their consciousness (not there yet), where it's almost impossible to distinguish between fantasy and mental illness, between the real, the surreal, and the allegorical.

Many of her stories have a strong tug of melancholy. Of longing for something that is not here, but possibly on the other side of here, tucked away, obscured by the here we're trapped in, by the screaming in our heads. Like the door in "Diamond Shell":

> "I figure," said the man, "the door took her into the centre."
>
> Shel couldn't help herself.
>
> "Of …?"
>
> He twitched.
>
> "The heart of things. The centre of this place."
>
> "What in God's name," said Shel, "are you talking about?"
>
> "She found a way out," he said. He added thoughtfully, "Or a way in."
>
> She was about to give him a piece of her mind when he hushed her. Held a finger against his lips and whispered around it.
>
> "Can't you feel it?"
>
> "Feel what?"
>
> "You have to be quiet," he said. Apart from the exasperated scream in her head, she was quiet.

Isn't that what all the best writing does? Open up our understanding of the everyday?

Biancotti does that over and over again in pared down prose and in conversations that slide into the absurd and back out again. I could read her dialogue all day long. And now you get to do so too. Instead of having to hunt these gems down in sundry magazines and anthologies on and offline, as I have, you get to hold them all in your hand. Together. The way they were meant to be read. I envy you.

Enjoy!

Justine Larbalestier

July, 2009

I. End of Days

Diamond Shell

People without walls learn to avert their eyes.

1. Last Day: Shel

The phone was ringing and that wasn't right. She squinted at the clock. It seemed to say 0280, and that couldn't be right either.

She fumbled for the handset, for the light, for the edge of the bedside table so she could navigate her way around the glass of water to where the phone—

She had it.

"Hello?" she croaked.

"Shel?" said the voice. "Did I wake you?"

It sounded querulous, uncertain, more a whisper than a full noise. She hadn't been able to make out the caller ID.

"Of course you fucking woke me," she said. "It's…" She checked the clock again. "After two."

There was a pause and then the tone went flat. Had they hung up?

Christ.

They'd hung up.

She fumbled for the lamp. The weak blue light of the phone screen wasn't enough in the middle of the night. Too blurry for her eyes to make out. Seriously, the middle of the night — she should just ignore it. Probably a wrong number anyhow.

She flipped over to the received calls and read the most recent one. It said Mish.

"Shit," she said.

She hit the call button. Engaged. She flipped the phone closed, opened it, hit the call button again. Engaged. Well, who the hell was Mish calling now? Two o'clock in the morning, for God's sake. It took eight minutes to get through. By then she was awake.

"Yeah?"

"Mish, shit, did you just call? Are you okay? You sound terrible. What's up?"

Her voice was still thick with sleep. So was her head. Something wasn't adding up, and it wasn't just that Mish wasn't the kind of person to call—

"It's not Mish," said the voice. A tremulous catch on the last syllable. "It's Ace."

Oh, great.

"Ace? Fuck," she said. "What are *you* doing with Mishi's phone? Where is she?"

Ace took a breath, or gave a sigh, or did whatever deadbeat junkie losers did when they didn't have a good answer.

"She's gone," he said. "She's… gone."

Shel was already cold, sitting up out of the bedsheets, back against the bedhead, free hand rubbing at her scalp, trying to force some wakefulness out of her skull, or into it. She was already cold, but that made her shiver.

What the hell Mish had ever seen in this no-good—

"Gone," she said carefully, "where?"

"Just gone. All her stuff's here, but—"

"Where's here? Where are you?"

"Mishi's place."

"Stay the fuck there," she said, "I'm coming over."

The cabbie knew dick about Pyrmont. Not a surprise. Pyrmont only figured on a cabbie's radar when there was a casino pick-up to be had. Nowadays Pyrmont was a backwater. Boatloads of migrants had passed through here in the fifties, arriving in Sydney with hope and glad hearts. Now hope was limited to what you could afford to drop into a slot machine. Or couldn't.

An anachronistic village on the arse of Sydney's only casino. A shag on a rock.

She gave the cabbie directions to Mish's apartment complex and handed him a twenty.

"Keep the change."

To his credit, he could at least follow instructions.

They pulled up on the corner opposite the cluster of high-rise apartments. On the street was an old man in a three-piece, skin pink all over his head, no discernible hair anywhere else on his body. Casino refuse, Shel figured. It took her a moment to realise he was urinating unselfconsciously into the gutter, the stub of his pink penis wrapped in both hands.

"You right?" she said, allowing a sneer into her voice.

His suit shone at knees and elbows. A dribble of piss escaped him and he turned to Shel, his lower lip sagging and his eyes like uncooked egg whites.

He nodded dumbly.

"Then stop pissing in the street," she suggested.

He muttered something that was lost in a thick accent and a drunken mumble. But he accompanied the noise by releasing one of his hands to give her the finger.

"Charming!"

She buzzed the number for Mish's apartment, buzzed and buzzed and muttered, "C'mon Ace" under her breath until the door finally clicked open. She shoved through into the too-bright, tiled foyer, and out the other side into a dark courtyard. There were five high rises in this complex. Mish's was the next one on the right.

2. Two Days Earlier: Mishi

Mish had moved to Sydney to be anonymous. Moved from a small sugar-farming town in North Queensland. Moved because in Halifax — her home town — there was no such thing as your business and my business. Everything was everyone's business.

Here the city's noise and bustle kept everyone else preoccupied. There were more people, but there was more privacy too. She could lie down in the middle of the road and no-one would do anything except politely look away.

She liked it like that.

"I'm sorry," said Mishi, "what?"

"I was talking about being invisible," said Shel.

"Right."

They were outside eating lunch in the grey of a city weekday, concrete and cement bookending the space where they sat with their salads on wide white plates.

Mishi wondered how anything could retain its whiteness in the leaden city air. She'd been starving before. Now she toyed with her food, smearing it around the plate. She hated eating here, outside with the thoroughfares on two sides, but it was one of the few places left where Shel could smoke. Another thing Mishi didn't like.

Shel was hard-edged, lost inside herself, calloused from hard living. But calloused in a good way, so she said. Calloused like a musician's hands. Toughened enough that she could produce something beautiful. That was Shel's spin on things.

"It's one of the drawbacks of a growing population," Shel said. "So many people wind up feeling, you know. Invisible."

She punctuated the statement with a plume of grey smoke and a wave of her cigarette.

"I like it," said Mishi.

Shel laughed. "Only you would *like* being invisible!"

Mishi didn't reply, so Shel added, "Do you know the percentage of women in the population of Sydney? Fifty-eight! Fifty-eight percent of all inhabitants are women. And single women outnumber married ones. So our odds are—"

"By how much?"

Shel hesitated. "Which bit?"

"Single to married. How much?"

"Oh," she waved her cigarette again. "I can't recall. What's it matter? The outcome's the same. Our odds are bad, Mish baby."

Mishi pushed salad around her plate with an oversized fork. There was no point arguing with Shel. It wasn't about the statistics or the difficulty or the inevitability of everyone else's failure. For Shel it was about the preciousness of her own imminent success.

"You're never short of a date, anyhow," Mishi said, supplying exactly the phrase she knew Shel was looking for.

Shel rewarded her with a smile. "Ha! Thanks, doll."

Mishi left most of her lunch uneaten, so afterwards she paused to pick up a sandwich in a convenience store. The label on the egg-and-lettuce promised "Made Daily", and then noted an expiry date. She took it to the checkout and raised it towards the smiling man behind the security screen.

"This expired yesterday," she said. "Do you give a discount?"

Steel security wires separated the man from his customers. Wide enough to let convenience products through, but not so wide that crazies could launch themselves at the till. She passed the sandwich through the wires so he could check the date.

"I can't sell you this," he said. "I'm so sorry."

He kept smiling while he said it, inserting the sandwich into some hidden space under the bench.

"I don't mind," said Mish. "I'll pay full price."

"Dan will fetch you another," said the man.

"There weren't any other egg sandwiches," she explained.

"I'm so sorry."

Dan was a skinny teenager with long arms, his elbows the widest part of his body. He returned holding a new Made Daily. Mishi took it without looking at it, paid full price, and carried it home still snug in its plastic skin.

Only when she was home, cross-legged on the floorboards did she pull the sandwich out. Chicken marinated in sweet chilli. She didn't like chilli.

She took a few bites anyway and stared out the French doors to the city beyond.

She liked the city best this way. Under glass.

Shel called her an anathema. She lived in the inner city, but so high up she felt out of reach of it. She could be anywhere in the world, hanging high above the accents. There was a sameness to cities like this one, but you had to be inside them to find it.

The casino squatted to the right of her field of vision like a black beetle on the water, its vibrant neon lights describing a wave along its roof. Part of the developers' plan to fit the casino into its environs. Symbolic of the harbour or some other cliché. That's how it'd been sold to the local residents anyway.

Mishi didn't mind the building. It was this kind of incongruity that gave the city its character.

She liked everything about the city. Liked its walls and its protective layer of noise.

3. Last Day: Shel

Upstairs on the twelfth floor, Ace was crying. Shel fought the urge to tell him to *snap out of it*. She was always fighting that urge.

One day she'd lose the fight and start shouting *snap out of it* until the world exploded.

He was sitting on the floor by the French doors of Mish's apartment, caught in a spool of pale glow from the city outside. The apartment was small, like a bunker, the view from the balcony its only selling point.

Shel crossed to where Ace sat. Beside him were Mish's phone, handbag, keys.

"What's going on, Ace?"

He lay against the wall like a crumpled doll, one knee up, hands loose in his lap. He whimpered but didn't answer in any verbal way she understood.

Shel backtracked, checked the bedroom, checked the bathroom. Both rooms empty, both painted in neutral white and beige. Both barely big enough for the furniture in them.

She swore for several seconds, then rounded on Ace again.

"What's going on?"

He turned to look out to the sky.

"She's not coming back, not this time."

She fought that urge again.

"You gotta help me, Ace. Help Mish."

She put one hand on the wall to steady herself, or stop herself from hitting him clean across the face. The wall was warm.

"How long since you seen her?" Ace asked.

"Uh," said Shel, "three days, maybe. We had lunch."

She brushed her palm along the wall, looking for the source of the heat. There wasn't anything that could heat an apartment from the walls. She knew that. She was a fan of architecture. Just like she was a fan of art and innovation and financial management and survival. Modern living made her a fan of all these things. She had to be, just to keep up. Just to get by.

"What about you?" she asked. "When did you last see her?"

"Not for weeks." He looked up at her. In the light from the casino she could see his eyes were puffy and pink.

She should probably feel sorry for him.

Ace was a weedy, overgrown kid who still dressed in skateboarding gear and hadn't yet acknowledged his receding hairline. He moved through jobs faster than Shel moved through men, and — just like Shel — he liked a certain type. He liked jobs in the entertainment industry. What most surprised Shel was that he kept getting them.

"Why are you here tonight, Ace?" she asked.

He shrugged, head lolling against the wall.

"How'd you get in?" she snapped.

"I never gave her keys back," he said.

Shel hesitated.

"Can you feel how warm it is in here?"

"Sure," he choked.

He pressed a palm to his eyes and sobbed. Crying for himself, Shel decided. Crying because he was too useless to know what to do except call someone who'd never liked him in the middle of the night to sob to about his missing ex-girlfriend.

"I'm calling the police," she said. "You got anything you want to tell me first?"

Behind his hand, he shook his head and sobbed.

The cops, when they arrived, were detached. Kind, but unpanicked. They'd seen stranger things, they assured her, and would be more than willing to list Mish as one of the city's missing. But beyond that they had nothing to offer. There was, after all, no evidence of a crime. No theft, no marks of violence, no goodbye note and most importantly, no body.

"You could take him in for questioning," Shel suggested.

She indicated Ace with a jerk of her chin. He was sitting on the lounge beside the other officer, torso almost concave in the soft upholstery.

"We could do that," the cop confirmed, "if we had reason."

"You could check security footage, right? See if she left any time recently, without her purse."

The cop was patient. "We could," he said. "If we had cause."

Shel, for once, had nothing to say. She was tired, confused, and the sun was still a couple hours off.

"Some people," said the cop *sotto voce*, "fake their own disappearance." He paused to let that sink in. "She maybe have something going on in her life that would cause her to consider that?"

Who doesn't? Shel thought. The deadbeat ex-boyfriend, the married man she was sleeping with, the no-hope job, the inflated mortgage for the apartment with no ventilation and the expensive view outside its French doors.

"No," said Shel. "I can't imagine."

4. Two Days Earlier: Mishi

Mishi had a set of cards. Long, narrow cards with meditative reminders on them. "Harmony" said one card. "Peace". "Worth". "Light". She shuffled them and drew out three to meditate on. Three was a random number. Meditation allowed room for the random.

This day she drew out "Adventure". "Surrender". "Serenity".

She lined the cards up on the floor and stared until her vision blurred to grey grit. She tried to find the way to inner peace. The escape, the surrender. The serenity.

5. Last Day: Shel

"I'll keep the keys, then," Shel said.

The cops looked to Ace, and she looked to Ace, and Ace looked back between them and shrugged.

"I'll need your name," one of the cops said.

They let her scour the apartment for a suicide note, searching all the drawers and the bedroom cupboard where most of Mish's stuff was crammed in fragile towers.

"Let me know if she comes back," Ace said as they ushered him out.

If. Not when.

They caught the lift together, uncomfortably cramped in a space that only just met building regulations.

"You need a lift someplace?" one cop asked.

"No," said Shel. "But he does."

Ace gave her a nonplussed look.

"Thanks," he said.

She waved goodbye outside the building and pretended to walk away. Once they'd left she crept back to the apartment complex, pacing it out, looking down sidestreets and going so far as to walk to the corners, scouring the spaces beside the parked cars and the insides of the cars themselves.

She didn't know what she was looking for. Mish, of course. Or some sign of her. A shoe, a bracelet, a hairpin, for God's sake. Anything.

There was nothing to be found, or if there was, she couldn't tell who it belonged to anyhow.

She circled back to the front of the apartment complex.

"Got any change, love?"

Shel was so intent on the ground she nearly walked right past him. It was his feet she saw first. They were bare but so covered in grime she figured at first he was wearing brown socks. He was homeless, she realised. Coat ripped at every seam, trousers so full of muck they could stand upright on their own.

"No," she said out of habit. "Wait, sorry."

She fished some coins from her pocket.

The man held out a hand. His palm, like the rest of him, was dirty.

"Thanks," he said. "Decent of you."

His voice was too loud, and he punctuated his polite statements with a bob of his shoulders. Like he was reciting something he'd learned a long time ago. He had a wiry beard and hair that stood up on end. He looked fifty but probably wasn't.

She went to move away but a loud exclamation from the man stopped her. Tourette's, she realised, noting the involuntary roll of his head and the click-click-clicking sound of his tongue.

"Not mine," he said, "not mine, not-mine."

"Sorry?" Shel said.

He was trying to hand her something, plucking it from the palm where she'd laid her change.

"Not mine," he said again, and his posture relaxed. "You gave me your key accidentally."

"What? No, I didn't."

Shel took the key and turned it over between her fingers. She felt in the pocket where it had ostensibly been, but found no imprint, no supernatural sign that the thing had ever rested there.

"I don't think it's mine," she murmured.

It was small and bright, like the key from a little girl's journal. It took her back. Afternoons on a window seat, rain outside, adults in other rooms. It was a long time since she'd felt like that. Hidden, secretive, lost in her own world.

The homeless guy shrugged and turned away.

"Tell me," she called, "you around here much?"

She moved towards him.

"Sure," he said. "Sometimes. More down by the casino. People going in, they sometimes think it's lucky to give money to a bum."

With a laugh.

Shel pointed back to the apartment complex.

"You seen a woman here recently, come out of the building?"

The homeless guy looked at her like she might be crazy.

"In the last two days," she persisted. "Short. Long dark hair. Wears trousers with oversized shoes and, and shirts with high collars. Even in summer."

Recognition was streamlining the man's face, smoothing out his premature wrinkles.

"You a friend?" he asked.

"Yeah, I'm a friend. You've seen her, right?"

"Maybe."

"Where'd you see her?"

He shrugged, looked to his dirty feet, looked away.

"You're not in trouble, I just need to know where she is."

The man shook his head and then his neck dissolved in a series of ticks and jerks. His hand fisted around the coins she'd given him. She waited silently, pretending more patience than she had.

When his attack subsided, he said, "I can't explain it."

"Sure you can."

"I can show you," he said. "But only because you've got the key."

"The — right. I've got the key."

She held it up so he could see it.

"Show me then," she prompted.

He turned and walked along the dark street, and she followed.

They walked the perimeter of the apartment complex, signified by a smooth eight-foot fence. Faux cast iron poles every half-foot, the tops bent inwards to make climbing impossible. With a rope you could drag yourself to the top, but you couldn't easily get over to the other side. And you sure couldn't get back out.

The homeless guy banked where the fencing parted from the sidewalk. He followed it around through a full tropical planting of tall ferns and an uneven groundcover.

Shel kept following. Nearly rolled her ankle a couple times, but managed to keep up. Just. The figure in front of her disappeared behind hanging palm leaves. She had to duck to avoid their recoil. She kept one hand on the fence while she followed, trailing her fingers along it. Tried not to imagine snakes and other monsters in the plants with her. Tried not to think about what it would be like to be dragged through here, or pushed or kidnapped.

Tried not to think about the fact she was following some stranger into the dark. The city, with its instant access to all parts of humanity, had made her nonchalant. Her mother would be horrified to see her here like this, alone but for a man she didn't know and the congestive anonymity of the dark.

Her ankle rolled again and she let out her breath in a hiss. In front of her the homeless guy didn't even slow.

"Hey, what's your name?" she called.

He didn't answer.

She stumbled to keep up and almost bumped into him when he stopped.

There was no noise except for the faint heartbeat of traffic and the more immediate sound of the wind. From here the dense foliage obscured even the power of the city lights. She could see the eastern edge of the apartment complex, the edge that fell away into the ocean.

She could feel the ocean winds on her skin and smell salt and tropical plants. It felt wrong, to be perched on the edge of a city and feel like you were in the middle of a jungle.

The wind ripped around them, through the trees, pulling at Shel's jacket. She folded her arms against it. In the moonlight she could just make out the dirty arm of the homeless man pointing.

"Your friend," he said, "that her apartment?"

Shel followed his hand.

"Which one do you mean?" she asked to be sure.

The man twitched as he counted.

"Third one down."

"Which building? Which side?"

He explained. She had to concede he was right. That was Mish's apartment. But from here there was barely anything to be seen. Only the tops of the French doors were visible over the brick balcony. A rectangle of Mish's ceiling, the light fixture on the balcony. She stood on her toes to be sure.

"Did you see something there?" she asked.

He nodded.

"When?"

"Two nights back."

When he failed to continue, she prompted him.

"And what the fuck," she asked, "did you see?"

"No need for the language," he said.

He gave her a hurt look. But in the sweep of shadow and wind it only served to deepen the darkness under his brow and exaggerate the curl of his lip.

"Sorry, sorry," she said quickly. "Sorry. Listen! Tell me what you saw."

He nodded, obliged.

"The woman in the apartment. The woman with long thin arms and small shoulders and hair that was straight and black and—"

"Yes," said Shel. "What was she doing, when you saw her?"

He chewed like he had a mouthful of cud.

"Opening a door."

A pause. Nothing but the wind and the night to fill it.

"Is that it?" she asked.

He nodded.

"She went through it," he said. "And she never came back.'

Shel fought the urge to run back to the apartment. It couldn't be true, her adult brain knew that. She'd looked in every room and the cupboard, too. It wasn't like the apartment afforded many places to hide. There weren't that many doors. The front door, the bedroom, the bathroom, that was it. Maybe the cupboard doors counted, but as small as Mish was, Shel doubted she was curled up in a cupboard somewhere.

Still, when she thought of it her heart leapt into her throat. What if, against all sense, Mish was curled like a shell in a cupboard in the kitchen. What if she was rolled, foetal-like and calcified, rocking in a grave behind the—

She pushed the images aside.

"I figure," said the man, "the door took her into the centre."

Shel couldn't help herself.

"Of…?"

He twitched.

"The heart of things. The centre of this place."

"What in God's name," said Shel, "are you talking about?"

"She found a way out," he said. He added thoughtfully, "Or a way in."

Shel was about to give him a piece of her mind when he hushed her. Held a finger against his lips and whispered around it.

"Can't you feel it?"

"Feel what?"

"You have to be quiet," he said.

Apart from the exasperated scream in her head, she was quiet. Her hair caught in the wind and she had to pull it off her face and hold it in a fist at the back of her head.

"You have to be *really* quiet," said the homeless guy. "Inside and out. Like you're meditating."

"Meditating?" she said. "The fuck?"

It was a knack she figured she didn't have. But since nothing else was forthcoming, she silenced herself and waited, watching the homeless guy. If it wasn't for Mish, she wouldn't be out here, standing in the midst of this, this damned darkness, this craziness.

If it wasn't for Mish, she wouldn't have tried. And maybe that was true of a lot of things. Mish made her feel anything was possible. That's why they were friends.

She stood and shut her eyes, trying for stillness.

"It's all about what you're prepared to witness," said her companion. "See?"

No.

She focussed on the glint of city lights on the water, the echo of traffic. She focussed on the meniscus of light where the night sky bled out over the lumps of buildings and bridge and light.

She was quiet enough and still enough for long enough to finally understand what he meant. Perched out here above the ocean, she could feel it. Something ancient and lost, something whole but with a missing piece at its heart. She felt the dread rise from the earth beneath her feet and crawl up her legs, making hollows in her skin.

She thought she was going to be sick.

Shel turned and stumbled from the space, falling more than once to her knees. Something was eating the space behind her. She had to pull herself along the fence to stop from being dragged backwards. She kept moving, the stink of squashed leaves and ground beneath her. It smelled wrong.

When she broke into the light of the street she stumbled, nearly into the path of a white minibus. She tripped backwards and fell, landing hard on the gutter.

"Stupid bitch!"

There were shouts and jeers from inside the bus as the rest of the dozen occupants joined in. Their echo added to the reassuring perfume of fuel fumes.

Shel got to her feet uncertainly. Her hip ached where she'd landed on it in the gutter. Her knees were scraped and raw. She was shaking all over, so hard her teeth were chattering.

She kept her back to the road and faced the dark space where the homeless man had led her. There was no sign of him. He was probably watching her from the dark. He would probably always be watching her.

She thought she would never be free of his eyes ever again. He had seen right into her. And the city with its mega-watt load of noise and energy and its million babbling examples of humanity had climbed right into his gaze after her and drilled into her core.

He'd been right. She could feel it. The whole fragile sugar castle of the city, with nothing for its foundations but two hundred years of loss.

6. *Two Days Earlier: Mishi*

Mishi had thrown away the other half of the sandwich. It was one am. She couldn't sleep and the meditation wasn't helping. She couldn't clear her mind. How desirable was that, anyhow? She'd spent a lifetime cultivating this mind. Clearing it was the last thing she wanted.

She roamed the narrow edges of the apartment. Looking for something, looking for—

The lights on the roof of the casino pulsed reassuringly. Always made her feel like there was life nearby. Something going on. People, if she needed them. Sometimes she went and sat in one of the bars, taking in the noise. She never stayed long.

But not tonight.

She sat back on the floor by the doors and wrapped her arms around her waist. To hold herself together. Figured she'd ride out the evening, wait for morning.

It was cold, with the night air dribbling off the harbour into her apartment. She leaned forward so her elbows covered her knees. For warmth, she told herself. A posture of obeisance to the world outside her window.

Strange.

Before her in the floorboards, a small key was caught. Angled into the gap in the wood point-first with only one round edge protruded.

She dug at it with a thumbnail, working it out of the wood. A small plain key, bright and practically weightless. She turned it over and over in her hand.

"Never seen you before," she murmured. "Where'd you come from?"

In the buzz of distant noise her voice felt wrong. She kept it to herself after that.

The key was light. She could feel neither its temperature nor weight. Was it metal? She tapped it against her forehead, trying to get a sense of it.

Nothing.

She bent her nails against it, trying to prove it was real.

The key defied her.

She dropped it on the floor, listening to the *ding* it made against the wood. Pushed it back and forth on the boards beside her meditative cards.

She wanted to feel something.

Adventure, she thought. *Surrender. Serenity. Like the cards said.*

She squeezed her eyes tight and tipped forward, bowing her head. She tipped and tipped over the key, bending at the waist, anticipating the smooth, cool floor on her forehead. Surrender. It was an escape, a release, stomach on her thighs, forearms over her head, face towards floor.

Serenity.

She tipped forward with a sense the floor would catch her.

When it didn't, there wasn't even time for surprise. Only a pure static feeling like emotional white noise.

She spiralled through the floor and out of reality like she was falling through a trapdoor. In one swooping gesture she was released to live free between the bones of the city.

Number 3 Raw Place

"It's new," Ted apologised.

The bank clerk stared flatly ahead. "Never heard of it."

Seated behind perspex, she was blurred around the edges like a crayon drawing.

"Maybe because we're the first to move in?" Ted offered.

The clerk didn't care. She pushed a thin piece of paper under the perspex and it came out sharp. Clean and white; not blurred at all. He was surprised.

"Should I fill this in?" he asked. He smiled, encouraging her to smile back.

She didn't. She just kept staring; the thick lines of her eyes unmoving. Ted wondered if he should take the form to a bench, or fill it in right there. Did she have to witness his signature? He looked around to see what others were doing, but there was no-one else. So he wrote where he was, using a pen on a string that was too short. He wrote with his hand all cramped up.

Then he slid the form back under the security screen and watched its edges blur. Like handing it to a deep sea diver; perspective skewing where the water began. The woman took the form with soaking fingers and held it in front of her face. She seemed to read it okay.

"Ten working days," she said, and filed it away.

Ted nodded, and returned to the house.

Walking home took over an hour. All uphill, too, so he had to do most of it bent forward, breathing heavily. He looked ahead once to see his roof pushing upward from the landscape like a flint. Apart from that one construction, and the road on which he walked, everything else this far from town was bushland.

As he climbed, the rest of the house emerged bit by bit and curled over him. He swore it was the house that advanced on him, and not the other way around. The thought made him dizzy and for a moment he believed that if he lost his footing and fell, he would be swept away to follow the road on and over the hill.

He hesitated by his front door. When he couldn't avoid it any longer, he slipped inside. It was gloomy and dark, even without curtains. In the lounge room the answering machine flashed twice and paused. Two messages.

"Hello?" said each voice. "Hello?"

They sounded confused. Ted slapped the delete button. More wrong numbers. Didn't these people check before they dialled? He crept upstairs to his study to wait for Jemma.

When he thought about it later, moving restlessly along the corridors, watching the afternoon light ripen to gold, he couldn't even say what his own phone number was.

"Hello? Is anybody there?"

Jemma was back right on time, like always. From the bedroom window he was able to watch her progress for a full ten minutes, climbing the arterial road from town. Her car began as small as a toy, winding through folds of green bedspread. Advancing, it swelled, until finally it was big enough to stop and let Jemma climb out.

"Here I am, Teddy!" she called.

Her long black hair was tied at her neck, and her cheeks were flushed. She held up two pizza boxes and made as if to throw them, laughing when he flinched. She hugged him instead, pizza boxes balancing on one arm, then dragged him inside.

"Good day?" she asked.

She pulled them both along the corridor to the kitchen, flipping the pizzas and car keys onto a bench. There was a spot on the hall table for keys, but she kept ignoring it. Ted didn't mind. It suited her, this careless abandonment. Brought a flush to her cheeks.

Jemma spun so fast it disoriented him. She fixed her hands to his shoulders and smiled, drinking him in. It always undid him, the intensity of her crystal eyes. He held onto her and tried not to feel washed away. He focussed on the forgotten pizza boxes.

"Credit cards," he said, distracting her, "take ten days."

Jemma's eyes went wide. "You went into town?"

"Uh-huh."

"And?" she asked, willing him to say he loved it. Loved the house, loved the town, loved it all. "Pretty, isn't it?"

"Oh, yeah," Ted assured her. He moved to the cupboard to get plates, and as he spoke, he addressed himself to the ceramics inside. "It's pretty. Very quiet."

"Just what we wanted, right?" Jemma said.

"Right," Ted said, although he couldn't remember what he'd wanted.

Jemma took the plates from him and cradled them to her chest. She had her head on one side, searching his face.

"Anyway," she said, "with our big, beautiful new home—" she leaned in softly to kiss his cheek, "—we won't need to leave."

Ted nodded and smiled, because she seemed to need him to. In reality, the house she loved so much belonged mostly to his father's designs, but he could never bring that up. Jemma would only wave her hands in the air between them and assure him his best work was yet to come. It didn't seem to matter to her what he did.

"Except," he said, "you'll have to leave to go to the office."

"Oh, sure," Jemma looked as though she'd already forgotten the conversation. "Well, there's *that*. Speaking of which, I've got a new project." She rolled her eyes to show him what she thought of new projects.

Ted laughed at last, watching her pull her clown faces, imitating her boss, whom he'd never met, and an apparently deranged colleague of hers. He reached for the pizzas, but something in the lounge room confused him and for a moment he swore it was a demon by the windows, biding time, its red eye blinking.

He froze.

Jemma followed his gaze.

"Oh," she breathed. "So you got the phone line working, too?"

She was already crossing to the answering machine, where the light flashed slowly. One message.

"No," said Ted. *No, don't play the tape.* "I mean, it's been working for ... a few days."

Jemma stabbed at the play button.

"Hello?" said the machine. "Hello? Who's this?"

There was a pause and a clunk as the caller hung up.

Jemma twisted, looking at Ted. "Who's this?" she repeated. "They're ringing and asking 'who's this'? What is that, a joke?" Then, more softly, she added, "The question is, who's *that?* Ringing us?"

She tried to grin, but it came out strained.

"There's been a few of those," Ted said. "They must be recycling the phone numbers. You know, using an old one somebody else had."

Jemma nodded, but she was slow to do it. Her knuckles whitened around the edges of the plates. "That must be it," she murmured.

She was staring at the machine. Ted moved around her to the delete key.

"Don't worry, Teddy," she said, brushing the back of her hand along his arm as he passed. "I'll take care of it."

Ted nodded. *Good*, he thought. He liked it better when she took care of things.

"Bob's Trucks and Services, no job too small. Hello, Bob speaking ... Hello?"

The house was too big.

Sometimes the thought struck him, like today, right after breakfast. After Jemma had gone and the place was empty. Then the walls thickened, ambushing him. Even the air was bloated. Not enough windows, so the darkness kept winding around him, wrapping his arms and legs like leaches. He was pinned, rocking in the centre of it, the house ebbing and flowing, and rolling like an ocean over him.

He had to get upstairs.

There, the light could still get in, and the air wouldn't be so thick.

He made a break for it, rushing across the lounge room, taking the steps two at a time, darkness pulling on his ribs.

In the study, the floor rippled with sunlight. *Much better*, he thought, red spots dancing in his eyes. He leaned onto the doorframe to gather himself. When he could, he crossed to the window, legs shaking. If Jemma could see him now, he knew, rubbing the cold from his arms, she would be so ashamed for him.

He sank into his desk chair, but spun it so he couldn't see the desk at all. This way, he faced the bay window at the back of the room. This window always seemed to lean in on him, the weight of the bushland too heavy to hold. It made Ted feel small, but there was a kind of safety in that. He felt contained. Today, though, the sight of all that mottled green bushland so close only added to the sense he was drowning. He didn't dare look away, though, because he knew if he did, he'd be forced to confront his desk. His empty desk, the blank slate, the daily reminder.

Jemma's gift to him. An architectural ensemble with an adjustable angle. Perfect, she'd said, for netting ideas. She'd treated it like a game. Still, Ted's ideas leaked away. His head was littered with half-formed creations. Bright, noble planes and sweeping curves. Open plan homes with atriums, mezzanines, grand staircases, sliding wall panels. Rooms for all sorts of lives. Once snared by the page, they dulled to grey.

He never discussed this with Jemma. She thought the world of him.

The desk still squatted at the corner of his eye, so he rolled the chair to the set of drawers where his plans were held. The drawers were old, made of dark wood, long and shallow and mostly empty. He couldn't bring himself to look at his old designs. He knew what he would find.

Instead, he opened the lowest drawer where remnants of his father's works were held. Fine, bold constructions with assertive, almost aggressive, lines and pencil marks so strong they sometimes scored right through the page. That, he thought — not for the first time — is what architecture is meant to be. A power with which to create new worlds for people. He put the stack of blueprints back in the drawer and replaced his father's notebooks on top.

Ted leaned back in his chair and rubbed his eyes. When he took his hands away, his vision blurred and danced. To his right, the bay window had come apart, and swung giddily like siamese ghosts. Ted blinked, waiting for it to pass. But when the window finally pulled back into focus, it brought something else with it. Something he hadn't seen before.

Foundations.

Bushland crowded the left side of his window, of course, and the road was a narrow strip on the right. But between them, he now saw, someone had begun work on a house. Square, concrete patterns in the ground, grey bricks stacked up. Wider and longer than his own house, but similarly proportioned. It was set back from the road, allowing space for what would undoubtedly become a small garden.

For no reason at all, it occurred to him that Jemma hadn't wanted a garden out front.

He stared at the space, allowing himself to be captivated by the idea of it, the potential, the new beginning. When he thought about it later, it occurred to him that he hadn't heard any building work. Nor had he seen any builders. Yet, there they were, rock-solid foundations almost as if they'd grown. As if the bush had finally tired of trees and plants and birdlife, and decided to throw up a home. Somewhere for people to plant roots instead.

Jemma had wanted to get away from it all.

She wouldn't like this at all.

"Radio TBR, we're here to listen. Can I take your call? ... Are you there?"

She hated it.

She'd come home, like always (this time, with Chinese takeaway), wrapping her arms around Ted, almost daring him to carry her inside. She'd thrown her keys at the kitchen bench and turned to get plates for dinner. Then she saw it. Above the sink, framed perfectly by the porthole window, the beginnings of the house.

"Brand new," Ted said.

"Sure is," Jemma replied. She moved to the glass and put her hand on it, looking out at the monster through splayed fingers.

After that they'd had dinner in silence and hadn't mentioned the new place again for two weeks. Ted was surprised by her resentment. He continued to live around the edges of his own home and Jemma's mood, moving from window to window, avoiding the dark at the core. He kept an eye on the other place. It was three doors up, or would be when someone got around to building doors between him and it.

The cement on the foundations had dried and construction workers had appeared. It all seemed so mundane. Lumber had been laid for floor framing. Ted forgot to wonder how they'd managed the foundations without him noticing.

"It had to happen," Ted consoled her.

They were eating toast by the french doors in the lounge, Jemma having tired of take-away.

She shrugged. "You think?"

"You can borrow cups of sugar," he said.

"What would I do with sugar?"

Ted nodded. True. The only thing he'd ever seen Jemma make was toast.

"I kinda like the idea of having neighbours," he said at last, but softly, not wanting to disturb her.

Jemma looked up at him. She was about to speak, but stopped abruptly.

"Did the phone ring today?" she asked, moving to the blinking eye of the answering machine.

In truth, the messages came most days, though Ted usually remembered to delete them. He never heard the phone ring, and assumed the tone was set too low. It didn't bother him. He didn't want to talk to anyone anyhow.

Jemma was playing the messages; something Ted had long stopped doing. The first voice was old. Perhaps a man, perhaps a woman. Hard to say. Next were two women.

"Hello?" they all said. "Hello?"

The final voice was young, a man.

"Pizza Palace," he said. "What can I get you today?"

"Why would a pizza place ring us?" Jemma asked.

"Maybe it's a joke," Ted suggested. "Or a new way to drum up business."

But his answer was a little too fast, because Jemma looked at him, frowning. For the first time, he saw her face at it would look decades from now. It was careworn, with a soft crease where her frown would sit. He felt suddenly lost. Where was he in that future?

"Let's get an extension in your study, Teddy," Jemma was saying, "so you can hear it." She added, nearly under her breath, "I'm sick of this."

"Sure," Ted replied straight away.

Jemma wrapped her arms around herself and stared out the windows. She was almost shivering, although the evening was warm. Ted didn't have to follow her gaze to know she was watching the new house where it lay with twilight pooling in the wooden frets of its floor.

Looking for all the world like rows of coffins.

"You break 'em, we fix 'em. Windows our specialty. How can I help?...?"

The man from the phone company was meant to arrive first thing. He didn't, of course. Up the road, the builders were back. Just four of them, draping the frame of the house with a tarpaulin. They must be expecting rain.

Ted was fascinated. He squeezed around the inside edges of his home until he reached the front door. It was early afternoon and the sunlight felt milky. Now that the place was covered — its modesty protected, so to speak — he had an urgent need to go over there, to sneak past the builders and peek under the tarp. He wanted to check nothing was still inside. He felt an odd mix of professional curiosity and greed. He wished it were his house.

It was then the van pulled up.

"Sorry," said the phone technician, squeezing out. "I woulda been here sooner only I had trouble finding the place."

"Yes," said Ted, "they haven't put it on any maps yet. Still, you could've called. We do have a phone, after all."

"Yeah," said the man, with indifference.

There were to be three extensions, according to Jemma's instructions: study, kitchen, bedroom. Ted pointed out all the places and then fidgeted, waiting for the technician to finish. It took hours, surely much longer than it should have.

The builders left silently and in the gathering gloom, the tarp shifted and itched. Occasionally it puffed out and then flattened, exposing the rib of a wall, the cheekbone of a window frame.

When at last he was able to wave goodbye to the technician, Ted found three more messages on the machine. He deleted them without listening.

Jemma was late that night.

"Who is this? Why do you keep calling?"

"What is it?" she asked.

She was staring at the house again, at the empty wall frames where the panels would go. The tarp was gone. Roof trusses extended across the cavity of the house. At the very top, towards the back, was a square shape like a cage.

Ted thought of it as the skull.

He shook his head vaguely. "I think I've seen something like it before, someplace."

He gathered his father's notebooks from the study. Jemma was curled up tight on the lounge when he returned. She shifted to rest on his shoulder as he flipped through the notebooks. Of all his father's works, Ted loved the notebooks the most. Pages of ideas and designs, all done in his father's hand. Notes were added alongside the most complex pieces, to decode them.

"Here," he said at last. "A widow's walk."

"A what?" Jemma started.

Ted read the accompanying note. "A small, windowed room at the top of a house. So wives can watch for their sailor husbands, returning from the sea."

"Only," Jemma whispered, "there's no sea here."

"No," Ted agreed, and felt the house rock shut around them. "I

37

suppose they'll use it as a kind of viewing platform. To look at the bushland. It's kinda nice, don't you think?"

"All those wives," Jemma said, "pacing up and down. Watching for husbands that never returned."

Ted squeezed her arm. "I meant architecturally, it's nice."

Jemma was quiet for a while, fingering a loose thread in the lounge. "I don't want one," she said.

Of course not, Ted thought. That wasn't what he'd meant.

She was quiet so long he thought she had fallen asleep. He waited as long as he could, listening to the steadiness of her breath. He had a cramp in his arm, and when he finally made to move out from under her, she said,

"Who's moving in there, Teddy?"

"Is that you, dear?"

Proper siding had been put up, although the widow's walk was still bare. The window spaces on the lower floors were huge, almost floor to ceiling.

Ted sat in a puddle of sunlight in his study. He was flipping through another of his father's notebooks, but he was staring at the house. Funny how it was the windows that gave a place its personality. This one seemed open and generous. The new people would need blinds, though, to stop neighbours looking in. He supposed he'd have to get blinds himself. Then they could start shutting each other out.

He noticed a page had come loose from the notebook in his lap. Pulling it free, he found it was a piece of folded blueprint paper, the edges shorn roughly with a ruler. Unfolding it, he found a house. With a widow's walk.

He'd been through these notebooks a thousand times and never seen this, but it made sense to him that his very need to discover this thing would make it so, at this time. Automatically he stood, pressing the blueprint to the window above the new neighbours' house. Even without looking he knew it was the same place. Window for window, wall for wall. Cut from the same cloth.

Ted turned and stalked downstairs, passing through the dark guts of his own home without a thought. He moved stiffly up the road towards the workmen. He did all this without vomiting, though he felt sick to his shoes.

"You," he said to the nearest builder. "Whose house is this?"

They all turned like bumblebees, sluggishly, gazing at him.

"Where did the plans come from?" Ted snapped. "Who's the foreman?"

"Problem?" said one of them. He was crouched by the steps, sorting nails. When Ted approached, he stood and gazed warily.

"I want to see your plans," Ted said.

"They're at council. Been there for months."

"I want your copy."

The man shrugged, indecisive. He rubbed his forehead where the hardhat marked it. Then he took Ted to his truck and — slowly, slowly — unspooled his plans across the bonnet. They each held a side of the paper flat, the corners folding over their fingers.

Ted scanned the print.

"This isn't what you're building," he said. "These plans are nothing like that house."

The foreman frowned blearily, unable to wake up. "I don't know what you're talking about."

Ted shoved his own blueprint in the man's face. "*This!* This is what I'm talking about."

The foreman peered at the drawing, chuckling at the old-fashioned handmade marks and shorn edges. He looked back to the pristine, computer-perfected plans on his bonnet.

"Are you qualified to interpret these?" he asked.

Ted was choking. He wanted to scream *how dare you*. Instead, he backed away, letting the blueprints roll loosely back along the bonnet. They were all watching him. Not with malice, but with a kind of listless curiosity. Ted could feel their eyes on him all the way to his front door.

He hid from the windows for the rest of the day, standing just outside their light. In the centre, the house was like ice, so Ted had to circle and circle, rubbing the warmth back into his arms.

As he passed the answering machine for the twelfth time, it sprang to life.

"Hello?" came a strange voice. "Hello?"

Ted snatched up the phone before he had time to think better of it.

"Who is this?" he shouted.

"Hey, what d'you mean?" said the stranger. "You called me, buddy."

"No, I didn't, I—" Ted began. Then stopped.

He put the phone back on the receiver.

It wasn't him. It had never been him.

Had it?

"Justin, is that you? Have you been calling? Why don't you come home? Say something, son. It'll all be okay, I promise. Just come home."

Jemma was back early, pleading flu. She was home before the builders had even left for the day, and she lay on the lounge looking at Ted with thick eyes. If it wasn't for her, he'd be at the other house. He couldn't help it. Something about what he'd seen that afternoon was nagging him. But Jemma was like an anchor, so he stayed.

Just before he drifted off to sleep that night, he realised what it was.

The new house didn't even have glass in its windows yet. But he swore he'd seen furniture behind its empty frames.

"Your call's important to us. Please hold the line."

He'd never noticed how quiet the bush was before. Not a birdsong, not a cricket. No cicadas, or the soft rush of creatures in the undergrowth. Pure silence. Like the countryside was a painted backdrop for an empty theatre.

The house was finished.

He hadn't slept for days, and perhaps it was fatigue that made the new place shimmer like that in the sunlight. There was an Arcadian glow to it, as idle and serene as an oil painting.

There was a verandah at the back of the house with a flat aluminium roof. On the second floor, louvres had been added almost all the way around. At the very top, the widow's walk had its siding at last, and large windows that would open out.

Jemma wouldn't look at it. She barely even looked at Ted. Not directly, anyhow, although he felt her watching. During the three days she had off sick, Ted retreated mainly to his study. She shuffled past his door every so often, bent over like she was dragging something invisible behind her. Eventually she had to leave and return to work. Ted was glad. It meant at last he could come up for air.

Sure enough, the new house had a garden out front, with piercing orange flowers and full green leaves. There was even a mat beside the front door. Ted would bet it said "*Welcome*", in warm, red letters. Behind the louvred windows of the second floor, blinds were pulled shut. But on the ground floor, where there were no blinds, reflections in the windows made it look like movement. Like somebody was in there.

In a heartbeat, Ted was outside. It was warm, almost hot in the sun. He didn't even feel the distance between houses anymore. One moment, he was by his window and the next, he was here, where the mat by the door did indeed spell out *Welcome*. There was a bright copper door handle in front of him and he twisted it, but it was locked tight.

So he went to the windows. There was an oily sheen to the glass, but if he pressed the side of his face against it, he could just make out the insides. Heavy curtains were pulled back on soft ropes. Beyond them the light was mottled and dense. It trapped strange shapes, shadows with rough-hewn edges like old wooden furniture. Ted had the impression these shapes had been sent to mark out the spaces where real furniture would go. It was as though the house was making plans of its own.

Ted moved around the walls, trying each window. They were all locked. He cupped his hand over the panes, breaking the morning glare, trying to see what was inside.

When he passed the back sitting room, he saw a man.

Though the man's back was to him, Ted could make out every detail of the clothes he wore. Dark trousers, pale yellow shirt, sleeves rolled up. He could see the colour of the man's hair. He was about to call out, but thought better of it and then a minute later, wondered why. The man was leaving the room. Ted hurried further around the house and caught sight of him climbing the staircase.

"Hey!" he called.

He rapped the glass with his knuckles. The man continued up. Not wanting to be left behind, Ted rushed onto the back verandah. This door was locked, too. He looked around for a way to climb to the second level. There was only the balcony railing, but when he pulled himself onto that and stood upright, he found the flat verandah roof was at eye level. With his left hand, he was able to grab hold of the nearest window frame. Wedging his foot against a corner of the building, he hauled himself high enough to hook his elbows over the gutter. From there, he dragged himself along the roof more by will than design. Eventually, enough of him was on the roof that he could roll over and pull his legs up into a foetal position.

His ribs hurt and when he sat up his shirt was torn and dirtied. He took a few breaths to steady himself and found he had never felt better. He was thrilled, fascinated by what was inside.

He crawled across to the louvred windows and peeked in. No shadows in this room and no blinds either. No mistaking what he saw. This room was fully furnished, complete with bedspread stretched across an old-fashioned bed. It was warm and rosy, the morning sun making it shine.

"Hey," Ted said softly.

The man was there. He was shutting a drawer in the dresser and turning back towards the door. Not once did he look in Ted's direction, not even when Ted began beating frantically at the glass.

There was no reason to think the man had gone up to the widow's walk, but Ted knew it was true. He looked to the roof above him. It wasn't possible to climb any further on the outside of the house. It was too steep and high.

But it was easy enough to begin pulling out the louvres, making a space to crawl inside.

"Is this a hoax? Stop calling here. I mean it!"

When Jemma got home, it was quiet.

"Ted?" she called.

She thought to call again, but knew he was gone. She checked all the rooms anyhow.

In the lounge room the answering machine winked nearly a dozen times. While she wondered what to do, she listened to all the messages, keeping her back to the French doors and the house beyond.

The final message was her mother's voice.

"Is that you, Jemma?" her mother said. "Have you been trying to call?"

"No," Jemma whispered, letting the tape rewind. "Not me."

The presence beyond the windows drilled into her back, so she turned at last. There it was, the house. It was perfectly complete, perfectly still. Some trick of the light made the windows glow so it looked almost welcoming.

She knew. She'd known all along. She hadn't wanted to leave that morning, but what good would it have done to stay?

She went at last to the new place.

There was no sound except for her shoes on the road. While she walked she pressed one hand to her stomach, one to her mouth. Twilight was descending, transforming the greens and browns into bruised purples. Beside the front door was a mat with black lettering.

Welcome.

"Ted?" she called.

The windows still shone, but whatever was behind was obscured by thick curtains. The frames were locked tight. She took her time circling the house, trying each window. She reached the back balcony, which seemed to float in the thickening dark.

"Can you hear me, Ted?" she called. "Come home."

Come home, come home.

She waited. There was no response from the house. There couldn't be, but she stayed anyway.

The bushland had become a wall of black to her left and above that the sky was a twisted mess of darkness. Standing in the silence was like being at the bottom of a tank. It was hollow here, and empty, and the walls felt thin.

"Ted?"

She was surprised her voice didn't echo.

Sometimes she stood, sometimes she sat on the verandah wondering how he'd gotten inside and why, what had compelled him. Eventually, the windows lost their evening glow and the world was as dark as it was silent. It made no more sense to wait here than it did to wait anywhere. So she went home, stumbling, almost crawling, searching out the front steps with her hands. She flipped on the hall light and the sudden luminescence was a slap to the face.

She used the phone in the kitchen to call. It rang three times before someone picked it up.

"Hello?"

"He's gone," was all she said.

"Darling. I'm so sorry," said her mother. There was sympathy in her voice but no real surprise.

Jemma filled the next silence.

"I thought it would be enough for him, but he kept wanting more. He kept adding things. Windows, everywhere, all these bloody windows. Every shape and bloody size. What did he want to see?"

"Oh, sweetheart," said her mother.

"All these stupid bloody windows, and not a moment to ourselves," she was rambling. She was crying.

"It's time you got out of there," her mother was saying, "and came home."

Home, thought Jemma. Good word. "*This* was meant to be our…"

She didn't finish. In the lounge room, the french doors gaped like mouths. They belonged to Ted, of course. Bigger and bigger windows, trying to let the outside in. Now it felt like the insides would be sucked out. Nothing protected her against the vacuum of the world.

In her mind it was all destroyed. She was tearing it down, pulling the buildings apart, ripping up the roads, laying waste to the damn bushland, the people. Folding it all back into itself like dough. She pictured it gone, just gone, and nothing left but dirt and this house and the other house, where Ted was. In case he was still there. In case he hadn't slipped right into the walls and been drowned by that place.

The new world was a bland, featureless place, and she promised herself it would be enough. At least for her, at least for now.

The porthole window above the sink gave her a perfect picture of darkness. It framed that other house, and she hated it for that. She used her free hand to press at the frame, kneading it, pushing at it the way someone might push on a flap of skin to seal over a wound.

"I can't leave him in there," she whispered.

"Darling," said her mother. "He was made to fit that world. But you, dear, you can't stay. It's not healthy for you. After all, it's not like he's real."

Tears rolled down Jemma's face.

Real, she thought, had never been the point.

Hush

"Shhhhhhhh."

Then later, "Quiet, Shep."

Another interval, then another. "Chasing rabbits, girl? Hush. We've got a journey ahead tomorrow."

Journey?

She opened one eye. Timmons was hunched in his chair by the fire, hands hanging in a loose clasp like an open clam.

He was getting old, Shep noticed. She noticed that a lot lately. How thin and white his hair was. How thin and white *he* was. And how the skin between his fingers and thumb when he reached for her face was slack and soft.

"Good girl, Shep," he said.

She heaved herself up and went to him, rested her chin on his knee and waited for him to scratch her nose. He obliged immediately. But soon the crick in her neck forced her to lay back down on the floor at his feet.

"Good dog," said Timmons.

Shep whined.

"Wake up, Shep. Good girl. Time to go."

It was morning. She knew this because the lights were off and a milky blur filled the windows. As close to daylight as they got nowadays. Dust covered everything, covered the world, covered up the light and the days and the seasons.

Timmons was holding out the lead and harness.

"I'm sorry, girl. We gotta do this, it's the law."

47

Insistent, he slipped the harness over her head and buckled it over her back while she struggled to rise. The stiffness in her elbows slowed her down.

She made a low growl that she hoped sounded like "where are we going?", but Timmons didn't answer.

They left the apartment and walked out across unscented turf to a covered carriage, black and gleaming like stone. A chestnut horse fronted it, and gave Shep a disdainful look as she approached. She stared imperiously back. Not because it was a horse, but because it was working class when she herself was clearly something better.

A man stepped from behind the carriage. A stranger with a wet face. Not wet like water; wet like drunkenness and want.

"There by nightfall?" he asked. "Only, the horse will need tending by then."

He said it like a challenge.

"Leave it with me," said Timmons. "I know animals."

The man chuckled. An odd sound, his laugh; a toneless, nasal thing, like he was trying to breathe through water. Shep stifled an instinctive growl.

"See that," he nodded, indicating Shep. "Haven't seen a dog in years."

He hunkered down in front of her and she let out a whine, then a grunt as his hand landed smack on her skull. He rubbed at her ears and pulled at the loose skin of her neck.

"Quiet, isn't she?" he observed. "Unusual breed."

"Last of her litter, too."

The man stank of sweat like onions. He was lean and rough. Calloused on his hands, face and elbows. Shep thought maybe he was a turtle hiding out as a man. There was something determined about him. But little that was slow, she sensed. She suffered the pull of his fingers on her ears.

"What was she before her mash? That what you call it?" the man asked.

Timmons nodded. "A scientist. A man."

"Yeah? My mother-in-law, she was undistinguished, if you don't mind me saying," replied the man. "Wealthy, though. Got herself mashed into a litter of kittens. Fitted her brain all neat into theirs. Most of 'em made it, too. They were five-gen. You types had it pretty much right by then, eh?"

Timmons nodded. "Shep here is one-gen."

"No! Thought they were all done for by now?"

"You just don't hear about them. We keep them pretty close."

"She a toy?"

Timmons shook his head. "No, she's not cleared for work with children. We didn't do the same extensive pre-mash testing as now…"

The onion-stink man made cluck-clucking noises with his tongue. "Too monstrous, eh? The kids I mean."

He laughed that drowning laugh again.

Timmons had a sad droop of a half-smile on his face.

"She's fine with me," he said. "I'm Timmons, by the way."

"Hendricks," said the man, and gave a kind of bow. Like he was proud Timmons had even bothered to ask.

He turned to the horse and gave the address.

"Sure," said the horse, eyeing Shep again.

Voice box, thought Shep resentfully. She clambered up the ramp and settled against the carriage floor. From the window she saw the bald Sun rise with clockwork smoothness, lighting the dusty air with opulent fire as it slow-dived upwards.

She dozed again, woke and dozed all day. Once she thought she saw a child's face, his mouth a perfect frozen O of terror, his pale hair clamped to his skull and his skin white under ice. She whined and rose with a start, ignoring the stab of pain in her back. But there was no child. Only the Moon, its engine bearing it skyward after its stint as the Sun. Moon and Sun were one globe. Artificial stand-ins for the real things, which had long disappeared behind dust and the detritus of human waste.

The carriage rolled on. Her uncut nails clattered on the floor as she turned in three tight circles and then fell rather than sat, back legs stiff and unwieldy.

"Steady on," said Timmons affectionately. He reached to smooth her brow and scratch her snout.

Shep made a hooting sound. "Roow? Ooow?" she asked.

"Who? You mean who are we visiting?" asked Timmons. He ran the back of one hand down the length of her jowls. "The sister of your mash-human. She knew you when you were Joseph Shepherd. We need to ask her…"

He drifted back into one of those sad smiles.

Shep settled with her head on his foot, lulled to sleep by the steady rumble of the carriage.

When she woke next it was because Timmons had moved his shoe out from under her. There was a thin line of drool smearing his toe and she whined in apology.

Timmons was at the carriage door.

"I had no idea how remote your home was!" he called, jumping to the ground.

"Remote all right. Last remote place on God's dull, brown Earth, eh?" came a voice that creaked and split with age.

Shep reached the carriage doorway and spied an old woman with gnarled shoulders and a loose housedress like a tent. She looked sure and cautious.

"This is Shep," said Timmons.

"Ha. Shep, is it?" said the woman, reaching out a hand, like they all did, to scratch at Shep's skull. Her fingers were like needles. "Bernese, eh? Bernese mountain dog. Swiss breed."

"That's right. You know your animals."

"I do that. Don't see a lot of 'em anymore. Labs take them all for mash, of course." She eyed Timmons bitterly. "Too many human brains they want preserving, they reckon. Can't keep up with demand. Can't afford to feed them all! But I remember when them was just good, old-fashioned pets."

"The Bernese were bred for their stable neurology."

"Right, right. Out of my league that neuro-mash stuff," said the woman. "Well, how you getting down from there, old thing?"

Timmons pulled out the ramp and the woman let out another *ha!* of exclamation.

"New-fangled things," she said. "And I suppose the horse is mashed, too?"

"I am," called the horse, making the woman laugh in a long series of *ha-ha-has*, bending forward so her gnarled back rose above her head.

"All this work on the brain," she said. "Still most people in poverty, farming's all to hell, food's to be stolen from fields when farmers ain't looking. Had me a good worker last year. Poisoned himself on potato plant. Go figure! Not the potatoes themselves, the berries. Ate the berries. Starving, he said! Died on my own lawn. Nothing to be done. No doctors out here. Well, come in then."

She gestured them to the door of her home. It was a modest place with a narrow front, three concrete steps, slit windows with a pale wash of light behind them. Only on the first floor, though. All the other windows were closed and dark.

"Local scientist asked if I wanted to mash the boy's brain. His brain! Got no animals for it, I told him, and no funds. Besides," she led them into the narrow corridor, "if he had a good *brain*, wouldn't have eaten those berries."

Timmons said politely, "Of course, it was your brother's work which made that question possible at all. Before Joseph, there was no neuro—"

"Yeah, yeah, heard it before," said the woman. "Straight through to the back. Front room's a mess, I'm afraid. Hardly ever get up the stairs anymore, so down here's all there is for me. Back courtyard. Not too cold out there yet."

Shep was shivering, her belly on the cold pavement, the bare Moon clicking across its programme above her. Timmons rested a hand on her neck. He was silent, lost in his head. She recognised this posture from the times he was working, trying to undo a knot in his mind.

When the woman returned she was carrying a tray with teapot and cups, plus a plate of flat biscuits. Shep didn't recognise the woman. A fault of time, she figured — time either acting on the woman's face or Shep's memory.

"Ms Holly, do you mind if…?" said Timmons, reaching for a biscuit and gesturing towards Shep.

"Feed the dog my good biscuits, eh? Well, fair enough. Don't know that Joseph ever liked biscuits, truth be told."

Shep sucked the crumbs from her teeth.

"You weren't much in contact with your brother in his later years, I understand?"

"Later years," said Holly. "Early years. Most of the years! Nearly twenty years between our births. Different mothers, of course."

She handed Timmons a cup with a delicate painted flower along its side.

"But I'm sure you must be aware of his pioneering work in neurology?" Timmons persisted. "He fashioned the entire process for mashing human brains to animal hosts—"

Holly bit into a biscuit triumphantly, crumbs littering her lips and spilling unheeded to her chest.

"I know it," she said. "Left nothing for his family, you understand? Don't know why he was so hung up on the brain. S'pose he was always trying to save his kid brother, eh? You know Joseph's history, I'm assuming." She leaned back, lost inside her own memories. "Brain the seat of the soul, and all that. Did he say? Why, that is. Did he say why?"

She looked vulnerable and hollow. An old woman in a floral housedress with a stained apron and stale biscuits in her pantry, unaccustomed to company. Shep rose from her spot on the floor and moved to Holly's side, allowing the woman's sharp fingers to find her neck. She felt a sudden wave of sympathy. Everything in the world seemed old nowadays, and Holly was just part of it.

"I'm sorry," said Timmons. "I was a junior when your brother was head of the lab. I didn't know him well."

Holly nodded. "Didn't like to fraternise, did he? Like that with family, too."

"You say his younger brother died? Your brother?"

Holly nodded, coughed, choked, spat a wave of crumbs into the air. She teared up and her face went red, and Timmons leaned forward in alarm lest she collapse. But in a moment the scene righted itself and Holly took a slurp of her tea.

"Henry, yes." She coughed. Continued, "Younger than Joseph, a year older than me. I don't remember him too well. Guess I was, what, three? Joseph was an adult by then. Twenty-something, I guess, meant to be looking after us, but he liked to sneak out all the time. Henry always followed. Wanted to be like his older brother. Some boys have that. Can't fight it. Wasn't a thing Joseph could say to stop him."

Holly told it to Timmons like she'd been there herself, but Shep didn't need the explanation. She saw it all in her mind, like a series of old photographs. Henry on the crust of the lake in winter, Henry bending to touch the ice and then falling headlong, a spray of water like a cloak fanning out to mark his fall.

"They found him," Holly asserted. "Four months too late, they did. The doctor said he must've found an air pocket. Small one. Suffocated in it. Darnedest thing. Wasn't drowning that killed him, it was the lack of oxygen to his brain."

Shep whined.

Holly reached to lift Shep's chin and peer into her eyes. She smelled of cookie dough and damp walls.

"Still in there, Joseph?"

She smiled.

"Shep's the last of the litter," said Timmons.

Holly nodded. "All this work to save his brain. And it was his liver that killed him. Joseph, I mean. If he'd turned all his science on the liver instead, might still be alive!" She gazed thoughtfully at Timmons. "So, what d'you want from me?"

"Permission."

"Aha. For?"

Timmons hesitated. "To let Joseph rest."

There was a whistle from Holly, a low, impressed noise. She leaned back so Shep couldn't see her face anymore.

Shep turned to look at Timmons but he wouldn't meet her gaze either.

"You want to put the dog down?"

"She's old."

"We're all old."

"Some months ago, she attacked a child." Timmons rubbed at his eyes. "It was … savage. His parents fund — or have funded, at least — a lot of the work in our lab. The child suffered head injuries. He's still in a coma."

Shep wracked her brain, but there were dozens of children's faces in her memory. She couldn't distinguish one from another. Only Henry was clear, blue with death and cold in the thawing lake.

"You want to destroy the dog for destroying a child?"

"She's become dangerous."

"So's your science, if you ask me. So's your penchant for killing animals. That not important? And is it that she hurt a child, or is it that she hurt the wrong child?"

She held up a hand to stop his answer. "I'd like to think it's all about the, what, the sanctity of human life, eh? But it's not that. No. It's the sanctity of the *chosen* human lives, the ones you think worth saving, the ones worth mashing. Nothing for the rest of us, though."

Timmons said quietly, "It's not … We think the bestial part of the brain is overwhelming Joseph. Wiping him out. We think Joseph is dying already. The brain is so malleable, you see, and the science so new. Joseph was a genius. If he'd lived we might have made more progress—"

"So," Holly interrupted with a triumphant laugh, "the dog is trying to survive. That what you're saying? The dog is eating the man."

Timmons didn't nod, didn't move, didn't acknowledge what she'd said at all.

"The one-gens were pure experiment. We've enabled them to continue as long as they can. To see how long the brain will retain its original mash. Other generations are put down earlier—"

"When you've had your fill of them? When they've fulfilled the purpose you chose them for? How humane."

Timmons didn't answer.

Holly humphed. "And Joseph's real brain? You kept it?"

"Lost—"

"Lost?"

"In an attack on the labs. Anti-research groups," Timmons continued.

"That's what got me out of research, you know," Holly said. "Animal rights groups."

"These particular ones weren't pro-animal," said Timmons. "They were religious—"

"Ah! The ones that claim the brain is the seat of the soul, hey? Wowsers," Holly spat. "They don't like researchers playing God. Full of self-righteousness, like everybody in this game. They're right, though."

"About the soul?"

"About Joseph. Playing God."

Shep snuffled and coughed, and Holly reached down again to stroke her ears. This time with more gentleness. When Holly next spoke, her voice had a new calm to it.

"An entire litter of pups," she said. "And what happens to the soul, do you reckon? Does it split, or are they replicas of the same soul? Does each soul carry the same stain?"

She grinned, an unsettling sight. The teeth in her head were discoloured and narrow, and the lines from her eyes to her hairline crowded her skin and turned her face into a loose mask.

"Such arrogance," she murmured. "To think animal nature is lower than human nature. To think we can use animals as ready-made teacups for the human brain."

When Timmons didn't respond, she added quietly, "Never struck you as odd, how many children's bodies Joseph was able to source? For his research?"

"In times of poverty," Timmons' voice was cold, "children—"

"Are cheaper?"

Holly's hand was still.

Shep watched them stare at each other unblinkingly, their silhouettes stark against the smoky dark sky.

Timmons rose to his feet. "Thank you," he said, "for your hospitality."

"Well. Not at all."

She saw them to the door, Shep limping with the pain in her hind legs. As Timmons operated the ramp to the carriage, Holly leaned down and addressed Shep one more time.

"Best thing for you, old girl," she said. "Joseph was so afraid of death he couldn't look away from it. But you don't need that, hey? Just need to rest. Nothing to be afraid of there."

Shep let out a soft whine. There was a comforting familiarity in Holly's presence and she found she didn't want to lose it.

"Joseph told me once," she said more loudly, "when I complained about the experiments on kids. He told me research is never clean. Progress relies on sacrifice. And a refusal to be reasonable, that's what he said. Think there's anything in that? Gotta be unreasonable to push progress forward, so he said. Can't take things lying down."

Timmons was harnessing a resisting horse.

"Up, Shep," he said, lowering the carriage ramp. Then to Holly, "I'm sure I couldn't say."

He climbed into the carriage and slammed the door behind him. Holly rested her hand on the window, staying them.

"Reasonable men," said Holly, "couldn't do what you do."

Shep turned to Timmons, but he was staring at his host with blank eyes.

"Funny thing about Bernese, though," she nodded towards Shep. "They're quiet. Rarely bark. Good with cattle. Good with kids, too. Not vicious. Not a vicious bone in their bodies. Can't see how you'd ever call them bestial."

She moved off and raised her hand in a wave.

"There, there, girl."

Timmons slumped in his seat, finger across lip, eyes fixed on the haze masking the horizon. She nudged his leg and he shushed her, but offered nothing more in the way of comfort. Shep whined once to herself and slept, the rumble and clump of their progress rocking her to sleep.

When she woke the sky was boiling pink and the desert beneath it was a blurred red. She rose stiffly, dull pain in her ribs and elbows.

Timmons was dozing, his chin on his shoulder and his arms slack at his sides. He looked washed out, as if dawn and wakefulness might never find him.

Shep sniffed the air. She growled.

Onions.

"What—" Timmons roused, but the rest of what he'd meant to say was lost behind a muffled cry.

The carriage came to an abrupt stop that sent Shep skidding. Timmons too had to hold onto his seat against the momentum.

Two men moved into the carriage, oxygen masks on their faces. One moved fast towards Timmons and pushed a cloth to his face. Timmons fought blindly, his cries becoming more distant until they stopped.

Shep moved to stand, splinters of pain shooting through her back. She landed a bite on the leg of the nearest man, and he yelped and lashed out with his foot. She was sent skidding to the far side of the carriage where she hit the wall hard. She let out a yelp and swerved back to the fray. But the other man leapt on her with a cloth in one hand, pressing it to her snout.

Timmons had fallen to the side, mouth open. Shep tried to call out, but her vision rolled and she fell choking into a darkness deeper than sleep.

When she came to she was on her side. The uneven floor dug into her ribs, bruising her with each roll and lurch of the vehicle. Loud music was playing and there was a stink of vegetables. She was in a van, she realised, its high windows covered in dark cloth. Impossible to tell if it was day or night.

She stiffened at the sounds of voices.

"Is he for my birthday?"

A child's voice. Shep tried to rise but her first few attempts were thwarted by the rough roads. Her back creaked and refused to bend, her claws scrambled for purchase. She struggled, finally, to a sitting position.

"That's right, son."

There was a man at the steering wheel. No mash-driver for him. She could smell animals, though, beneath the reek of onions.

Onions.

She craned forward. The smell was unmistakable. Sure enough she spotted Hendricks, their onion-stink stable owner. The man who'd given them the horse and carriage. She whined to herself. Where was Timmons?

She moved closer to the back of the seat. From there she could make out the halo of hair that marked the child sitting beside the driver.

"He's a she, son," said Hendricks. "She's very rare. And smart! Ever seen a dog before, Huck?"

There was silence from the boy, but his hair spun in the Moonlight.

"What about in books? You seen dogs in books?"

"Sometimes," said Huck. "Sometimes they bite."

Hendricks chuckled, wet and snide. "Those are old books. Dogs don't bite anymore. They're just like people now."

"Yeah?"

"Good people," Hendricks assured the boy. "Hand-chosen for their brains. Well, not your grandmother, she chose herself. But this one, this dog, was a scientist."

There was a photo hanging from the rear-view mirror, a boy with a grin as wide as his face, eyes screwed up against the light. With the Moon behind the photo like that, the boy looked blue. Like he was suffocating, Shep thought. She tensed.

She edged closer, the radio masking the clack-clack of her nails. There was a growl trapped in her throat, but she held it there.

"She'll keep you company when Daddy's at work. See?" Hendricks was saying.

"Okay."

Beyond the windscreen the night loomed starkly. To the right, Shep saw the rough earth edge of a cliff rising above them. On the other side of the car, nothing. Just night and the Moon.

"It'll be just like having a grown-up looking after you."

"Okay," said Huck again.

Shep eased in close. Her snout was just above the boy's head. She could smell the sweat in his hair and the dirty synthetic clothing he wore. He needed a bath, she thought with unaccustomed clarity. He should be clean.

A sneer pulled her lips above her teeth. She watched the small skull beneath her, the tender mechanisms of its little brain sliding in and out of place. She eased back and placed her front legs on the seat.

The growl escaped her then.

The man turned in a daze, the smile still on his face.

Shep pushed forward, aiming to snap her jaw around the boy's neck.

Protect the brain, she thought. Protect and preserve the brain.

The pain in her back snagged her and she came up short. Her jaw clamped down hard on the child's skull and the impact sent a shudder all the way to her chest.

She'd never liked the taste of blood.

The boy screamed and screamed. He tried to pull away but Shep was too strong. She shook him almost gently, trying to work her way to his neck.

He was screaming without pause, his hands held out stiff in front of him.

"Let go," shouted Hendricks. "Let go of my boy!"

He had one hand on the steering wheel. With the other he landed a punch to the side of Shep's head. She grunted but held fast.

He punched her again. Again and again until her grip loosened.

The boy tipped forward, exposing the back of his neck and Shep dived for him, grabbing hold of the skin beneath his hair. Her back erupted in a fierce pain like fire.

But at least after that the boy stopped screaming.

Hendricks' face had gone slack. He wasn't watching the road, Shep noted. He was staring at Huck with the expression of someone waking from a dream.

"Huck," he whispered.

He reached for his son with both hands.

Shep tried to shout a warning, but it was muffled against the boy's neck.

Free to follow its own nose, the van slid towards the edge of the road and off and out, arcing across the empty air towards the Moon.

Seven Ages of the Protagonist

Age Six

She develops an aversion to seafood, occasioned by her grandfather's heart attack. It's his ninety-eighth birthday. The family is gathered in white plastic chairs around an excessive mound of fried "fisherman's basket".

Grandpa topples without warning face-first into the sticky mess of his plate and lies there, forehead smeared with tartare sauce, shattered crab claw stuck to his cheek by the drool emptying from his mouth.

Our protagonist gags with hand to her face.

The grown-ups react more slowly. It's left to the waitress to call the paramedics.

When they sit Grandpa up again, his lower lip is sagging into the oxygen mask and his eyes are loose and wet in his head. His skin is mottled purple and white. His dark grey tracksuit pants are stained where he's wet himself. He stinks like piss and Ajax and deep-fried fish. His gaze rolls about the room and fixes on her, our young protagonist.

She's ashamed for him.

She looks away.

She spies her grandmother. Shock has wiped out the old woman's wrinkles and turned her pupils into pinpricks. She's holding out two large notes to the shell-shocked waitress, but saying nothing.

She's trying to pay the bill.

"Take it," says her grandmother finally.

She refuses to look at her husband. It's business as usual around the old man's edges.

But the smell of seafood is henceforth associated with fear for all of them.

Age Twelve

At a family barbeque she meets Roy, the son of a friend of her mother's. Roy's only outstanding trait is Down's Syndrome. In the process of eating a sausage in white bread, Roy unceremoniously shits himself.

Our protagonist is the first to notice because, confined to the children's table even at her mature age, she recognises the stench.

Roy grins with a mouth full of teeth like loose stones. His eyes, however, have a blank cool gleam. He laughs in grunts, his fist wrapped around his sausage sandwich almost obscenely. Then he reaches his other hand into his pants and pulls up a sticky, stinking brown mess. It oozes through his fingers and fills up the jagged spaces under his bitten nails.

When he pushes his hand toward the tomato-sauce smear of his own face, our protagonist jumps up and leaves.

After that, predictably, she never eats another sausage. Nor does she attempt Rocky Road, Maltesers, chilli con carne, peanut butter, coffee, most Indian food or chocolate ice cream for several years.

Age Sixteen

To fit in, she develops bulimia. It's not about her weight at first; it's about bartering vomit stories in the schoolyard.

She becomes familiar with the texture and tang of bile. She learns to identify components of a meal in the stringy mess of muted colour along the walls of the toilet bowl.

Milkshake, she discovers, is too viscous to be enjoyable when purged. But orange juice retains its flavours remarkably well.

She talks it through with Jenny, her best friend.

Jenny has thick blonde hair like cold noodles, and discoloured brown buckteeth. Jenny's mother says the colour comes from exposure to the air, but our protagonist knows otherwise.

Over the course of the next two years she watches Jenny's teeth worsen. Jenny develops soft downy hair across her face, yellow brittle fingernails, and an unfixed gaze. Jenny, in the absence of food, becomes mean, unfocussed, irritable.

But she looks great.

Age Twenty-three

She's backpacking across Europe. Living in public spaces, showering in shared bathrooms, sleeping in bunkbeds in large, crowded rooms. She's never felt so alone.

She learns to ask for "a table for one" in eight languages. She eats what the locals eat or what she can find or — when she's feeling vulnerable — something familiar. She's startled to find that carpaccio is raw, and French chefs will sell her an entire duck intestine.

It's explained to her that diseases from "duck intestinal mucosa" are rare. These particular ducks are force-fed for days before their intestines are claimed. It is suggested she try it fried.

It tastes, rather inoffensively, of herbs. But takes hours to chew.

It's in Europe she discovers coffee. It makes her sick half the time and anxious the other, but she drinks it to fit in. Her gut is never quite the same, but she likes to think she is opening herself to the world, inviting it in through her mouth.

Age Twenty-five

After more than two years she returns home and spends seven weeks organising her photos into albums with an elaborate cross-referenced index. "Church", "sunset", "mountain", "statue", and so on.

Her mother photographs her one day, leaning forward over her albums with a self-conscious smile sliding off one side of her face.

Our protagonist is so horrified at the image of her own thick arms, her round chin, the slope of her breasts inside her loose shirt that she spends the next several years on diets.

Detox, liver cleansing, grapefruit, no fruit, vegetable soup, low-carb, no-carb, nothing-after-six-pm, vegetarian. She tries them all.

This can't be right, she thinks. *How can I live an entire life this way? How can I spend all my time with nothing on my mind but food?*

She wants to slice out the piece of her brain which feeds her the obsessive thoughts.

This state of affairs goes on longer than she would like.

Age Forty

She is a healthy weight, according to her doctor, though her waist refuses to return to its girlish proportions. She hated her figure when she was fifteen. Now she'd give anything to look like she did, even in the most unflattering pictures.

The hormones she's on make her hungry. The diet pills clog up her insides. She hasn't touched a cheesecake in twenty years, but she does love to lick the salt off corn chips.

Her favourite indulgence is white bread with a smear of butter.

Age Fifty-one

She's on a plane, going home. Alone.

The American she's been dating (her last great romance, so her friends suggest) had taken her to meet the family and eat the local delicacies.

"Prairie oysters," he says proudly, offering her a plate of round fried *hors d'oeuvres*.

The oysters squeak against her teeth and then explode warm fluid over her tongue.

"Yuck," she chokes, "what is it? Eyeball?"

He laughs, fried shit stuck to his teeth, chewed colourless mass coating his tongue. When he tells her what prairie oysters are — in this case, bull testicle — she slaps him right across his face. Releasing a spray of masticated membrane across the room.

She feels, for the first time, extremely satisfied.

Silicon Cast

fetch. For those who can afford it, who cannot fetch themselves. I reach for objects on the high shelves and prepare my clients' baths, help them to undress. Even wash them, if they desire it. I am a maid for the rich, a concubine for the wealthy. I facilitate.

None of them have strength enough to do it for themselves. They sit with careful expressions of ennui, crafted by the finest surgeons. The criss-cross of technological perfection in their skin means they can never sag. And under their skin, there are now only artificial implants, shaped and sculpted, held in place by nylon strands, grafted onto muscles that have atrophied. They can't even raise an arm, a hand, but they can gaze at each other if you sit them together and turn their heads for them.

Dressed like dolls, posed in their fine furniture, they have no need for muscle or movement. They look just so perfect. So beautiful. Reclining in fine rooms, carefully lit. Delighting in each other's splendour.

But the hands they feel are mine. Or rather, the hands they cannot feel. On the days when I am too tired for their demands, and the money does not seem like enough, I wonder what it would be like to slice them open. Whether their liquefied insides would spill out like soup, or whether the bodies would remain upright and intact while the blood flooded onto the floor.

This evening I visit the home of a wealthy man. I'm not even sure how he earned his money, or if he did, but he is a special client of mine. And there is a particular service he requires — one that I have grown fond of. Bala, the sole servant of the house, lets me in.

"Good evening, Brosia," she says. "The Duchess tonight."

"His favourite," I reply. In the overhead light, Bala's new cheekbones send half her face into shadow. I smile approvingly. She must have paid a fortune for those. I toss my head a little, so she may admire the gloss of my new auburn hair, but she gives no sign of her admiration. I put my jacket and shoes in the closet by the door and smooth my hands across the front of my skirt. Then I ascend the stairs to the salon where I know Londar is waiting. My satin dress whispers in the silence. Tonight I feel a tingle of anticipation, but it is not solely because of the Duchess.

I do not knock. Londar's hearing is not so good. It is deemed a low priority by his medical team, and so is not attended to. I open the door, and the hundreds of mirrors in the room all reflect my face above the burgundy dress. As usual, I pass a critical eye over the reflection of my features. I like the sharp angles of my face and the full roundness of my figure. But also as usual, I pick out a dozen little things that need some extra care. My eyes could be larger, and my nose smaller. Perhaps I will adjust those features next.

Then I turn to look for Londar. It takes me a moment to place the real man within all the reflections. He is in the centre of the room, sitting in his armchair, elevated thirty centimetres above the dense carpet. As I walk towards him, the mirrors make me feel as if I walk as part of an army, swarming towards Londar, closing in on him.

He sits as still and perfect as a painting. The sheen of the lanterns reflects in his skin. He is one of the most beautiful men I have ever touched.

I can hear his unnaturally steady breathing as I near him. Londar's chair is of a rich brocade, and he wears a sheer slip, studded with pearl buttons in a straight line. I can see the perfect circles of his nipples through the cloth. I look into his preternaturally bright eyes. He can still move his eyes. He rolls his blackened irises to the chocolates he knows are at his elbow. Bala always leaves chocolates on a silver tray just there. They are sweating lightly in the heat of the room.

I sit on the edge of his vast armchair and it bobs for a moment under my new weight, but then the air pressure adjusts and we both float calmly, my bare feet brushing the thick carpet beneath me. I reach for the fattest chocolate, glistening darkly in the lights, and then lean over him.

His eyes roam my face and body but find nothing of interest there. There is a spasm in his jaw and I delicately part his lips with my littlest finger. He is one hundred and seven years old, and at the very height of his beauty. His skin is smooth. It glistens like the chocolate I hold. I place the brown ball on his tongue. Even that has been tightened and recoloured. He makes no move to crush the sweet, or suck it. He just sits with his mouth open and the chocolate on his tongue, softening with the warmth of his body.

I close his mouth for him and smile. He gulps his dark saliva and a little of it wets the corners of his mouth. I wipe it away with a silk cloth. I smile again. He looks away from me to his own hands, resting in his lap. His hands are perfect, as smooth as gloves. No hairs, no wrinkles. There are not even any lines to show where his knuckles are. Tiny gold threads have been placed there subcutaneously. He is so proud of his hands. He likes to have them visible when his visitors call.

And tonight he expects an important visitor. An old lover. She must be nearly one hundred and thirty by now, the Duchess. She will be arriving the old-fashioned way, by carriage, and she will be bringing her full-time carer, Jareth. I have not seen Jareth in many months. He is, like me, not someone of means. Not handsome, not wealthy, but he has invested, like I have, in some of the basic cosmetic enhancements that keep us in employment.

I hear the clatter of hooves as the carriage arrives. This is a conceit, because horses are not used for labour anymore. But the Lady likes the sound of hooves, if not the smell of animal flesh. And since she and her guests only ever enter the carriage from the back, never the front, real horses are not necessary.

I rise and go to the window. I can feel Londar's eyes burning into me as I move about the room. I place a hand on the velvet curtain and draw it back. Outside, the city is dark. Few people spend time in the streets anymore. From the window, I can see only walls and walls of similar windows, all curtained. I look down at the carriage as it pulls up to our door. It is black and dome-topped, smooth and straight in front, but gilt-edged at the back, with ornate doors and false windows that allow no view in or out. I know that the inside panels of the carriage show electronic images of sweeping countrysides.

As the carriage doors open, light tips into the street like milk. Jareth steps into the white pool of radiance and looks up as I look down. He raises his left hand in a gesture I remember well. I nod at him. In his right hand he holds a small control. He thumbs a dial and the Duchess glides out of the carriage on a pale yellow lounge.

Even with the harsh light of the carriage behind her, I know she is glorious. She lies half on one hip, all the better to display the tight curves of her body. Her knees are half-bent and her feet rest against each other. Jareth has tucked her arms in close to that famous hourglass torso. The shadow of her head bleeds across high, neat breasts and a tiny waist. I cannot see her face in the shadow, but her white-blonde hair cascades and curls around her shoulders and the cushions she rests on. The lounge jostles slightly as it begins its ascent up the ramp into our building. Jareth walks behind it.

I go over to my old man and whisper into one shell-like pink ear, "She is here."

The edges of his lips jerk momentarily. I turn his lounge so that he can face the arched doors of the salon, where the Duchess will enter.

The doors swing silently open and the Duchess floats into the room. She is even more beautiful in the flattering light of the salon. Her bronze skin shines and her hair is a platinum halo. Her eyes are huge and bright and her lips have been shaped into a sensuous smile. She wears a long gold dress, gathered around her ribs and falling away at her thighs to reveal her varnished legs. I hear Londar release a long, rasping breath as she moves closer to us. I hope his new lungs can cope with this.

Jareth steps into the room after the Duchess, his hands on the control that moves her chair. I smile at him. He smiles back at me, revealing teeth that are only slightly uneven. His hair is white this time, and his face is broader than I remember. I still feel a genuine warmth for Jareth, although our work keeps us apart. Once, I thought of him as a brother.

"Brosia," he says to me, with a laugh in his voice. "How lovely you are."

"And you, Jareth," I reply. My pulse races at his compliment.

As the Duchess glides silently past me, I notice that Jareth has even painted the nails of her feet and hands. Tiny desert landscapes in orange and red. I raise my eyebrows a little, but such attention to detail made Jareth famous. Twelve years ago, he could have had any client he wanted. But Jareth had been seeking something else: one perfect masterpiece to call his own. The Duchess had some natural charms and enough money to buy more. Jareth realised her potential. I have no doubt that he tends to her every need with the utmost professionalism. And she has indeed become the talk of the social columns all over the world. Her surprise appearance at a ball two days ago is still the leading story.

I acquired many of my own clients when Jareth moved into his new position. Occasionally, those that can still talk will mention Jareth. But always with bitterness. As if he betrayed them by specialising with just one client. He would not find work with them again. I hope the Duchess will look after him.

As the Lady's lounge settles into position, I turn Londar's chair. A little too quickly, because he wobbles slightly as I grasp the headrest to stop the spin. Jareth is turning the Lady's lounge so that she and Londar may gaze at each other. Her face is like stone and her eyes are unfixed. I place both hands on Londar's shoulders.

Jareth tosses the control box towards me playfully, but I miss it and it drops into the carpet. He raises his hand, palm up, in a gesture that tells me that tonight I am to commence the proceedings. Jareth and I have done this many times before. It is calming to do this work with an old companion. Sexual jealousies died in us both many years ago.

I begin by reaching my right hand down and across Londar's shirt. I trace my fingers clockwise around his sharp nipple, showing darkly through his white shirt. Then I press all my fingertips into his hard torso and trace four straight paths to his sternum. I know he can feel none of this. His eyes jump from his lady friend to my hand and back again. As I reach the middle of his torso, I finger one small pearl button, slipping it through the buttonhole. I slowly, slowly move my hand down to the next button, feeling the smile on my face as I do this.

Jareth has pushed the Lady's lounge so close that I could reach out and put my hand on her thigh, but I do not. That is Jareth's job. I notice that Londar's eyes are fixed on the Lady, and I know that Jareth must have begun his Duchess's response.

I turn my head slightly and from the corner of my eye, I can see that he is stroking her face and hair, scraping the tips of his nails along her hard cleavage. Londar's mouth has become slightly ajar, and I reach down with my left hand to push his jaw gently back up. I swirl my hand over his face and look up quickly to catch the Lady's eye. She is still, but her eyes are bright. They stare at Londar, at the pocket in the base of his neck.

I move my hand into her line of vision, caressing Londar's firm flesh. Then I draw my hand down again, hoping to draw her eyes down too, to the pearl buttons I am unclasping for her pleasure.

Her eyes do not move. Jareth's hands are loosening the ties of her gold bodice, pulling back the cloth to reveal those perfect breasts with their dark, oiled nipples. But her eyes are completely still. She has not made one move nor taken one breath since she entered the room.

"Jareth?" I whisper. "She does not move."

Jareth continues to reach his hands along her ribs and tiny waist. She lies still and naked under Jareth's caresses and Londar's gaze. I wait for Jareth to signify to me that he has heard me. For a long time, he looks only at the Duchess. I can hear Londar breathing, and if I chose, I know I could also see his glossy chest rise and fall, but there is no such movement or sound from the Lady.

Jareth turns his head up to meet my gaze. His hands work slowly across the Lady's flesh, but his face shows no pleasure. He holds my gaze for a moment and then he drops his eyes to Londar's face. I look down quickly, but Londar shows no realisation of his Lady's unnatural stillness. He has become used to it, after all. And perhaps his eyesight is also fading, like his hearing. Perhaps the dimness of the room will save him from the realisation that the Duchess is not alive.

After a moment, I continue unbuttoning Londar's shirt. I notice with a touch of contempt that my hands have become unsteady. I struggle to pull Londar's shirt from his body, revealing his own sculpted torso, so fine you could count each artificial rib and muscle. I know that the implants sit like bubbles under the skin, held in place by strands of nylon. Surgeons will slice through any tissue just to get the right suspension.

I continue to knead Londar's flesh, working my way down his body, timing my movements to fit with Jareth's own, building to a climax only Londar of all the people in the room will appreciate.

Some time later, when Londar is satisfied, the clothes are pulled back across the sculpted bodies of our clients. I try to catch Jareth's arm as the Duchess departs. He dodges my touch swiftly, but stops in front of me. The Lady's couch hovers motionless in the doorway.

"Jareth," I say, stepping in close, so close I can smell him. I open my mouth to speak, but I don't know what to say. I hold up one hand close to his face, but I do not touch him. Jareth gives an almost-shrug and steps away. The only sound is the regular churning of Londar's breath behind us.

"I need the job," he says.

I nod at this. I understand that need.

"She chose this?" I ask. It is the only way I can think to ask all the questions running through my mind.

Jareth looks down and gives another shrug. He does not say. He will not tell me who controlled the Duchess's internal compulsions, who stopped the mechanics of her unnatural heart or the respirator that governed her lungs.

He manoeuvres the Duchess soundlessly from the room. I stand in the doorway for a moment, then I cross to the window for the second time this evening. The golden lounge of the Duchess glides into the carriage. For a moment, Jareth's shadow stretches along the street, then the light is extinguished as he closes the doors behind him. The carriage rolls away into the night and I am left in the room with the silent man behind me.

I return to Londar. I bend in to look at his irises. It is impossible for me to see anything there. Grief or oblivion. Whatever Londar feels, he is alone. In the artificial warmth of the room, the chocolates have melted.

I pick up the tray and take it to the kitchen. Bala looks up at me as I enter the room, but gives no welcoming sign.

"Long night, tonight," she says. "I thought you would never be going home."

I stretch my arms out above my head, trying to ease the stiffness in my back. I look closely at her and notice that one of her eyes is larger than the other.

"Goodnight, Bala," I say.

"See you next time," she says, turning to her reflection in the window beside her. Behind that reflection, the city waits silently.

I nod.

"Yes, Bala," I say. "Next time."

Stone by Stone

killed him quickly. *Bam!* One blow to the head with a metal pipe and Jacob went down fast. Like an empty coat, all the stuffing gone. Just *fwoomp*, and he was on the ground. Hit his head on the floor again. Thud. A heavy, wet sound from a body that didn't care anymore. And it was over.

Funny. I wasn't really prepared for that. Thought it would take longer. I stood over him for a moment. Killing time. But it didn't matter. I could stand there for the next four days if I wanted. I had an eternity now. So did he, if you believe that kind of thing.

Jacob was indifferent on the concrete floor, and I left him there under the narrow blaze of a bare ceiling bulb. Stepped over his crumpled legs and walked away from him. Didn't dwell on his full lips, his dark eyes, now closed. Didn't admire the sweep of hair along the back of his neck, the sharp shoulders, hunched against cold concrete. Didn't need to. Memories can be so bright they overshadow the present.

Plenty of time to reminisce later. I walked to the southern end of the room. I'd already begun to build a second wall inside and parallel to the original one, leaving just enough room between for my repose. This space I estimated at just over three quarters of a metre, once the equipment was moved and the bricks laid.

The inner wall reached my mid-thigh. It was over half a metre tall and built of exactly forty eight bricks and eight half bricks. Just tall enough for me to step over. Which is what I did, swinging my legs like a toy soldier.

I surveyed the space. The bricks were stacked in two rows against the original wall. Two hundred and fifty-six bricks and thirty-two half bricks, carefully counted. Couldn't afford to get that wrong. Camping torch in the right-hand corner. Battery life: six hours. A bag of dry mortar and five buckets of water lined up like sentinels. One empty tray for mixing. Plus the little step-ladder, gloves and finally, my brand new trowel.

Perfect.

Secure behind my little wall, I turned and shot a glance at Jacob. *Damn.* Hadn't realised. In his sudden descent, Jacob had landed facing the other way. His left shoulder jutted up like a sail without wind, obscuring his face. I thought about stepping back into the room and moving him around, but the blood was already seeping from the wounds in his skull, and I didn't want to disturb its natural pattern on the floor. The police might wonder why he'd been moved. Let them choke on it, with their badges and notebooks and their damn eyes. Watching everything. Let them tell his family they didn't know why, couldn't see why – oh, *why* – he'd been killed. Random violence. So heartbreaking.

Let them tell his damn wife.

I poured some mortar into the empty tray, adding water sparingly. Mixing it into a thick grey sludge and smiling at the ease of my success.

"So far," I cautioned myself, my voice hollow in the empty room.

Jacob had intended for this basement to become a wine cellar. Never quite got around to finishing it, though. He wasn't good at finishing things. Still, he'd dug out a civilised retreat from the damp ground under the house, cemented a floor, two metres by seven. Built walls in red brick nearly three metres high. Even — inadvertently — made enough room here for me, under his house in which his children will grow up. Two boys, perfect pictures of their daddy.

But don't worry, I'll keep my word. No one will ever know about us.

I put down a layer of mortar on the little wall, slathering it like shaving cream across the rough bricks. I wasn't worried about the workmanship. Jacob was strictly amateur. The walls he'd built were jagged with dried mortar pushing out between the bricks.

"Lilly hates this room," he'd told me.

Enter The Wife. Lovely, lovely Lilly. I never saw her in the flesh, but her picture was in every room of the house, except this one. Crowning glory: one massive portrait in the lounge. Larger than life. Jacob loved to stand beside it, destroying my attempts to ignore the monster wife. He liked to admire — though he would never admit it — her brush-stroked face and round clear eyes. Her sweet mouth lightly creamed with lipstick. There were even dimples in her cheeks, for chrissake. And her hair! A dozen soft golden hues formed a halo above her face and cascaded past her shoulders. Must've cost a fortune.

I wanted to burn that portrait. Wanted to watch her skin smoke and blacken, her eyes dissolve. But this way was better. This way had a kind of irony that appealed to me.

"I'll tell her, about us. Every detail!" I used to say fiercely.

"Darling," he'd smile. "Why spoil it?" Then he'd lean in close. "This way, we can be together."

Forever?

No, not that.

The wall reached my waist now. I laid the next row of bricks, carefully buttering the last one with mortar and sliding it into place. Tapping each brick with the heel of the trowel, I made sure the row was lined up with those of the neighbouring walls. Didn't want any gaps at the top that might let in light or air.

The first time he brought me to this house, I moved like a ghost. Afraid to touch anything in case my hand went through it. I didn't belong here. Family photos and heirloom furniture. Carefully-marked "Wedding" videos stacked under the television. Crystal glasses "from her mother". And more than that, I began to sense that Jacob enjoyed my unease. From then on, he made sure we met nowhere else.

Chest-height now. I looked at the wall forming under my hands, mortar hardening in the cracks. I looked at Jacob with his back to me, left arm outstretched across his body. The utter quiet unnerved me suddenly. It seemed to crowd the room.

Will I really suffocate, or will the silence drown me?

I knelt quickly to mix more mortar. The weak light coming from the cellar made this difficult to gauge, but I didn't want to turn on the lamp just yet. Wanted to save the battery life for when I was alone. Entombed.

How long would I lie there when the wall was done? That was the only calculation I wasn't sure of. It might take days to die. I couldn't stand that.

Four more rows and the wall nearly reached my shoulders. In the dim light I could barely see my feet. It was like standing in a black quicksand. I focussed on the wall. It had to look just like the others or they might come looking.

The lamp, when I flipped it on, slashed the walls with sharp harsh patterns of light and dark, wrapping my legs. It was almost more disturbing than the simple twilight haze of before. Still, I kept it on.

I was trying hard to compromise between using just enough mortar to close any gaps and not so much I'd run out. Jacob didn't cross my mind again for a while. Plenty of time for reflection when this was done, the lamp turned off, the ladder tucked away at my feet.

Lovely Lilly, darling wifey, was away four more days according to Jacob. Long enough, I hoped, to get the job of dying done. She'd come home, search the house. Eventually, she'd think to check the cellar, where she'd find her precious husband collapsed like a forgotten deck chair in a storm. Then she could collapse and sob over his cold body, her flaxen hair falling like a shroud across his face. Bemoan her fate and call out to her gods.

Why! Why!

What a touching scene it would be. Her dimpled cheeks wet with grief.

I wondered if she would. Maybe there was more to her angelic head than met the eye. Maybe she'd stand over him, cigarette between two fingers, pulling her lip and looking quizzically at her dead husband. Doing the sums in her head. How long until the insurance kicked in.

No. I was just projecting now.

The wall was up to my chin. I worked more slowly, checking the straightness of the rows. Time for the ladder. It was more awkward now because I had to step across the mortar and then pick up the bricks one or two at a time, returning to the ladder. My heavy shoes felt clumsy on the narrow metal steps, but I didn't want to drop a brick on my foot. Breaking a toe now would be extremely frustrating.

Seven years I'd waited, with him never once saying he'd leave Lilly but me always wanting to hear it. Staying home in case she left the room and he could call.

"Darling, I'm in my study, thinking of you. What are you wearing?"

Seven years of making excuses to my family until they forgot what I looked like. When was the last Christmas I hadn't spent alone?

I was mixing mortar again, checking the bricks were straight, that the wall didn't lean in or out. The lamp still shone harshly, making its flat shadows in my little room, my sepulchre. It took me two steps to comfortably reach the top of the wall now. Only three rows left to go. Brick after brick going into the wall. My arms and shoulders were burning, but I didn't stop.

Two rows left, a brick lathered in my hand. As I was about to place it, I heard a sound in the room where Jacob lay. I stopped, my right arm dragged down by the weight of the brick. A voice. Jacob's voice. I could never forget the sound of it, after the phone calls and promises. No, wait. There had never been promises.

"Huuuuuuuuu…"

He moaned, long and low. Like he might never stop.

Perhaps it was his death rattle, that animal noise he made. Perhaps his soul flew out on that noise and spun into the heavens, abandoning me at last.

"Sssssssssssss…"

The sound went on and on, a croaking hiss.

Don't tell me he's lying there in agony. Condemned by the one who should have loved him most. Abandoned, betrayed! Tossed aside like an old toy. Jacob, my poor Jacob. This wasn't how it was supposed to be. I never, never meant for you to die alone.

"Sssssssuuuuuuuuhhhhhhh…"

Don't tell me I'll spend eternity with that noise. What if they never find him? What if we lie three feet apart forever, him sprawled like a forgotten puppet while Death pulls on his strings, opens his mouth and pushes that noise out of his decayed body with an unholy wind.

Sweat formed on my face, running down my neck. With a growing sense of my own betrayal, I pressed my palms against the wall in front of me. The mortar was almost completely dry.

Jacob.

Trapped in my grave, it was too late to save him. The decision was already made. I couldn't get out if I wanted to.

By the time the noise stopped, as it had to, my arms were shaking.

I had to crouch on the ground for a moment to pull myself together. I didn't look over the wall. Didn't want to see what was there.

There was no other noise for a while. No voice. No scraping sound as someone dragged themself towards the stairs. No. It wasn't happening. Jacob was as dead as I was, both of us just waiting for the final puff of life to release us to the void or what comes after.

With a shaking hand I placed the brick in the wall, the mortar almost dried already. Went down the ladder for the next one. Cement splattered the walls and my clothes as I finished that row, started the next.

Last row.

There were only a few bricks left now.

"Suuu…" Jacob groaned, the sound amplified in my little chamber. "Susan."

I froze, caught in the act of bending towards the mortar, the lamp glaring into my eyes. My trowel extended, its point trembling. His voice. The voice that edged all my fantasies with guilt and desire. *Jacob, Jacob*. My heart leapt at that sound.

"Susan."

Weaker this time. I slowly pushed the trowel into the mortar, pulled it back thick with sludge. I went back to putting the bricks into that tiny space between wall and ceiling.

"Susan." It was a whisper now.

My hands no longer shook as I picked up the last brick. I pushed it into its slot, carefully lining it up with its neighbours, not tapping it too far with the trowel. Blocking out all light from the room where Jacob lay. Then I switched off the lamp.

Susan.

That's not my name.

Pale Dark Soldier

(1) It begins with the death of a judge. Early one morning while the sun's a milky glare in the sky.

Stop.

Wait.

The beginning shouldn't belong to the judge. This isn't his story.

Let's start again.

(1) It begins with a girl, slip of a thing, mousey and plain. She grows up to be accused of murder and the judge (an ordinary man predisposed, apparently, to suicide) declares her innocent and sets her free. The first thing she does with her freedom is go to his funeral.

She wants to see them cut the world open and rest the poor judge inside. She hopes it will be peaceful.

It isn't.

Afterwards she doesn't know what to do with herself.

Not a good way, she acknowledges, to begin.

(25) It ends with fire.

(1) OK, let's find a good beginning.

Let's forget the judge, because that's what she's trying to do, and let's start here, on the fat silver slug of a bus with the sun shining red through closed eyelids. Shadows of trees and birds and telegraph poles smear black bruises into her nightmares, but she stays resolutely asleep. It's better than her waking life.

A new beginning, they'd told her at the remand centre the day before. A new beginning. She'd thanked them for it, too, and meant it. Thank you.

Her forearm stings and when she does finally stir, it's to look to the crooked maroon lightning of her newest cut. She's amazed she still bleeds red. Surely it's all darkness beneath her skin by now?

Had she a god to pray to, she'd pray right now, right here on the bus that sheathes her from the sun. Instead, alone, she rests her forehead against the warm glass and stares and stares.

(2) After the funeral there's another bus. It moves on and through and when it stops, it stops on the edge of a town. She finds no words to describe this town and likes that about the place, likes that it feels forgotten. She thinks "forgotten" would be a good feeling too, soft and swollen. Like a biscuit left to soak in warm tea. Yeah. Yeah, she could get used to that.

She wraps her arms around herself and shivers because this much brightness makes her feel cold. The sun beats down so hard it turns the street to white like porcelain and the rubbery grass to soft white sheets. She squints into the light and spies a caravan park. She likes caravan parks too. Likes their promise of transience.

This one, though, up close makes no such promise. The rusted caravans squat and lean on bricks, not wheels, and the grass beneath them is long and jaundiced.

She decides to stay anyhow.

It's years before they find her again.

(3) When they do, they send two cops in deep blue uniforms who say, "We know it's you, Oscine."

She winces. "What is?"

She's thrown that name away.

The first cop is large and breathes heavily. The fat of his face pushes his features apart. His colleague is younger, fitter, milder-looking, effectively androgynous. Never speaks.

"This murder," says the first cop.

"I thought it was suicide," she says.

"What? What suicide?" He pauses, chews the inside of his cheek.

"Judge Rodan?" she queries, because Judge Rodan's is the first death she thinks of right then.

"Rodan? Hell, that's ancient history, girl," sneers the cop. "I'm talking about a helpless old man, two days ago. We know you did it."

His chin wobbles when he speaks. She likes it, likes to watch, but sees him become self-conscious under her stare.

She asks, "How?" Curious.

"Don't get smart with us!"

"Okay."

She doesn't mean to.

The cop's face is fat-red, fat-purple. "I'm not shitting you, lady," he snaps, "we're onto you, we're watching you."

She nods. She doesn't blame them. She would watch her too, if she were them. And she wants this cop to like her so she tries to be agreeable. She finds herself wanting to ask him to say her name. Her real name, the new one, the one she chose for herself. Goes so far as to open her mouth to form the question (the cop staring all the while with red-rimmed eyes).

She can't though, in the end. Stands there instead with her mouth hanging open, singing a silent note.

The cop apes her expression, wobbles his face at her, mocks and sneers. Finally says, "You got something you want to say?"

She presses her lips together, shakes her head, watches the cops retreat from her caravan to their car.

"Don't mess up!" shouts the cop.

She shakes her head again. She doesn't intend to mess up at all.

(4) But freedom is one of those things. Sometimes you run from it when you don't mean to.

(5) Long after the cops are gone, well into dark, into night, she sits outside and lets the mosquitoes steal schooners of blood from beneath her skin. That's when she sees it. Near her elbow is a new red line to go with the pale pink scars of the rest.

She calls the marks her soldiers.

Failures every one.

(6) Time slows down or it speeds up and sometimes all you can do is push through. She does that now.

It occurs to her there is often a point where everything in life is different, where everything spins and tips and changes. She starts to look for it then, a point, an instant when the incomprehension of all that has gone before fades into a future that seems oddly, convincingly familiar. A kind of prescient déjà vu.

She feels herself leaning forward, looking for it.

(7) There's a memory, but memories can't be trusted. Memories are impositions, stitching patterns onto moments that haven't earned it. They make sense of things that make no sense. They're easier.

Still. There's a memory of washing her hands under a tap. The tap's outside, behind a house she doesn't recognise. Water spills red into the rough cement drain. Beneath her fingernails are red stains that take much careful rinsing.

There's broken brown glass under the tap, a smashed beer bottle. In the memory, she's careful not to cut her fingers on it.

Later, she laughs at the irony.

(8) More cops.

These ones follow her in a slow black car like a thickened flea. They pull up beside her at the local shop where she goes to avoid the freezing cold light of supermarkets.

The cops ease out of the flea and walk with her until she stops. She can feel the bottle of orange juice warming under her arm and against her ribs. She holds it close while she turns to confront the newcomers.

The first cop is a man, has a deep tan, thick eyebrows. His jaw rocks constantly because he's chewing gum or something like gum. Tobacco, maybe, some other thing. The other cop is a woman with a pale face that is both slack and sharp.

"You're not untouchable," says the woman cop. She's young, hard like flint, hair shorn. Hands thick and square but with short, pointed nails.

"Of course," the girl replies, slip of a thing, more of a woman herself now.

"Don't give us shit!" chews the man.

"Okay," she says. The politeness is routine.

"Getting sassy, are you? Shirked the system too many times, think you're above it?"

"No."

No. It's true.

This latest in a long line — a lifetime — of cops looks her up and down.

"And what's with all the fucking scars on your arms? Some kind of tribal shit? You into some fucking tribe shit I should know about?"

Easing the juice out of the way, she looks at the puckered skin (white like spiderweb) of her own forearms, the result of decisions begun by a girl she doesn't remember being.

"No."

"No," seethes the woman cop, leaning her pointed hands on her hips, "what?"

The woman who was Oscine blinks. "No shit?"

(9) Inside, it's dark. The kind of dark that has nothing to do with light.

(10) The shrink they appoint is old and white-haired.

"Do you know why you're here?" he asks.

"They want to keep me in prison."

"If you're guilty, they want to keep you in prison."

"No," she corrects him. "They want me to be guilty."

"Why would they want that?" the doctor asks. He's nice. Has a calming smile.

She blinks. Why get into it?

"I know you're a shrink," she says, changing course.

"That's right. I told you when we sat down, didn't I?" He gives that calming smile.

"Did you? I forget." Her head doesn't work too good anymore. She's forgotten how to smile, for instance, if she ever knew it.

"Does that happen a lot?"

"How much is a lot?"

He chuckles, turns his smile to his lap, pulls it up again.

"Miss—"

"Skel," she whispers. She's never said it out loud before.

"Skel? Is that what you like to be called?" His tone is conspiratorial. At her nod, he continues, "What's it mean? 'Skel'? Is it a family name, or a name you got from a place, a person?"

"I made it," she says. "It means me. It's all me, mine. I made it."

She's beginning to sound like a crazy woman. It frightens her and she shuts up.

"Skel," he acknowledges, but the rest of the conversation is forgotten.

(11) "What's she say, doc?"

"She says she's still looking for the right one."

"Right one? For what?"

"For murdering."

Pause—

A sigh. A gesture to a newspaper, an easing in the chair, a stretch and a move to release his pistol from his holster, push it onto the desk, a look at the shrink with a wry smile. "I could give her a few suggestions."

A shared chuckle. Isn't life the same all over, hey?

(12) When the moment happens, she doesn't recognize it. Too much like all the others before it, the ones that held no change. And maybe that's its secret. It's the fact there's one more moment in a seamless

string of moments where nothing happens and nothing continues to happen that tips her. Skel, waiting for a change, goes quietly sane.

(13) The person talking now is maybe a shrink, maybe a cop. She's all light and no shade, and Skel can't quite look at her without wincing.

Skel sees things in tones but not colours by now. Even the wind has stopped being invisible. It has a jagged, numbing shape and it twists up light and dark into long braids.

The unidentified person puts the pad of one finger gently to the whitest scar on Skel's arm. "How old is this one?"

The touch is soft.

Skel is shrugging. She's lost track of the soldiers and of the dead. She's very, very sorry for all she's done.

"We x-rayed you, of course," says the stranger. "We found pins. You put sewing pins in your arms. Under these scars, here. See? This one and this one and all of these along here. Why do you do that?" When Skel doesn't reply, she says, "Does it make the pain go away?"

But she must know the answer to that already. If the pain had ever gone away — even for a breath, for a second — there'd be no need for so many scars.

The doctor asks, hesitating on the words, "What does it feel like?"

Skel shakes her head.

It feels like nothing, not unless she runs her fingertips along the bumps, and then it feels like piano keys budding under her skin. Or teeth. It amazes her what the body will appropriate and claim as its own. Memories are the same kind of thing.

She's not sure how long it's taken her to answer, but then she finds herself saying, "The cut stings and burns sometimes, a little. You'd expect that, right? But it's not so bad. The worst part is right before the cut is made, knowing what's coming. Sometimes it's best not to know. When the cut is made, I push the pin inside and feel a slight pressure. Then nothing. I push to make sure the pin's there — even if I can see it, I make sure. It's hard to trust your eyes sometimes.

"Then I tape over the top. Tight. The skin heals up fine, like nothing's even changed." She flexes her wrist up and down. "I don't feel them at all anymore. See?"

It's weird, though, because she does feel something, and it's something like presence and loss, an absence with thickness and weight and shape and range.

She adds, "I think I must be guilty?" And it's a question more than anything.

(14) Sometimes, alone in her cell, she's tempted to make new marks. Just to give the woman's fingertips a place to land. Sometimes she worries she already has.

(15) They keep letting her out and back in. They begin to call her "institutionalised". Skel doesn't mind, though it's not a name she would've chosen for herself.

"How is it," says a stranger, "that you keep getting away with it?"

Skel tries to retreat, but the person mocks her, mimics her, shifts to follow. Skel stares, furious. She blinks away some of the wool itching her eyes. She takes a wide step to her right and the person in front of her is cut in half lengthways. Like an axe through the middle, one half of her face and torso and one leg, all disappear.

It's then Skel realizes the figure is constrained by the blunt edges of a mirror.

(16) The doctor says, "I'm going to suggest the scars relate to the sins you've committed. That is, when you commit a sin — in your eyes — you cut yourself."

The doctor says, "What do you think of that? Does it make any sense to you?"

The doctor is wasting her time. Skel's entire life is incoherent. Nothing makes sense. Nothing relates to anything else. That's how Skel knows she's sane. She's stopped expecting sense. She's stopped seeing patterns. She allows things to fall apart.

(17) The doctors say, "She appears lucid, coherent, but detached. No apparent delusions. Extremely reserved, but not entirely lacking in affect — that is, emotion," they supply for anyone who doesn't know. "Further, she does not particularly respond to any of the medications the State will legally allow us to administer. We must surmise she is sane."

They add, "Well, as sane as you and me."

"What we can't work out is what she wants. What motivates her."

(18) The cops don't like it, don't care what she wants. Maybe it's the way she was raised or perhaps some entirely personal or imagined disappointment. Whatever. It doesn't change what they know she's done.

"Life hasn't worked out the way she wanted," some of them say. "Welcome to the goddamn world."

After all, they reason, most people are disappointed or bruised somewhere along the line and most people don't end up murdering other people. Much as they might like to. They grow up, they get over it or if they don't, they store the disappointments away where they will do least harm. Least harm to others, that is.

The cops congratulate themselves on their compassion.

They call Skel "unholy" and "a machine" (two descriptions Skel herself sometimes wonders at, catching herself unawares in the middle of something. But who gets to decide what is unholy? And aren't we all just a little governed by what may be called mechanics? Even biology has identifiable aspects of machinery).

(And what, while we're at it, is the sum total, the end result to the world, to others, of "harm"?)

(19) Half the battle is working out what you want. The rest is working out if it's okay to want that. Somewhere in the middle, you often get

the very thing you've been wanting and waiting for. When you do, it's usually by accident and generally too late.

Knowing this does not make Skel — or anyone — happy.

(20) She's outside again. The sky is so thick with damp and cloud as dense as mud. She almost believes she can dip her hands up into it and carve herself a space. Grey like prison, like death. She thinks to drag it down over herself.

(21) On the bus she stares and stares. It occurs to her suddenly, her brain a-fire, that she has no love for landscapes. The places she's seen (and there have been few so far) are almost always empty, narrow and thirsty. Once, though, she'd seen rainforests that lived on meanness and sweat. She'd liked that. The world is an inhospitable place and she likes it to look that way. It's a particular bitterness of hers. Ugly, hard, gruesome, that's what she thinks the world should look like.

Burned would be even better.

She passes through the space where a small bushfire has been. Even in the air conditioned bus she can smell the ripe scent of burnt, though there's no smoke left. Only pitted blackness on both sides of the road. Skel rubbernecks her way through, ignoring the leers and grins of her fellow passengers. It's beautiful here. The world is all black chalk. The world is ebony salt.

Split open, cracked, peeled apart, the earth reveals the darkness beneath. It's comforting. She would like to lie down in one of those splits and rest. And rest.

This is what she wants now. To burn down the world.

(22) Skel is sure she's being followed.

She keeps spying movement from the corner of her eye and imagining it means something. She figures whoever's following her probably wants the same thing she wants herself or else why would they be all the way out here?

She's carrying a chemical cocktail in a backpack. Lack of mechanical knowledge means she wasn't sure what would light the best, so she's brought a bit of everything. It's not like she could ask advice, not for what she's doing. Consequently, she has kerosene, methylated spirits, paint thinner, solvents of various names, and petrol. The petrol was the hardest to source. She had to go to a service station and make up a story about a beat-up car she was restoring. (*Got it at auction*, she said, *a friend is fixing it for me, I'm not really sure what kind it is. It's black, though, and round like a bug.*)

They only sold petrol in large cans, so back home she had to pour it into milk bottles to fit in her backpack. The fumes made her head spin. They slapped upside her brain at the point where her eyebrows meet, bypassing her nostrils entirely. When she screwed the last lid back on, the bottle warped. It felt soft in her hands. Skel handles it gently like a child, like hope, careful not to crush it. It is her new beginning.

She's at the dry edge of a park, miles from rivers or hoses or houses or streets. She's taken half a day to walk here, and she's dizzy from thirst and the weight of her pack. Nevertheless, she rests the bag on the ground gently and squats beside it, legs like rubber. She hasn't given herself a way out of this plan. But she's calm. She's never been so calm.

She's also armed. So when she next spies a movement, she spins, razor blade in hand, spins and almost topples, catching herself with her spare hand against the ground. Her knees click and ache, feeling like uncooked gristle.

There's no one there. There never is, she finds. She can't remember the last time someone was there.

She goes back to pouring petrol on the ground, angling her face away from the fumes. By now she's old and her knees have stiffened. It's taken her a while to come at this plan. She frequently has to change position, taking time to unfold herself and sit flat with her legs straight out, resting on one hip and then the other. Where the petrol touches her thigh it feels warm.

She hesitates on lighting the match.

She wishes she had someone.

(23) "What's your name?" Skel asks. "What's your name?"

(24) The wind doesn't quite whistle and doesn't quite scream. It could be an answer, and Skel thinks she could find herself in that answer if only she could make a word to match the noise.

The first match is whipped clean by the wind, and the next and the one after that, but Skel is determined. She wants the world to plaster over where she's been. *What is death*, she wonders, *what is it?* A stupid hangover from Sunday School and the random philosophising of a misspent youth, most like, but Skel still wants to know. Wants to understand the journey before she begins.

She hunches over the new match. Its flame stumbles and starts and finally holds, and she stares at the point where it turns blue. Misleadingly serene, that soft, clear blue. Deceptively round and pure. The contrast is gorgeous, and she forgets, for a time, everything that's happened to that slip of a girl she was.

When the match warps and withers to black and the flame dies again, she understands she is faced with a choice. She doesn't shirk it. She takes as long as she needs to work out what she wants. She lets the moment stretch and stretch, wanting, making sure.

At last she nods, yes, and the plan continues to unfold.

"What's your name?" she whispers, to absent somebodies she's grown to miss.

"I'm Skel," comes the answer.

"No," she says, turning to look for a stranger, "that's my—"

No one's there.

Just the wind, hushing her.

Skel pauses, because in a way it's all beginning to make a certain sense.

And because the fire, when it hits, hits faster than thought, faster than light, and stops everything that ever had a chance of going before.

II. End of the World

Coming Up For Air

S he had a scar on her hand she didn't remember getting. Probably happened in the last data crash. It was a crazy time. A lot of things were screwed up then. Planes fell out of the sky. Hospitals were forced back to guesswork when all patient records, all treatment records, were lost. Hell, the scar wasn't the only thing she didn't remember. She'd probably forgotten her own name during the Great Data Fog of '09.

"Mistakes happen," Egan said. "Don't take it hard."

He was standing by the windows, side-on to her. The whole office was windowed. It was like floating in a high-rise air bubble.

"Sure," she said. "Just surprised. Thought Adelaide would be the last to fall."

He grunted. "You and everybody else."

The city was ideally suited to farming. The winds were consistent and strong, the connection to the national grid was reliable and the urban population wasn't as dense as other places in the country.

She'd helped establish the Adelaide farm ten years ago. Back then it was all about progress, ways forward. Hope. Now, not so much. Progress of a different kind, she guessed. Weren't they calling it devolution — negative evolution — nowadays? Forward into the past.

"I hear you're pretty good," he said. "Not the best, but we can't afford the best."

"Thanks," said Maggie without irony.

"You were there for the big one of twenty-thirteen, right?"

She nodded, but didn't offer any more.

"Not your baby?" he prompted.

"Sydney? No. I was a lackey for that one."

"Fetched the coffee, that sort of thing?"

"Well, not that much of a lackey, no. I mean…" She shifted in her chair. "I was new to this line of work. If I had to do it again, I mean, looking back…"

She let the sentence hang itself.

"Yes?"

"A lot of things could've been done differently if we'd known better."

"Sure," he agreed. "We were all novices, then. Didn't understand the politics of what we were doing."

He moved away from the window and sat on a lounge, one leg crooked across the opposite knee. Maggie had to swivel her chair around to see him. Nice office, this. Roomy. You didn't get one of these if you weren't prepared to undo a few mistakes. But even then it was just a waiting room for a bigger office. Egan was on his way up.

He was young, but not as young as he looked. He wore his suit in an offhand way, like someone who wore suits to impress people but pretended not to give a damn himself. It was a carefully crafted balancing act. His hair was combed back to emphasise the narrow lines of grey that worked out from his temple.

"For instance?" he asked.

"I'm sorry?"

"What would you have done differently?"

He was bored, probably not really listening. He had a budget, she had a price. This was just an obligatory waste of each other's time so they could claim due diligence on the contract.

"Well." She took a breath and tried to look like maybe she hadn't been rehearsing this all morning. "They were too light on the comms. They figured if they didn't tell anyone, no-one would panic, right? But of course when it all hit the fan, no-one was prepared. That's really where they got into trouble. You rock one boat, the waves spread all over the place."

Egan chuckled. "Nice."

He pulled back, withdrawing into his suit. He was ready to end the interview.

She pressed on, "They shut the power off overnight, figuring no one would notice, there'd be less going on. But the trouble with that is—"

"Most backup programs run overnight," he supplied.

"Exactly. So halfway through everybody's backups, the power cut out. Not only were the systems corrupted, so were the backups."

"No fallbacks," he agreed.

"Not a lot. Unless you were part of a really big org."

"Lot of those," he observed.

"Not enough to go round, though."

"Sure."

"Plenty of the smaller places, and the individuals, families, whatever. They just re-use the same disks over and over. You screw up Thursday's backup, there's not necessarily a Wednesday. Right?"

"Right." He stood and moved back to his desk.

Maggie swivelled in her chair, keeping an eye on him.

"Like I said," she continued, "more comms. Get people prepared. Get their expectations managed from the start."

"And there'll be no panic?"

"Oh," she said carelessly, "I've worked half a dozen of these jobs now. There's always panic."

He nodded.

"So what happens when it goes wrong?" he asked. "What happened with Sydney, for example?"

She sighed.

"Well, Sydney, that was different."

There'd been a power surge when the new eggs went online. People built their electrical facilities pretty robustly now, but not robustly enough for the kind of power that got unleashed. Fritzed everything. Servers fried, backup drives burned, circuits overloaded during the buzz. Too much heat. Data got done, basically. And routers. VOIP was zapped, TV and radio stations went down, air conditioning went off.

"The price of generators went through the roof after that. People learned to be paranoid," she said.

Egan snorted. "Paranoid is good?"

"Paranoid is smart," she said. "The only people with generators back then were the people who owned transistor radios."

He grinned. "Those things still exist?"

"You'd be surprised."

"So. Disaster recovery planning? I take it someone had a contingency plan?"

"In a lot of cases, we *were* their contingency plan. We were trying to steady power supplies, after all."

He was thoughtful. He sat in the large executive chair behind his desk and shuffled some papers in front of him. One of those papers she recognised as her CV.

"This time?" he asked, scanning the page.

"Comms, daylight—"

"Community consultation?" he asked wryly.

"Well I wouldn't go that far." She returned his grin. "I mean, unless you have that kind of time. When were you thinking of doing this thing?"

"In about three months."

"Then you don't have that kind of time."

He shook his head and smiled. "They told me you were a cold fish."

"Is that a problem?"

"Not for me," he said. "Exactly what we're looking for."

He gave her a thoughtful look and leaned back in his chair, silhouetted against the grey sky.

Twenty floors up, they should've had a pretty good view of the city. It was down there somewhere, underneath a halo of smog. From here even the black solar balloons that formed the top layer of the wind farm were barely visible. Too far away, and the city haze closed in on every side.

"How many? In the farm? I see one, two … five?" he counted.

"Twenty-two."

"That many?"

"Two of them are on your own roof."

He glanced up at the ceiling.

"And when you take them down?"

"Phased approach. Another thing we learned from Sydney. We'll use a small team and we'll do it one at a time. No more sudden moves. It'll take longer but it'll be safer," she said, adding, "about a month," before he could ask.

He reached up as though he might be about to stroke an invisible beard. When his fingers reached his bare chin, he paused.

"You sound like you know what you're talking about," he said.

But there was a question in his voice, so she said, "There's been no problems since Sydney."

He raised an eyebrow. "None?"

"You ever heard of any?"

"No," he admitted.

"So how about you just let me do my job."

Maggie's team consisted of one other electrical engineer, Josh, two Maori security guards, and her. Small was better. Less noticeable.

The Maoris, Iraia and Tui, called each other "cousin", but she didn't know if that meant they were related, or if it was just a nickname. Why not? After all, she called them "consultants". Another made-up label. Nobody needed to know otherwise.

The communication strategy had been thorough, but not thorough enough to let people know *exactly* when she was coming. She figured that would be counter-productive.

Still, some people were apparently waiting.

"Arrived target one," Josh said over the intercom. "Access denied."

"ETA three minutes," Maggie said. She was in the car with Iraia and Tui. "Trouble?"

"About five foot four of it," Josh replied.

Tui snorted, his heavy hands resting in his lap. Iraia chuckled.

Josh had gone on ahead to scout for trouble. Target one was a soft target. Mid-week, residential, a thirty-five storey apartment building on the east edge of town. She figured it would be most quiet then.

Josh was easy to spot. He was at the back of the building, dressed discreetly, in dark brown, like a cleaner or an electrician. It was a uniform that usually provoked the least questions. But in this day and age, everything was questionable. He stood with his pack against his leg, hands on hips. In front of him was a woman with her arms crossed, barring his way.

"This your boss?" she asked as Maggie approached.

"Yeah," Josh said. He inclined his head towards the woman. "Owner."

Maggie nodded.

"Ma'am—"

"Ma'am?" said the woman. "What is that meant to be, sarcasm?"

Maggie ignored her. "We have the necessary paperwork, the State's permission—"

"You don't have my permission."

"We don't need it, ma'am," Maggie reminded her. "The egg on your roof—"

"Egg? That the wind farm balloon?"

Maggie took a deep, deep breath. Let it out again.

"Yes, *ma'am*, that's the farm item. Which you don't own. The Government does. And now the Government wants it back. As per their contract—"

"To move it where?"

"The farm's being shut down."

The woman was slight in a hungry way. Her mouth was set hard and the lines on her face suggested that was habitual.

"People rely on that power," she said.

Maggie didn't argue.

Most places, the farms weren't profitable. Wind was too irregular. But here above Adelaide, slipstreams were fairly regular, power was good. It was probably enough to service the local area pretty cheaply. But with just one farm left, it would require too much to maintain the expertise needed to service it.

She could try explaining all that to the owner but she figured it would be wasted.

"And you rely on the rent?" she asked instead.

A muscle throbbed in the woman's cheek. "I got kids to feed."

"And you're Mrs…" Maggie checked the paperwork. "Owens?"

"Yeah."

"I'm sorry, Mrs Owens. The Government is making reparations—"

"Don't cut it, though, do they? Reparations. Fancy word meaning 'next to nothing'."

"And you can apply for hardship benefits."

Owens snorted. "Me and everybody else. Take a number, is that what you're saying?"

Maggie didn't hesitate. She had full authority here and a kind of diplomatic immunity under federal law. That gave her the power.

"I guess that's what I'm saying, yeah."

Josh looked from one woman to the other. Owens' gaze was steady on Maggie. It was like standing in a wind tunnel, that stare. It drowned out everything else that was happening.

"Well," said Owens. "Fuck you very much."

But she stepped aside.

"Getting a bit hairy there, boss. Thought you might need us to step in," said Iraia. "Right, cousin?"

"Right," said Tui.

"Yeah, you guys were a big help," Josh observed.

"If we'd known you were being held up by a skinny white woman, we would've come running, Josh."

Iraia slapped Josh on the shoulder and Josh grunted.

"That's probably enough," Maggie suggested.

The lift was a slice too small for four people when two of them were two-foot wide each. The packs were between them on the floor. Winches, rifles, mesh metal butchers' gloves, scythes, two small generators, currently balanced on top of each other.

"The Government want the balloons back?" Tui asked.

"No," said Maggie. "Just the electrical stuff. The turbines, tethers."

"That's what we have to escort out?"

"Yeah. That," said Maggie, "and us."

"It's like we're going backwards," Josh observed. "I reckon I remember putting this one up here in the first place."

"And the balloons? Can we keep those?" Iraia asked.

"They're good for nothing. By the time we're done there'll be holes all through those things," said Maggie.

"The material's still all right, though," said Iraia.

"They're not much more than garbage bags."

Iraia shrugged. "Could be a market for garbage bags."

Maggie waved her hand. "Do what you want. Just get those turbines out of here."

The horizontal-axis turbine lay like a massive bullet, its round metal casing a metre across and rotor blades spinning dumbly. Four huge feet kept the whole thing screwed to the roof, with a quad of guy-wires adding further stability, pinning the porcine shape either side. The balloon tethers stretched from its snout straight upwards.

"We gotta get that off the roof?" Iraia asked.

"No, they've got military planes on standby for when we unscrew the damn thing. I just have to call when we're ready."

Someone had planted a garden around the twenty-centimetre bolts that held the thing's feet in place. The braided metal cable, seven centimetres thick, stretched into the grey sky with a jasmine vine wrapped around it. White flowers nodded and the cable shifted slowly back and forth.

"What a mess," Josh observed. He took a deep breath. "Smells good, though."

He laid down his gear and added, "Too bad about the Owens family, hey?"

"The Owens family," Maggie observed, "and every other family losing their cash cow."

"Well, when you put it like that," Josh said. He busied himself with his gear. "What about you? When we tear down the last wind farm, you got a new cash cow lined up?"

Maggie didn't answer. She dropped her bag and pulled out the shears. "Let's get this junk out of the way."

Good thing they'd kept the vines away from the rotors. Could have plunged eight city blocks into darkness if they'd done otherwise. Somebody was maintaining the place.

"How's the balloon get the wind into the turbine here?" Tui asked.

"It doesn't. They're different systems," Maggie said. "This turbine is one egg, catches the wind coming over the roof. The smaller one, on the balloon, sources wind higher up. Built-in redundancy. If one fails the other keeps pumping out electricity. That's the theory, anyhow."

She braced for the inevitable joke about wind, but since she'd learned to say "catching wind" rather than what the rotors were really doing — passing wind, pulling it through the fat turbine's body — the men were blessedly quiet.

With the vine littered in pieces at their feet, she pulled out the first winch and began clipping it into place around the base of the cable. She kicked aside the layer of dirt in the makeshift garden bed so she could extend the winch feet to the ground.

Josh knelt and drilled it into place. The cable creaked against its new casing. With the winch they'd pull the balloons into reach, deflating them for their final descent to the roof. Hopefully the roof, anyhow.

"How low do you think we can get it before we shoot it?" he asked.

It was a careful calculation. Too high, it could deflate and fall over the side of the building. Maybe break a window. Or land on another rooftop where someone else might scavenge it before they could reach it. Damage and injury, public outcry, whole project out of control.

Just like Sydney. A few of the eggs had fallen out of the sky of their own accord, of course. Wind hadn't been consistent enough to hold them in place.

Maggie put a generator in place. It would mechanise the winch, meaning they wouldn't have to drag the thing out of the sky by hand.

"Winds are pretty high," said Maggie. "We'll have to get it down real low to be sure."

"Great," said Josh.

"Gloves on," Maggie replied.

This was just a precaution. In case the generator failed. She'd only had to resort to manual work once. Nearly tore her arm off doing it, but at least she hadn't fallen off the roof. She was the first to admit it wasn't a good backup plan, but that's why she had two winches and two generators. And Josh. And spare gloves for the security guys, not that they knew it.

Josh flexed his fingers inside the gloves.

"Ready?"

She nodded.

The rooftop generator had a lever to turn it on and off. She wrenched it around to the off position. Ironic, really. They were carrying generators all over the place with them because this powerful turbine in front of them would run out of juice when the egg got low enough.

The rotors slowed, the blur of their movement giving way, revealing dark blades like paddles.

Josh squatted, connecting the leads from the winch to the generator, then powered the generator on.

Nothing.

"Crap," he observed.

"You got the leads around the wrong way, cousin?" Tui called.

"Doesn't matter," Josh called over his shoulder. But he flipped them anyhow.

Still nothing.

"Grab the second generator," Maggie said.

Down one contingency already.

Josh swapped them over. The new generator chugged to life. She gave him a thumbs up and they backed off from the noise. The winch began to draw in the metal cable, wrapping it backwards into its guts. *Like pulling on the tail of a dragon*, Maggie thought.

They settled in. The winch would take an hour or more to drag the balloon into sight from over a hundred metres up. Just under what the Civil Aviation Authority deemed an acceptable height.

Maggie thumbed her palm-net to the weather page. South-westerlies. Five on the Beaufort scale. Strong breezes. There'd be spray coming off the ocean. White crests like bird wings. When this was all over, she was going to take a break. Maybe teach herself to surf.

Josh leaned forward and raised his voice over the sound of the generator.

"So, about that job?"

Maggie frowned. "You looking to line something up?"

"Can't afford to be too long out of work," Josh confirmed.

"Maybe you should send your CV to that government guy, Egan. He offered me something."

Josh looked surprised. "What is it? A desk job?"

"Yeah, I think so. I said I'd think about it."

The generator noise made conversation tough, reducing their voices to staccato words.

"Not gonna wait for the next round of power fads?" Josh asked. "Gotta be something new, right? We've tried sun, wind and ocean. I figure next they'll find a way to make electricity from dirt."

Maggie grunted. "Yeah, they did already. I think it's called coal."

A shiver of tension went through Josh's body then. He was focused on something behind her. "Thought this was a residential building?"

"It is," Maggie confirmed.

"So how'd they get access to that kind of firepower?"

Maggie turned. Four men had come through the door to the stairwell. They were tall and well-fed. Obviously not from around here. And they were carrying rifles. Big ones.

The Maoris had seen them, too. They were shifting their weight, reaching for the handguns at their waists.

"Just here to talk!" one of the strangers called.

To their right the generator continued to drag in the balloon.

Maggie moved forward to meet them.

"You Mr Owens?" she said to the first man.

"I'm Farris," he replied. "Local council."

"The State's offering compensation for councils," Maggie said.

"You know there's a sick girl in the building, right?" Farris countered.

She nodded. "Iron lung. I heard. We took provisions on your power supply. Should be no interruptions."

Josh interrupted. "Shouldn't she be in a hospital?"

Farris grinned. "You offering to pay?"

Josh shifted on his feet. "Guess I'm not."

"Electricity keeps her breathing, and that's one part of the equation," said Farris. "Rent keeps her eating, though."

"Right, Farris," said Maggie. "I'm going to have to ask you to leave. The Government is still renting this space and these men," she indicated Tui and Iraia, "get edgy with civilians around."

"Civilians," said Farris. "That's appropriate. There's a war going on, after all."

Maggie didn't respond.

"You taking all of them?" Farris asked. "Hills area as well?"

"Already got those," said Maggie.

"They were the biggest money-spinners in the state."

Maggie said, "They also needed the most service. Cyclic stresses on the axles and bearings. Winds over forty miles knock the turbines around too much. Cables wear on their hinges. Rotors need replacing."

"Right," said Farris without interest. "Aren't you the walking encyclopedia."

He moved in closer, close enough that he was almost nose-to-nose with Maggie. He smelled of aftershave and tobacco, in that order.

Behind and above Farris, the black balloon had come into sight, swinging its turbine beneath it like an udder. Maggie focussed on the man in front of her.

"I'm going to ask you one more time," she said.

She said it low. Standing this close to Farris there was no need to raise her voice. She pulled a handgun from the back waistband of her trousers, beneath her jacket. The intruders watched her do it. They didn't look worried.

"Please leave," she said.

Farris smiled. "Are you threatening me?"

The tobacco got stronger when he opened his mouth. She tried to stop a sneer.

"Not at all," she said. "It's for the balloon."

Beside her Josh did the same.

The guns were heavy and small with long barrels. They really were meant for the balloons, but since they carried real bullets they'd work just as well on human flesh.

It was clear Farris hadn't been planning on dealing with people carrying guns. He stalled, looking from her to Josh. He was probably only here to save face, Maggie figured. One last-ditch attempt to show the local community the council cared. She wondered if he was planning on spending the reimbursement on community programmes or a better class of thug. So far these ones hadn't done him much good.

"You might want to get out of the way," said Maggie.

She shifted to her right so Farris was out of shot. She took quick aim at the solar balloon and raised the gun.

"Wait!" said Farris.

He jerked the end of her handgun, sending the bullet wide and low. It bounced off the roof-top turbine with a clang.

"Wait," he said again. "What happens when you decommission all the eggs?"

Maggie hesitated.

"You're out of a job, right?"

Josh looked at her, but she ignored him.

"What if we kept you on the council payroll? Your team, too?"

"As?"

"Wind farm service team."

"You got any idea how expensive the parts are for those turbines? You'd be paying double whatever you could pay us just for replacement parts."

"Nope," said Farris. "But I do have an idea of where they're junking the pieces. Should keep us supplied for a few years."

Maggie shook her head. "Sorry, we've been sent here to do a job."

"I can pay you more," Farris said. "Think they'll ever notice one missing turbine? There's always accounting mistakes."

Maggie moved as though she were lowering the gun. She took a careful look at the balloon where it rode the tether down to the roof. Without even really aiming, she fired.

The balloon puckered, rocked, and groggily increased its speed towards the ground. She fired again, winging it.

Farris had instinctively moved out of the way on the first shot. Now he glared at her.

"You won't even consider it," he said.

"I considered it," Maggie replied. "You think you're the only one who's looking for a black market in electricity? This isn't the way to do it."

"Oh no, Little Miss Encyclopedia?" Farris sneered. "Then what is?"

Maggie strode across to where the balloon was rapidly falling, wind whistling through its black plastic. But Farris was there ahead of her. He snatched the small turbine from the air above her head and cradled it to his chest like a baby. The slack of the tether trailed from the turbine to the winch.

Tui and Iraia were approaching fast. Escort the turbines, that's what she'd told them.

"Wait!" said Farris.

"You don't own this," Maggie said. "Build another farm, sure. Micro-site it in a park, or even better, out at sea. Somewhere no-one else can access. There's plenty of places for your own wind farm. It's not the environment that let you down here. It's the politics."

Farris considered. He opened his mouth, but a sudden jerk on the cable pulled him off his feet. He was dragged bodily towards the winch.

Josh shouted, "Let go!" just as Maggie leapt over Farris' prone body towards the winch.

Farris released the turbine but his hand must've been caught. He gave a yell as the turbine met the winch, then screamed as his fingers were crushed between them.

By then Maggie already had the generator off, but it was slow to shut down. Farris' hand was caught up to the wrist and the way the blood was pulsing out made it clear he'd hit a vein. Maggie balled up the black plastic of the balloon and pushed it against the winch.

To Iraia she shouted, "Call an ambulance!"

Farris was ashen.

"Lifts weren't working when we got here," he said. "Guess because of the generator. If the ambulance even gets here—"

"Save it," said Maggie. "Josh, unbolt the winch. Now!"

She flipped out her palm-net and speed-dialled the number she'd been given. She was thinking on her feet, activating another contingency.

"Sergeant Tobin," said the phone.

"Sergeant, target one, time to send that military plane," she said. "Only, there's been a change of plan."

"I can't authorize a change in plan," said Tobin. "Upstairs doesn't like it."

"Then they'll hate this," she said. "But I'll trade you. The generator for a fast rescue. Got a man down."

"You crazy?" Tobin asked. "We're not here to rescue your team. You'll lose your job over this, ma'am."

Maggie switched off the device.

Well, hell, she reflected, *she'd been planning on losing her job anyway.*

Watertight Lies

"You know who has good air conditioning? Banks have good air conditioning."

Pete was hanging upside down from the cave roof, lowering the monitoring jack into the pool below. Though "pool" was probably too generous a description.

Further back on the roof, Gabrielle took a more traditional approach to the problem of hanging upside-down. She was spread-eagled, alternatively tipping her head to watch Pete's progress, and more frequently leaning her forehead on the cool rock above her. She took deep, concentrated breaths, pressing her fists to the sides of her temple.

Pete often said if they gave him a desk job, he'd wither and die.

Gabe would've killed for a desk job.

"I worked in a bank once," she said.

"Yeah? Did they have good air conditioning?"

"Mostly they saved it for the customers."

"Well, those two-faced, snake-rat-bastards," said Pete calmly. "What'd you do there?"

It was how they checked in on each other, this bland back-and-forth, making sure no one was panicking in the confined quarters of the cave. The water, four metres below, glowed green under their head lamps but the rest of the cave was so thick with blackness you could almost chew it.

"Cleaner," said Gabe. "Dyslexia, again."

Pete's light wobbled as he pulled the jack free and wrenched it back up towards him.

"Man, you got a bum steer with that dyslexia. I thought they could treat that?"

"Yeah, yeah." Gabe bit back on a pulse of nausea. "Trouble is, I get so freaked out whenever I have to take an exam."

"Sucks," observed Pete. "Three canisters. Enough for a good sampling. Head up?"

Gabe pulled her head back towards the roof before realising he meant "head to the surface".

"Hell yeah, let's do it," she said.

Pete clicked the sample canisters to his chest harness and spun easily on his axis. That's how he made it look. Effortless, like he was being held upright by the hands of heaven.

"I heard they're banning elephants from zoos," he said.

"Elephants?" How did he find out about this shit? "Why?"

"They need too much water, of course," he said blandly.

Gabe was annoyed. "Oh, oh, right, the elephants, the *elephants*."

Her harness shuddered and she gasped, grabbing for it with one hand, keeping the other one pressed to the roof.

Shit. Shitshitshit*shit*.

"Gabe," said Pete with total calm, "we're about four metres above water. You fall here, the biggest worry you have is getting wet."

He was lying, of course: there was barely enough water to cushion her fall. But he was also reminding her that if she wanted to go postal, now wasn't the time.

"Right, right," she said. "Save it for the surface."

Sweat trembled in her eyebrows. She rubbed at it with a gloved hand and realised she was shivering. She took more deep breaths and then turned, infinitesimally slowly, in her harness. There was nothing, nothing in the world but her and a narrow circle of light. Outside that was a thick weave of darkness and Pete's voice, droning on and goddamn *on*.

"Talk to me," he was saying. "Talk to me."

"What?" Her own voice was thick, shuddering. She was still turning though, turning to face the way out. *Getting out,* she was chanting to herself. *Getting out, out.*

"You like elephants?"

"I … never thought. Yeah, yeah, I like them. They're conscious of death. They have … graveyards."

"Whoa," said Pete, drawing it out. "Welcome back, Little Miss Morbid!"

"Salt," she said.

"Did you just call me a shit?" Pete joked.

"No, salt. I heard they used to tax it."

She was carefully adjusting each of the links on the waist of her harness, attaching the hooks at her collarbone to the bright-red climbing ropes on the roof. "In China. And in Jordan, they fought the first war over it. It was precious. That's where the saying comes from. 'Worth your salt'. See?"

"Salt, eh? Well, precious, you and me must be rich as all get-out. Let's hurry back up there and find ourselves a casino and some smack, Gabriella."

"Just Gabe, thanks," she said.

Pete pretended to ignore her. "I'm gonna fill my pockets."

"Your what?"

"Pockets. With salt."

She was working carefully and methodically (*like a machine*, Pete had described it, *move like a machine*), snaking her way back along the static ropes they'd laid on the way down. She checked each handhold, tugging slightly to confirm it'd take her weight. Of course it would. Of course. They'd come down this way, right?

She didn't let her mind go down the path of what wear and tear the ropes might've taken on the trip down. They were brand new. She didn't think about the climbing disasters she'd heard about. She just kept moving forward, jamming the spikes of her boots into the roof, taking one step at a time. Pete had told her never to let her imagination run away with her. If she started getting antsy, she should just start thinking about her favourite food. Start listing it. He said this sort of job pre-selected for people who loved food.

"Ironic, hey?" Pete was talking again. "They dump a desalination plant here, and then they realise there's water underneath. You'd think they'd have checked for that."

Pete had been first coming down but now Gabe was in the lead. It was easy. The bolt anchors were already laid. She only had to join the dots. It was a mixed blessing, heading back up and out. A retreat from the claustrophobia underground, an ascent into the hot, dry heat.

Gabe's elbows were trembling and she had an ache in her left wrist. *Relax, relax.* She focussed on each hand as she lifted it. Pete kept up his absurdist theatre of mundane conversation behind her, betraying none of the impatience he must be feeling. He couldn't pass her here, not without unhooking himself from the safety rope and chipping out a new route.

Panic was beginning to destabilise her.

Left hand. Right hand. Left … hand. Right, c'mon, right … right.

"Sorry, Pete, sorry."

Even her voice held an edge now, shaking as much as her fingers.

"Take it slow, el Capitano. No rush. The desert will still be there when we get back. Even if that's tomorrow."

Pete made it sound easy. Just hang around — literally, hang here on the roof and the walls — all night.

She couldn't tell if it was the danger or the dark that scared her more. She swung her helmet left and right, lighting up the space around her.

Cheesecake. That was her favourite food. Beer-battered chips. Tacos with a mild chilli.

Pete kept at his trademark humdrum dialogue until Gabe stopped answering every question with "I'm sorry" and began to engage again.

"Got pain going on in your neck?" he asked.

"Yeah," she said.

"Relax it, take the weight with your abs, loosen your shoulders. Pull your neck back in line with your spine," he said, like he was reciting something.

He was right, though. Usually was. She felt a little better. Not that it was her neck that was bothering her.

"Okay, I'm moving," she said.

She was.

"Moving is good."

He fell into constant reassurance, his voice never wavering. Always calm in a crisis, was Pete. Always a team player. He even picked up each one of her feet and moved it forward himself, forcing the front of her body to keep up.

Moving is good. Gabe kept that in mind, dragging herself forward like she was moving through tar.

Finally he said, "We gotta be near the fissure. I can feel it warming up here."

"You can?"

Thank God, thank God.

Gabe couldn't feel anything at all. She was so hot from fear and overexertion she figured she wouldn't be able to feel for days. The sweat dripped from her forehead and she had to keep turning to spit. She was hypersalivating hard.

Hot chocolate made from Mars Bars and cream. The Heart-Attack, they called it. Came with a tiny cookie on the side in the shape of a bear.

She leaned her forehead away from the rock and caught the shaft of light on water that signalled their upward path. Soon they'd be off the roof, rounding the corner to scale the wall upwards nearly thirty metres to the surface. Relief made her elbows tremble, but Pete was still pushing at her, still shoving her forward.

"I'm gonna miss this place," he said. "Great air conditioning this far underground. Maybe I could set up an office."

Gabe was so relieved she actually laughed for the first time the entire trip. "Lousy commute, though."

"Yeah. I could be a shut-in. Then all I'd have to do is telecommute."

"I don't think you'd get wireless broadband under a hundred feet of rock."

"Perfect."

Gabe hurried forward, almost slipping, aiming for the gap in the roof. Most of it was natural, but explosives had been used to widen it enough for human entry. She hooked into the spot beside the deepest rock cuts and leaned her head back so she could feel real sunlight on her face. This far down, there wasn't much of it. Her helmet thudded into the opposite wall, just a metre away.

"Ouch."

Here Pete was able to detach from all but the belay rope that held the two of them together. He came up beside her, working the rope into its device to keep just the right amount of slack. His ginger beard parted into a grin.

"Now for the easy bit," he said.

He took a gulp of water from the flask at his chest and passed it to her. She nodded gratefully. The water was warm, but at least worked to clear the spit from her mouth.

"You lead," said Gabe.

"Aw, now c'mon. You got us all the way here. I can't take over. It'd be like stealing your thunder."

Gabe shook her head, rubbing a gloved wrist across her nose. "Steal away. Seriously. I'll be right behind you, taking it a little slow."

"Shame," shrugged Pete. "I was developing a real foot fetish back there."

She backhanded him across his shoulder. He laughed and — God bless him — climbed in front of her, carefully arranging hooks and harness until he could rejoin the static rope. They'd used rappels to go down. Now Pete was feeding the static rope through an ascender. It'd let him climb up easily enough but provide some steady friction if he started to slide downwards.

Gabe took a moment to lift the walkie-talkie velcroed to her top left pocket.

"We're on our way back up." Then she followed Pete, relief filling her lungs with every breath.

"Roger that," said someone from the ground crew. It wasn't Susan's voice, though, and she was usually the one who answered. Funny, that. Usually the ground crew was a lot more chatty, the way Pete was.

"You like gardening?" Pete asked.

"Nope," she said, but she'd never been more pleased to be asked.

They chatted naturally all the way up, until finally Pete stuck his head over the lip of the fissure and paused.

Beneath him, Gabe nearly ran her head right into his spiked boots before she stopped.

"Gentlemen!" said Pete.

Susan wouldn't like that.

Gabe reeled back as Pete lifted his spiked toe and waved it in her face. What the hell was he up to? She thought he was reaching for another foothold, but when the boot continued to wave like a warning, she crouched back instinctively.

Then a voice she didn't know said, "Why don't you come on up out of there?"

Who the—?

"I'm planning on it," said Pete, the cheerfulness never leaving him. "Why don't you put down those guns there and I'll step right up."

"Mostly when someone has a gun pointed at you, it pays to shut up and do what you're told," said the voice.

"You bet," said Pete. "I just figured since I've been alone in this hole for so long, we could chat a bit. I'm lonely, you know?"

Gabe hunkered down beneath him, silent, peering up at the blank blue sky and sweating into her suit.

"Alone?" The owner of the voice must've turned to someone else then, and asked, "How many down there?"

"One."

That was Susan, an edge of resentment clear in her tone.

"Bullshit." Another unknown voice. "You'd send someone down there alone? Un-bloody-likely. So why don't you and whoever's got their head up your arse just ease up out of there, and *then* we'll chat."

There was movement, and then a shadow a metre to Gabe's right.

"Hey little lady," said the shadow. "Come on up after your buddy, why don'tcha?"

Cover blown, Pete climbed from the hole.

Gabe followed. The owner of the shadow had retreated back into the shade of the blue canvas awning, rigged that morning by the ground crew.

Shit, they had guns all right. Rifles, to be precise. There were two men, strangers in faded checked shirts and akubra hats. Probably out hunting. They'd probably mistaken the research station for … she didn't know. She was trying to work out what was going on, but it was making no sense.

The canvas leant them impenetrable iron silhouettes in the bright heat of the day. To either side of the strangers were the monitoring systems and survival gear, the esky of food, the small water tank. Everything, in short, that was needed to maintain life in this desert of a place.

Gabe blinked, trying to adjust her eyes to the high-contrast of outside life. She looked to where Susan sat cross-legged on the ground, the skin on the backs of her hands red from sun exposure, her lips white and scaly from the salt-dryness of the desert. She must've been sitting there for hours. Susan squinted back at her but said nothing.

Anthony was back under the shade of the canvas, but he was tied with his wrists to his ankles, his face in the dirt, his dark skin even darker in the shadow of the canvas. If it wasn't for his white shirt she probably wouldn't be able to see him at all. She couldn't tell if he was even breathing.

"What's all this, then?" asked Pete. "You had a party and nobody invited us?"

"Funny," said the first guy. "You're on my land."

"We've got permits—"

"Not from me. This bit here, this is mine."

"Well, I'm sure it's a misunderstanding," said Pete.

"Well, I'm sure it is."

The man doing all the talking was middle-aged, she saw now — white-haired, skin like an old leather handbag. He held his rifle at waist-height, balancing it over his forearm. The other man was younger, his face mostly obscured by the rifle at his shoulder. Both of them stood in the shade of the canvas, their faces a deep blue darkness.

"Say, could we join you under there? It's a killing heat out here."

"Not until you explain what you're doing to my land."

"We're testing for potable water."

"Potable?"

"Drinkable."

"Well, now," said the man with a grin. "Well, now. We got us some water, eh? What d'you think of that, Geoff?"

The younger man, Geoff, nodded. "Guess that must be worth something."

"Reckon," said the older man.

"Might be," said Pete. "If it's drinkable. I'm Pete."

"That's nice."

"I didn't catch your name."

"What you need my name for?"

"Nothing, unless we need to talk business," said Pete.

The man hesitated. "Ross," he said.

"So what's the problem, Ross?"

"The problem, Pete, is you seem to be stealing my water."

"Not stealing, Ross. Testing. We're just here to test the water."

"I still don't think I like that, *Pete*. Gotta protect what's mine. Could be worth a small fortune, water this far out."

"Sure, sure. We got no jurisdiction apart from testing."

Pete's tone was friendly, but his words were authoritative. Ross went quiet, thinking it through.

Gabe was standing furthest from Ross and his buddy. The fissure was at her left and the men, and Pete, were directly in front. She'd unconsciously stepped behind Pete as she'd climbed up, coiling the belay that still bound them in one hand, leaving some slack.

She saw Geoff, the young man, raise his head from his rifle sight.

"Dad. I think it's Malcolm."

Gabe looked. A jeep was rolling along a road eighty metres or so out, throwing up a fan of dust like the wake of a boat. As it got closer it changed course, heading straight at them across the dirt.

"Yeah, that's Malcolm all right."

While they waited for Malcolm, Pete tried to negotiate to get Susan water or shade. Ross shrugged him off; said Susan had quite a lip on her, bit of sun would do her good. His face in the blue shade didn't seem to move, even when he talked. He held the gun casually but never took his sights off Pete.

"She's a quiet one," he said of Gabe, pointing with his chin.

"Oh, just get her onto the topic of salt," said Pete. "She never shuts up."

Ross looked around him. "Damn salt. They're trying to ruin this place, dumping salt on it. Never be able to use this land for anything, anymore. No farming, nothing. One thing we don't need more of, is salt. Am I right?"

Gabe wasn't sure, but he seemed to be staring at her. "Right," she said.

Malcolm's dusty white jeep pulled up with a grunt on the far side of the fissure. A slim man jumped out, narrow at hip and shoulder, filled with an anxious energy.

"Ross, what the—" He caught sight of the guns. "What the *hell* are you doing?"

"Reclaiming what's mine," Ross said with steel calm.

"Government's renting this spot, Ross. From me. It's my land."

"Bull*shit* it's your land. What'd they give you to rent *my* land, you lying bastard?"

"Look—"

"I own this goddamn land, you scum! Been in my family for

three generations. I own it, and I'm keeping it. Between you, and the Government here, and the fucking junkies who keep stealing the copper right outta the water pipes, I'm bloody lucky I'm still standing."

"Listen," said Malcolm, holding both hands up at chest height. He looked concave, shoulders rounded, chest hollow. "Boundary lines put this piece here on my side. It's all on paper, Ross. It's all legal."

"Fuck legal!"

Ross spun to face Malcolm across the fissure, swinging his gun around with him. He probably didn't mean to — that's what Gabe suspected the first time — he didn't mean to, but his rifle jolted and went off. The bullet snagged Malcolm on one of his skinny shoulders and he spun, going down on one knee.

"Shit!"

Malcolm held one hand to his shoulder, suddenly dark and wet despite the sun.

Pete moved towards him, probably meaning to help, but there was another gun retort and Pete seemed to bend at the middle, falling, falling into the fissure. He didn't even say a word; just fell right into that stupid damn hole.

"*Pete!*"

Gabe fell and flattened herself on the ground. The belay rope snagged on her hand, crushing it. She was dragged to the edge of the fissure before she knew it, arm extended over the side. She jammed her boot spikes into the ground as the rope rapidly uncoiled into the void.

Susan was beside her on her knees, crying dryly, gulping and gasping. "Pete." Her voice was a croak.

He was hanging, unconscious or dead, face scraped red from the rock, arms and legs dangling, in the small gap of the fissure, a dark red pool where his stomach should be. He rotated slowly on the rope, bumping the sides with knees and helmet.

"Pete!"

"Oh shit, Dad, oh shit."

Gabe spared the young man a glance and saw him standing with his gun lowered to one side. Anthony, lying bound on the ground, had twisted around to see what was going on. Even in the canvas shadow she could see where they'd beaten him. His mouth was crooked from swelling and one eye was swollen shut. He was shifting, moving backwards on his side, out of the way of Geoff's rifle.

"Dad, aw, Dad, I … I don't have the stomach for this. I'm a farmer for god's sake. A goddamn salt-of-the-earth farmer. "

"No, you *used to* be a farmer. You think you can get a crop out of this dirt again? This is the new world order, son," said Ross. "Wake up and smell the fucking napalm."

Gabe craned her neck back. In front of her, Malcolm was getting slowly to his feet, still clutching his ruined shoulder.

"You goddamn idiot, you goddamn, stupid, fucking idiot." This from Malcolm. "You're both going to prison for this. Don't you worry about your fucking farm! You just shot two people."

"Shut up," Ross was still calm as stone. His eyes flickered briefly to Anthony and then dismissed him. "I didn't shoot anyone."

"You shot *me*, you fucking psychopath! One of you shot that government bloke! You goddamn headcases."

"I doubt we'll be seeing him again," said Ross.

He must've missed the belay rope that still bound Pete to Gabe. Or else…

"As to you," continued Ross.

He raised his rifle and fired, shearing off the side of Malcolm's head. Malcolm spun on one toe and seemed to hang upright for a split second. Then he crumpled to the ground. His arms lay at his side, palms up to the sun, his legs bent under him.

"Jesus," croaked Susan.

"Son, hand me your rifle."

Geoff was sobbing into his palm. He gave Ross the gun without question and took the other rifle when Ross pressed it to his chest.

Ross said, "You never would've been much of a farmer anyhow, son."

Geoff had stepped into the sun. In the light he looked gentle and fair. And confused, holding the murder weapon across his body like a shield. "Dad?"

Ross shot him once and Geoff folded neatly to the ground, the rifle hitting Anthony across the face. The second man grunted.

"You goddamn son of a bitch," said Anthony.

He half-rolled backwards into a bank of monitoring equipment, bringing it down on top of himself. The tall metal sample cupboard toppled and hit Ross hard on the shoulder.

Ross staggered forward, the rifle thrown from his hands. He didn't even hesitate, just pulled a handgun from the back of his belt and began firing at Anthony, cursing loudly.

Without thinking, Gabe grabbed the static ropes and swung into the fissure. She didn't even hook her harness to the safeties, just started climbing down, hand over hand, fast as she could.

Time was slowing. She wasn't letting her imagination run away with her. She was focussing, she was climbing, she was thinking of deep-fried honey prawns with salt-and-pepper squid. Salt again. Stop thinking about salt.

Ross's shouts above her seemed way too close, too close for comfort. She kept climbing, spiking into the walls with her boots just long enough to guide her other foot. She headed down.

She felt weight on the ropes and looked up to see Susan climbing, too, sneakered feet scraping the rockface. It must be killing her bare hands. She skidded down the rope and screamed, hitting Gabe hard on the shoulder. Gabe steadied herself, hooking the safety to her harness. She did this almost without pause, without thought. She was still climbing down, down into the dark where it was safe.

There was more shooting and suddenly Susan jumped and went slack, spilling from the wall and falling. She hit Pete on the way down and their weight dragged Gabe further into the fissure, gloves whistling against the static ropes. If she let go, she'd be a goner. Just like Susan and Pete. Two holds popped from the rockface and she grabbed on. There was a thud and a splash as Susan hit the ground beneath her.

Another shot ricocheted off the wall to her right. Then there was clicking as Ross discovered his gun was empty.

"Fuck!"

His voice already had an echo. She must be pretty far from the top already. Her hands were shaking, but she kept moving, just kept moving. Pete's weight on her harness made her back ache, but she kept moving. She didn't look up to see Ross reloading his gun, she didn't look down to see Pete's still body sprawled against the dark.

"You can't steal my fucking land! You can't take my goddamn water!"

She just kept moving down into the quiet, cool dark, where she could take a moment to wipe the sweat off her face. She'd stop there and drop down to the water (the potable water, it better be, that damn drinkable water, she was thirsty as all hell) and check on Pete and maybe see if Susan, if Susan…

How long did it take to die from poisoned water, anyhow? No, don't think about that just yet.

She kept moving, just kept moving, shushing the jagged sounds that came out of her throat. All the while replaying every stupid word Pete had ever said about keeping your head and about circus elephants and about every damn thing.

The rope went suddenly slack and she had to dig into the sides of the rock with her boots and hang her finger over the hold on the wall. Someone at the surface must've cut the rope. Okay, okay, she'd still be able to climb out. She'd lay some new climbing holds, that's all. She could do that.

Pete was right. He was right, this'd be a good place for an office. She'd stay here until tomorrow if she had to, longer if she needed. She'd head back into the underground cave where Ross couldn't see her head-lamp and she'd stay within the circumference of that tiny amount of light and after a while she'd … she'd…

Try not to let her imagination run away with her.

The Distance Keeper

Toby checked his watch. It was one minute to six in the morning. Too soon.

He rocked onto his toes, looking from his verandah to the empty space in front of him. Not exactly empty, not really. But empty in a way that defied the objects in it. That reduced the dead and living equally. He had to stop himself from thinking: dead and dying. Geoff wanted him to think positive.

It was hot already. Here and there eucalypt trees stood like the ghosts of soldiers. Caught out, upright and surprised. Dead in their boots, he couldn't help thinking. Pellets of sunlight shot through the branches to hit the dusty ground. Toby breathed in deeply and smelled — nothing.

He checked his watch again and it was six o'clock. Exactly. He started down the stairs. Not leisurely, but not quickly either. Pacing it just so. Like he did every morning, leaving at the same time, walking the same way. He was very careful about it.

On the horizon the trees looked like they curved around the Earth, wide-angle-lens-wise. Made him feel like he was in a fishbowl full of dust. He looked down instead, checking for cracks or the telltale signs of fading in the elastic of the world. His worn-out boots scuffed the dust into the air around him so he moved in a haze.

The ground was so dry he could almost walk in the footprints left from yesterday, marked out in the dirt. Here and there he saw the tracks of animals. Tracks only. He hadn't seen an animal in months. Not that there were less animals. Just more space. Toby kept track of distances and he knew. But Geoff said no, that couldn't be right.

It was right. The world was stretching like a rubber band. It was pulling taut, ready to snap. Ready to fling them all into space.

He walked the distance between his property and his neighbour's. The road was empty. Even the birds were silent now, having sung their tunes to the wide morning and then waited, propped up invisibly in the trees, for the next event. The next day or night or what would come.

Geoff said there's a time for doing and a time for waiting. Toby was trying to work out which this was.

He resisted the urge to check his watch again.

When he reached Geoff's place, pacing himself along the worn path, he was sweating. He wanted to run up the stairs and into the shade, but forced himself to use the same stride he used every day. Not too fast and not too slow. He stared through the heat haze into the shadow of Geoff's verandah. The screen door was ajar and behind it, Geoff's front door was still shut. Must have been a bad night with Melissa again.

Toby stepped gratefully into the silhouette of the house, walked the three steps to the verandah and stopped to check his watch. Six forty-seven. A whole two minutes longer than yesterday. That was the biggest difference so far. Add that to the ten seconds from Tuesday, the thirty seconds from the day before. It had been building for weeks. And it was getting faster, the rush to explode overwhelming them.

The house was no cooler inside, but the darkness was a relief after the bright morning light. There was no one in the lounge room so he went through to the kitchen. Last night's plates tipped precariously over the sink. No sign of breakfast yet. He took off his hat and rubbed his head hard, wiping the sweat away. He was thirsty, but there was a line between letting yourself in and opening kitchen cupboards to find a glass. He sat at the table and waited for Geoff.

It took a while but Geoff finally appeared wearing a crumpled shirt and no shoes.

"Been here long?" he asked, nodding hello at Toby.

"Nope. Four minutes," Toby nodded back. "Shed today, Geoff?"

"No, not the shed today. Back fence. We'll take the truck."

Geoff pulled a glass from the edge of the sink and filled it with water. Seeing the thirst on Toby's face, he held the glass up, tipping it in Toby's direction. Not enough to spill anything, but enough that Toby nodded yes-please. Geoff got another glass from the cupboard.

The two men sat and drank silently until the glasses were empty.

"'Nother?" Geoff asked.

"Sure."

After the second one, Geoff stood up and began shifting plates and cutlery around.

"Have to make Mel some breakfast first, Toby. See you outside?"

Toby wanted to talk about the distance, but he bit his tongue. Geoff was engrossed in his task, his back to the other man. Reluctantly, Toby went through the kitchen door into the heavy sunlight. He sat in the truck, leaving the door open optimistically for a breeze. There wasn't any. He fanned himself with his hat and dangled his legs over the faded grass, waiting.

Another quarter hour and Geoff appeared, this time with boots on. He came round the back of the truck, checking on the fence-mending equipment.

"Keys in there, Toby?"

Toby leaned round the steering column. "Yep."

Geoff started the engine before he was even in his seat and they jolted forward with the doors slamming shut.

"Hot," Toby said.

"Yeah, sure is," Geoff replied. "Mel's having a hard time of it in the heat."

They rode on for a while, staring at the day, both men with an arm out the window.

"Forty-seven minutes today, Geoff," Toby said.

"Yeah?"

"Two minutes more than yesterday," he said, in case his friend didn't understand. "It's speeding up."

"Accelerating, you reckon?"

"Yeah. Accelerating."

"Maybe you're just getting old. Slowing down." Geoff laughed, knowing Toby was only three years older than him.

"It's not that…" Toby began, clenching his fist around the window frame as the car gurgled along the path. "It's the world, Geoff."

"Yeah, the world. Everything's getting further apart. Like you said," Geoff rubbed his face. "Like we need more space out here, hey?"

"Stretching," Toby murmured.

"Stretching?" Geoff sighed. "And then what, hey? Think it'll burst? Think the guts of the Earth will all come whooshing out!"

Toby was silent, wondering. In his head he saw it kind of like pulling a sticky bun apart with your thumbs. Some of it would tear and some of it would hold together, but you couldn't tell where.

"I dunno," he said at last.

"You don't know," Geoff replied, like he'd tasted something bitter. "Anyway, aren't you ever two minutes early?"

Toby looked out the window. Sure, some days the world pulled in again. But the net effect was an expansion. He didn't want to tell Geoff that. He wanted to be positive.

"Anyway, maybe you're just walking differently," Geoff continued.

"It's not me."

"But it could be, eh? A bit faster, a bit slower. I mean, you can't be exactly the same every day."

"Yes, I am."

"Toby—" Geoff began, then stopped. He let out a long sigh instead and in the heat, Toby could almost see the air swirl in front of them.

"How's Melissa?" Toby asked, to change the subject.

Geoff had to pause a while before answering that one. He chewed his lip and glared at the landscape. "She's having a bad week. Doctor says she should stay in bed now until the baby's born." The truck hit a pothole and lurched upwards, its front wheels off the road. Then it jolted back down with a screech of metal twisting. Geoff didn't seem to notice. "She doesn't want to go to the hospital yet."

His voice faded and they sat in silence again.

"How long?" Toby asked.

"What?"

"How long? Until the baby."

"Oh. Three months at least," Geoff rubbed his chin, wrestling the steering wheel one-handed. "We're so cut off from everything here, hey, Toby? I mean, what if there's an emergency? Maybe I should take her to hospital anyway. Maybe they could find space for her there."

"Maybe."

They reached the fence and Geoff switched off the engine, leaving the gear in drive. As they pulled the roll of wire from the back, he said, "Hey, Toby. I gotta go into town tonight. The bank's open late and I have to see them about the loan. Can you stay with Mel? She's on her own all the time. Might do her good, you know? See somebody else's face for a change." He grinned under the patina of dust.

Toby hesitated. "Uh. I dunno, Geoff. Don't know much about pregnant ladies."

Geoff laughed. "Don't have to know anything, Toby. Just … you know, be there if anything goes wrong."

"I don't want to do that," Toby muttered, pulling at his collar.

"Look. Nothing's going wrong. Just stay with her. To make me feel better. Hey? I'll bring you some beers from town. I'll even drive you home. You won't have to walk for a change. What do you say?"

Toby didn't like the idea at all, but he nodded at last, watching the relief on Geoff's face.

They spent the day there at the back fence. Around midday they sat in the shade of the truck and shared water from Geoff's flask. Toby tried to pull out a stem of grass to chew on — more to pass the time than from real hunger — but the bottom was as dry as the top. Once he thought he felt the earth tremble under them. He waited, but it didn't happen again.

"Twenty-eight minutes to get to the fence today, Geoff," he murmured around the grass stem. Longer than last week, but he couldn't be certain with Geoff's driving.

"Sure, Toby."

"Think it's time to do something?"

"Do what, Toby?"

When they finally left the fence, it was evening. Close to seven, but the sun still bristled against the ground. Geoff was silent on the way back, his face drawn.

"What time's the bank?" Toby asked.

"Eight. I'll be late, I suppose."

Melissa was dozing when the two men entered, Geoff leading the way upstairs to the bedroom. Toby leaned in, not wanting to break the threshold. It was dry and dark in there, space enough for the bed and a cupboard with no doors. There was a little fan on a windowsill, but it wasn't moving.

"Power shortage?" Geoff asked, indicating the fan.

Melissa nodded, smiling sleepily. She lay diagonally across the bed, a thin white sheet ballooning around her belly.

"Hey," she said. "Hi, Toby."

"Hey."

"Still keeping time?" she asked, her smile widening.

Toby had to think about that one. Then he realised she was asking if he still measured the distance from door to door. Geoff must've told her.

"Yeah. Two minutes longer today."

"Yeah?" She laughed. "You need one of those kilometric things — you know, you roll them along the ground and they click over every metre."

Toby hadn't heard of those but he nodded again, hopeful. "Yeah," he said, moving around the doorway a bit more. "Where do you get those?"

"Don't know. Maybe next time you're in town ask at the hardware store."

"Don't encourage him, love," Geoff laughed. "Hey, maybe Toby will make you some toast later."

He looked questioningly at Toby, who shrugged assent.

"I'll check with you later, Melissa," Toby said. He backed out awkwardly, leaving the couple alone.

Geoff came downstairs a few minutes later, flipping on a light as he entered the lounge room.

"Power's back on at least."

Distantly, Toby could hear the fan whirring in the bedroom.

"Check the phone, hey, Toby."

Toby picked up the phone by the lounge. It was dead.

Geoff let out his breath in a long sigh. "If it's not one thing, it's another. Anyway, I should be back by nine, nine-thirty," he picked up some manila folders from the sideboard. "Help yourself to whatever you can find in the fridge. Torch is in the kitchen drawer by the back door. And thanks, I appreciate this."

Toby nodded, fiddling with the cuff of his left sleeve.

"I'll give you a lift home when I get back, eh?"

"Nah, it's OK. I'll walk," Toby said, unsticking his watch from the sweat of his wrist.

He wanted Geoff to go, so he could finish his meeting and get back sooner. So Toby wasn't left with the pregnant woman lying dormant in that dark room upstairs. Geoff shrugged and left, the screen door slamming shut behind him.

Toby settled into the silence of the lounge room. He stared at the deepening night in the back window, fingered the worn knees of his trousers and waited. There was nothing else he could do.

When the window opaqued to black he looked around the room instead. Most of Geoff's furniture was hand-me-downs from his parents. Toby had helped move it into the house, dragging the brown lounge up the stairs, angling it through the front door. Then the chipboard table, the aluminium edges snagging on the doorframe. Three chairs. No one knew what'd happened to the fourth.

By ten-thirty Geoff still wasn't home. Toby was examining the few old paperbacks on a shelf of the sideboard. He did this nervously, to pass the time. His reading wasn't good, so he flipped through them, occasionally lighting on a picture caption or chapter heading.

A shadow passed over the world. Toby swayed giddily, dropping the book. Another shadow, longer this time. Upstairs, the fan coughed and was silent. Then the lights went out and stayed out. Toby gripped the sideboard, swinging the other arm out to his side, searching for an invisible assailant.

He groped his way carefully towards the kitchen and trailed his hands along the bench towards the door. The moon bled weakly through the window, bubbling along the uneven benchtop.

Upstairs Melissa screamed.

Jolted, Toby shouted back, "Coming, Melissa. Hang on!" Perhaps the dark had frightened her.

She screamed again, and Toby struggled through shadow towards the drawer.

"Hang on!"

In his panic he pulled the drawer right out of its slot. It smashed to the ground, spilling tools and string and rolls of Gladwrap across the floor. Toby sank to his heels, hunting for the torch, pushing the wreckage out ahead of him until his fist closed on its rubber barrel. It rattled as he grabbed it, nearly falling apart in his hands. He had to twist the top back on as Melissa screamed a third time.

"I'm coming!"

The corner of the table punched his hip as he ran. He twisted the top of the torch until it glowed, racing up the stairs with the light dancing crazily. The corridor stank of corrosion. In the bedroom, he swung the torch towards the bed and caught Melissa's face in its glare. Black shadows pulled at the side of her nose and filled her open mouth. She screamed again.

And the lights came on.

The bed loomed brightly, dwarfing the room and its two occupants. Blood soaked the sheets wound tight around Mel's legs. It pooled darkly in places, spreading itself along fissures in the old mattress. Mel held her palms out to Toby and they were stained with blood, too.

"Jesus," Toby hissed.

Melissa sobbed, her body convulsing with each guttural cry. She was wet with sweat and blood.

"Oh, Jesus," Toby said again.

He still gripped the torch, its beam pointed at the ground.

"Towels," he said, moving dizzily out of the bedroom. He went to the bathroom, then the cupboard in the hall, pulling out all the towels he could find. He brought the armload back to her.

Mel's knees stuck up like wire coat hangers from the tangled mess of the bed. She was hugging her huge belly, tracing red smears through the sheets. Toby tried to clean her face but she slithered away with a jagged groan and began retching into the pillows.

He felt sick, leaning over her with the stench of blood choking him. He stumbled to the window and took a lungful of fresh air.

"Do I call somebody?" Toby asked, then swore, remembering the phone didn't work.

Behind him, Melissa cried. Great aching dry breaths half-muffled by pillows. In the dark outside, Toby could make out twin yellow lights in the distance. Headlights.

"Geoff," Melissa said very softly, still crying.

"He's coming," Toby said, focusing on the lights. "Geoff's coming."

He turned back to Melissa, lying wasted in her drying blood.

"I'll go get him, Mel," Toby promised.

Toby had never prayed, but he prayed now, running from the room and down the stairs. The door slapped closed behind him as he leapt from the verandah into the dark. In the distance, Geoff's lights seemed to hold fast. The truck's familiar gurgling was almost too faint to hear.

Toby ran. He ran toward the lights, straining against the distance and coming up short. Sweat rolled down his back and the sound of his breath smothered everything else. But still the truck kept its distance.

Gasping for breath, his body turning to jelly, he slowed and stopped, nearly falling. Pain laced his ribs and his eyes were blurred. He bent double, hands on his knees, sweat dripping from his face. When he craned around to look for the house, he found it shrunken between earth and sky far out on the horizon. From here, he wouldn't even hear Melissa scream. If she still could.

"I'll never—" he gasped. Never reach it.

He turned back to the truck, swinging his head like a wounded animal looking for an out. But he was trapped by the terrible space.

His gut ached and his feet wouldn't lift. Tiny yellow points like pin pricks marked the place where the headlights lay, remote in the dark. As he watched, they shrunk further into the wide night.

He knew what it meant. More than anyone, he understood what the world had come to. Melissa was lost somewhere behind him and Geoff in front, with the distance pressing them all apart.

"No," he sobbed, "Please, no, no, *NO!*"

There was a rumbling under his boots. He fell to his knees and leaned forward, pressing his face to the earth. In the moonlight, he tried to make out stretchmarks in the ground. Pushing at it, digging his fingers into the hard ground. Trying to hold on.

He waited.

Six Suicides

The Hitcher

Del was woken by snoring. Not hers. She sighed, shifted, pushed at the face resting against her neck. She squinted at the alarm clock and read the first number — four — but couldn't be sure of the rest. Middle of the night and she was at that see-saw point between drunk and hungover.

The snoring continued. She slapped at his face lightly.

"Niall!" she grumbled. "Shut up, man."

The snoring stalled.

"Huh?"

He rolled away from her, darker than the dark room, his shoulder rising like an ocean wave. There was the sound of him groping on the nightstand, the drag of a metal watchband. He held up the watch and the green LED lit up the side of his face. It took her a while to realise he was angling the watch not to read its time but to illuminate his face.

"Who's Niall?" he said.

Del liked to think it was all behind her. All the mistakes, missed opportunities, the struggle for understanding, the struggle to be understood. That was the gift middle age was supposed to bestow.

"Sorry, man," she said.

Drunk, in the dark, she'd gotten lost inside her own head. Niall was gone eight months. When friends asked what happened she said the relationship ended when she couldn't bear to be hated anymore.

That was a lie.

She would've gone on being hated if only he'd stuck around.

The stranger put the watch down on the bed between them and lay on his stomach, snoring, until the sun came up. Curled on her side, she watched him through half-closed eyes. Not her usual type. A little young, lean but soft like he didn't take care of himself. Probably didn't eat right and didn't exercise but hey, who was she to judge?

Later the sun streamed through bare windows and he rose and dressed, taking his time. Left without waking her from her feigned sleep.

She sat up just enough to light a cigarette, took a long drag and wiped ash from the sheets.

What the hell *was* that guy's name?

She smoked three cigarettes before getting up for the bathroom, walking with her head thudding and one arm across her breasts in case anyone looked in the windows.

There was a half-empty glass of red on the bathroom bench. She tasted it — sour — tipped it down the sink, caught sight of herself in the mirror. This morning, like every morning, she couldn't help noticing the paunch around her middle, the orange-peel skin on the tops of her thighs. She spun the shower taps and let the mirror steam over.

The shower made her feel better, but the feeling lasted as long as the hot water did and then she was on her own again. Her towel was missing. Weird. Men had taken trophies before, but never a towel.

She walked, wet and naked, to the kitchen. There was the stench of something fermenting. Kebab wrappers, half-eaten contents on a benchtop now scorched by sun. Her towel was on the floor with a red wine stain stretching end to end. She bent to retrieve it and her brain sloshed in her skull. The room swung and she thought for a second she was going to throw up. Shit, she'd always been able to hold her liquor before.

The nausea rolled over her and exited at the back of her skull. She leaned on the bench, feeling sticky, pinpricks in her neck and armpits. In the heat her skin was already drying. By her elbow was a page from a notebook. She captured it, turned it over and over between her fingers. It was a single line, 'See ya, Delcina — cheers, Karl.'

Whoa. She'd told him her real name. Must've liked this one, must have felt a connection. It was only then she remembered where she'd met him. Group therapy. Well, where else was she meeting people lately?

She tried to remember what the hell they'd talked about and came up with an image of him at a diner, all young up-start and know-it-all. She made a tut-tutting noise against her teeth, but grinned.

The young were better at connection, she figured. It was easier because it was less rare. You worried less. If you screwed it up you could find someone else to connect with. Music, food, philosophy, sex, whatever. You got older and most of that stuff mattered less. Survival mattered more but surviving made you scared.

Karl had an expression that implied that he could hold onto it forever. Like life and the living of it was going to be easy. She knew that look. She'd seen it in the mirror for the first twenty years of her life. She wasn't sure where it went after that.

The white of the notepaper contrasted with the nicotine-yellow of her fingertips and the dark grey city grit under her nails.

She bent it in half and dropped it into the mess of kebab leftovers, then swept the lot into the bin.

The Loner

This was a mistake, he saw that now. This going-for-a-beer-to-swap-ideas, sounding-board-let's-help-each-other-out thing.

"I'm thinking of quitting the group therapy thing," Karl said to distract her.

It worked. She stopped chewing, oil-stained fingers stilled on the mess of soggy cheese melt in front of her.

"How come?"

"I'm not buying all this magnetic connection stuff," he shrugged. "You think Doc Gilberd believes it?"

"Oh, yeah. She's mad for it. I've been seeing her for years."

When Del talked she pushed the greasy lump of toasted cheese into one cheek. Sodden bits of white bread stuck to her tongue. He looked away, back to the table. Picked up his burger experimentally. Found it cold.

"Yeah?" he murmured.

"It works. For me, at least. I feel less, you know, alone, I guess."

She ripped up more cheese and dropped it in her mouth.

"That could just be the group," he said. "Doesn't mean the magnetic—"

Del grinned.

"What?" Karl asked.

"Nothing, you remind me of someone," Del said. "Too space age for you, is it?"

She pulled on her beer, leaving greasy fingerprints on its neck.

"No, I get it. All matter is affected by magnetic fields, whatever."

"Okay. So what more do you want?"

Karl shrugged, shook his head.

"You want to know why it works, not how. Right?" she said. "But if it works then it's not about 'why'. I mean, when you get to my age—"

"Right," he said.

He hated that. "When you get to my age," whatever. Some people used their age as a weapon instead of what it really was: a wound.

"Guess I need a timeout," he murmured.

"You got a lot of friends older than you?" she asked.

"Why?"

"Just, you were saying something before about life defeating people."

He sized her up. A woman on the wrong side of forty, wrong side of angry, wrong side of over. What was her life but eating bad cheese sandwiches and patronising people she barely knew? No wonder the boyfriend left. What was his name again? Karl had met him in the group a while back. Neal, he thought. Something like that.

"Yeah, I guess I got older friends."

"Must be frightening. Always looking into your future," chewed Del.

Karl eased back, pulled his wallet up to the table.

People like Del were all about the "can't", he figured. Can't look into the future, can't go it alone, can't relate to a new idea. He would never give up his passion or intelligence for the sake of self-delusion and a five-dollar cheese melt. He knew the traps of age and other people.

He was going to make it alone.

"My treat," said Del.

"Not at all."

He laid a few dollars on the table and stood, unhooking his jacket from the chair.

"You gotta be someplace?" Del asked. She wiped her mouth on a napkin. "Because if you don't, I got a place."

Karl hesitated. Maybe there was a way to salvage this waste of an evening.

"Sure," he said.

"I think we're really onto something here, hey?" she said.

"Oh," said Karl, "sure."

The Keeper

The bus was overheated to make up for the European winter. Niall thumbed his phone open and shut, occasionally working through his address book to Del's name.

He pressed the entry experimentally. A name and a number, all that was left. He checked the reassuring "No Network Available" message on the LED screen and pressed the Options button.

"Delete this entry?" asked the phone's small grey screen.

The bus lurched forward and Niall hit the window beside him hard enough to knock the phone from his hand. He was thrown sideways against the passenger beside him.

"Sorry," he said.

Zara gave him a sleepy smile. "That's okay."

Her bronze skin caught the light as she shifted. She lay back against her seat and sighed into sleep. Sweet kid. Gorgeous, he couldn't help noticing. He'd met her last night in the hostel. She seemed lonely, like him. No harm in being lonely together.

He turned back to the phone. He'd met Del a decade and a half ago in group therapy. She'd made him feel unimportant and he'd liked it. No pressure that way.

She swore the group therapy worked. Some crazy psycho-magnetic thing meant to bring a balanced mind. She used the group as her personal harem half the time. Back then she'd been thirty-something, settling into a belated adulthood with steely pride. He was nearly thirty, wanting to prove himself.

In the end, maybe that was the problem. Maybe that, maybe everything.

He stole another glance at Zara. She was younger than he remembered being. How could anyone let her out into the world with a face that beautiful? Heavy dark eyes and round mouth, smooth cheeks and curls of glossy black hair around gold earrings. People were drawn to her. He saw that. He felt it himself. Nearly twice her age. He just wanted something beautiful in his life, that was all. Everything else was too hard.

"Delete this entry?"

Niall hit Confirm and the phone gave a jarringly cheerful melody.

"Entry deleted."

He went through the phonebook again and again to make sure all history had been deleted. It was the only way forward.

The Seeker

Zara was running to—

She wasn't sure yet. She didn't have a name for it.

A few months past her eighteenth birthday, past the time she'd left the home where her mother had died rather than live, and her father was living without the courage to die.

She figured there must be another option. There must be another house.

"You're young," that's what everyone said.

They sensed her mad rush towards maturity, towards love and the touch of someone else's skin, towards assurance, dignity, independence. Everything!

Mostly it was only people on the wrong edge of a relationship — like Niall — who understood what it was like not to have someone. He hadn't said it, but she recognised the raw look of loss. It was the look her father had all the time. The slack face and sloping shoulders. It was easier to connect with someone who'd lost something, she found. They were more open.

That night in the hostel she'd met Niall, sipped liquor from a flask and told him the truth: no one had ever asked her on a date.

Niall had looked surprised, then thoughtful, and finally convinced. He'd chuckled wryly, leaning forward on crossed arms. It was late and most people were asleep already. He'd just arrived, a backpack still rested by his chair while the hostel staff counted beds to see if they had room. He didn't look nervous. Zara envied him his freedom.

"You're too beautiful to ask out," he told her.

He'd taken a swig from the flask and offered it again. She'd swallowed and tried not to cough while Niall tried not to laugh.

"Well," Niall said. "I'd ask, of course, but—"

"I accept," Zara replied at once.

Niall had raised his eyebrows in faint astonishment, then looked away, embarrassed. He'd caught sight of the book she'd been reading, *How to Connect*, by Doctor Stephanie Gilberd.

"I know her," he said, unexpectedly.

"The author?"

"Sure," said Niall. "She's my shrink. Well, was. Magnetic resonance therapy, right?"

Zara had nodded, looking at the author photo on the back cover. A smiling, grey-haired woman with glasses.

"She looks too young," Zara said. "To have grey hair, I mean."

Niall grinned. "She's older now."

"I was in therapy when I was ten," Zara told him.

"Yeah? Lot of kids in therapy these days."

"Not where I'm from," said Zara.

"Your folks put you in therapy?"

"Folks?"

"Parents," Niall supplied. "You had nightmares, or something? Behavioural problems?"

"I don't know," Zara admitted. "I don't remember. My mother died. I suppose it had something to do with that."

"Right," said Niall. "I can see how that would be hard."

Just like that. No fanfare. Just a nod and another sip from his flask. She liked that he seemed … like he'd already put his demons to bed and wasn't struggling anymore. But after a night talking with him she'd realised it wasn't that. It was just that he'd gotten used to the struggle.

Zara hesitated. "Did you have depression? Is that why you did magnetic therapy?"

Niall nodded effortlessly. "Yeah, maybe."

"Did it cure you?"

"Maybe."

He was tapping one nail on the metal flask, a kind of quiet s-o-s, barely audible.

"Do you believe in Doctor Gilberd's theory?" she asked. "The idea we're drawn to each other? Our resonances—?"

"I guess it makes sense," said Niall. "Each one of us a kind of compass, seeking balance rather than true north. Or whatever. Been a while since I've read the book"

Zara smiled. "You got it pretty much right."

The hostel manager had arrived with good news. Just before Niall had picked up his pack he'd said, "I'm leaving tomorrow. On the bus to Venice."

"Not staying in Rome?" she said. "Not going to see the Vatican? The museums?"

"I've been to Rome before," he explained. "Rome is done. The Vatican is done."

He'd winked and she'd laughed at how easily he dismissed an entire culture.

She was old enough to know she should be careful who she travelled with, careful who she flirted with, careful where she went. She'd been careful all her life and right then that felt like a long, long time.

Rome was done.

The flask had replaced her blood with something warmer. She said, "I've always wanted to see Venice."

"Yeah? You should be careful what you want. You know what they say about Venice?"

"What's that?"

"See Venice," said Niall, "and die."

The Pusher

Parham sat in front of the TV most days and nights of the week. Sometimes the phone rang. Usually a cousin whose name he'd forgotten — there were several of those. Sometimes, like now, it was an old army buddy.

Never Zara.

"Remember that land mine victim?" said Medhi down the line.

"Which one?" said Parham.

It was their game, to pretend that the faces of the victims had been lost inside their memories.

"The amputation."

Parham grunted. "Which one?"

But he knew. It had happened fifty years ago but they spoke about him every time. Thirteen years old. If he'd lived, he'd be sixty-three by now. Still twenty years behind Parham.

"He was a screamer," said Medhi.

People mistook Medhi's manner for coldness. It wasn't. He'd lived with that boy dying for fifty years.

They sawed off his leg at the upper thigh. He screamed every minute of it. Not just from pain, from the shock. There was no way to hide the sight of his jagged, ruined limb. There weren't any sheets and the anaesthetic wasn't enough to knock him out.

"My son, the great doctor," said Medhi, "is using magnetics for healing now."

"Magnetics?"

"Can you believe?"

"What does he heal with magnetics?"

"Wounds, he says. One woman, he said, a paraplegic, had a wound on her stomach that wouldn't heal. Tried everything."

"Skin graft?"

Medhi paused. "Maybe. Who can say? The great doctor could tell us, but *ai*. I'll ask him next week when he calls. Anyhow, he bandaged the wound and taped a magnet to it. And it healed."

Parham snorted. "How long did that take?"

"Two months."

"So they left it alone for two months and it was healed?"

"With a magnet."

"They kept up the cleaning and changing bandages?"

"Of course! Those magnetic doctors aren't barbarians!" Medhi guffawed.

"So, are you sure it wasn't just time and attention that healed the wound?"

"You ask me? My son, the great doctor, would know."

"Of course."

"Also, he's now using magnetics to treat depression."

"What does he know about depression?"

"He's a Great Doctor," said Medhi, and Parham could hear the how he capitalised the words.

"So he tapes magnets to people's hearts?" Parham asked.

"Heads, I think, but I'm not sure if they're taped. Perhaps they hang them in socks from their ears."

"Perhaps they use helmets."

"Yes, yes, that would be the way," Medhi replied. "Or perhaps they just imagine magnets and *poof*, the depression is gone!"

"Science isn't magic," said Parham, welcoming the old argument.

"Yes it is," said Medhi. "It's magic with a different vocabulary."

Parham chuckled, like he did every time.

"How's Azara?" Medhi asked.

He'd been expecting the question.

"She never calls."

"You were always too harsh with her," said Medhi, predictably. "She needed more compassion growing up."

"I did what I thought best."

"A girl needs a mother."

"She had aunts."

Medhi grunts. "You drove them away, too, Parham. Sorry to say. But a friend needs to tell a friend the truth now and then."

Parham couldn't disagree. It was how he'd lived his whole life. With the truth. And few friends.

"We've been through thick and thin, Medhi," he said.

"Without that we'd have nothing to talk about."

After Medhi hung up, Parham thought about magnetics. Superstitious foolishness. What could magnets do for wounds? For problems of the mind? The young surely knew nothing.

Still, he went over to his computer. The internet was always slowest this late at the night. He sat in the dark in front of the heat of his computer screen, reading about magnets and wounds and depression in between bouts of net timeouts and pinwheels of death and his own exasperated cursing.

"Synchronous resonance," he muttered.

Absorption of energy. Cause and effect, interaction of tissue and magnetic field.

Rubbish, he thought. He scanned pages of research, adjusting his glasses when they rested too heavily on the bridge of his nose.

Some said it worked, some that it didn't. Normalised the heart rate, claimed one study. Normalised? What was normal across a population? Parham had seen too much, done too much, lived too long to believe in simplicity. Life wasn't simple. It was a chaos of chance and circumstance.

His phone beeped. Medhi, up late, too. Forgot to mention his daughter's divorce. Time marched on, was the conclusion. Parham texted his sympathies and returned to the screen. Medhi should discover email. It was cheaper.

Alleviated depression, yes. Alleviated resistant depression, no. Resistant. What's the difference? Parham wondered. Did they label it "resistant" if it failed to respond to their magnets? How was that science?

One site said, "Remember that humans are electro-chemical machines. Coils of electricity can be used to produce magnetic fields."

Were they suggesting humans could create their own electrical fields? What, roll into a foetal position and find yourself able to control iron filings? Or wrap your arms around another human being and...

The world was a crazy place, he'd known that for a long time. And this was as crazy as anything else he'd heard.

One more "page not found" message and Parham hit the power button. Forget it. He sat in the dark listening to the whirr of the fan as it slowed and wondered how Zara was. Where she was. He'd bought bank bonds when she was born, put money into an account every year. Given her the whole lot when she turned eighteen. Told her it was for her education.

She'd used it to get away from him.

That's one thing he didn't like admitting even to Medhi. He and his own daughter, they were like strangers.

The Loser

She knew the answer before she asked the question, but she asked it anyhow.

"And how do you feel about her now?"

She tried to focus, failed, slipped back into her own thoughts, missed the answer.

"Have you contacted her since?" she asked.

The answers continued.

She struggled momentarily to remember this client's name — started with K, she thought — and sent a quick glance at the clock behind his left shoulder.

Kevin, Keith, Karl...

All matter is affected by magnetics, that was the theory. Six hundred years of theory. Flesh and blood held prisoner by the thick thudding iron centre of the world. The magnetic core.

The problem, for her, wasn't so much one of matter, of substance. It was the other stuff. The insubstantial stuff.

She wanted to believe in the concept of a soul.

She'd published seven books, counselled over eight hundred clients (she specialised in group therapy. As her ex-husband liked to point out, this unfairly upped her numbers), been married twice, pregnant twice, given birth once.

Had no children.

At nearly seventy that final startlingly empty statistic was unlikely to change.

"If you could talk to her now," Gilberd said, and faltered.

K. looked at her quizzically.

"Yeah?"

"If you could talk to her now, what would you say?"

Gilberd's mind raced. Her child, her second child, the unaborted one, had died at birth. Been born dead. She still couldn't believe how that fierce little life had neglected to take its first breath. Amala, she was to be called. A name to grow into. Instead, a name used once on a miniature gravestone outlined with engraved flowers.

In the hospital, groggy from an epidural, feeling like her back was breaking, Gilberd had unwrapped those tiny fists herself, counted the perfectly even fingers. Held her thumb into the child's stilled feet, marvelled at the perfect toes.

The problem was the heart, she was told.

Wasn't it always, she'd replied, and started crying. Never really stopped. Sitting bolt upright in her counselling chair over three decades later she could feel the tight centrifuge of grief beneath her sternum.

"How do you think she'd respond?" Gilberd said out loud.

God, how would she respond, her own daughter? Given a chance, given voice, given a life outside someone's imagination.

Life was dangerous, all of it. People died all sorts of ways. A woman had electrocuted herself making coffee. It was in the paper. Intent on her fix, using an old coffee machine with an exposed cable. Groggy, tired, rushing to work, probably, spilled water on the bench, tried to mop it up with a hand, and *sayonara*. It was so easy to die.

"She really got under my skin," said the client, finishing some line of thought.

Stephanie *mmm*ed non-commitally.

"You still feel a connection to her?"

"I dunno if that's right," said K.

"No?"

"I mean, I can't stand her."

"Sometimes," Gilberd said, "we wind up drawn to the wrong kind of person, for the wrong reasons."

"Yeah? Like why?"

Why.

The pregnancy was successful. They'd been trying for three years. The very normal nine months that succeeded their efforts was reassuring. She'd been worried the teenaged abortion would ruin her chances. Destroy her womb or bruise her karma or something.

Pregnancy consumed her, every detail. She journalled every change in her body, every obsessive thought. They couldn't settle on a name, so decided to wait until they could look into their daughter's face once she was rescued from Stephanie's womb.

Rescued was the wrong word, of course.

Amala, when she was born, looked normal, smelled normal, felt — until she grew cold — normal. She'd rocked the baby back and forth, back and forth. Dan was beside her but she wouldn't let him touch their baby. The failure was all hers. She had to fix it before she could hand her little girl over.

Amala's name meant "hope". It meant "pure". Perhaps she should have named the girl something else. Perhaps it was the weight of her mother's expectation that killed her.

She'd wanted to consume the tiny shape back into her body, make her whole, add in whatever piece it was that had gone missing in the birth. Surely it's lost inside her now. She can feel it rattling around inside. The piece that keeps her bound to her lost daughter forever. If there is a forever.

She hopes not.

Dan had left some months later, apologising for appearing heartless. Not for being heartless. Just for appearing like it.

I guess I thought the baby would help the marriage, he'd said.

Is that what you thought?

Pregnant women repulsed her. Children mesmerised her. The laws of magnetics, attraction and repulsion.

When she had the painter back in to undo his work in the nursery — the metallic yellows and greens in thick stripes — he didn't ask why. Returned the room to a subdued eggshell white without a word. There wouldn't be another child in Stephanie's life. Dan was gone. She was too old to start again.

Amala joined the other child, the earlier one, the gender-unknown, medically-removed child. Ghost babies on ghost umbilical cords, tethered to her like invisible balloons. Her unerring lodestones.

Stephanie took to moving slowly, her children drawing her backwards into the past.

That's why she'd gotten into magnetic resonance therapy. It was a sublimation of her disordered connection to her children. It was her desire to yank the cosmic cord that connected them. Amala would be thirty-five by now, had she lived, and Stephanie still found herself looking out for her daughter. Searching for her, rather than watching over her.

She's tried to outwit God. She's pleaded for it to be made clear. She's wanted to know why her children died.

I want you to help me see the word "school" without sobbing.

Another client of Gilberd's was a woman whose son, age six, was snatched from his school. Never returned. The woman hadn't come looking for a miracle. It was escape she was after. Release. Not from memories of her son, but from the knowledge her son was never coming home from school. She preferred to think of her son as a dream.

Gilberd had bought butchers' paper, a whiteboard, paint, permanent markers. They'd written the word "school" on every surface, in every colour. The woman had never learned to stop sobbing. But she had learned to cope with crying, to make it bearable. And since that was all they could do, it became enough.

"We need to disrupt the connection you feel to her," Gilberd said. "Are you ready?"

Karl, Keith blinked. "I guess so. Ready for what, exactly?"

Gilberd hesitated.

"Ready," she said, figuring it out as she formed the words, "to be untethered."

Life's Work

ike the devil from holy water, Ruby thought, watching Tara shrink from her.

"Sweetie," she told Tara, "I'm your mother, not your nurse. You want a lock on your door, *you* go buy one."

Tara had retreated to the threshold of the kitchen, glaring. There were beads of sweat on her forehead.

"Besides," Ruby continued, "you're a grown woman now, for chrissake."

She stalked past Tara, forcing her to spin out of the way. In the hall, Ruby collected her hat and bag, and slammed the front door behind her.

She didn't have time for this. There was God's work to be done.

"Hello, Mrs R."

Ruby shielded her eyes against the afternoon sun.

"Oh, hello, George," she smiled. "Working on your front lawn again? Mind my daisies, now."

"Those damn daisies will outlive both of us, Mrs R," George rumbled. He spat good-naturedly at the pile of cheerful flowers. "Say, are those new earrings?"

Ruby turned a proud profile to her neighbour and patted her ear.

"George, you are the most observant man I ever met! Yes, they are new, matter of fact."

"Fifty-three years in fashion teaches a man to be observant. That, and my own dear wife. Rest her."

They observed a moment's silence.

"Say, how's your youngest coming along, anyhow?" George asked.

"She's too old to be acting like a baby," Ruby told him. "But the doctors say patience." She rolled her eyes to show what she thought of patience.

George chuckled and nodded. "Patience is a virtue. Especially in the old!"

They laughed, feeling young.

"And now this old woman has to go, George." Ruby put her keys away and snapped her purse shut decisively. "Business to attend to." She smiled and turned towards the front walk.

"Business?" George made to spit again, but held it in when he saw the look from the corner of Ruby's eye. "What business you got, Ruby? I thought we were all retired in this street."

Ruby strode past, calling back over her shoulder, "If you could be a little more retiring, George, and a little less nosey, I think this street might be a better place."

"What's the point of retiring if I can't be nosey?" George shouted.

Ruby raised a hand in farewell and stepped onto the sidewalk.

Left behind, Tara walked unsteadily up the stairs. On the top step she felt darkness tug at her back. She ran for her room and shoved the door shut behind her.

Take a breath, hold for three, she told herself. *Like the good doc says.* Her lungs weren't working and she was shaking all over. She pushed her dresser across the door, blocking it.

Darkness stood in the corridor, shifting from foot to foot. When Ruby returned early that evening, it dribbled back downstairs to greet her.

"No, she's still in her room," Ruby said into the phone. "Every once in a while she sneaks out to use the bathroom. Then straight back to her room."

She paused, listening. On her wrist dangled a gold bracelet with a thick lock. She spun her hand, watching the bracelet catch the light.

She was aching all over today. In her street, it was called "growing-old pains". Like growing pains, but without the promise. The voice on the phone was small and tinny. Less than two hours by car, but by phone, a lifetime away.

"Suzanne, I'm out of ideas, I swear. The shrinks say let her be, then I'll let her be. She can find her own way."

There was another pause, where Suzanne either agreed or disagreed with the self-help sentiment.

"No, sweetie, you don't have to come," said Ruby. The wrist with the gold bracelet rested on her thigh. "See you when I see you, sweetheart."

Ruby hung up the phone, rubbing her eyes. Last night she'd dreamt of red curtains. The image was still burned onto her retinas, painting red streaks across the grainy morning.

Yesterday in town, she'd found the gold bracelet spinning in the air. It wasn't the first time she'd received such a gift. Like a down payment from the gods, she'd thought, delighted. Gods, plural. For in that clarity of that moment, she realized her life-long mistake. All this chaos and doubt in the world. It couldn't stem from just one divine soul. There could be hundreds. And one of Them had chosen her.

Well, Ruby Reynolds, she sighed, *time to work.*

She began by going through the kitchen drawers.

Old Tony tapped softly at the back door. It was raining lightly but not enough to bother him. Normally he didn't have to knock. Just do the gardening, then pick up the envelope with the cheque in it. Mrs R always left it on the top step. She was the best customer that way. But today, though the cheque was right there, something else was bugging him.

"Yes, Tony?" Ruby said through the screen of the back door.

Tony squinted at the ghostly shape behind the screen.

"Hey, Mrs R. You're looking well," he said, taking off his hat and holding it in front of his heart. He always said that to Ruby, "you're looking well", even if he couldn't quite see her. Ruby liked being treated like a lady.

"I'm very busy, Tony."

"Oh? Yeah. OK, then," Tony said. "Only, I was wondering. Do you know about the yard, Mrs R?"

"Of course."

Flat, like that.

"Right," Tony hesitated. "You sure, Mrs R? Only there's a big hole in it. Like someone's been digging. But with something real small."

"I said I know, Tony, of course I know. My grandson. He's building a goldfish pond."

Tony couldn't make out Ruby's face at all. It was almost like her voice was coming from some place else.

"Well, I could help him build one of those," he said. "He'll need to seal it, and all. Can't just drop water in a hole. It'll all drain away," Tony offered. His head was beginning to hurt from the squinting. "How old's the boy, anyhow?"

"He doesn't need your help, Tony. He has his father." Ruby's voice was sharp as thorns. "Oh, and Tony," she continued. "I hate to say it, but, I won't be needing the gardening done anymore."

The rain had stopped, Tony realized, although bright sparkles were trapped in the screen.

"Oh? Your son-in-law going to do it all, Mrs R?" Tony asked, polite as he could. Only death itself could take Old Tony's good customers away from him. "Because if it's the money or something, I'm sure we can work it out."

"No. That's fine, Tony. Thanks for your help." Ruby was shutting the wood door behind the screen. "Goodbye."

Tony put his hat back on and stared straight ahead, thinking. Something weird was going on. Because as sure as he was standing there, he knew three things. Knew them like he knew his own soul. One was that — from the ache in his left elbow — they were in for more rain before the end of the week. Two was that the hole in the yard had been carved with something no larger than a spoon. And three was that Ruby Reynolds didn't have any grandkids. Or any sons-in-law, for that matter. The retiree grapevine never got that stuff wrong.

Ruby's arms were plastered with mud to the elbow. She hummed as she worked. She'd been up most the night. She'd never been much of an artist, but she was drawing on all her hard-earned skills as a mother of two not-so-successful daughters to make something truly special.

This one, she decided, scraping mud from her hands, would be better. A body fit to house a god. Or — she laughed out loud — a goddess.

"Mama?" called Tara. She was hunched on the dresser, leaning against her door. In the corridor the footsteps stopped. It was late at night, and only extreme hunger could make Tara call out.

"Mama?" she called again, unsure.

"What is it?" Ruby's voice, muffled and tired.

Tara jumped off the dresser and pushed it out of the way. She opened the door enough to peer out. Ruby stood like an ink stain in the corridor's shadows.

"Have you had dinner, yet, Mama?" Tara asked. The darkness made her nervous, and it took all she had to keep the door open between them.

Ruby didn't answer for a while, only rubbed at her neck like she was petting a dog. Then Tara realized it wasn't her neck exactly, but something around her neck. Like a fallen halo.

"I'll get you something. Since you're determined to stay in your room," Ruby told her at last. "I'll fix it."

"Thanks," Tara said, ashamed. She was still frozen in the doorway, staring at the pale white circuit on Ruby's neck.

"Is that a necklace, Mama?" she asked.

In the near-dark, Ruby chuckled. "You like it? Genuine pearl."

"Where'd you get a necklace like that?" Tara asked.

Ruby gripped the pearls with both hands.

"Found it," she said. "Payment for services rendered." She chuckled, then added. "Don't go in the kitchen. I'll fix you something."

She moved slowly down the stairs. Tara pushed the door shut carefully.

"No," she said. "I'll stay right here."

"Listen," Tara was whispering. She didn't know why except that she didn't want Ruby to find her here. Her palm was sweating on the receiver. She was sitting on the floor of the lounge room, her back against the wall, her feet pointed at the stairs, ready. In the kitchen to her right, Ruby had the radio blaring and she was humming at the top of her lungs. "I'm telling you. Something's wrong."

On the other end of the line, Suzanne was silent. Tara could feel her thinking she didn't have time for Tara's craziness.

"She keeps…" Tara began again. "She keeps *finding* jewellery. Every day, I swear she's got something new."

"Maybe she's finally decided to spend some cash on herself," Suzanne suggested, her voice thick with cigarette smoke.

"What cash? She doesn't have enough cash for the things she's bringing home."

"Credit, then," said Suzanne. "Which is great, because how the hell are *we* going to pay?"

"And she talks to herself."

"So do I."

"Not like this," Tara hissed. "Not like someone is talking back to you." Tara raised a hand and pushed a jagged nail into her mouth. "She's even got a name."

"Who?" Suzanne asked.

"Whoever Mama's talking to!" Tara spat a sliver of wet keratin at the carpet.

Suzanne didn't say anything for a while, but Tara could hear the sharp inhalation of smoke. *Please God*, she thought, *please God.*

"Tomorrow, then," Suzanne said finally. "I'll drop by. Sit tight, little sister."

"OK," said Tara. "Don't tell Mama."

She hung up quickly. Ruby's humming grew louder as Tara shot up the stairs.

Suzanne was knocking loud enough to attract the attention of every nosey old so-and-so in the neighbourhood.

"Where are they?" she muttered, and then realized she was talking to herself. Tara wouldn't like that.

She knocked harder, hitting her fist until her knuckles were white.

"OK, damn," she told herself.

She stepped back, looking up at Tara's window. The sun reflected from the panes, turning them opaque.

She bent and began fumbling in the pot plants at the side of the door. Mama always kept a spare key in one of them, but she couldn't remember which one.

"Well, if it isn't the *other* Reynolds gal," came a voice. "Been a while."

Suzanne looked up at the man next door. What was his name again?

"Hello," she smiled.

"Big yellow pot at the back," said George. "Is Mrs R away, then?"

"Away?" said Suzanne. "Um. No, not at all."

"Probably sleeping in," said George. "Keeps her curtains closed a lot nowadays."

He gestured at the windows where the curtains were certainly closed.

"Found it," said Suzanne. She held up the key. Probably Mama just wanted the old busybody to leave her alone. "What about that window? See anyone there?" she pointed at Tara's room.

George squinted obligingly, leaning into the daisies. "Well, I guess I don't see that far anymore," he said.

"OK, well," Suzanne smiled, unlocking the door, "thanks for your help. Bye-bye!" George looked as though he was about to say more, but she shut the door firmly behind her.

Inside was stuffy and dark.

"God, did something die in here?" Suzanne whispered, regretting it with a sudden superstitious dread.

She edged towards the staircase, flipping on lights as she went. The rooms were deep and still, almost like they were underground. Suzanne paused at the bottom of the stairs. She didn't really want to do this alone, but what else could she do? Go and get that nosey old neighbour to hold her hand?

Grimly, she started up the stairs. *I swear*, she thought, *if something grabs my ankle, I'm marching right the hell out of here and never coming back.* Tara, she decided, could find her own way out.

Upstairs, the corridor was in shadow. Tara's room was the first on the left. Suzanne grabbed the doorknob like it was a lifeline. The door was stuck.

"Tara?" she called, forcing the panic out of her voice.

Inside, she could hear furniture being moved. Lots of it. What, did Tara have her whole room piled against the door?

"Thank God," Tara said. Her face was red and streaked with tears.

"What the hell's going on?" Suzanne asked. "Where's Mama?"

Tara squeezed out into the corridor.

"Can't you feel it?" she asked. She wrapped her arms about herself, shivering.

"No," said Suzanne, although in truth she did feel something. There, at her back. She spun but the corridor was empty.

"Let's find Mama," she said, putting a hand protectively on her neck.

She started towards the master bedroom at the end of the corridor, Tara close behind. Passing the half-closed door of the bathroom, something caught Suzanne's eye. She leant to her right and slowly pushed the door clear.

They were silent.

Ruby sat in the bath, a pool of cold brown water barely covering her thighs. Along her shoulders and chest, brown stains marked where dirty water had dried.

"Mama?" Suzanne asked softly. "Mama, are you okay?'

Ruby smiled toothlessly. Suzanne moved into the bathroom. Leaning towards her mother she smelled piss.

"Fetch a towel," she said to Tara. "Mama, what's happened? Where are your dentures, for chrissake?"

She knelt beside the bathtub, trying not to breathe too deeply. From this close, she could see that most of the sediment in the water had settled to the bottom. When Tara came back with a towel Suzanne wrapped it around her mother's shoulders. Ruby was dry, but Suzanne rubbed her back anyway, trying to force some warmth into her mother.

"I've been busy," Ruby said, her words slippery. "I've been working."

"You don't have to work, Mama. You're retired. You've earned yourself a break now."

Ruby kept smiling, showing pale pink gums. Her bones pushed up softly under her loose skin. Suzanne didn't want to stroke too hard in case she rubbed her out completely.

"Tara, go boil the kettle, will you? Mama needs hot tea."

When she heard Tara's footsteps on the stairs, she said, "What have you done to your hair?"

Ruby reached a hand to claw through the uneven grey spikes.

"Cut it," she said.

"My God! And your nails! Did you cut them too?"

Ruby nodded, laughing.

"Yep! Yep! Cut them off. Needed to."

"Well. The other thing you need to do is get out of this bath right now," Suzanne told her firmly.

"I'll need my eyes," said Ruby.

"Yes, of course you will."

Leaving her mother under a warm shower, Suzanne went to check on Tara. She found her frozen in the kitchen doorway, one hand over her face. She turned to Suzanne, pointing wordlessly into the kitchen.

Suzanne looked over her sister's shoulder and glimpsed the kitchen table. Dried mud was strewn from one end to another. As she moved into the room, Suzanne recognized the shape. It was the figure of a woman with large breasts, tiny narrow arms, and a spiky cloud of silver-grey hair. Her mother's hair. Then she looked into the mud-doll's face.

"I found her teeth," said Tara unsteadily.

"Oh, *Jesus*," hissed Suzanne. She turned and ran from the room.

Bless these poor hands, Goddess, that only seek to serve. I meant to build for you a body of clay. A perfect expression of your divine presence. To repay the favour you paid us, fashioning us from the world's dirt. So that you could walk amongst us and feel the pain and joy of what you made, and deliver us from the sickness that has prospered in your absence.

But I have failed.

Do not abandon me now.

"To be honest, Ms Reynolds — may I call you, uh?"

The doctor checked quickly through his manila folder. He had two streaks of grey in his hair which he brushed straight back from his face.

"Tara."

"Tara. As I—"

"And you are?" Tara sat in the chair offered and looked up at the doctor.

"Doctor — ah. Right. Matthew."

"Thank *you*, Matthew," Tara said. "You were saying?"

"Yes. Er. Your mother's a fighter," he smiled, taking the chair behind a wooden desk. "I'm afraid, however, that her health is in decline. We must prepare ourselves for the worst."

Tara looked at him steadily. "What's that, then? The worst?"

"Well, the worst for these patients is of course…" he paused, fixing her with a preacher's stare, "dying."

Tara dropped her gaze to the narrow desk.

"I expected your sister might be here, also," the doctor said, flipping the pages of the folder.

"She's busy," Tara said.

"Of course," said Dr Sharpe. "Is she the One?"

"What?" Tara asked. She took a deep breath.

"The one with the panic attacks?" He tapped the folder in front of him.

"N— yes," said Tara, nodding. She tried to smile, but her face felt heavy under the makeup. "Yes, she's that one."

"Well, it can be difficult for afflicted people." He gave Tara a sad smile. "Tara, your mother's stroke has affected her terribly. You will find her much changed, I'm afraid, almost a stranger. You may be shocked."

Tara raised her chin. "I'll cope," she told him. "How long does she…?" Before she could finish the question, her voice dried up.

"How long does she have?" The doctor rubbed his jaw. "Months. Years. It's almost as though the body doesn't know when to quit."

Tara stood groggily and moved towards the door. The doctor grasped her elbow and steered her into neatly landscaped gardens. White-haired patients turned to stare.

"I understand you found her? After the stroke?" said Doctor Sharpe.

"Suzanne and me. We found her in the bath."

"There was some reference in the report to a totem," said the doctor.

"What happened to that?"

Tara looked at him and saw a gleam of curiosity. The same expression she'd seen on the faces of Ruby's neighbours when the ambulance arrived. Suzanne had stood on the top step of her mother's house and screamed at them.

Stop staring at her! Stop fucking staring!

"Is this a professional interest?" she asked the doctor.

He looked at the grass apologetically.

Tara saw her, then. Sitting in a plastic chair. She was dressed in old blue trousers that had begun to pill, and a black-and-red check shirt. She looked like she'd robbed a lumberjack. The clothes hung loosely, old and faded.

"Hello, Ruby," the doctor said.

"Mrs R," Tara corrected him. Mama had always been Mrs R to men like this. "Hi, Mama."

Ruby looked small, stripped of her jewels and her house and all her meaning. Tara leant down, trying to kiss the old woman's cheek. Ruby flinched and raised an elbow in defence.

"Careful," the good doctor pulled her back. "It's the stroke. Causes aggression in some patients."

Tara straightened mutely, her throat too tight to speak.

"Don't worry. She can't really hurt you," He patted Tara's arm reassuringly. "Come and see me when you're done. We'll discuss some of the arrangements."

Tara sat beside her mother. There were brown stains on the lumberjack's shirt.

"How are you, Mama?" she asked.

Ruby wouldn't meet her eye. She sat with one hand folded over the other. Tara wanted to reach out and grasp her mother's hands and say, *it's all going to be OK, Mama.* But that wasn't true. She took a deep breath and held it. One, two, three. Let it go.

"I hate it here," said Ruby, so quietly Tara almost missed it.

It's all going to be OK, Tara. Breathe. Just breathe.

"I'm sorry, Mama," Tara said. She brushed a hot tear from her cheek.

Ruby shuffled her hands in her lap. On her left hand was a silver ring Tara didn't recognize.

"What are you doing here?" Ruby asked, twisting the ring.

Tara had to lean in close to hear. Even Ruby's voice had shrunk.

"I came to visit you," Tara said.

"Not you."

"Yes, me, Mama. I came to visit."

Ruby straightened, staring intently ahead.

"Goodness!" she hissed.

"What?" Tara asked.

"Godless."

Ruby was still staring. Tara turned, expecting to see somebody, but there was only the careful hedges and neat lawns. She turned back to her mother.

"Godless?" she asked Ruby.

"No, no, no," Ruby said. She plucked at the buttons of her shirt. Tara searched for a tissue in her bag and found a fast food napkin. She wiped her face with it.

"Oh, Mama. I'm sorry. I'm sorry I can't fix it for you."

"Didn't work," Ruby said. "Couldn't work."

The tissue came back smeared black with mascara. Tara wished she'd brought a mirror. She sat with the stranger her mother had become for an hour. Sometimes Ruby smiled, but mostly she frowned and shook her head at nothing.

When a nurse came to take Ruby to lunch, Tara strode from the hospital without looking back. By the time her bus arrived, she was curled up in a corner of the bus shelter.

Suzanne put down the borrowed shovel. Jesus, how long was it since she'd been in the garden? Her back was aching. It'd taken all morning to dissect Ruby's crazy mud pie.

She'd begun with decapitation. Standing on a chair, she'd taken aim at the thing's thick neck with the shovel. It'd dried hard, and Suzanne needed all her weight to push through it. *Crunch*, and the head jerked free. A wave of nausea swept her up as she stared into the shallow indents meant to hold the eyes.

She felt worse with each crack of the shovel through the mud doll's body. Ruby's fingerprints covered its skin. Suzanne tried not to look too closely. She carried the pieces one by one into the yard and dropped them into the hole.

Standing over the dismembered shape, she scratched at the red welts on her arms. Great, allergies. Probably the bugs. It'd take a week for the swelling to go down. She kicked the pale grey limbs at her feet. Stupid damn doll. What was Ruby thinking?

The hard mud rocked back into place, oblivious to her rage. She kicked it again, stubbing her toe and shouting.

"Goddamn you! Goddamn you, stupid *bitch*!"

Shit, now *she* was talking to it. She looked about guiltily. By the back steps she spotted a tap. *Now, there's an idea.*

There was no hose, so she fetched the largest saucepan she could find and filled it with water. Little by little, she drenched the doll pieces until they were soft. Then she smashed them with the shovel, crushing the shape back into dirt. There wasn't enough mud to fill the hole, so she added shovelfuls of earth from the flowerbeds and smoothed it all over until the ground was level.

Ashes to ashes.

She was wet from head to foot. Even the smokes in her pocket were damp. Never carry a saucepan at speed, she told herself, managing to light one anyway. She inhaled deeply.

"Gotcha," she told the black stain at her feet.

Suzanne took the shovel and stuck it in the ground like a headstone. When the first cigarette was spent, she lit another, picking tobacco from her tongue with grubby fingers. She wondered what to do next.

Insects buzzed her face and far away a siren wept. She stared at the ground, willing the hideous doll to crawl from its grave. A kind of vindication for all Ruby's mad effort. When it didn't she was almost disappointed.

She lit her third cigarette, picturing the wide, grey face of Ruby's last work. Its blank, trusting stare. There should be, she thought, a better way to say goodbye. She finished the last cigarette, considering it.

"To hell with you," she said at last.

The Tailor of Time

The Tailor of Time sat at his sewing machine, stitching night to day.

He joined the clear cloth of dawn to a full bright afternoon like a circus top. Then he smoothed on a panel of smoky rouge for dusk and finished it off with a thick purple evening. Brushing his hand over the result, he felt a thin echo of satisfaction.

The Tailor worked with a minimum of noise or fuss. He suffered only the occasional grunt or shrug (to indicate "this is done" or "bring me cloth"), aimed at the tyros who also worked in his rooms. The tyros were pale, bald children that could pass as the Tailor's own. They looked like a ramshackle circus, dressed in scraps of cloth that tied at waist or shoulder. They worked at the Tailor's demand, darning or mending or gathering whatever needed to be darned, or mended, or gathered.

The Tailor ignored them. He existed in a meditative cocoon, his voice so unused it had all but healed over. His mouth sagged like a pocket, his eyes drooped like the shoulders of an old suit and his whole body slumped like a smock on a hanger.

Only his hands remained steady, darting leanly under the light of his sewing machine and out again before they could be caught by the quick, sharp tooth of the needle. In and out, swift as the very machine itself. In and out.

With the day laid out in cloth before him, the Tailor added a hem, threaded a drawstring through both ends and slung it like a cloak over a bare globe to his right.

Thus dressed, the globe was spun onto tracks like the tracks of a train, where it butted against other globes and sloshed with the weight of water in its guts.

The water served to hold it steady.

Dismissed, the globe and its partners creaked and shuddered, working their way along the tracks that circumnavigated the room. They passed the industrious tyros, the bare stone walls and heavy curtains of the room. They passed towards the arched window in one thick-cut wall, and would have passed out, but here they snagged and pushed back, bubbling against each other.

Coming through the window was a man. He shoved his way into the chain of gowned globes and climbed into the Tailor's room.

The tyros saw him first. In a sudden frenzy of panic they fell into a silence even deeper than their usual quietude. One ran towards the Tailor and stopped, confused, unsure how to encroach on her master's concentration. One ran towards the man, the stranger, and halted just as cautiously as her cousin.

The Tailor was unaware of the alterations in the room, sewing night to day, day to night. Until he received a bobbing tap to his elbow from his most recent globe (having scuttled back along the tracks), and jumped hard in his seat.

His finger snagged in the great machine, and the Tailor cried out to see the cruel incisor pierce all the way through. Blood beaded in the whorls of his fingertip and spilled onto the cloak of time he was making.

"Oh!"

The first clear sound he'd made in a hundred years.

"Ouch!"

The second.

He stepped off the foot-pedal at once and rescued his stricken finger, pulling his bloody hand free. He drew the injured appendage to his lips to taste the unexpected saltiness of his mistake.

On the cloth with the bloodstain, war broke out for a day. It commenced seemingly from nothing and returned there just as quickly. History would refer to it as the War of Hours.

The Tailor, however, was not concerned with this. He looked up to find the cause of the commotion and caught at once the eye of the intruder. The man had completed his expedition through the window and now stood surrounded by tyros up to his waist.

The tyros divided their gazes between the stranger and the Tailor, chewing the blood out of his injury.

The stranger said, "You the Tailor of Time?"

The Tailor, mouth still entertaining his finger, nodded.

"You make the cloak of time that clothes the world, you determine night and day, the colours, the length of hours, the pattern of seasons and years?"

The Tailor nodded and shrugged so that his ear travelled painfully close to his shoulder. He hoped to signify both regret and well-intentioned acceptance.

"Then my name is John Avery and I have a favour to beg."

The Tailor cleared his throat but the first sounds to come out were not words. He had to try twice more before he managed to say, "Beg it. John Avery."

Avery drew breath. "Tailor," he said. "You are largely forgotten where I'm from, and many places besides."

Not forgotten enough, it seemed. Though the Tailor was engaged in the act of polite conversation, it did not escape his attention that Avery had breached walls which had not seen a visitor in hundreds of years.

Avery was not privy to the Tailor's befuddlement. He dragged an empty stool to the Tailor's side, and rested his elbow on the table where the machine sat glowering and grinning.

Up close Avery was older than his spryness belied. Much older than an adventure like this warranted, climbing walls and windows and rooms, vaulting or swimming, surely, the moat which still must hug the base of this fortress. He had a light beard that deepened to faded brown at his ears. His hair was thick but receding, lending him a horned look. And he had long, wiry eyebrows over narrow brown eyes. He looked kind, but sure, and careful.

"I paid witches and bribed fools," he said. "I followed dreams and rumours from elders and madmen, seers and scientists. It took three years."

"And," said the Tailor, voice still thick and unpractised, "what do you want?"

"Time."

Of course.

"I want you to slow down time for a day. No, an afternoon. A set of hours, even. Just some small, very small, amount of time."

The Tailor let out a bark that might've been a cough, might've been, instead, some descendent of laughter.

Avery continued, "You expected me to ask that."

The Tailor nodded.

"You want to know why I ask?"

A grunt, meaning "naturally".

Here it came, all sorts of tales of great deeds and discoveries to be made if only time would permit. Of acts of humanity planned and mistakes to be rectified. Of love to be given or taken, of fears that must be faced, of favours to be returned. Particularly to the Tailor, if only he would grant this one wish.

He tried not to roll his eyes as he faced this newest petitioner.

"I intend to waste it," said Avery.

"W— ?"

This was new.

The Tailor spread his hands and gestured Avery forward, indicating with the tilt of his ear that he should repeat the request.

"Waste," said Avery, leaning in and enunciating carefully. "I want some time to waste."

"Because…?"

"Because that's exactly what youth is meant to do."

The Tailor paused, even more confused than before. John Avery, he was convinced, was not young. But was he mad?

"I would waste every precious second. I would engage in all the childish pursuits my old-man frame would allow. I would run after dragonflies and kick at puddles in the mud and roll in grass and thread plastic spoke rattles onto my pushbike, I would—"

"Spoke rattles—?"

"Because this girl," said Avery, reaching into a pocket, "deserves that, don't you think?"

"Your…?"

"Daughter, yes."

The Tailor drew breath.

He was trying to clear the constriction that threatened to overwhelm his throat and stomach and ease the tension that dragged his shoulders backwards like broken wings.

Avery held a photograph of a girl (of — what? — seven, eight years?). Sunlight limned her fair head and lay on the top curl of her grin. She was squinting, standing by a pushbike with one hand gripped to the handlebar, one hand curling the seat.

"This is Bella. Some days she can breathe," said Avery. "Some days she can even ride her bike. Some days she gasps and coughs up the fluid that is drowning her from the inside out."

He let this sink in.

"Unlikely I could repay you, Tailor, understand."

Not even a favour traded.

What was the Tailor to make of this?

He dropped his hands to his lap and sat, looking lopsidedly at his visitor. Then he gazed around at the drapes, the thick stone walls and finally, to the childish tyros who had returned, by degrees, to their work.

He looked at the chain of globes emptying from the room, the spill of blood on the cloth still caught in the machine, the floor and then, his own lap (filled with threads and scraps of cloth). He shook his head slowly like he was waking from a dream.

How had he…?

How did any of this…?

How could…?

"One problem," said the Tailor, voice heavy, "I don't know how."

"You…? Oh," It was Avery's turn to pause. "Is there someone who does?"

The Tailor gestured broadly. "No. Only…" he paused.

"Yes?"

"Perhaps the Engineer."

"Okay?"

"She built everything."

"An engineer?"

"*The* Engineer."

"You've met her?"

"No," he grunted at the impossibility of that idea. "Well, once. Saw her, more like. But she was … I called out to her, but perhaps she didn't hear. She was busy."

The Tailor couldn't find any other excuses for the way the Engineer had looked at him. Blankly, like he was a swatch of fabric and she was thinking what to do with him.

"Okay," Avery looked like a man trying not to give up. "And she made this strange place?"

"Some suggest she built all of everything that there is."

"Oh? Okay. And what does she do now?"

The Tailor shrugged. "Maintenance?"

Avery nodded, thumbing his beard thoughtfully. "Can she be found?"

The Tailor was uncertain. And even then, he explained, it was unlikely she could be prevailed upon. The Engineer was cold and unyielding, like the stone that made up this place.

Avery leaned back, clenching his hands over his stomach almost in prayer. He stared at the stone ceiling. "Unlikely…" he repeated.

They say time heals all wounds, but it wasn't as true as this: time, most often, runs out. Avery was thinking that then, as he leaned his chin into both hands beside the Tailor's grand, grinning machine. He stayed there, bowed, for a long time.

When he spoke, his voice was muffled by his fingers. "Then how…?"

The Tailor had never granted a request. Had, in fact, attempted to make sure he was in no position to hear them.

But now, stalled in his work, he couldn't *not* consider John Avery and that cheerful girl with the sunlit grin who looked directly from the photograph like she might leap from its shallow page.

"Bring her here?" said the Tailor.

But here there were no dragonflies, no spoke rattles, no mud. And could such a small girl travel the whispers and rumours it had taken Avery just to reach here?

No. The only way to do it was to stall the globe. And not just any globe. What they needed was to stall the globe that was in use, the one determining time at that very moment.

The Tailor reached out a hand to Avery, but hesitated, uncertain, and said instead, "I will help you, John Avery. Somehow."

For Bella, with the smile like daylight.

Avery stood to leave, the plan agreed. On a good day, when Bella could breathe without help, he would send word.

"You'll know," said Avery, cutting off the Tailor's next question. "And Tailor—"

"Welcome," nodded the Tailor. "You're welcome."

He left the way he'd arrived.

The Tailor returned to his sewing as best he could. His focus was gone and he was aware of the dull throb of his injured finger, and how the injury made him cautious now, lest he wreck some other part of him in the maul of the machine.

Almost at once the machine hit a snag and ran rough temporarily, and he was forced to reach for the pouch of tools in his pocket, to poke and prod it open and check its gears and screws, discover a loose one and right it, then return to his work. This he did as required while he waited.

Also while he waited, he drew in several of the tyros at a time, their bald heads shining in the light of the machine, and he lead them through what to do and how to clothe the globes.

Just in case there was ever another Tailor needed.

The word from Avery when it arrived, was a whisper carried on whispers. It breached the room, starting with the tyro nearest the window and working its way around to where the Tailor sat ready.

"This is the best way to tell you that today is a good day for spoke rattles and dragonflies, dear Tailor," whispered the nearest tyro.

"Time," replied the Tailor, "has come."

He rose from his machine and watched as his training took effect. The tyros shuffled into position, two of them dragging the swathes of cloth up to the machine; another two feeding it through.

Unsentimentally he left them to it, straightening his spine with effort and pausing a moment to savour the release of standing upright. He crossed to the tracks where the globes travelled and climbed, unsteadily at first, but with increasing assurance. He pushed out a gap in the line and pulled himself along, nose bumping the sheathed globe in front while the ones behind caught at his toes. He crawled, hands gripping hard to the track, knees pressing painfully.

The window caught him on each shoulder and threatened to dislodge him. He had to back up and remove his cloak and thick shirt, then clamber forward again naked to the waist, skin trembling from the effort, elbows alternatively locking then shaking.

When he breached the other room he took a moment to get his bearings. There was a passage, the track snaking across to exit another window just as small as the first, light glowing messily from the other side. He approached and squeezed through, scraping his upper arms, awkwardly pinning his wrist under him and wrenching it enough that it ached.

After the second window was daylight and a sheer drop over which the tracks meandered in confused circuits.

What a crazed, hellish design he'd found. What singularly unfriendly efforts had been spent constructing this track and the struts that suffered its support. And then affixing the lot to a cliff at angles and heights that sent the senses spinning.

But of course this was exactly the point, he realised. The maker of the machines did not want for interference. The Engineer built monsters so others would think twice about abuse or ownership. She made them unfriendly with all the purpose and intent possible.

He thought again of those blank eyes and the unsmiling fixture of her mouth, and none of it surprised him after that.

He took a shuddering breath and then another. He kept his chin high so he wouldn't be tempted to look down.

The globes here had stalled. To move forward, he would have to climb over the top of them. He clasped each one in turn, pulling it into the shadow of his belly and then pushing it back between his thighs to where it washed against its followers. The soft thud and glub of the waterlogged spheres behind calmed him.

Still, he cursed his newfound friend more than once and then cursed the crazed mind of the Engineer who'd built this thing. But he couldn't go back on his word. If he failed, the memory would nag and fill him up and leave no room for anything else. He had, as he saw it, no choice.

He gripped hard, chin between shoulders, forcing himself to breathe, to squeeze his eyes shut against the inertia that dragged at him. He focussed on stilling the tremble in his arms and isolating the ache in his knees, willing both into ignorance.

Only then did he find the focus to look ahead for his quarry, the globe that determined the current day. And there it was — that had to be it — a globe that stood alone on a plinth, lit from above and below, held steady and rotating methodically.

The lights made it look as though it floated. It rotated slowly, already shifting from a pleasant pink dusk to a throaty, overcast day. He didn't remember sewing that one. It hadn't seemed special in his machine, nor had the cloth inspired him as he ran it through his hands. And yet, here it was. The day John Avery had deemed a good day.

He crawled forward, slow but sure, traversing the track in-between. He passed another globe and another, closing in on his prey shining with the bliss of its being.

One final globe and at last he was there. Now all he had to do was stall it. He needed to wedge something into the mechanism to hold it steady. This way he would give John Avery those hours he'd asked for.

The Tailor stood upright on the tracks with the gaping void on either side of his feet. His ankle shook and nearly gave way, and he had to wave his arms out straight on either side of his body to keep himself right.

He stabilised, and let out a slow breath that was too passionate for a sigh.

The globe, by now, was rotating closer and closer to night. Soon it would slip its mooring and sail off along the track to where the other used-up days sat, their coats faded from the harshness of the spotlights. Soon, soon the day would be done, and the Tailor's promise unaddressed. And he had come so far, climbed so far, was even now perched precariously above the sheer drop that emptied out to nothing but a grey horizon.

In his pockets were all manner of implements and needles and miniature tools to mend the machine. His pockets, however, were all in the coat he'd left on the floor of his room.

He took a moment to curse.

Then he leaned over the globe and found the tiny mechanical catch that kept it isolated, and he wedged his thumb against it — that lean, learned thumb that had been used to pinch and hold and size the demands of thousands of years of sewing.

Almost too late he realised that wasn't the right spot. A latch opened outside his hand and he had to swiftly move to keep it from closing.

There was a grinding noise as the globe attempted to dislodge, and the whole world quivered and seemed as though it would topple.

But it held, the clicking latch pressed back on the Tailor's sinewy thumb. It held and the bank of globes behind him waited dutifully, and the globes in front continued to bounce along, oblivious.

For one full rotation he waited. Then he waited another and another, averting his face from the dull glare of the spotlights (dimmed but not extinguished, signifying night). He held himself in place with one strong hand gripping the appendage that kept the lights and plinth together.

The cloth grew faded.

Slowly at first, then like a day where the sun refuses to rise or set, the cloth faded as if smog covered the world. He should let go. Soon he should let go. One more moment, one more…

Brown patches of burn appeared gently, the soft cloth falling to ash. By then his thumb was so stiff with the weight of the latch that he couldn't even be sure he was holding it anymore. And finally with a click, the globe rolled off.

For a moment, no globe took the plinth.

The Tailor had to haul himself bodily over the spot, convinced he would fall, his knees so stiff and shoulders so weak he couldn't feel when he was touching the track and when he wasn't. He moved out of the way, willing the next globe into place.

Sure enough, the next globe rolled onto the plinth, latches and catches working perfectly to hold it steady.

The Tailor was too spent to even breathe a sigh of relief. He made to lower himself to the track, reaching out a shaking hand and bending to an awkward squat. He offered a silent acknowledgment for John Avery and his daughter, hoping it had been enough. Surely it had been enough.

He was so wrapped in his thoughts that at first he didn't realise his hand had missed the track. His own hand, on which he relied every day, and now it fell beyond safety with an almost pre-ordained determinism. It dropped in something akin to slow-motion and pulled the rest of him with it.

His inside elbow scraped the track, following his hand. His chin snagged, but it wasn't enough to hold him.

And then he was falling.

Head first, body unfolding behind, swooping with an uncanny grace. Plummeting through grey.

He fell and—

He fell and—

He fell.

Nothing caught or saved him. He plunged into the gap afforded by the precipice. He dropped towards a grey void that could've been anything but ultimately turned out to be stone and earth.

He fell and hit the hard ground.

He died.

The impact shook free the Tailor's soul, which blossomed and ballooned above his crumpled form and then spread thin like a bubble exploding.

When it rose past the windows of the place that used to shelter him, only one witness was there to see it. Not the tyros, still busy at their work in the Tailor's room, bald heads bobbing almost in time to the needle on the great machine.

It was the Engineer who leaned from the window, round-eyed with bemusement, reaching with short, stocky fingers for the suds of the Tailor's soul. She rubbed with finger and thumb at the smooth stickiness it left on her skin. She frowned and gazed and wondered what other force could call her tailor-man away, and to where. What higher force could there be, she thought, than an engineer?

As he drifted from her reach and travelled, uncertain at first, then with increasing urgency into the grey-blank sky, she merely stood, paying heed to the last of her lost man.

The Engineer seemed — seemed, only — more human than her fellow occupants in this strange place. Were it not for the blank, calculating eyes and the permanent downturn of her mouth, she might be mistaken for a child of — what? — seven or eight. But she moved with the steely calculation of an intellect that had observed thousands of years.

One more Tailor, she calculated, had just been lost. The best one yet. One more disappearance, one more example of the only remaining mystery in a world she once believed herself to have built. It frustrated her. But frustration, like all emotions, was barely more than an intellectual effect. What benefits others received from emotions, she had never determined.

The remnants of the Tailor were all but gone, a bare shimmer in the distant air. The Engineer dismissed the sight, turning from the window. She slid to a seated position with her back against the stone wall, and pulled out a strip of plain cloth and a white tailor's pencil. She looked thoughtfully to one corner of the ceiling.

Then, balancing the cloth on her knee, she wrote:

'The Tailor hopes…'

In bulky, childish script.

She licked the tip of the pencil and chewed her lip and thought. She drummed her thumbs on the bones of her knee. Then she continued, '… hopes there were dragonflies and mud and spoke rattles for your bike and more…'

And more.

Then she crumpled the note in her fist, since cloth and pen marks cannot travel through whispers and rumours. John Avery and the unmet girl, Bella … if they were to be reached at all … must be sought in the traditional way, through muted words and the spaces in-between the words.

The Engineer leaned back to feel the smoothness of the wall behind her and to wonder idly, idly, what places she might visit. That is, if she could travel whispers and rumours, beg favours and elicit curses, roll across silence, across water-coloured skies. She wondered what more there was and more there could be.

King of All and the Metal Sentinel

King of All regarded the sky with his one good eye.

"I am King of All I Survey," he mused. "Named after my mistress's father. And since I survey this — the sky! — so I must be master of it."

The thought pleased him. He moved his head slowly from side to side, servos whining in his long neck.

"I am King of the Sky," he told the granite-faced goblins to left and right, news they took with stony solemnity. "King of All," he added to himself.

After the decades on this roof, any voice was comforting. Even his own.

He began another slow circuit along the wall walk, pausing to greet each of the six familiar towers like an old friend. King had a tottering limp, his right rear leg sticking on every forward movement. Backwards was okay, but without rear video feed the prospect was daunting. So King continued forwards. Or, to his mind, without a backwards glance.

His limp wasn't the only legacy of the accident.

"Accident," he muttered out loud.

He was sure that's what it was.

With his back welded stiff from the blast thirty-five years ago, there were other things he couldn't do. Like chase his tail. Or make the movements necessary for going down stairs. Up stairs was fine, but King had run out of stairs that went up. And so he lived on the roof, weathering the seasons as best he could.

From the corner of his eye he spied the flowering corrosion of scorch mark along his metal back. When it rained he could hear water sloshing around his insides. Luckily, most of his programming resided in his head — an anthropomorphic touch for which his creator had been proud.

"No harm done," he consoled himself every day. It was a lie, but he allowed it. "Still ticking," he told himself with a grin.

The turbine in his chest hummed in reply.

King missed the warm, dry insides of the castle. He even missed his fellow mechanical labori. Some of whom, he supposed, might still be active. But they'd been programmed for only the meekest of work and in King's experience, not one had been fitted with voice-com. The Queen, who loved silences of all kinds, found voices unnecessary in servants. She made an exception only once for her daughter's new toy. Provided he never spoke in her presence.

"I can't hear the ocean with you making all that noise," she'd whisper hoarsely, towering over above him in a mountainous satin gown.

In her rooms at the castle centre, the ocean was a bare murmur. But here on the roof it roared and wailed like a wounded thing. The Queen, he reflected, would hate it here.

He trotted up to a favourite spot on the parapet and reached his front legs onto the embrasure edge. Easing himself upwards, he pushed forward and out so he could peer over the battlement of the castle's inner wall.

In front of him the shorter curtain wall wrapped the castle, separated from King's own by a space of nearly ten metres. The curtain wall was the castle's first defence, and it stood braced against the onslaught of forest and plain and — directly to his right — ocean. King looked down to the space between the walls and examined again the vivid green grasses beneath him. Slowly, he swung his head to the left, holding it at the edge of its range. He waited, poised in that position as if frozen.

Thirty-one minutes later the sun glinted off a metal sphere 200 metres below. King attempted the tail-wagging program, but found the routine corrupted. He followed the smooth progress of the metal body beneath him, turning his head to keep the shape in sight. It slid through the long grass, skimming the edge of the inner wall. When it disappeared around the corner, King let out a soft electronic whine.

He spent the rest of the afternoon there, watching the sphere appear and disappear at exactly forty-seven minute intervals.

Sentinel QR73X8 — S-QR, for short — continued his rounds of the castle all day. He was executing a non-native program — one of his own design — and he was well aware that he wasn't intended for surveillance work. But in the absence of any other fit sentinel units, he had appropriated the role. And once he'd made that decision, he was determined to stick to it.

Fallen Guards dotted his route. They were three times his size and equipped with weapons and protocols he couldn't begin to understand. They were also completely inactive. Some were burned from the fires that had fallen from the sky. Others merely lay there, as pristine as the day they were bought.

"Because we need more power than you," Chief Guard, KS-X93Z9, had explained. "The back-up solar panels on the guard house were all wiped out by comets. And now the uranium pulley from the castle is jammed. Without a steady supply, we're done for, Toy."

S-QR had absorbed the information solemnly. The panels on his tiny hut in the rose garden were mercifully undamaged, but it seemed impolite to mention this.

Reflecting on that conversation now, S-QR realised he'd just passed the Chief Guard's resting place. He paused, reversed direction smoothly, and skimmed backwards to pay his respects.

The Chief lay close to the outer wall, sinking, decade by decade, into the long grasses. His body appeared undamaged, although the cameras lining his upper quadrant were blank.

"Not really a sentinel, are you?" said KS-X93Z9 the day S-QR arrived. "Not built for it. Not tough."

S-QR had to concede to the correctness of that. "OK," he had said.

KS-X93Z9 had sat stolidly in the air a moment. "So, what are you?"

"A ... novelty unit," he'd told the shape hovering above him.

"Novelty unit?" KSX-93Z9 had replied, more with surprise than cruelty.

"Yes. For the Queen's garden."

"Well. Queen's man, eh?" rumbled KSX-93Z9. "Not so bad, then. If we ever need help patrolling the Rim, we can count on you, eh, Toy? Think you could handle that?"

S-QR reflected. He had only one weapon, added as an afterthought by his programmer, and not really designed for defence: a small laser with which he could turn props into smouldering rubble on command. Intended solely to create mirth in an educated audience.

But he could see well enough for any patrol. Three-hundred-and-sixty degree data from twenty-eight separate visual feeds dotting his spherical frame added up to one extreme 3D image of the world.

"OK," he'd agreed.

He had set to work learning his new task, rushing after the larger units in their rounds. The Rim Between, KS-X93Z9 had told him, was by definition the route currently occupied by a sentinel unit. So wherever he was, it was his duty to protect the inside. Repel the outside. Most of the time, the Rim they patrolled was the space between the high inner wall and lower curtain wall of the castle.

That was forty years ago. S-QR still patrolled the Rim Between all day long. Protect the inside, repel the outside. That was the idea. His databanks had corrupted only minimally over the decades since he'd taken up sentinel responsibility. Some days he couldn't remember which was inside and which was out. But since very little appeared to challenge him, it didn't seem to matter.

So long as he remembered the Rim. Wherever he was, he controlled the Rim. He was determined to continue his rounds for as long as order held.

In the intervening years, the ground had become gorged with weeds. It bothered him that the castle should suffer this disrespect. But there was little he could about gardening, lacking arms. It bothered him more that, with the northern gates now hanging from their hinges, the dense tangle of woods was leaning in towards the Rim. And behind the fallen gates, the ocean boiled for miles into the horizon.

S-QR continued to guard the Rim all that day, like he did every day, until purple twilight brushed against the walls. Lacking proper night-vision, he made his way back through the thorny vines to his hut, dragging the Rim with him.

"I am King of All I Survey," King told himself. "I am King of the Night."

He sat by the door that led back down into the castle. The blast thirty years ago had been terrifying, but the continued absence of his mistress, Keagan, disturbed him more.

Keagan was a young princess of ordinary childish cruelty, or so King believed. She was prone to tearing madly about the castle and desiring to be chased, although always resenting being caught. She liked to eat her supper on the floor with her favourite toy and never enjoyed having her hair combed. All this King learned quickly as they roamed the castle's rooms. He became expert at predicting human behaviour, but never really felt he understood it.

They never ventured outside without permission from her parents, who took turns doting on and then ignoring their only daughter. In contrast, young Keagan was King's central focus. She demanded almost all of his attention. Which suited him fine, because he had a lot of attention to give.

"You're not to go outside without me, King," Keagan had told him the morning she unwrapped him from his box. "Not ever! That's no place for indoor labori. Stay inside."

"Understood," said King, with a grin.

"See that?" Keagan had pointed. "That's a sentinel."

King had looked out the window at the massive floating units. They were huge, and patrolled the castle grounds with a synthetic single-mindedness he wholeheartedly admired.

"They'll kill a little unit like you," Keagan had promised. King hadn't quite understood the threat but he'd taken note of Keagan's expression and nodded sombrely. He'd searched his databanks, but killing and being killed were not required concepts.

"If they kill you, you have to play dead forever!" explained Keagan.

"Play dead" had no more meaning to King than "lie still", but judging from Keagan's solemn stare, forever was a long time.

So King fetched, followed and generally radiated good will as best he could.

Then the lights had come out of the sky, sizzling through the castle walls, burning furnishings and flesh equally, upending labori too slow to dodge them. King had stuck close to his young mistress. Not out of fear, which he'd never learned, but out of respect for Keagan's evident distress. That's what a pet is for, King had thought gladly, to love his mistress.

He'd followed Keagan into her mother's room, populated by an army of the Queen's personal labori. The metal units were holding aloft towels and brushes in various of their arms, but otherwise they appeared aimless. They skittered across the carpets, frequently bumping each other in their chaotic haste. *Something has them rattled*, King had thought. *The Queen won't like this.*

"Mummy!" Keagan had screamed then.

King wasn't sure what possessed her to say that. The Queen was obviously not there. Certainly, visual input led him at first to believe that the shape on the floor was the Queen. The resemblance was very close, right down to the satin dress fanned out around it. However, the olfactory data had been radically incorrect for that conclusion, and there was an absence of familiar bio-chem information. Perhaps Keagan had not processed that yet.

The next fireball caught Keagan along the top of her head. She continued to kneel upright for nearly a minute, during which time, available visual input re-confirmed to King that this was indeed his mistress silently balancing in front of him. But as the shape fell towards the carpet, the other, contradictory data overwhelmed him.

King remained in the room for three seconds more. He was confused. Keagan's input had suddenly disappeared right in front of him. No, it had morphed somehow, as if the real Keagan had travelled out of the room on the blast that smote the walls, leaving behind something that, if bio-chem information was to be trusted, could only be classified as "food".

King had no need of food. Dodging the distressed labori, he bounded from the room in search of his mistress.

S-QR peered uncertainly into the darkness around his hut. At any moment, the Rim could be breached. In front of him, in the darkness, he knew the Queen's garden lay neglected. Mechanical labori that had once tended it were frozen in place, shears extended towards vines that now wrapped their bodies. Like most nights spent here, his problem-solving protocol sorted through his databanks and again came across the one unresolved issue it found there. It was the problem of intent.

S-QR knew all about intent. He knew there were two kinds of movement to be expected on the Rim. Movement without purpose, like the wind through the grass, was random, safe, ignored. Purposeful movement had an aim and a kind of order. Climbing a castle wall in order to breach the Rim, that was intentional.

For this kind of action, there were two outputs. Challenge, or attack. Challenge was easy; it activated a phrase in the voice box. Attack — which S-QR had hoped to avoid ever using — fired the laser on the base of his body.

Recognition of intent, S-QR reflected again, was not the problem. The fault lay in his gate-program. It was the gate-program that choreographed all the other programs. It was the one that dealt with dual input/output commands. It assigned status, multitasked, blocked inappropriate responses. Or, at least, it was supposed to.

S-QR remembered the incident thirty-five years ago. An indoor unit had been loitering near the shadow of the inner wall. Small, square, no taller than S-QR himself, but ground-dwelling. Just as he'd located it in the visual field, it had begun to trot towards him. Whether it was outside trying to get back in, or inside trying to get out, he couldn't tell. But it had violated the Rim, and so he had approached with the plan to—

Challenge! he invoked.

Attack, responded his gate-program.

The laser blast, though weak, was nevertheless strong enough to flip the other unit into the air. S-QR hovered, shocked, afraid to try any of his other programs and yet wondering at the status of the fallen foe. But since the unit had been flung deeper into the shadows of the inner wall, it was lost to his weak sight. S-QR had waited there nearly seven minutes but had seen no further movement. Eventually, too worried about the Rim to stay, he rushed away to continue his patrols of the outer ward.

Since then he had numerously invoked the test procedures, only to find them corroded or perhaps incapable of the tasks for which they had been designed. To his horror, he was unable to determine his own procedural status.

But S-QR was a soldier, however self-promoted, and he was determined to do the best he could. He reflected again on the plan his problem-solving procedure had established. It awaited only the appropriate stimulus. Then he would invoke the Attack program and hope the cross-wires went both ways, resulting in the Challenge execution. It was a dangerous plan, but he was aware that he had become a dangerous unit.

And that frightened him.

King had roamed the castle for twelve weeks after Keagan disappeared. He was programmed with a high mischief tolerance and abundant nuclear energy, so he was rarely bored. He roved up and down the stairs, looking for input from his mistress. He checked behind every open door and under every piece of furniture. Then he checked it all again. By that time most of the other labori had wound down, frozen in their final acts of obeisance.

There was no sign of the King or Queen or his little mistress. Finally, he decided to go outside. This was against the direct order of his mistress, but King had decided that perhaps it was a game she was playing, and she had been waiting for him in her mother's garden since she'd disappeared. Testing his loyalty.

The idea tormented him.

He jogged up to the door by that led to the gardens.

"Door, open!" he commanded, just as Keagan had numerous times.

The door slid open and King stepped hesitantly outside, cautiously scanning the panorama. He had never been this far without Keagan before.

He spied a round metal unit and, fixing his best grin to his face, loped towards it.

The sudden blast knocked him off his feet and flipped him high into the air. He landed on his back in the shadow of the door. Axons in his neural network popped and the wires in his back sizzled. Recovery programs began their calculations; positing and revising estimated restoration chances a hundred times each second.

Unrecoverable damage 15%. Recoverable damage 30%.

Unrecoverable damage 20%. Recoverable damage 35%.

Remembering Keagan's threat about playing dead forever, King lay completely still, silently regarding the massive grey wall of the castle through his own upturned legs. The stranger, denied any further input, eventually moved on.

By steadily working his right shoulder into the ground, King managed to flop onto his side. His back legs were stiff, but by using only the front ones, he slowly regained his feet.

He limped back through the open door, into the dark surrounds of the castle.

"Door. Shut."

Eighteen hours later, having climbed to the first floor to continue the search for Keagan, King of All He Surveyed discovered his inability to go back down. In the absence of a reason not to, King continued to climb the stairs, one landing every second or third day, until he reached the roof.

The sky was donning its pre-dawn grey when King made a new decision. Since he could no longer use the stairs, and since Keagan was quite obviously not on the castle's roof, King would go down. Straight down. Over the edge of the parapet.

Satisfied with the plan, he trotted clumsily over to the wall and eased himself upward. He looked over the edge. The base of the wall was still wreathed with shadow, but he had excellent night vision. The metal sphere was nowhere in evidence, and would not make his first appearance for — King glanced sideways at the sky — nearly an hour.

He hoisted his back legs up onto the wall, relying on the power in his shoulders. Balancing a moment, he deliberated again, listening to the roar of the ocean.

"Nothing to lose," he decided. "Can still be King of the Sky from down there."

Slowly he leaned forward, tipping his nose towards the earth, pushing his toes against the stone, straightening himself out like an arrow. His front paws were on the very edge of the battlement. With little effort, he rocked forward. Then he fell into space, hurtling through the pale morning towards the ground.

It was a bright clear day when the sentinel began his rounds. As usual, he felt re-energized after a night in the hut. He skimmed out of the rose garden into the outer ward. Halfway around the Rim he noticed an awkward silver form on the ground. S-QR paused by the unfamiliar shape. He observed for some minutes. It seemed to lack any intent whatsoever. Without a reason to stay, and worried again for the Rim he patrolled, he hesitantly moved on.

Three full circuits of the castle later, the thing stirred. As S-QR rounded the corner, he saw it half-lifting from the ground. The little sentinel remembered his plan and sped towards the shape in all haste. It was finally time. Hoping desperately for co-operation from his gate-program, he commanded:

ATTACK.

"Who goes there!" he found himself shouting. It was the first time he'd heard his own voice in over thirty years. In his relief, he nearly sped right past the foreign shape.

"I am King of All I Survey," said the shape, moving its head with difficulty towards the voice. As the other met his video feed, S-QR thought he read recognition, then fear, in its hesitation. And the sentinel recognised the intruder, too. A figure that had stayed at the forefront of his databanks for thirty-five years.

"Should I play dead?" the figure on the ground asked, seemingly of itself. It froze, upright, staring at the sentinel implacably.

The sentinel froze, too, gingerly feeding the input/output gate in his programming.

"State your position," he shouted.

The figure continued to stare blankly.

"In the clan, state your position!" S-QR said.

"Ah! I am a laboro, an internal unit for the Princess Keagan. My name is King."

"An internal laboro?" S-QR paused. Processed. "Then you must stay inside. Do not cross the Rim!" he proclaimed.

He regretted having to send the unit away already, but order had to be maintained. King seemed to sag a little, but nodded dutifully. He rose stiffly to his feet and began with wavering steps to move towards the door.

"Not that way!" S-QR shouted. His Attack sequence was adjusting smoothly. He wondered what the Challenge sequence would invoke, but, lacking proper input, did not feel tempted to try it.

"But I'm going inside," replied King carefully.

"You are crossing the Rim. Internal labori may not pass the Rim. Besides," the sentinel was shouting, "that way is outside."

At least, he thought it was. He wasn't really sure but didn't dare ask the other, since this might compromise his authority. For three decades it had not mattered which was inside and which was out. Only the Rim mattered.

"So where am I now?" King asked after a moment.

"You are on the Rim Between," S-QR informed him, "since you are beside me and I must be on the Rim. None may cross." The sentinel's voice was softening as he spoke.

"Then, how do I get inside, from the Rim?" King asked.

S-QR had no idea. He had been on the Rim so long, he wasn't sure how to get off it.

"My programming does not allow me to say," S-QR replied.

The two units regarded each other for a minute.

"So I'll stay here?" asked King eventually.

Sentinel regarded the small grey shape with its face tilted up towards him, noted the tremor, not quite fully pronounced, in its tail section.

"That would be acceptable," he said, "provided you do not violate the Rim and do not go outside. No place for an indoors unit. But I must continue my rounds." He began to move away, leaving the stranger beside the wall.

That seemed to go well, he thought. From the cameras along his body, he could see King tilting his head to the right, watching him go.

"You are welcome to assist me, if you think you can keep up," Sentinel shouted.

With a grin, King began to stumble after the guard. It gave the sentinel a new kind of feeling to watch the unit totter after him. "If you think you are built for this work," he added more softly.

King looked up respectfully.

"You know, I am King of the Sky," he offered as S-QR slowed down to his pace.

Sentinel regarded the sky above him through eleven of his visual units. He was impressed.

"Then you are king of a vast empire, indeed," he said.

III. End of an Era

Problems of Light and Dark

I. First Light

Lennie's dad was a long time dying.

"Like a shirt on the line too long," he laughed.

"I never leave shirts on the line," Lennie's mother replied.

Papa grunted. "Not blaming you."

It was how all their fights started.

"You put terrible ideas in your young boys' heads. They'll grow up weird."

"Nothing wrong with weird."

Papa chuckled and spluttered, then he coughed. He coughed like he might burst. Mama patted his shoulder and reproached him in equal measures.

"She thinks she can argue the weirdness away," Papa told Lennie *sotto voce*.

The cancer wore Papa down until he was just a sliver of skin wrapped around that wracking cough. He was in the hospital by then. Didn't say much after that, weird or otherwise. Just one thing he repeated over and again.

"Lights out. Lights out, lights out."

"Hush. You scare them boys."

Lennie's mother shushed her husband and shushed her sons in turn, silencing their whimpers. Then the tinny silence would start again. The one thing that hospitals excel at, that flat, expectant quiet.

Lennie backed up against the hospital walls with his brothers, the narrow waste of their father taking up the entire room.

"Lights out! All little boys to bed!"

Papa in earlier times, ushering his boys to bed sergeant-major-style.

Lennie and his brothers would squeal and run in mock rebellion until Papa caught them and lined them up like little soldiers.

Papa's hair would be mussed from too long leaning against the side of his armchair, but he'd snap his fingers to his forehead in a sharp army salute. They'd stand with their backs straight, bellies sticking out, arms rigid by their sides. Then they'd salute and stumble, march, sprint to their beds.

Then Papa would tell them bedtime stories. Frightening tales of sandmen and ink monsters and eels that lived in air, that slid and slithered in dark corners, waiting for little boys to go to sleep so they could suck the life from under their little-boy skins.

"Ernst, don't you scare them boys," Lennie's mother would call.

"They're not scared," he'd reply. "Are you?"

He would poke their ribs and tickle until they squealed.

"We're not scared, Mama!" they'd shout, halfway between hilarity and horror.

Lennie, though, was scared to the roots of his soul.

Papa would say, "In the future, what will you be, Lennie Sobczak?"

Lennie leaned into his father's familiar scent of nicotine and sweat.

"I'll be in the circus!"

"The circus! And what will your talent be?"

"I will be Amazing!"

"Yes! That's a great talent!" Papa assured him.

Days went by in the hospital and Papa smelled like disinfectant. His face was as blank as old soap and the skin of his neck hung loose. His eyes were rubbery, and his hair — his hair was still mussed like he'd been dozing in his armchair again. Mama couldn't bring herself to cut it, but she smoothed it with her hands and trimmed his beard and crooned resentfully.

"You shouldn't do this to your boys," she said.

Her accent was always strongest when she was upset. Sometimes she wielded sing-song cadences and foreshortened vowels like her voice was a sword.

"Go, play outside," she told her sons. "It's not healthy for boys in a hospital. Nothing can grow under these fluorescent lights."

They filed silently into the sun and sat in the grass and practiced waiting. They were waiting for their father to die, but mostly they didn't know that then.

On the bus home their mother implored, "Get a trade. Plumber, electrician, builder. Don't work in an office like Papa did. It's those fluorescent lights. They kill you. They killing your father."

When the lights went out for Lennie's dad, it wasn't the office job Lennie blamed. It was the darkness.

In Lennie's mind, all the hospital visits became one and all the bus trips became one and his one chance at childhood was lost in transit between them.

II. Spotlight

"Huh-and now," booms the circus ringleader, "ah-preSENTing the NEWest member of the Reed Family Circus! A man with a remarkable talent for LIGHT!"

Lennie stands in the curtains outside the circus ring, waiting for the drum roll to build. Beside him is Marcel the Strongman, thick arms folded across his broad chest. Even in the shadows his oiled skin shines. To the right of the Strongman is Susan. She's tall, built like a whip, with long brunette hair all the way to the small of her back, and a beard like a young Santa. She's plaited her beard and tied ribbons into it and studded it with small brooches in the shape of butterflies. She is, undeniably, a striking woman — but not necessarily for the right reasons.

The ringmaster, Oscar, wears top hat and tails. He stands tall, a wide smile beneath his waxed moustache. Oscar loves the spotlight. He would do the whole show himself if the public didn't want horses and monkeys and acts of daredevilry so much. He struts from one side of the ring to the other. It looks as though he's making eye contact with each and every audience member. It's an illusion, Lennie knows. The spotlight is blinding. Oscar can't see a thing where he is.

As the introduction continues Oscar puffs out his chest in his waistcoat and flings his arms wide.

"Ladies and Gentlemen!" he booms. "The Huh-MAZING Electric Man!"

Oscar spins on his booted heel and holds out a hand to where Lennie waits.

"Go to it, Lennie," says Marcel.

He slaps Lennie on the back and Lennie stumbles forward, almost falling. Susan catches him by the arm and gives him a hug, returning him to upright. She grins and Lennie hopes the shadows hide his blush.

Once he regains his gait he jogs into the ring, stopping only when he reaches the very centre. The spotlight whites out his vision. Once Oscar exits Lennie could be alone in the tent and not know it. He feels it, though, feels the eyes of the audience daring him to impress, to astound, to amaze. He can smell their anticipation.

The drums belt out their hollow rhythm and then, with the clash of cymbals, silence descends.

And the lights go out.

There's a gasp from the crowd and thunderous applause. Lennie bows and nods.

In the dark, he glows.

It's an illusion, of course. The glow of his skin is bioluminescent paint, his white suit highlighted by a standard blue light. Nothing magical or amazing about it when you pull it to pieces. But it's a crowd pleaser. Lennie looks electric.

He makes a tour of the ring, turning and posing so they can see his blue-painted skin, his white shirt. He's careful to paint his neck to within two centimetres of his collar and no closer. A spill of paint would compromise the illusion. The result is that his head appears to float above his clothes — and his hands seem equally disembodied — but it only delights the crowd more. Children rush forward to touch the Amazing Electric Man. Like magic their fingertips begin to glow. They squeal and hold their hands up in the dark.

When the applause winds up Lennie pulls out his trump card. He grins at the audience and a stream of light bursts from between his teeth. The crowd goes into an uproar.

The tiny torch in his mouth is battery operated. He can operate the switch with his tongue. Another trick, turning the light on and off, lighting up his cheeks from the inside. He buys the torches from a mail order magic shop. It works every time.

The spotlight snaps back on and Lennie's brilliance is lost in the light. When Oscar returns to the ring with his waxed moustache twitching, he offers Lennie a broad wink.

"Puh-LEASE thank," he says, "the huh-MAZING Electric Man! Ladies and gentlemen! And now! The BEARDED lady!"

Susan storms the light, chin thrust forward in defiance of everything she is. Lennie blows her a kiss and resigns his place in the limelight with one last gracious smile.

His father told him he'd be talented.

III. Leadlight

"Mum says you're wrong about the dark thing," said Frank. "She says when people die, they go into the light."

It was early, the day of Papa's funeral, the day before Lennie's ninth birthday. The air was already fuzzy with humidity.

Frank seemed to expect a response, but Lennie just shrugged. In his mind, death and the dark were all messed up. Darkness and death. He was learning early that most people found his ideas weird.

"Uncle Theo says humans run on electricity," he told Frank. "He says humans just get worn out. Like, the electricity leaks out over time."

"Yeah? That's funny," said Frank.

"He says you can't tell how much time."

"What?"

"How much time you get. He says it depends."

Frank was standing on the wire fence that bordered the marsh that, in turn, bordered the west end of town. It stank of corned beef and stewed vegetables. It stank like that all year round. Frank complained about it constantly, saying the smell made his belly ache.

"My dad's radio's like that," said Frank. "The batteries wear out. He gets mad if we use it 'cos they wear out faster. Then he has to get more batteries."

Lennie tried to say something under this breath, but Frank — whose folks had no manners, according to Lennie's mother — said "What?"

"I said there's no batteries in people."

"Yeah? Too bad. You can always get more batteries."

Frank leaned down to scratch a scab on the side of his knee, pushing a grass stem into it. In between examinations of his knee, he rubbed at his nose with a bare arm.

"It's pretty easy to fix a radio. I took the batteries out once," he gave Lennie a gaze from his narrow blue eyes, "but you gotta put them back in the right way or they won't work."

He was small for his age, Frank Johnson, but even his weight made the fence sag. Lennie's mother said Frank was malnourished, but Lennie figured it was just the way Frank was. He fidgeted all day long and probably at night, too. He needed a lot of energy. Probably Frank would wear out fast the way that he fidgeted.

"I'm supposed to be at Papa's funeral," said Lennie.

"I'll come with you if you like," Frank offered. "I had to go to my aunt's funeral once."

Lennie hesitated. He was hiding out, hoping if he stalled long enough the funeral wouldn't happen. Frank shrugged.

"What'd she look like?" he asked, fast before Frank lost attention.

"Who?"

"Your aunt."

"Ah, nah, she was in a box. You couldn't see any of her."

"Really?"

Frank rolled his head on his neck. "Sure. Come on, we'll go, hey?" Like it was no big deal.

They took it slow because the heat was strong. Frank's bare feet burned on the roadway and were scratched by thorns and prickles if he walked too far from its edge.

So they walked single-file on the loose pebbles bordering the bitumen, Lennie in his best shirt and long shorts. He rubbed the heat from his face and left greasy handprints on his shirt.

What passed for a funeral home in Lennie's town was a cold white building like a single tooth jutting from the dirt. It sat under the spread of a gnarled canopied tree. Dark red, fleshy flowers covered the top branches, making the shade of the tree so heavy it was like stepping into the maw of a cave.

No sign of anyone when they approached.

"We're too late," said Lennie, unsure whether to be glad or ashamed.

But then Mrs Monk stepped out of the doorway, camouflaged in a crumpled black sleeveless dress. The loose skin of her arms jerked as she waved the boys in. Frank trotted over obediently and Lennie followed, concentrating on his friend's dirty heels.

Mrs Monk grabbed both boys and pushed them all the way up the centre aisle of the parlour so that everyone saw they were late. The minister even stopped in his recital to give Lennie a complicated look — a kind of disapproving sorrow.

His brothers sat either side of his mother, whose face, when she turned to him, was thick with rage and anguish. She reached out and dragged him close, her palm under his chin. It was then that Lennie began to cry.

His mother said nothing, only sent a confused glance over Lennie's shoulder. He turned and saw Frank's face as close to ashen as it was ever going to get.

"Wow, they opened up the coffin," said Frank. "It's like he's made of rubber."

And Frank vomited right there in the parlour, all over the dense green carpet and his own bare feet.

IV. Skylight

Lennie makes it all the way to thirty-three years old. Mid-thirties, mid-life crisis, middle of the road, still living the out-of-date childish fantasy of running away to the circus.

"Is this dumb, what we do?" he asks.

Beside him, Susan grunts. "What, you want an office job?"

She slaps him on the arm, leaving behind a stinging red imprint of her hand. She has wide hands and heavy arms, but her fingers are narrow and tapered. She could be a hand model. Her hair is tied back but her beard is loose and, recently shampooed, soft as the down of hair on a baby's crown. She combs her fingers through it as she drives, keeping the tangles out.

"I guess not," Lennie says.

They're in the cabin of Susan's truck. This is the best truck to ride in, because Susan makes sure the suspension is perfect, the tyres are well inflated and the gear changes are smooth. She does it because she doesn't want to upset the elephants in the trailer she pulls.

"Still reading all those science books?" Susan asks.

Lennie admits he is. "My mother says I should study medicine. Fix my broken, crazy head."

Susan chuckles.

"Sounds like something your mother would say, at that. Not that I can understand much with that accent."

The sun's setting behind them, sending caramel glints of light into the rear vision mirror. Lennie finds this time of day eerie. He's spent his life reading about light, chasing light. First in switches and circuits, then in turbines and later in fireflies, glow worms, fungi, bioluminescent invertebrates from the bottom of the ocean. Always looking for that trigger, block, mechanism, hope, miracle that could keep light alive.

Finally he's begun to read about human physiology. But the easy meat-and-motion of human anatomy, the twitch and thud of electro-chemistry — none of it seems to explain life. Or maybe it just doesn't explain the living of it.

"I'd work at a power plant," Lennie says. "I mean, if I left the circus."

"Well, that makes sense," Susan replies. "The Amazing—"

"Don't call me that," Lennie cuts in.

Susan falls silent, navigating the truck to a stop at a red light.

"Sorry," Lennie says. "Only, what I do isn't amazing."

"It looks amazing," Susan says. "And the audience loves it."

"Because they don't know how it's done."

"It doesn't mater *how* it's done," Susan says.

Lennie doesn't respond.

"Always respect the audience, Lennie," Susan says. "If they say it works, it works."

Lennie sighs and rubs his broken, crazy head. Susan squeezes his knee. Her fingers are hard like tent pegs.

"Ow," he complains, and she snorts.

He sits with one elbow sticking out the cabin window, enjoying the last of the setting sun on his skin. Winter's coming and the daylight doesn't last as long. Lennie hates the night.

The cabin rolls and bounces along the roads, following the trail of the other trucks. Nearly a dozen by now. Reed Family Circus is the largest in the country. Not that there are any original Reed family members left. Oscar claims to have won the whole kit in a poker game, though no one's ever seen him play. Maybe a win like that has made him afraid of losing.

"That's weird," Lennie murmurs.

"What's that?"

He holds out his arm. "Look at this bruise."

On his forearm is a long, rectangular bruise, its edges neatly marked. Susan glances from the road.

"What's that shape?" she asks.

She tries to pull his arm closer while glancing away to the road.

"It's exactly like…" Lennie says.

He moves his arm back so his elbow is out the window. The bruise on his arm exactly matches the shadow of the side of the doorframe.

"It's like the shadow made the bruise," Lennie says.

"Not because of that paint you use, is it?"

"I don't see how."

As the sun sinks lower the shadows grow and the bruise expands. Around his legs the darkening cabin seems to grab hold. He can feel his feet become crushed, his legs aching with dark.

"Suse?"

"What is it?"

"Turn on the light, please," Lennie says, a shake in his voice. "Please, Susan, turn on the light. Please. Oh my God, TURN ON THE LIGHT."

V. Kleiglight

Circus folk look after their own, but that night it's all they can do to keep Lennie safe from the dark. Everywhere a shadow touches him becomes an aching bruise.

They sit him in the caravan he shares with Marcel and two others. He's naked, surrounded by every lamp and torch they can find. Eloise the tarot reader brings all her candles. She arranges them in plates on the ground at a distance from Lennie's chair. She huffs each time she has to lower her impressive bulk to the ground, and groans each time she rises.

"Thanks," Lennie murmurs.

"Are you feeling any better?" she asks.

"A little," he says, though it's not true.

The light holds the worst of it at bay. Oscar tries painting Lennie's skin with the luminous paint from his Amazing Electric act, but it doesn't help. The paint creates its own shadows. When they wash it off there they find bruises like the strokes of a paintbrush.

Wherever shadows touch his skin, it burns and bruises. Between his toes fat shadows wriggle and ache like leeches, and there's a searing pain in his armpits and behind his knees.

Susan returns from town with a bag of candles and new torches. She politely averts her eyes from the naked Lennie where he shivers and sweats in the middle of the radiant altar of light. She reaches out to give his shoulder a reassuring squeeze, and despite himself he flinches.

She steps back until her shadow falls on the floor and not on Lennie.

"We should take you to a hospital, Lenn," she says.

"No hospitals," Lennie says.

"What's a hospital going to do?" Oscar asks.

Oscar's booming ringmaster voice is subdued.

"They'll have better lights, for one," Susan reasons.

She sticks out her chin in that familiar defiant way, the jewelled butterfly brooches winking.

"They'd cut him up," Marcel says. "For science."

That puts an end to the conversation. Nobody quite believes him, but nobody wants to risk it. Marcel has elicited the enduring fear circus folk feel for the more mundane.

"Anything else we can do, hon?" Susan asks.

Lennie shakes his head and suffers a lancing pain through his jaw. He hunches forward in his chair.

"Hand me that desk lamp," he says.

She does so, proffering an old-fashioned green thing with a round shade and a flexible neck. He places it in his lap and trains its light on the shadows on his belly and chest. When the lamp grows too hot for his knees he picks it up by its metal neck and holds it out in front of him until his palm burns. Then he drops it to his thighs again. On and on he goes with this, balancing the pain. Bubbles of sweat sizzle on the lamp's metal shade.

The others wait outside the heat of the lights.

"What do we do?" Oscar asks.

"I'll sit up with him," says Susan. "You go off to bed. Someone has to be awake for tomorrow. We'll need to work out what to do with this."

The others leave without argument. They're tired from the packing and moving of eighteen people and thirty animals. Elephants never want to move and lions are resentful almost all the time. It's the people that get restless to move on.

Susan settles into a seat by the door, wrapping her arms around herself as if she's cold. She can't be, in the heat of all this light.

"Thanks," Lennie says.

"Don't mention it."

Lennie's skin prickles like pins and needles in the thin shadow of the hairs on his chin. He raises the lamp to his face for a moment of relief, shining it under his brows and into his nostrils. He opens his mouth so the light can release the pain in his gums.

There's a migraine birthing at the back of his skull. He shuts his eyes and sees bright, rolling paisley. It gives him vertigo. He leans back so his face can be soothed by the bare ceiling bulb above him and the paisley explodes into yellow swirling flowers. Lennie shudders. He tips forward into the heat and the awful light.

Outside he can hear the growl of the generator powering the lights. Occasionally he also hears the brief trumpet of the elephants and the snore of the lions, but only when the generator coughs and splutters. When it does, Lennie feels his own heart skip a beat in answer.

VI. *Nightlight*

Some have argued — his mother, for example — that Lennie's physical reaction to the dark comes merely from his obsession with it. The bruises and aches are a result of his mind's fear and he should, it's been suggested, snap out of it.

Lennie thinks differently. He figures, if anything, his fear of the dark was prescient.

He figures that when it comes to darkness — when it comes to the consumptive nature of "the void" — it isn't a question of looking away sooner. The question is whether or not it has always been too late.

For Lennie, this new horrifying effect of light on his skin is merely the logical result of the inevitable. Like a relationship that was always destined to fail.

VII. *Twilight*

"We could turn this into an act, you know," Oscar says.

"What?"

It's late afternoon, and Lennie is sitting in the full sunlight with a lamp trained on the shadows under his chin.

"We could bring you out in the spotlight," Oscar says, "then hold something above your skin — something small, like, a pencil. And then you could show the crowds the bruise in the shape of the pencil."

"I guess," says Lennie.

"It would be amazing. Like real magic!"

Lennie is only half-convinced.

"Don't go hurting Lennie!" Susan calls.

In all the days and — worse — the nights since this started, she hasn't left his side. She's stayed up with him and arranged the candles, replaced globes, shone lamps on him when his own arms let him down.

She has circles under her eyes nearly as dark as her mascara.

"What are you, his mother?" Oscar retorts.

Susan offers, "You want me to call her?"

Oscar admits he doesn't. After that he leaves Lennie alone.

Lennie sends Susan a weak smile and Susan winks in reply. They've fallen into that easy kind of intimacy where silence says as much as speech. Lennie's never felt so calm, so relaxed with anyone. He figures at first it's just fatigue, but his mother's voice keeps coming back to him. If it feels like love, she used to say, it probably is.

Lennie blushes to think about it.

It's coming up to two weeks after Lennie's first brush with the shadows, and the results haven't been improving. He's been hitting the books like crazy, forced to find answers alone during the long nights while the others sleep. His roommates have found space in other caravans, and Susan has moved in. She argues — convincingly — that someone needs to keep an ear out for the generator, and she may as well do it from the room where Lennie studies.

"You don't have to stay," Lennie says.

"You," says Susan, "shut up."

She curls into a bunk and falls into a fitful sleep. Lennie is half-asleep himself, stooped over the desk lamp, letting it burn his thighs, listening to Susan's gentle snores.

Outside the generator does the inevitable. It stutters and sounds as though it might fail.

Lennie is snapped from his doze.

Susan stirs and snorts but doesn't wake.

"Suse?"

She grunts.

The generator picks up again, chugging like a pig at a trough. Lennie breathes a sigh of relief. He squints at the room through the glare of lights.

He freezes.

Shadows bubble like fungus at the edges of his radiant altar, dripping from the corners of the ceiling with ominous intent.

There's a loud bang that shakes the room. Then a noise like the tinkle of piano keys. Hot glass sears his calf and Lennie jumps.

One of the lamps has exploded. Its burnt filament stands upright, blackened and bare beneath the shadows dripping down from the ceiling.

Susan leaps from her bunk, confused, her hair tangled and wild.

"They're exploding!" Lennie cries.

Another lamp bursts, sending hot glass into the air. They both duck.

"Holy…!" says Susan, snapping into action. "Hold on!"

She runs for the door and the failing generator.

The lamp in Lennie's lap begins to sizzle. Lennie gives a yelp and jumps from the chair, spilling the lamp from his lap. It pops and goes out.

A fourth lamp begins to hiss.

"This isn't happening," he pleads.

But when the next lamp shatters Lennie makes a run for the door. In a chain reaction, explosions rock the room. One by one the lights go out. Each explosion paints the walls in over-exposed whiteness for a moment before the shadows set in.

Lennie ducks as glass spins past him. He gets to his knees and crawls across the floor. Another lamp explodes and he drops to his belly. Sweat spills into his eyes.

"Suse!"

He helter-skelters towards the door, dragging himself on his forearms. Dark tie-dye shadows sweep down the walls.

Suse, for God's sake—

Lord only knows what he'll find when he reaches the door. It's not dawn yet, but death in the dark seems preferable to death by a thousand hot cuts from exploding bulbs. He figures he'll take his chances.

He gets to the door and reaches for the handle, stealing himself for the crush of darkness outside.

A voice whispers right beside his ear, so close it's like his own earlobe is talking.

It says, "Lenn, hon?"

He screams.

VIII. Limelight

The generator is up and running again. Oscar arrives to help Lennie replace the broken bulbs and then they sit up until dawn. There's no sign of Susan.

"I'm telling you, the dark got her," Lennie says.

His voice is dense with fear. The dark, the worst thing he could imagine, and Susan disappearing into it.

Eloise rushes in, gasping, dressing gown askew over her shoulder. Marcel is right behind her, looking powerful even in faded pyjamas.

"I just heard Susan, right inside my room!" says Eloise.

"What?" Lennie says.

"She told me, 'don't turn on the light'," says Eloise.

Lennie takes this in. "So what did you do?"

"Well, I turned on the light," Eloise says. "I thought she was just being modest."

"Susan?" Lennie asks.

"Modest?" Oscar snorts.

"But when I turned on the light she wasn't there. So—"

"You turned it off again?" Lennie asks. When Eloise nods he asks, "And?"

And with the light off, Eloise explains, Susan's voice could be heard dropping into the room with the descent of darkness.

"She's in the darkness?" Oscar asks.

"She is the darkness," Lennie says with sudden understanding.

Darkness, the absence and opposite of light. It makes sense to Lennie, whose skin has come to tolerate only the light, that there would be someone for whom only the dark would be endurable. Someone who had always offered him a kind of balance, a strange kind of normal in a life that had never invited it.

Lennie moves towards the door and stands on the stoop with the prickle of darkness in front of him and the pain relief of light protecting him from behind. He feels the pull of shadows on his chest, a kind of sticky, oozing feeling followed by the dull thud of bruising.

"Suse?" he calls.

She answers immediately. "Guess I spent too long obsessing about the dark, Lenn. Once your bruising began."

"So where are you?"

"Everywhere!"

Except, she goes on to explain, where there's light. She talks about the stretch of her limbs and the rapid expansion, she supposes, of her cells so that she fills all the darkness she can reach. But when someone turns on a light, she has to chase the shadows to someplace safe.

"Like water running off dishes when you pull them out of the sink," she says.

"Sounds weird," Eloise murmurs behind Lennie.

"It is," Susan confirms. "But think, no more diets. No more trying to find something that fits. No more…"

Lennie grins despite himself. Few people would welcome transformation the way Susan has. Few people, he supposes, have had the opportunity.

"Maybe what happened to Lennie is contagious," Eloise suggests.

She doesn't sound worried, only curious. But Oscar cuts in.

"Wouldn't this make a great double act!"

Dawn is breaking and Lennie anticipates the relief of it on his skin. It's been months since the bruising began. He misses touch, the simple skin-to-skin contact that, once upon a time, didn't result in agonizing marks.

Around him the lamps are arranged like children waiting for a bedtime story. He makes sure to keep up his stock of candles and bulbs. He does this on overcast days when the shadows are less powerful. Bright days leave him with welts and sprains and on those days it's his friends who fetch and carry for him.

He runs a thumb along the pale marks on his calf and reflects, not quite randomly, on life after Papa died.

"My family thinks I'm crazy," he says.

Susan hmmms from the darkness of the doorframe. "Maybe they're right. But sometimes crazy is the only option."

It's true. The craziness of his path is already chosen. If he wasn't meant to explore it, why is he here? Why is he sitting, sweating in the light, one ear out for the gurgle of the generator, talking to a disembodied bearded lady in the dark? Why would he even have been born if it wasn't to pursue light?

"I've found some new experiments," Lennie says. "With bioluminescence. You know, glow in the dark invertebrates and such."

"Invertebrates?" Susan says.

"They make their own light. Real light, not paint."

Susan says, "You thinking of doing the same?"

Lennie nods, and feels the pull of shadow under his skin. "I start tomorrow."

"You scared?" she asks.

"Nah," says Lennie without conviction.

It's not the experiment that frightens him. He thinks of telling her that, but how could he explain? His mother's voice is in his head, pushing him towards some culturally inadequate idea of normal. He sees his father dying, always dying, in his memory.

IX. Feather-light

"Ready?" Susan asks.

"Nearly," Lennie replies.

Susan's voice echoes from every shadow, every fold in the big top's curtains, every dark pocket of space. Lennie, from practice, walks carefully along the edge of the voice and the darkness that holds it. The meniscus of shadow is like the skin on warm milk.

"Nervous?" Susan asks.

Lennie hesitates. "Maybe."

"You're pacing."

"Right."

He coughs hard, thumps his chest to clear it. Then he scratches at the skin of his neck. It's the evening of their first show, and Lennie is dressed in the white suit he's used to donning for a show. He braces himself for what lies before him in the ring.

"You haven't said how the treatment went," Susan says.

Lennie says, "We'll see, I guess."

"Huh-And NOW, ladies and gentlemen! In our special evening performance for the grrrrOWN-up only, we PRE-sent-huh, the most astonishing duo this side of the grave! Brace yourselves for a look into the dark side! Yin and yang, light and dark, substantial and insubstantial, space and flesh. The huh-STONISHING duo, Lennie the Lightman and the Unseeable Susan!"

Lennie strides forward towards where Oscar stands in the centre of the ring. The light when he steps into it is like a wall. Everything outside the light ceases, for a moment, to exist. Marcel's encouragement cuts out like the line has been cut and despite Oscar's reassuring wink, Lennie feels alone.

He wonders how his challenge to nature has gone. Will the circuitry — the delicate path that carries life's signals — hold? Will the speed of his assault on the darkness wear out the batteries?

When Oscar leaves, Lennie takes a gentle turn on his heel, arms high, letting the audience look at him. He knows he doesn't look astounding. Just a man in a white suit. The illusion continues as he takes off his jacket and vest, his shirt and shoes and stands in socks and trousers, bathed in light.

The audience waits politely. He can hear them outside the lights, shifting in their seats, shuffling their feet against the sawdust. Lennie raises his hands again and then, as if conducting an orchestra, he lowers his wrists gently.

As he does so, the lights begin to dim.

Lennie pauses as if thinking. He raises his hands again and the lights return to full.

He takes a breath. In theory, this will work, but in practice he is about to leap that gap between faith and knowledge. There is nothing for it, he's realised, but to live.

Then he lowers them almost all the way to his waist.

"Here goes nothing."

By the time his hands drop to his side it is as black as pitch in the tent.

X. Delight

The audience, like Lennie, takes a moment to adjust. The thick darkness is an assault, a personal apocalypse where gasps and nervous murmurs can be heard from the crowd.

He hasn't seen a dark like this — really looked into it — in months. Full, rich dark. A waterfall of chocolate syrup.

His eyes fashion a kaleidoscope of compensatory colours in red and green paisley. He's so taken up with this unexpected visual onslaught that at first he can't even tell if it's worked. Is it panic or pain he's feeling?

When he hears the crowd draw a collective breath, he's sure. It's worked.

His skin glows a gentle blue. Then pulses into green, then white, then coruscates into mottled colours like fireworks under his skin.

The applause is thunderous. But it's the next bit that really floors them.

"Bioluminescence, ladies and gentlemen."

It's Susan's voice, whispering in the ear of everyone in the audience simultaneously. There's screams and deep shouts, and when the surprise wears off there's self-conscious laughter.

"Lux," Lennie adds. "From the genes of jellyfish of the Celebes Sea—"

"Spliced with human enzymes and released as a virus—" Susan picks up the story.

"—that causes a rash—"

"—on the skin of a man—" says Susan, "which transmits the code right into the man's very genes. To create this amazing display of light!"

Their back-and-forth continues as Lennie's skin continues its kaleidoscope glow. He examines the absence of shadow between his fingers and in the crook of his elbow. He holds his hand over his stomach, arm, chest. No shadow, no pain, nothing. Only light, strange, pulsing light, pushing the shade of his hairs far enough upward that he can't feel it. So constant and complete he can't even see the rash that carried the genetic code into the cells of his skin.

"Good show, Lennie," Susan whispers. "Amazing."

"Nah," Lennie says, "it's just illusion."

"So's everything, then," Susan reasons. "Doesn't make it less real."

"Well, I guess it's all in the perception."

"Exactly, science boy. Exactly."

He hears the chuckle in her voice and feels her gentle weight wrap around him.

The First and Final Game

will enjoy telling you this story, Martin. I have your eloquence at last. I will enjoy caressing your cold still hands and delighting in my own pulse.

Martin.

You have that blank stare of the dead now.

It is my first day as a flesh and blood human being. I have been standing, staring out this window until my eyes burn. Sharp white daylight turns the bay into flat glass and slices cleanly across rooftops. Across the water, houses squat behind high hedges, hidden from their neighbours. Electricity is irregular here, and so are phones, but the privacy is absolute.

You could kill every single person in every single house and hardly anyone would disturb you. It's that kind of place.

That's what made it so perfect for us.

Some of my new knowledge I have pulled from memories I found in this house. Some of it comes from my intimate acquaintance with your own cruel methods, Martin. You gave me life.

I have existed since the first moment you embraced your evil. I was born in darkness and chaos in a realm that twins your own. Perhaps you would call it Hell. I had no word for it when I was there.

Martin, can you hear me?

Ah, but you just stare and stare. There is no answer from that place. I will tell you the story.

This morning was a crystalline summer morning. The loudest sound was the water sucking at the banks of the bay and the sound of you knocking on my door. I knew it was just a matter of time before you found your way here. That's why I killed the boy.

I needed a place to wait for you. He was only — what? Six, perhaps? I reached out from the darkness that engulfed me, feeling for one bright soul, and I snuffed it out. His parents have gone back to their small, safe apartment in the city. Gone to bury their only son in a neat little cemetery far away. What they saw here — what I showed them — was too frightening for them to stay. The house they left empty is mine now. This house and your life.

You strode up the unused driveway, through the untended garden. Don't tell me you didn't notice. It has been months — perhaps years — since the boy's death, and the garden where he played is dense with weeds. But you were drunk on some recent success, and perhaps you felt my calling too strongly for such details.

You really should have paid more attention.

Not that it would have saved your life. By the time you reached my front door it was too late. But, Martin, I think it has always been too late for you.

And I suppose in a remote suburb of weekend retreats and rich holiday homes such as this, an overgrown garden is not so surprising. After all, you could not have expected to find *me* here. How could you even conceive of such a thing? I barely understand it myself.

I think I am what has become of your soul.

With your fist against the door, it began. My summons to this physical world. And in a room in this house, a storm raged. Dark clouds massed, ballooning out and then falling in on themselves, congealing into flesh and skin. My heart began to beat. My blood began to flow, pushing veins ahead of its rush. I had a head, a face. Arms. I had eight perfect fingers and two broad thumbs on the ends of my long hands. My legs slid, unformed, across the floor — pulled from the mass of my body.

I opened new eyes to look about me. It was the dead boy's room. Briefly I saw the walls decorated with little boy colours and little boy toys. But then reality replaced these images and I saw the room empty.

You knocked again and every splinter in the house hummed. I felt the echo through new-formed ribs. I rolled onto the balls of my feet, regarded my legs, my hands. I stood for the first time as the rest of my woman's body formed about me. I thought only of your hand on the timber doorframe.

I pushed myself towards the stairs and began to descend. Through the thin glass of the front door, I could see your outline. Your shadow was as sharp as if it had been cut from the sunlight itself.

I knew you. I knew exactly when you had made your first kill and when you had started to enjoy it. And when the murders began to bore you. When the games had been introduced.

"Shall we play a game?" you asked the strangers, your unwilling playmates. "Shall we see if you can live until morning?"

Or evening, or afternoon. It depended, of course, on the time of day you began.

In the empty hallway I stood and reflected on what I would need. A light, floral dress to tickle my knees. Chairs for the hall, a hat stand filled with hats, a vase of flowers. It came easily from memories in the house.

I reached for the doorknob and tried to twist it. The door was locked and my new flesh was still soft. The metal knob pushed painlessly through my palm, ballooning out of the back of my hand as if — I now reflect — my body were an elastic band. When I pulled my hand away from the door, my palm bounced back into shape.

In my mind, the tongue of the lock drew back from the doorframe, nestling into the bulk of the door. And because I could imagine it, I willed it to happen. I didn't even have to touch the doorknob: it spun anti-clockwise and the door swung towards me.

Warm sunlight spilled in and lent my new skin a buttery gleam, distracting me. When I glanced up, you were there. Looking for all the world like a gentleman caller. With your hands clasped loosely behind your back, you waited for my greeting.

Voice, I thought, forming vocal chords in my throat. I said, "Hello?"

My first word.

You smiled a practised smile. I did respect you, Martin. I respected your apparent fearlessness. You must have known the risks. The fragile layer of trust you depended upon to isolate your victims. But that was part of the thrill, wasn't it?

You blinked into the darkened interior of the house, pushed your face against the screen door. Waited in silence for the first signs of my discomfort. This was how all the games began. One person to play the victim, and one the killer.

I waited, too. I didn't know how to show discomfort, or even how to feel it.

Then you frowned at me through the screen and I watched your expression with fascination. My own face, I suppose, was blank.

"Hello," you said. "I am staying with your neighbours, Mr and Mrs Leigh. We need some…" you paused, reflected, "…eggs. For breakfast."

Your memories too, were mine. I could see the Leighs. Of course they were dead. Locked safely in their lounge room where no one would find them for weeks. Mrs Leigh sitting almost upright on a lounge. Her husband reclining in a chair, his head bent too far backwards. They were so still it was like an oil painting.

I saw it all as clearly as if I had been standing beside you in the room. But I merely said, "Eggs," thinking about the empty kitchen.

"You killed me."

I was startled. I thought it was you who had spoken. But it was the dead boy. His whisperings began like a buzz inside my skull. I wondered if you had heard him too, but you gave no sign of it. You reached emphatically for the screen door handle, wanting to come in.

"Would you be so kind…" you were asking, pulling on the handle. Leaving the request unfinished and smiling at me.

I was concentrating hard to hear you over the boy.

"Yes," I said, mimicking your smile. Feeling it wrap onto my face and enjoying the sensation of it. "I would … be so kind."

I reached gently for the door and unlocked it, although I had no key. Something else you didn't notice. You just kept smiling at me, gazing into my eyes as you stepped through the door. Testing for weaknesses, watching. Waiting to see if you could frighten me. But not paying enough attention.

I looked at your hands as you reached to close the door behind you. Gloves. To leave no trace. White gloves, as pure as innocence.

"Your hands?" I asked.

"Ah," you told me, with a regret that went no deeper than your face. "Terrible dermatitis." It was a well-practised excuse.

"Of course," I said, and felt my smile widen of its own accord.

You were looking with open interest across the things I had composed in the hallway. When your gaze reached the vase, you stopped.

"Those flowers are incredible," you said.

I turned to look. They were indeed incredible. The result of a childish imagination, I realised. Something the boy had fed me from his memory. Vibrant reds and purples sprayed across huge drooping flower heads. Leaves spiralled against the wall, twisted around the vase itself and dropped almost to the floor. I could smell their sweetness even from where I stood.

"Killed me," hissed the boy.

"Yes," I replied, to you.

Caught up in the sight of those flowers, I lost focus. When I pulled my attention back, I saw you looking at me. Examining the floral dress and noting the bare feet.

"The kitchen." I turned to my left and lifted a hand to point. You gestured for me to go first. That suited me fine: it gave me time to visualise what I would need in that room. A table. A refrigerator. A chopping board, much marked.

In the empty room these things began to form. When we stepped across the threshold it was complete. A lace curtain danced for a moment although the window was closed. There was even a salad half-made on the bench. Another contribution from the boy. I knew it was the wrong meal this early in the day, but I left it there as a clue for you.

"This is such a lovely area for a holiday house," you were saying as you followed me. Even with my back to you, I knew you would be smoothly surveying this new room. "I am thinking of buying a place here myself."

I moved through that long kitchen like I was walking down an aisle. At the far wall, I spun slowly back to face you. Your gaze travelled the room and lingered, finally, on me.

Next you looked at the bench, the salad, and frowned. You frowned again at the dust on the fingertips of your glove.

"Killed," said the boy.

I still had the smile on my face, but I was feeling another emotion altogether. It was the beginning of contempt, I think, or pity. I expected more from you. You were my first, Martin. You were too easy.

"Would you encourage me? To buy a property, I mean," you were asking.

"Encourage?" I said, admiring your killer's physique and the shine of your eyes. "Yes." I leaned back against the bench, feeling its cold edge digging into my palms. I said, "Of course."

Perhaps I should have waited, toyed with you some more. But the boy's naggings were like a headache now, and I thirsted for your reactions.

"The refrigerator," I prompted, with an upward gesture of my hand. You were puzzled a moment. "For your eggs?"

"Ah," you said. "Yes."

So we kept playing the game.

I was building something special for you inside that refrigerator. I was so eager to see you open the door that I dug my fingernails right through that kitchen bench. The flesh I wore was getting stronger.

The door swung out towards you then and I wasn't even sure which one of us had opened it.

Silence, except for the boy.

"There are no eggs in here," you said, and your voice was soft and harsh all at once.

Did you feel a quickening in your pulse? Did you think it was the excitement of the game? Or did you realise you were afraid? I think you had forgotten how to recognise fear. But on some level you must have known death was beside you. Surely you knew that. Tasted it, the way I did.

"Ah, no," I said, with an expression of … remorse, I suppose. Then I asked, "Do you recognise them?" Even murderers have people they love, sometimes, but there was no one left to you now.

I couldn't stop my smile. It stretched so widely across my face, my muscles were beginning to hurt. Then I laughed. I couldn't help it. I leant forward and laughed at you as you closed the refrigerator and turned towards where I stood. Not towards the door, the exit, but towards me.

You did not speak. I pushed my hands against my mouth to smother the laughter.

Then I asked, "As there are no eggs, shall we, instead, play a game?"

Was it making any sense to you yet?

Of course, you didn't answer the question. Maybe you still believed you had a chance. If not to win, then at least to live. If you could only work out what the rules of this game were.

But there are no rules in my games, just as there were none in yours. And Martin, as it turns out, you were not such a master game player.

"Who are you?" you asked me carefully.

I grinned. I'd thought by now you would recognise our kinship.

"Or what? What are you?" you asked.

"Ah, so you have worked out that much, Martin!" I said. "But you created me. Can you not tell *me* what *I* am?"

I guess you couldn't. And the need to know has died in me now. You turned and walked carefully from the kitchen, back to the front door. Of course it was already locked. I imagined you twisting the handle fruitlessly, pulling off those white gloves to grip the door.

I guess we both had a realisation then. You realised the importance of hope. In the absence of it. And me, I realised that I had a talent for this game. I could pick up right where you left off. And do it so much better.

"Can't get out that way, Martin!" I called at last.

When you came back into the kitchen, the gloves were gone. I sat at the table and laid my hands palm-down on its soft wood.

You sat silently opposite me. There was no bargaining or pleading. There was no panic or fear on your smooth skin. For a moment, even the boy was quiet.

"Guess what's in my hands," I said.

You said nothing. So I turned my palms upwards and held them out towards you. In my right hand was a knife, old and worn. Did it look like a trick of the light? The way it wasn't there one minute and then there the next. Except, of course, it was your knife. A player never forgets a game piece like that.

"How many died with this one, Martin?"

I knew the answer already, of course. That's not what I was after. I just wanted you to respond to me. The knife was between us, but we looked at each other.

"Do you understand why you do this?" you asked me.

That surprised me. Meaning was something I had not sought. Meaning for what I was, sure. But not meaning for what I did. I did it because you did. Now the question haunts me still, more definitely than you do yourself. I find I cannot answer.

"Do you?" I asked, your words infecting me. You gave no reply. I leant across the table and said, "Martin. Do *you* understand?"

Martin, Martin. Why did you have to ask?

You shook your head slowly, silently. At the last moment you were still incapable of grief or pity, even for yourself. You cheated me. I am your legacy and I am tormented by this one unanswerable question.

Inside my head, the boy suddenly started to scream and scream. He had no need to pause for breath.

"Kill me," you said. "That's why you're here."

"Kill him," said the boy, halting his own screams with an eager whisper.

In the dark place, something stirred.

Some people die in peace, Martin, but we will never be allowed that luxury.

I smiled again, more slowly this time, but it was not a smile of pleasure. I wanted to reach out and smooth back your hair, tell you it was all going to be okay. I imagined the beatings of your heart, the steady flow of blood through your body. I imagined your spongy lungs.

"Ah, Martin," I said, as your blood slowed and mine flowed faster. "I already have."

And the boy at last was silent.

Stealing Free

Thrice-born Salamander, supple-limbed and edgy, was not at home here. He drummed his dumpling fingertips on the echo-drum of a hollow log, and waited.

"Salamander, you never were good at it," said ample Kingfisher.

The kingfisher arranged jade-tipped, onyx-sheened feathers in the melting sun. He had time to glare at the horizon, then to turn his cold-coal stare to the rushes by the lake's edge, before Salamander even bothered to reply.

"Good at what?"

"Waiting," spat Kingfisher. He spun his head suddenly back to the river, his eye caught by a sinewy ripple.

"Right," said Salamander, craning his neck to follow Kingfisher's gaze into glare-warmed water. He added a mutter beneath his breath.

"What?" Kingfisher, all poor-impulse-control, could never resist the bait.

Salamander shifted, his eyes like the pits of pawpaw. "I said, I can't help trying to see what you see."

"Ha!" said Kingfisher. Then, "Does it hurt?"

Kingfisher seemed long and mean, but wasn't. The ripple was gone, so he twisted back to his pale-skinned companion.

"No, no, no, it never hurts." Salamander whipped his blue-jasper tongue at the air.

"I think you do it on purpose," said Kingfisher.

"Why would I do that?"

"Maybe you're bored."

"I'm bored right now, all right."

"Maybe you like making me go out of my way, fetching and carrying for you and bringing you back to the river for mending. Picking up your pieces," Kingfisher said, iron in his voice.

"I know you do it out of kindness, and care," Salamander soothed. Kingfisher was his friend, and Salamander understood the duty there. He knew what was owed.

"This is the fourth time you've—"

"—third—"

"—that you've grown that leg back, for a start."

"Right. Oh, this leg? No, only the second."

"When's your—"

Fat-lipped Barramundi broke the surface then, unexpectedly close. Kingfisher tried to smooth his surprise, but the ruff of feathers at his neck gave it away.

"She'll see you now, Mudpuppy," said Barramundi, and plummeted with a flick of her tail, the silver of her scales like a neon streak.

Kingfisher swung his beak in a slow left-right. He glared balefully at the absence of Barramundi. "Best of luck with—"

But Salamander had already gone, following the fish to the place where the gatekeeper lay.

"—that."

Salamander was not a mudpuppy.

Descent #1

The Empress (self-declared) was a spotted gudgeon who lived in a cave that was never warm. Her chequered skin was pink-green-grey beneath her scales and the constant sway of her tail gave her a restless air. Eels attended her, swarming her sides like oily ribbons and bumping into each other with careless grace. The floor of the lair was littered with bright, smooth pebbles gathered into clumps of colour. It was the Empress's pride, and she personally oversaw the design, updating it seasonally or more often as was her mood. Today, the floors were in almost vertical lines, first white then brown, with a determined streak of black along each edge.

"We need you," said the Empress, "to steal. For us, something. From the Monster's hall. A prize beyond. Price. For us. For here."

Her mouth was always curved down into a sneer, but it was worse when she spoke. She lay on a flat stone that was almost an altar. She had lived so long that the stone was slightly curved beneath the swing of her weight.

"Why me?" asked Salamander.

"It is a saltwater. Thing. And we know you. Are able. To deal with saltwater. Since your last. What do you call it? Rebirth?"

"I'll need my other arm first," said Salamander, not disagreeing with her. My arm, he thought, and a plan to get out of this. "I'll need to get my strength back." He waggled his shoulder at her, where the stump of his arm was growing.

"We. Shall try to. Help you hurry. That along," she said.

The Empress's powers were part magic, part force, and Salamander never knew which to expect. She might try to cure him with charms, or she might very well order other slaves to pull on his nascent arm and drag it out of him like he was a coil of rope.

"I've done more than lose an arm in your service," Salamander said, pitching his voice to sound respectful, not accusatory.

"And we. Are grateful. Waterdog."

The Salamander was not a waterdog either. "Perhaps some end to my service is in order?"

A gravid pause.

"We have taken. Care of you and. We have fed. And kept you and. Watched over you and. Performed such rituals. As might enhance your returns. To life. You know."

Salamander spoke carefully. "I know."

"We. Are. Still. Owed," she said. She almost sneered. "Where is your. Honour? That we. Enjoy so much? Where. Your duty?"

Salamander felt the heavy truth. No job could discharge the debts he'd incurred. He owed the Empress his life, more than once. He felt for a heartbeat the bitterness that all owned things feel.

"So," said the Empress. "Say when. Until then remember. We value you. Whatever you. Need."

Asymptote

"Not always the same arm! Sometimes a different one," Salamander was saying.

"Right, right," Kingfisher was unconvinced and worse, almost indifferent. "So they're arms because…?"

"These have elbows, see? This arm will have an elbow when it's finished growing back."

"I think mostly the same arm," Kingfisher cut across Salamander. "I think you're lazy—"

"Lazy! How—"

"—or too slow. Or maybe you just need to swap trades. Stealing's no good for you."

"Stealing's what the Empress asks of me."

"Then get used to growing back your arms."

Kingfisher got in the last word by huffing out his iron wings and flying straight out at the sun.

Salamander, one of a kind, self-regenerative optimist, slipped under clear waters and walked with the barest trace of awkwardness on three legs, across pebbles as mottled-brown and perfect-smooth as his own skin. The stump of his shoulder was lighter under water. In truth, there was an ache, but it was just beyond his edge where his arm would finally be when it grew back. Each re-growth was faster, as if salamander limbs pushed themselves forward once they knew the way, running like putty along memorised lines.

Above, Kingfisher blurred and shimmied, a dark tear in the cloth of the sky. Now and then he swooped and his voice came hollow, words lost in echo.

Salamander inched ever on, spreading pads of fingers wide to find purchase, his mind less on the task ahead and more on questions of a personal nature.

Flight

Salamander walked and swam and walked for eight days in the direction of the ocean. On the way, he surfaced but rarely, shooting out his pale blue tongue for bugs along the river's edge. Reaching the ocean, he paused, finding his breath, swallowing up the salty water until the stinging on his soft skin and throat and lungs stopped long enough that he could release himself into the beat of the waves.

It wasn't so bad, he told himself. It wasn't so bad.

The ocean smelled of tin, whereas he was used to the fulsome dank stench of the upper river. He tried not to let it get to him. Seagulls swarmed until he dipped and wiggled forward through dense water, blinking often (the salt-world was a blur to him). When he rose again, the seagulls were grey-white specks sticking close to shore. This far out, they found no purchase. Only air, and air is an empty thing at the best of times.

On a buoy, abandoned to the waves, a lone pelican squatted with her webbed toes spread, dramatic black-white wings folded. She blinked at Salamander with curiosity, sweeping her pale pink beak over and around him. The empty sack of her throat wobbled as she shifted her head back and forth, trying to hold him with yellow-black eyes that looked painted to her head.

"You?" she said, piecing him together between her disparate pupils.

"I believe we may have met," said Salamander.

"I believe," she said, "you were the one to steal the trap that held me, Salamander."

"Of sorts," Salamander replied patiently. "You had a torn plastic bag wrapping your foot, and I unsheathed you."

"Stole," said the pelican, with satisfaction.

"I hate to disagree, since we have this cheerful history," Salamander said, the sun prickling where the water didn't reach on his neck and face, "but I believe it's only stealing if you take something someone else wants, isn't it? I mean, if you wanted that plastic bag, that would be stealing, yes, but otherwise—"

"—what is it?" Pelican asked.

"Just taking, I should imagine."

"I find the distinction pointless," said Pelican.

She was joined, then, by another pelican, one that straddled the side of the buoy awkwardly, wings spread for balance.

"Pelicans," said Salamander, addressing them both (for now there was neither room nor reason to address either one individually), "I could do with a favour."

And that's how Salamander stole many miles from his trip, carried safely in the throat of a pelican (he wasn't sure which), and how the debt came to be paid between the unique salamander and all the saltwater birds. For a time, at least.

Should he need a ride back, he was assured, he would be one debt in their favour. Even, he made them declare, if he was in pieces, they would carry him back to the start of the river. There, Kingfisher would find him and take care of the rest of his journey. He heard a throaty promise, ensconced in the gullet of the giant bird, and let it rock him still.

Salamander wasn't worried. He always paid in trade what he could not steal.

Descent #2

What the Empress called a Monster was an octopus, mottled honey-mustard in colour, and graceful. She lived alone in a cave like a craw. Two fat rocks marked the entrance. To leave the cave, it might be that she rolled the rocks away with her long arms. No, wait. Legs (there were no elbows). But she never left.

Salamander watched for three more days outside the cave, saltwater grating on his skin, his new arm throbbing from the long journey. He fended off the strangest and most voracious of creatures while there. The worst, a dim-witted, twenty-armed starfish. Purple-red-grey, it moved dully like a stomach on thick fingers, and Salamander chose simply to ignore it until it dragged itself away.

Sand pressed into the soles of his feet and he shifted his weight awkwardly. He gauged there was space enough for him to get inside the cave. However, if the Empress was at all correct, the treasure would require the removal of the boulders. She was expecting him to ask for help, most like, but he didn't intend it.

The octopus must be hungry. Its legs were spilling from the cave like seaweed, drifting across lumpy corals. Between the boulders its head bobbed stupidly like a fishing fly.

It must have spied something then, because its brown colouring gave way swiftly to yellow; deep blue rings blurring-bright along its legs and sides. Salamander startled. The concentrated pulse of colour was like two personalities struggling for the same skin.

Deftly, one leg snagged a passing something that crawled the ocean floor and wore a suit of blue shell. Salamander guessed a crab, but his eyes weren't adjusting right to the salt. The water hung heavy like taffy. He supposed he might not be able to do a trip like this again.

The octopus and its would-be crab disappeared inside the cave, one last bob of the bulbous flashing head marking their passage.

Salamander was used to the many forms of panic. Stage-fright-panic, nearly-getting-away-with-it-panic, about-to-admit-defeat-panic, and the panic that came right before dying, for which he had no clear name, the panic that flooded the mind and locked fast on the body. The panic he felt then was somewhere between stage fright and dying. He knew the octopus was deadly, its shocking colours the sign of passion.

Salamander never planned far ahead. It was, according to Kingfisher, what made him such a lousy thief. But in the three-day wait he'd thought perhaps he could steal into the lair of the monster secretly, through cunning alone. Now he was worried. The poison she used on her prey was harmful enough, but he understood of this creature that she had another, more deadly poison that she would release if threatened. The flash of blue brilliance still hard in his mind, Salamander grew alarmed. Cunning of the type he himself possessed (i.e. minimal) didn't feel like quite enough protection.

He did then what he always did when troubled. Marched boldly across the ocean floor towards the source of his anxiety and hoped for the best.

At the cave's edge, he peered past the rocks to check for clear passage. Once assured, he squeezed himself through the narrow gap. He picked his way over a couple of colourful open maws that he guessed (despite his groggy eyes) were sea urchins, their prickly mouths feathered with thin, bright beards of tentacles. His tail brushed one urchin and it contracted in ecstasy, colours rippling in patterns of concentric pleasure.

On the walls were many scuttling things, wisps of biology that could have been coral, could have been fish (probably seahorses, Salamander guessed, from the speed of some of them whirring past his head with dumb intent).

"Tut-tut-tut," said several of the wisps at once.

"Oh, shut up," Salamander muttered.

He wondered if they'd spin ahead to warn the monstrous Octopus, but they seemed to prefer hovering around him, apparently fascinated by his careless arrival. Perhaps they were afraid of her, too.

"And no gift?"

Salamander froze.

"Beg pardon?" he asked of no-one in particular, since the voice came from nowhere.

"No gift. What I mean is 'you haven't brought a gift'. Oh, over here. Here!"

Salamander looked towards the sound and saw only the seam where the wall of the cave met the sandy floor. Then the seam moved towards him and he realised it was a sea snake, pale yellow, flat at the tail but curved high closer towards its bullet-brown-head.

"You'll need a gift, most like," said Sea Snake. "And you haven't brought one."

"Tut-tut-tut," said the seahorses.

Salamander did a quick inventory of his possessions. "This could be bad," he said, since he was, indeed, carrying nothing at all.

"Unprepared?" enquired Sea Snake. "Curious. Here, take a little something from the treasure room before you reach her chamber at the end, there. She has so many gifts from so many better prepared visitors, she won't even remember."

"But er, what if I choose something she particularly likes?"

"Tut-tut-tut."

"All the better. Who doesn't want two of what they particularly like?"

Salamander hesitated, trying to gauge the snake's honesty.

"I hadn't known," said Sea Snake, impervious, drifting away, "that we snakes could grow legs. And yet, here you are, my odd, brownish, leggy friend. And so, I will help you choose a gift."

Salamander did not correct his new brethren, the snake. Instead, he followed her into a room in the cave filled and dripping with all sorts of stolen things. Strange shapes that had become soft and muted by the corals and creatures that now lived on them. Shapes that were small craters and some that were long stemmed things and other oddities most probably from ships. Somewhere in here, too, was the treasure the Empress desired.

"How did you grow your legs?" asked Sea Snake.

"Oh. You know. Um, magic?"

The snake cocked her head attentively. "All right," she said, when there was nothing more forthcoming. "Not as interesting an answer as one might hope." Then, "Take these."

She indicated with an elegant nod three strands of white saltwater pearls, tied together with seaweed and knotted with oyster hair.

"You know," Salamander said carefully, almost idly, "what would be really good?"

"Yes?"

"A stone."

"A stone?" asked Sea Snake. "Would that really be so good?"

"A, um, a beautiful stone. That glows pale as the moon, white with a delicate fissure through the middle, like the tiny map of a river."

"Tut-tut-tut."

Salamander was of course describing the very thing he'd come here for, all the while ignoring the whirring, irritating seahorses and keeping his eyes on the countenance of the snake, to best gauge her responsiveness. Sea Snake reared and rose, zigging languidly through the water. "I know the very one. A perfect piece of smoothed selenite in a silver setting, yes? Used to be her favourite."

Salamander suppressed a skip of delight. Why, with the help of his so-called brethren, this might turn out to be a successful theft yet.

They had to dig for it, through strange, hollow objects that clunked against each other when dropped, and shreds of faded cloth. But there, beneath it all, was the treasure the Empress had described.

Salamander was slipping his fingers into the coral and slime on its surface, cleaning it and congratulating himself earnestly, when he felt the hard, rough edge of the crystal. Except, the crystal — this crystal, the one the Empress craved — should not be so rough.

"The saltwater…" said Salamander.

"Yes," said Sea Snake. "Corroded the metal and corrupted the crystal, discoloured and roughened it. Yes. I remember now. Not such a good gift after all, perhaps."

Salamander stared at the dull exterior, river landscape hidden beneath.

"I suppose," he said, "there isn't any other?"

It wasn't until then that he noticed the tut-tut-tutting of the Seahorses had stopped.

"Oh, no, no, there's no other," came a hard whisper, not from the snake, but from the door, where the Octopus now rested.

She swept into the room, nearly filling it, the floating sack of her head bobbing above them. The colours of her skin began to bubble and roil. She still carried, in one long leg, the shattered carcass of her lunch. Around her scuttled tiny crabs like moving jewellery boxes, their crystal legs silent against the walls, their eyes precarious on stalks above their heads.

As the Octopus flared brilliant-blue, and Salamander attempted to remember how to speak, one small crab said, "Heard of you."

"Me too," said another, bright shell of a thing beside the unpredictable bobble of the Octopus's head. "Heard you lost your legs a lot. See how pale the new limb is. Hellbender, aren't you?"

Sea Snake scoffed but was otherwise silent, fitting herself along the edge of a pile of treasures. She regarded Salamander with keen eyes.

Salamander, meanwhile, flicked his gaze back and forth between the wall of enemies. "Um. No. A salamander. Hellbenders are different. Though it's probably not uh, an important point right now."

"Anyone," said a partner crab, scuttling along the wall towards Salamander, "anyone would think you don't know what you're doing, losing pieces of yourself. Throwing yourself away, in a way."

"Yeah, you must be bad at stealing."

"Yeah. Maybe sometimes you lose your head."

Salamander trained black eyes front-forward. "If I did, it'd grow back."

"Yeah?" said a jewel.

"Yeah?" said the other.

"Yeah," Salamander said through flat lips. "Did last time."

He kept a poker face, waiting for a challenge. When none came, he stood up as straight as he could and looked to the Octopus.

She said, "You steal often?" Interest piqued.

"Sometimes stealing is the honourable thing," said Salamander.

Then a plan opened up in front of him, and he looked deep into the Octopus's eyes. There was no time for caution or second-guessing, so he said straight, "Explain to me, if you would, where the flaw is in this."

The Octopus stared, her tiny beak motionless. When Salamander was finished telling his plan, she suggested there wasn't much in it that was flawed at all. She agreed right there and then.

Ascent #1

The journey home always seems to take longer.

Three strands of white pearls were around his neck and, though pretty, their true value for Salamander was more practical. They were used to harness him to three Sea Snakes, who pulled him up and away towards the buoy where the Pelicans waited.

"God speed," said one of the Snakes.

The Pelicans, who preferred all debts to be paid, even those owed them which they didn't yet need, tried to convince the Salamander to part with a strand of his pearls. He wouldn't hear of it.

"No," he said. "When the time comes, you find me, and we'll be even again then."

They dropped him as far inland as they dared (since it was a foreign place to them), and Salamander continued along the river bed on foot, the strands of pale glowing pearls dragging and bouncing on the ground and threatening to dislodge at any moment from his neck. He kept pulling them back on with fingers like fat buds. And one other piece of the trade he carried, pushed along gently in front of him, rolling unevenly and constantly requiring correction to its path: an oyster shell. The largest oyster shell that had ever been found, claimed the Octopus, clasped in the disembodied claw of a mighty crab, long dead. She'd promised the claw would need to be prised open with great force.

Saved from a time-consuming journey, Salamander reached the Empress within barely a day of leaving the Octopus's place.

"Pearls?" asked the Empress. She rocked in slow anticipation, eyes mournful, mouth downturned. The eels blanketed her sides, moving even closer when the salamander arrived.

"Mine," said Salamander. She would assume them stolen.

"Your bounty. Then," she said.

"That, and my freedom."

The Empress didn't blink, only stared at him with eyes sticky-soft but hard and mean.

"What is. Free? Are any of us. Truly? Free." In her gulping monotone she added, "You have the. Prize?"

Eyes black-blank, giving nothing away, Salamander said simply, "Yes."

"You do?" There was almost amazement in her voice.

"Are you surprised? And tell me, why should I give it to you?"

The Empress would have smiled in faint derision, but her face would never let her. Stiff as a mask, her indifferent profile said, "Because. You gave your. Word you would. Steal this thing for me."

He sighed, as if in defeat, paused a moment for drama. Then he shoved the shell forward until it came to rest in front of her. The Empress shifted first to one side and then another, rolling her eyes at the object. Even through the stillness of her face, confusion was apparent.

"This is it?" she asked. "And ... how. To open it?"

"Yours to find out," said Salamander.

He stayed to watch, standing outside the cave and feeling the smooth pull of freshwater on his skin. He took deep swigs of the stuff and delighted in its sweet weightlessness. Inside the cave, the Empress struggled.

First she mouthed the claw with great consternation, pulling on it with her fleshless lips. Then she tried dropping it, hoping the weight would shatter the thing (it didn't) despite the water's impedance.

"You could ask for help?" suggested Salamander, noting almost smugly that she pretended not to hear. The Empress would never risk having to share. Instead, she batted at the shell in rage, knocking it against the edges of her cave, pushing and pressing at it with her stony mouth until her skin tore in several places.

Finally she pushed the shell against the wall, wedged it in the pebbled floor of her cave, and managed to wrench the crab claw loose. Showing a dexterity he hadn't thought she possessed, she twisted herself nearly in half, working up enough energy to slam her jaw into the shell, and slam and slam again, until the claw sprung free.

She nosed greedily into the gap between the shell halves. Inside, a single stone glowed with dull intent, wrapped in its metal setting. The Empress opened her mouth in delight, leaning into her gift. The brightest, smoothest stone she had ever…

"Wait," she said.

At last.

"This isn't it," she added, her words coming out in a rush.

"It is. The crystal that fell from a ship to the bottom of the ocean, that struck the back of a sleeping stingray, startling it into flight? So that when he skimmed the Octopus's — the Monster's — hall, it was dropped and then recovered by one of her long limbs, and coveted, and carried inside so that she might gaze on it forever? Is that the one you meant?"

"Yes," said the Empress. "No."

"It is," Salamander assured her. "It's the very one."

There was a pause, during which the Empress listed to one side, her eye fixed on the Salamander.

"Oh," he said. "Wait. You're wondering why it's so unalluring? Why its milkiness does not give way to a soft transparency that reveals, at its core, a tiny landscape with a river? Is that what you're wondering?

"Yes," sneered the Empress.

"No."

"No?"

"There's every chance you knew all along, of course, of how the saltwater had blunted and tarnished it so the Octopus threw it aside. And you sent me there anyhow. But I think only that you couldn't decide what you wanted more. The stone, or my failure to acquire it. Either way, you have no intention of ever letting me work off my debt. Do you."

The Empress didn't answer. The invisible venom from the Octopus had already kicked in, the stuff carried in the clamped-shut shell. It had trailed into her revolver-eyes and the cuts on her hard-edged mouth. She moved her head in thick confusion, noting, probably, a darkness like twilight setting in unexpectedly, and unexpectedly fast.

Paralysis was next. The slow beating of her tail stopped and her eyes crystallised into perfect opacity. She drifted to the floor of her prison. The eels wafted, bemused, into the space she'd left behind. They lowered themselves to her fallen corpse and those that got too close died with her.

Diversion

And here's what happened in the Monster's hall.

Salamander, true to his word, explained to the Octopus that he was going to steal from her. He did not ask her permission or her good grace, because stolen it had to be, to fulfil the contract. One thing he did ask, though, was if there was a further trade he could perform. Did the Octopus ever desire something from the river? Freshwater pearls, say, their pink-grey skins perfectly rolled?

One favour he did ask, which he could not steal.

"Name it, odd little thing," said the Octopus, her voice a reedy soft rasp coming from the tiny beak of her mouth.

"Some of the venom they say is lethal, that you possess in your bite," said Salamander. "I ask you to trade it freely, and I will repay with some other favour."

"Favours," said the Octopus, supposedly a monster, "are given, they can't be paid or repaid. That's my code, at least, and I will hold you to it."

She agreed to the favour and vowed to live with the curious little leggy creature in her debt.

"You can always claim—" began Salamander.

"Yes," the Octopus interrupted. "And can choose not to. And can decide."

Ascent #2

One year to the day a blue bullet streaked the sky and came to land on branches above Salamander's head.

"Kingfisher," acknowledged Salamander.

"Salamander." Kingfisher sat brood-chested, steel green in the sun. "How goes it with the collection?"

"Fine."

"Customarily tight-lipped," observed the Kingfisher. He focussed on something far away.

Salamander blinked slowly. Said, "I believe I have enough, now."

"Good, good," agreed Kingfisher. "Anxious?"

"No."

"Nervous? A little?"

"No. What do I have to lose?"

Kingfisher spun his beak around as if his head was on a coil. "I would say 'life', but you've lost that a couple of times already."

"A-yup," said Salamander. "And no one to piece me back together with their magic this time. No need for you to fetch and carry, either, so there's a bonus. But, I gave my word."

"Powerful magic in itself, that. For many of us."

Salamander would have shrugged, but lacked the musculature. "You don't get to choose a moral code, I think. You're born with it. It's in your—"

"—your what? Your bones?" interrupted Kingfisher, a scolding tone. "And if you can grow new ones, then what?"

Salamander didn't answer. He moved as if sighing, his belly expanding beyond his ribs and taking a moment to settle back in.

"Here goes," he said, by way of goodbye, and slipped beneath the water.

"Goodbye," said Kingfisher.

Free

"Are you, now, free?" asked the Octopus, rolling subtle-grey-pink freshwater pearls along the sand in front of her.

"Yes."

"Free of service, or free of guilt?" she looked at him softly over the stab of her beak.

Salamander paused, eyes like black beads. "Both. Either. Is there one without the other?"

"There's choice," said the Octopus, tiny eyes steady under her enormous head. "That's perhaps all there is?"

Salamander inclined his chin in agreement. Outside, he knew, the Pelicans sat in saltwater, awaiting his return. "I can't stay long."

"Tut-tut-tut."

"You know," said Salamander, ignoring the interruption, "sometimes, the things you value most can't be bought at all."

The Octopus absorbed this quietly. "They have to be taken?"

Salamander nodded, "Sometimes, they even have to be stolen."

Summa Seltzer Missive

"Tizzit?"

"Tizz...? Er, yes," said Polly. "Yes, this is it."

Polly Daley was once described as a walking Gone to Lunch sign in the empty café of life.

"Whenzel lunge?" asked the girl morosely.

"Er, *lunch* is whenever you want."

Polly Daley's hearing was going. She wasn't sure whether it was biology or lack of use. She was only thirty-six or so. She didn't mind the loss. She mostly didn't need to hear.

"House and stanza?" said the girl.

"I stanza — stand, I mean! Stand it just fine, thanks. I do," said Polly. Twenty years in the mailroom of Streck & Serge Shipping and she'd stood it all that time.

But then, Polly Daley was a kind of "not". Not so much empty as absent. Not so much hopeless as someone who had put all hope aside. Left it on a bench someplace and forgotten to return. Not unhappy enough to be truly discontent, not any-other-kind-of-anything to be otherwise or else.

Polly Daley was empty like an ice cream cone where the ice cream had melted away. Not like one that had never seen ice cream; that was a different kind of empty. An expectant kind. And Polly had no expectations.

She liked mornings best, when the mailbags showed up like thick, grey slugs, bloated with daily missives. She would split their skins and reach

231

both arms into their guts to dig out the envelopes. These she spread across the floor, sorting by size until it was time to dock them in the honeycomb walls of pigeonholes around her.

Afterwards, she'd step back and admire the delicate spectrum of coloured envelopes, like pale threads in a tapestry. Or settled snow (though she'd never seen snow, she thought, with a twinge of almost-resentment).

It was quiet, her life, but it was all hers.

Until the girl showed up.

Late, Polly couldn't help noticing.

The girl was called Caroline Something (she didn't catch the surname) and she was there, in Polly's mailroom, because Mr Streck had told Polly that kismet is wombing. By which Polly took him to mean business was booming.

It was true.

The usually neat, fat mailbags had begun to bloat and bust (like old suitcases, Polly thought, with reason). They leaned drunkenly and leaked their contents across the floor. Still, Polly would have preferred to be left alone with her room. She'd offered to work longer hours but Mr Streck had brushed the suggestion aside.

"Wouldn't hear of it," Polly translated him as saying.

Caroline was young, with long black hair and pale powdered skin. Her lips were shadow-bruised and her eyes were dark pools of spilt ink. She wore a loose ebony dress that ended at her ankles where her black lace-up boots began.

The dress looked homemade and home-dyed. Here and there, spots of green satin winked through. On her inner elbow, for example, was a mark like a tiny treasure map. When Caroline spoke, Polly found herself staring at that odd little piece of escapee cartography.

Staring and staring.

"Watch me," Polly directed.

The mailbags were already empty, slouching like empty stomachs to be filled again. The envelopes were gathered across the floor. Polly scooped up a handful and moved across the pigeonholes the way a maestro might traverse a grand piano. She raised each pale envelope high, allowing Caroline — behind her — to clearly see the addressee.

Then she darted her hand into a pigeonhole, came out clean, swept up another white wrap. Down with her arm, up, shift left or right, forward and back, the crescendo building. She worked tirelessly. She was a windstorm caught up in its own momentum, rushing to—

Caroline sneezed, and the image shattered.

At the end of the first day Mr Streck — the only living partner of Streck & Serge Shipping — stopped in.

"Howza guitar lounge?" he boomed. He winked at Caroline, then turned hesitantly to Polly.

"We're getting along just fine, thanks, Mr Streck," said Polly.

"Yeah. Mime, tanks," added Caroline, sending Polly a wink in turn.

Polly smiled uncertainly. It seemed a gesture of friendship, though she was out of practice with spotting those. She nodded her appreciation and Caroline nodded back.

The girl — Caroline — settled comfortably into a pattern of her own and they spent their days together apart.

For which Polly was entirely grateful.

Months of companionable silence passed.

Then Caroline said unexpectedly, "Gonna tonner summa seltzer missive?"

"Sorry?" asked Polly.

"I said," sighed Caroline, shifting her gum into one cheek, "Going. To the. Summer. Social Mixer?"

Polly wasn't even sure what that was.

"You know," Caroline enunciated carefully. "To mix with people. Socially."

"Oh. No, I've never been to one," Polly puffed up her cheeks in what she hoped was a cheerful smile and returned to the mailbag.

"Cow song in a pig's ear?" said Caroline.

"I beg your pardon?"

"How long," with a sigh, "Have you. Been *here*?"

"Well," Polly considered. Decades, she realised. "A … while," she said instead.

Caroline chewed thoughtfully, fixing her dark eyes on the wall to Polly's left. "I sink," she said, (meaning "I think"), "we should go, by golly!"

Polly smiled. "'By golly!' I haven't heard that for years!"

Pulling out her gum, Caroline shouted, "I said, 'hey, *Polly*'."

Next came shopping, with Polly inadvertently launching the journey by saying she had nothing to wear, and Caroline progressing the adventure by insisting it was time she did.

It was hot. Christmas-hot. Shops had bulging shelves, shoppers shone with a kind of glad seasonal anxiety, and everywhere there was tinsel and bells and bows and banners that applauded The Festive Season.

Festive Season. Always sounded so anonymous to Polly. Though why should she care *what* they called it? She wasn't Christian anyhow (well, she didn't think so, she'd never really thought about it) and it wasn't like she had family to celebrate with. She usually just wanted to get through The Festive Season without injury or insult, please God.

Caroline, by contrast, grinned a wide chocolate grin at all the foil brocade. It was, she told Polly, "Precarious!"

"Precarious?"

"No! *Hilarious*, I said."

Caroline grabbed hold of Polly's elbow and navigated the crowds like a champion yachter, ebbing patiently when she needed to, lending her weight to alternatives where she could. Eventually they washed into a shoe store, where Polly found herself deposited on a narrow lounge.

"Ear," Caroline said, dropping sandals at her feet, "fry peas."

Polly tried these and these. She liked those, but hated the ones over there and wondered how anyone could decide anything at all when there was so very much of everything.

But then a spark caught her eye. A splash of red, a glitter of rhinestone that pushed up from the floor. A heel that was tall, but just so, straps that were sheer and yet firm. It was, breathed Polly, plucking it from the ground like fallen fruit, it was just, "Beautiful!"

"Yeah?" said Caroline, and she looked dubious.

In a bed of pure white tissue, its mate was found. Before she knew it, Polly's stockinged feet were slipping between the straps. Her translucent toenails shone as pale as onionskin in the glare of overhead lights. Her insteps arched, her ankles flexed, the sandals slid along her feet.

"Up?" Caroline grinned, crouched like a crow on the floor.

Carefully, Polly stood. She took one experimental step, then another, and then she crossed the floor, the crowd of shoppers parting before her. It was like walking on fairy floss. No, it was like *dancing* on fairy floss. Like flying over fairy floss from a great height.

"You'll have to paint your toenails, then, I'd say," Caroline said, drawing breath to repeat herself.

"Yes!" said Polly. "I will."

Caroline started. "What?"

"I will. I will have to paint my toenails!" Polly said. "Won't I, just?"

She gave a little twirl, fluttering the heavy weave of her sensible tan skirt.

The black pools of Caroline's eyes were widening.

"How…" she said. "Wow. How do you feel?"

Polly felt the way butter must feel on warm toast.

"I'll have them!" she cried.

Of course she would.

Buying the dress, by comparison, was remarkably uneventful.

The shoebox was kept by her bed, the dress on the wardrobe door, for all the weeks it took to wait.

In the meantime, Polly continued to live around the edges and the spaces in-between. A sliver of seat on a bus, a gap in a queue at the bank. She didn't want for much. At night, returning from the office to her modest apartment, she would balance take-away on her knee and gaze towards the television. Noise from the train station below buzzed her walls and rattled windowsills.

She was doing nothing but waiting.

The date arrived (at last) and Caroline was late (as usual) and wore black — of course — but this time her long hair was pinned up in huge loops over her ears. She waved from an old station wagon that had been painted dark matte grey.

Polly settled into the voluminous passenger seat and Caroline sent the car lurching forward and it was as easy as that. They were there.

The Mixer was in an old hall. Gold fairy lights blinked along the eaves and coloured streamers hung across the walls. Waiters brandished silver trays with sparkling glasses.

"Looks good," Caroline said, swiping two glasses of champagne from a tray.

Polly sipped at the champagne. She felt exposed. Her bare shoulders caught a warm breeze and the dress tickled her knees. She tried to look about herself while trying to look like she wasn't.

She gazed instead at her sandals — strange, bright, red, gaudy things — and she felt glad. She blinked up at the crowd and for a minute thought the rhinestones in her shoes had given her afterglow. Except afterglow was meant to be the reverse of the colour that had burned your eyes, and what she saw was red. Definitely red. Bright red, a thick stab of it.

She frowned, squinted, blinked hard several times. She saw it again. A flash, a flare of ruby behind the crowd. She stared.

It couldn't be.

"That's not…" she began, turning to Caroline. Or rather, to the spot where Caroline had been because Caroline, inconveniently, had disappeared to mix or mingle, or whatever-it-was they were meant to do. Polly looked back to the crowd.

Oh, no.

Oh, it definitely was. She was sure of it now.

It was Santa.

Arms flung above his head, knees bending haphazardly, a wide, red man in a Santa Claus suit was dancing erratically. His majestic white beard flopped against his broad chest. A red hat, fur-trimmed, sat high on his forehead. Two bright red cheeks jutted up, shining with sweat, and possibly within his beard there was a jolly grin.

On his feet, in strange deference to the season, was a pair of brown leather sandals.

Polly drank it in with a single glance, and two other things she noted. The first was that he was the only one dancing. And the second: there was no music. Absolutely none at all.

Santa skewered her with his gaze. His bright white eyebrows shot up and waggled. Bopping and jerking he started towards her, nudging people out of the way with his huge belly.

She froze. She felt a blush crawl her cheeks and wondered if she was quite the same shade as his suit (or her shoes). The closer he got, the more she could hear him humming, but even that was out of time to his dancing.

He was just about to reach her and she was just about to speak — unsure what on earth she could possibly say — when a shadow fell on her.

"Mr Streck!" said Polly, by way of objection.

"Call me Kevin," Mr Streck insisted, nearly throwing his glass of champagne at her.

She ducked and tried to lean around him.

"Did you see…" she began.

"Look at you, then, Polly!" said Mr (Kevin) Streck. "Barely recognised you! Who'd have thought! Having a good time?"

"Well, I—"

"Good! The band's about to start. Do you like jazz music?" He took a quick chug from his champagne glass and just as quickly refilled it from the bottle in his other hand.

"I'm not sure," Polly said, scanning the room.

"Good, then," Mr Streck said, swaying. "Bit of a change from the mailroom, eh?"

Polly had to agree with that.

After which Mr Streck moved — thankfully — away.

"Mailroom is it?" came a voice to her right.

She turned and found herself looking up into eyes that were a sharp crystal blue.

"Yes," she smiled, feeling the heat return to her cheeks. "I'm Polly. From the mailroom."

"I'm Santa," said Santa cheerfully. "No, really!" he added when she laughed. "What? You think they give these suits to just anyone?"

"But you must be boiling!" she said, still laughing.

"Boiling, baking, steaming and stewing!" he confirmed. "Like a pudding! But to the point, what's a delightful woman called Polly, like you, doing in a mailroom?"

Polly leaned in conspiratorially. "Why, sorting mail!" she replied.

It was Santa's turn to laugh, and he did so generously, throwing his head back and *ho-ho-ho-ing* with both fists clutched to his red suit.

Polly took another sip of her champagne and grew bold.

"And where," she asked, "is Mrs Claus?"

"Ahhhh," Santa leaned in with a sorrowful smile, preparing Polly, it seemed, for the worst. "I made her up."

"No!"

"Yes! Would you guess, it's less unusual for a family man to be climbing chimneys than some unattached young ruffian. And hey, see this beard—"

"No!" said Polly scandalised. "It isn't real?"

"Oh, it's real," said Santa. "I just wanted to know if you could see it. Stop laughing. I'm quite proud of it."

A waiter swerved by them then and Santa relieved the man of his tray with a quick swipe of his gloved hand. He proffered the tray to Polly where she saw, arranged in neat rows, tiny castles on squares of white bread. Like a chess game, she thought. She popped a rook in her mouth.

"Marvellous," she told Santa, choosing another. "The best chess pieces I've ever tasted!"

"Oh, I think that might be the champagne," he told her.

"Really? In the bread?" she asked, and was surprised by a long drawn-out and gleeful *ho-hooooooooo*.

There must have been champagne in all the food, then. Also in the lights and the jazz music and even in the smiling faces that floated past. Polly hardly needed to take a sip from her glass. All she had to do was stand there with Santa opposite her and wait for the world to turn.

"Why don't you tell Santa all about yourself," said Santa.

So she did. Little by little, she told him about her life. Or rather, the life of the Streck & Serge mailroom, which was a different life altogether (although she didn't quite know that yet). She told him, for instance, how the seasons came and went, summer producing wild bouquets of correspondence that thinned markedly when winter approached. She told him she knew when the company was recruiting, when they were late paying debts, when business was good and when it was bad. She ended by telling him, quite inadvertently, how sometimes it seemed she was standing just outside life and watching it pass by through tiny plastic windows in business envelopes.

She told him about the new girl, Caroline, and apologised because of course she shouldn't still be calling her the new girl. Caroline was old now.

"I know Caroline, of course," said Santa. "She's a good stick."

Which Polly told him was a strange thing to say.

"You did say 'stick', didn't you?" she asked, suddenly afraid.

"I did."

Eventually she even told him about the day she came home from high school to find two stuffed suitcases in the hall, heavy with portent like pregnant ravens. And how her mother had swept by with a quick, "Darling, I return to the mother country, you're on your own, I'm afraid."

And how Polly had eventually come to wonder, as the memory hardened and hollowed the way overworked memories do, whether her mother had actually said "You're on your own. I'm afraid."

"I mean," said Polly, "she'd never even been to Europe before in her life, so how could it be a mother country, right? No wonder she was afraid."

Santa kept a kindly, twinkling gaze on her the whole time, standing with his sandalled feet apart, his thumbs looped through his belt, while the party swung back and forth around them.

"Do you really find this so interesting?" Polly asked at last.

Santa chuckled. "Starboard," he said.

Which made no sense at all, until Polly glanced to her right and saw Mr Streck jiggling wildly towards them.

"Oh, hell," she said. "I think he's drunk."

"Marvellously!" agreed Santa.

At which point Mr Streck reached out towards Santa and placed a hand firmly on his neck.

"Santa!" said Mr Streck. "I never did thank you for that bicycle!"

"The one when you were six?" enquired Santa politely, "or the one when you were ten?"

"Ten!" shouted Streck. "No, wait. Both! Why, I'd forgotten! How did you … ahhhhhh!"

And here Mr Streck laughed, lifting his hand from Santa's neck in order to waggle a finger at him. Then he fell fortunately and unexpectedly backwards, shouting, "Lennie, old boy!" at someone else entirely.

Polly watched him being carried away on the drift of the crowd. Then she turned back to Santa speculatively.

"You know," she said. "I think you really are. You are *the* Santa."

"Oh, ho," said Santa, "did you ever doubt it?"

"I don't know," she said, looking inquisitively at her shoes. She bunched her toes and pushed up against the straps.

Santa leaned in close.

"Are they magic?" he asked.

"What?" asked Polly, startled. "My shoes? How do you mean?"

"Well, it's just that you're looking at them like they might give you an answer."

"Oh," Polly gave a half smile, feeling her face grow hot. "I almost thought they might."

She paused, wondering how to explain it.

"You see, my hearing is usually…" but she trailed off.

Perhaps she should just show him. The real Polly, plain Polly. Polly without pretty gaudy shoes. Polly like a paper bag when the lollies are gone. Like a muddy old shirt that's been dropped in a hot wash and all its colours have run.

Her arms prickled, but she gave her glass to Santa anyhow and bent to her sandals. She slipped the straps away from her heels and straightened again, stepping backwards while Santa reached out an elbow to steady her.

She stood barefoot.

"There. Say something."

Santa watched her silently, silver eyebrows raised. She had time to notice that the band was packing up, the waiters were clearing the glasses, and most of the guests had gone home. Mr Streck didn't seem to be anywhere, and Caroline — well, that might be Caroline, that shadow inside a shadow at the far end of the hall.

Polly had time to wait and wonder whether fate could be, if not avoided, then at least detained and held in a headlock until the time felt right to confront it.

She had time even to wonder where her mother was, what patch of Europe had most felt like home in the end.

"And," Santa began after that long, long pause. "What exactly would you like to hear, Polly from the mailroom?"

Polly stared. "What…?"

Santa gazed back at her in bemusement.

"I said—" he began.

"Yes," Polly interrupted. "I heard you. I heard every word."

Santa chuckled. "Oh! Is that so strange?"

"You have no idea how," Polly breathed. "Say something else."

"Anything in particular?" Santa replied. "A limerick? A sonnet? Some rhyming couplets from Pope? I hope not, because I don't know any. I could tell you a joke. Have you heard the one about the talking horse? Perhaps it will resonate."

"No," she said. "I haven't. Tell me."

So he told her the one about the talking horse. And the one about the polar bear that goes to a bar, the one about the drunk on the bus, and the one about the woman and *that* Freudian slip. He told her every joke he remembered, and when he ran out, he made some up with much apology and laughter.

They had to sit eventually, because Santa claimed — in a clear and even tone — that his feet were well and truly killing him in those new sandals he'd bought.

"You know what I mean?" he asked, sitting down hard and rubbing his ankles.

"Not really," Polly smiled.

She sat with her chin in her hands, one bare foot curled under her, sandals forgotten beside her chair. They talked until the sun glazed the tops of the hall's arched windows. Once, Caroline drifted over and leaned across Santa's shoulders like a piece of bent black wicker, proclaiming she was tired, and going home, and if anyone needed a lift they'd better speak up now.

Polly smiled, trying to hide her disappointment. She almost rose to go but Santa held up his hand to stay her. He said that though the reindeer had the night off, he could still offer her the use of his sleigh — provided she didn't mind that it was actually an old, red hatchback with some decisive rust along its frame.

She didn't mind at all, of course.

That whole ride home she spent with her head turned sideways, gazing at him, and he, in turn, pretended not to notice. In front of her building, he returned her look with a cheerful smile.

"So I guess you have lists to check," she said.

"Twice," he winked.

"And then there'll be stockings to fill."

"Indubitably!"

"And will I be on your list this year?"

"Well, hmm, you have been very, very good, Polly from the mailoom. I'll see what I can do."

"You know where to find me, then."

"I will likely need to return so my memory doesn't fail me," he smiled.

"Tomorrow?"

"At the very least!"

"Are you really, really old?"

"Impossibly."

Polly didn't mind. She liked impossible things.

She exited the car and watched it skim along the street, barely touching, until it rounded a corner and was gone.

Then she climbed the stairs all the way to bed, shoes still in hand. Her windows buzzed and rattled with the noise of the train station below.

To Polly Daley, right at that time, it sounded for all the world like a skidding jazz beat.

The Razor Salesman

"Can't tempt you?" he asks. He holds open a small port filled with shining razors. They rest on folds of blue velvet lining. Single blades, men's razors for shaving, women's razors. Even razors for children, made all of bright plastic with softened edges which are plastic, too. Can't cut yourself on those.

"What would I want with razors?" Ellen replies.

The razor salesman doesn't say anything. His skin is grey like overchewed gum. His trousers are perfectly pressed, a high, neat ridge ironed straight down the front. The sun is setting behind him, painting a golden outline across his neck and smooth, round face. He is wearing a grey suit and black shoes, and the sun wraps gold foil around his shoulders and sides. Beside his left shoe is another briefcase. A larger one. Why does he need so many razors?

"Who buys all these?" Ellen asks.

The razor salesman is smiling with a thin, lipless mouth.

"People like you," he says, but he doesn't elaborate.

Ellen decides she doesn't like him. She can make that kind of decision very quickly. But it's a shame he's not selling something else, something she could use. Home delivered, and everything. What a waste.

She shakes her head and shuts the door firmly. Turns back inside and sighs. The house is a mess again and the boys are shouting upstairs. Bloodcurdling shouts, like maybe they're being murdered. Ellen waits for the silence of a successful homicide, but it doesn't come. *I guess they're still alive, then*, she thinks. Not without humour.

The washing machine bangs against the laundry wall. Probably tearing all the clothes to ribbons. She goes to the kitchen, twisting her hair into a bun. She only keeps it long so she can do this. And she only dyes it so she can keep it long. She's not ready for short, grey hair just yet.

The grocery bags are sprawled across the far bench, intestinal in white plastic. She misses brown paper bags, even though she barely remembers them. There's something poetic about paper. She fixes a fast dinner, exactly enough for three; she's not feeding that rotten little Andy from next door again. It's not her fault if his mother isn't much chop.

"Boys!" she shouts, sliding grilled chicken onto plates. "Dinner!" There's rice with bits of defrosted vegetables and a few leaves of lettuce. "Dinner," she tells herself, dividing it up evenly. Ellen, a grown woman, eats only as much as a ten year old boy. It's enough.

She drops the plates on the table as she passes through the dining room to the stairs.

"Boys!" she calls again.

She stomps up the stairs, kicking her shoes into her own room. Of course the boys are playing video games with Andy.

"Isn't it time you went home, Andy?" she asks firmly.

"No, Mrs Croydon," Andy answers, as sweet as caramel sauce.

"I think it is," says Ellen, feeling nauseous. She often does, with Andy around.

He gets up without another word, just as Ellen is thinking of saying, "not another word, Andy". He turns to Ellen and for a moment, he is faceless. A blank space fills his head. Ellen backs away instinctively, gripping the door edge behind her. It's only an illusion. The sun is setting behind him and the room's dark with only the video screen glaring blue. Andy is smiling sadly, the weight of the world on his little shoulders. Ellen suddenly feels sorry for him.

"Geez, Mum," says Karl, getting up stiffly from the floor. He's ten and too old for his mother. He gestures to Matty, who is two years younger and still accommodating.

The four of them plod downstairs, Ellen in the rear. She notices that the boys look as tired as she feels.

"Andy was a bit quiet today," she says to Karl as they sit in the dining room.

"He's cut up about not making the softball team," Karl tells her.

Cut up, thinks Ellen, that's a funny thing for a little boy to say, but she doesn't tell Karl she thinks he's a little boy.

It's only well after dinner, after the plates are in the dishwasher and the last of the shopping is shifted from plastic intestine to wood panelled cupboard, that Chess starts barking. Ellen realises she's forgotten to feed him. She tips canned mush into his bowl, but he ignores it. He's barking at the locked back door. Just to be sure, Ellen goes through the house shutting and locking all the windows. She goes to bed with a torch and a meat cleaver, for reassurance, and listens to the house groaning.

The next day is an instant replay of the last. Breakfast bowls left in the sink (at least they made it that far), hurry to work, rush through work, home again at sunset. There's the knock at the front door. Ellen isn't at all surprised to find the razor salesman on her doorstep, briefcase in his arms, the last of the afternoon light glinting wetly from his razors.

"Good day for it," he says. "Can't tempt you?"

Ellen hesitates. The razors, lit up by the gold sunset, look almost like jewellery. They are very clean. She wants to slide her fingers over the glossy edges. She doesn't even think that it will hurt. She's reaching out, towards the case the pulpy salesman holds, and she's not even scared. The salesman is perfectly still, waiting.

There's a bump from behind and Chess appears, sticking his long wet snout past her legs. He sniffs appreciatively at the salesman and the briefcase by his left foot. Then he grins, the white patches across his eyes all innocence. Ellen snaps out of her daze.

"No, thank you," she says. She grabs Chess by the collar with one hand and tries to shut the door. Chess is a heavier dog than that, and Ellen needs both arms and her full body weight to drag him back out of the way. He slides across the polished floor, toenails clattering. Ellen pushes the door shut with her knee.

Razors. What would she want with razors?

She makes sausages and mash from yesterday's shopping and calls, "Boys!" then "Andy!" automatically. "Time to go home!"

Karl and Matty come down the stairs almost straight away. Unlike them, she thinks, and she's glad.

"Andy's not here, Mum," says Karl, rolling his eyes.

"Oh." Ellen pauses, a plate in each hand. "Where is he, then?"

"Don't know," says Karl. "Wasn't at school today, either."

"He wasn't?" Ellen puts the plates in front of her uninterested sons, who shrug. "Hmm. Perhaps I should go and see his mother. Check if he's all right."

She thinks: *I could also ask if she's being visited by that weird salesman with the razors.* But with the washing up and then the vacuuming and Chess barking — this time at the rumbles from the drier — she doesn't.

It's nearly a week since she last saw Andy, and Ellen is in the supermarket again. Can't seem to keep food in the house for any period longer than five days. She doesn't know how her mother ever managed, only going to the supermarket fortnightly. She sees someone else's mother in aisle eight. *Sally's? No. That's Dan's mother.* Ellen nods hello, but she doesn't want to interrupt. Dan's mother is talking to someone in an urgent whisper, hand partially covering her mouth. *What, is she worried about lip readers?*

When she sees Ellen, Dan's mother says, "Oh!" with great authority and gestures her over.

"Ellen, isn't it?" she asks. "This is Jayne. We were just talking about poor little Andy. Isn't it sad?"

"Andy?" asks Ellen. She wants to pretend she knows what this woman is talking about — she hates to be caught out — but it's too late. The fear is already in her voice. "What is it?"

Jayne answers. Ellen knows this type. Gossip is like ambrosia to them. "Mel was just telling me about how poor little Andy died yesterday. His lungs, the doctors say."

"Yes," Mel, Dan's mother, continues, "he suffocated. He's dead."

"Oh my — goodness," says Ellen. "Andy!"

The other women nod, flooded with superstitious relief. It hadn't happened to their children.

"Such a nice boy," says Mel.

"Yes," says Jayne. Then adds, eagerly, "I don't know how a perfectly healthy little boy can just suffocate like that!" The women exchange glances.

"They say it took days for him to finally … you know … pass," says Mel. "Poor little thing — must have been quite painful."

Jayne says, "I'm not implying anything, of course, but … well, what're his parents like?"

They look to Ellen, but she shrugs.

"To be honest, I've never met Andy's parents." She finds she can't stop using his name. She wants to call him "poor Andy", over and over again.

Jayne and Mel are nodding wisely.

"Just as I thought," says Mel. "Kept to herself, did she? Cut herself off from everyone? They do, you know."

"Well…" says Ellen. She looks away. She wouldn't know what Andy's mother did.

Ellen buys hot dogs and thin buns. She hugs her children tightly when she gets home and they flop in her arms like rag dolls.

"Guys," she says, "have you heard what's happened to Andy?"

They shrug listlessly.

"Yeah," says Matty. "He was in hospital for three days. That's what Jeffrey says."

"And he died," adds Karl.

"He suffocated for days and days, and then he died," says Matt.

Ellen nods and tries to find words to say. She can't. The hotdog skins have split, but she wraps them in buns anyway. They eat on the lounge room floor, watching TV. The boys don't play video games that night. Ellen keeps sneaking glances at the front door, but the razor salesman doesn't come back. She wishes he would. She needs another grown-up right now.

Poor Andy, she thinks.

Ellen goes to sleep and dreams of frozen soldiers.

"Daze and daze," they tell her. "Daisy days."

The razor salesman doesn't come the next day. Or the day after that. Ellen waits each evening near the door. Her trips to the supermarket become shorter, the door to the laundry stays closed to hold in the sounds of the rattling machines. She doesn't want to miss the knock at the front door.

He leaves her waiting for a week.

When he returns, it's midday and Ellen is still at home. That morning when she went to wake the boys she found their breathing shallow, their eyes swollen. She tried to drag them out of bed, but they slid to the floor, yawning. She couldn't get them to school. She worried what an ambulance would cost her, so she maintained careful vigil with the car keys in her hand.

"Good day for it," the razor salesman smiles.

If he notices Ellen's breathlessness or the fear in her grip on the door, he doesn't show it. She is struck all over again with how clean he is, how neat his suit is. How — she realises, looking closely — he has absolutely no facial hair whatsoever. Not even eyebrows. She moves onto the step with him until she is pressing right up against the open briefcase. To her right, Andy's house stands empty. A bright yellow and red "For Sale" sign stands straight-backed on the front lawn.

"Good day for what?" Ellen asks. It's rude to stare, but she stares anyway, looking for something in his face. She's not sure what.

"Can't tempt you?" he asks.

Ellen finds him repulsive, this close up. She's careful not to touch him.

"What would I use razors for?" she asks, meaning, *what do I need to do? What's coming?*

The razors are slices of red sunset in their velvet lining. They look like children lined up asleep on a wide bed. There are, she thinks, enough razors there for all the children in the neighbourhood. She thinks of Andy, suffocating for daisy days.

The razor salesman doesn't say anything. He only smiles, his face like vanilla pudding.

Ellen stares at the razors. They're meaner-looking than she remembers. More effective. Cutthroats and switchblades dot the velvet pockets. She hesitates.

"Is this all you have?" she asks. *Is this enough?* she thinks.

The salesman's smile broadens. He nods approval, closing the case and placing it by his right foot. Then he picks up the other case, the one that has sat silently on his left side through every visit. It's almost a suitcase, she notices. He turns it so the handle is pointing towards Ellen. Then he draws open the top, very carefully, like lifting the lid on an antique grand piano. The sun is behind the horizon, so the salesman has to angle the case into what's left of the light.

Inside are knives as long as Ellen's forearm. Cane knives and scythes. Some taper to fine points, and some are shorn off straight across the top. The light swims along them as the salesman subtly shifts the case. There are no blemishes, no tarnishes, no smudges from where someone might have touched them. Ellen's fingers itch.

"This one might meet your needs," says the salesman. He lifts a meaty hand to point, balancing the case in an elbow. He's indicating a long blade with a jagged edge like a saw, but finer. It has a thin, sharp point. Ellen reaches for it with both hands. The metal is cold, and in the shadow of the salesman's body, it looks like it's been carved from solid oil.

"It's very dark," says Ellen.

"Perfect," says the salesman, "for your needs."

Ellen traces the handle of the knife with a fingernail. It's sharp like needles, and there are grooves where her fingers might fit.

"Try the grip," the salesman smiles.

Ellen picks it up. He's right. It is perfect. Her hand was made for it. The balance and weight guide the blade almost without any effort from her. She experiments, manoeuvring the knife out to her right so she doesn't cut either herself or the salesman.

Then holding the knife up between them, she asks, "How much?"

The salesman's expression doesn't change.

"What's it worth to you?" he asks.

Everything, she thinks, everything I have. But she knows better than to say that to a salesman. She keeps a poker face. She's not some easy sell.

She reaches into her pocket. In her hand are the car keys, so she holds them out to him. The salesman nods, half-shrugs. It's enough. She drops the keys into the slot where the knife was.

"Congratulations on your fine purchase," says the salesman. He picks up both cases. "Good luck."

"Wait," Ellen says, licking her lips. "What…?" She wonders how to phrase it. "What are the instructions?"

The salesman points at her with a corner of the smallest briefcase.

"You've got all you need, madam," he says. He may mean the knife, but Ellen thinks perhaps he means else. Perhaps he means her.

He carries both cases to the edge of the sidewalk and turns left, not looking back. He doesn't take the car — not yet, anyhow.

Ellen shuts the door and locks it soundly with one hand. She goes to the bottom of the stairs and listens. The boys are silent. She creeps up the steps, cradling the knife almost like a child. It's dark up there. She flips on the light and the knife gleams dully. Its handle is dark brown and perfectly smooth. She can't believe it's been made. It's so perfect she thinks it must have been grown, the way she was grown. Grown to fit each other.

She finds Matty and Karl on the floor in Karl's room. Chess is stretched out beside them. He's the only one who looks up as she comes into the room. He thumps his tail on the floor and seems to smile. Ellen sits beside him and rubs his head a moment with her free hand before looking at her boys.

Matt is stretched out on his stomach in front of her. She pushes him over by the shoulder, holding the knife high, pointed at the ceiling. There are thin, silver strands like spider web over Matt's face, covering his mouth and nose. She can even see the puncture marks where the thread breaks the soft skin of his cheeks. Some of the strings have grown quite thick. They must have been there a good while. Strange she never noticed them before. But then, she thinks wryly, we're all a little strange.

Having the knife in her hand is making everything clear. She pulls away as much of the thread as she can with her fingers. It's strong and sticks to her like fairy floss. Her nails are full of the stuff and she can't use that hand anymore. She has to lower the knife carefully to Matt's face and squeeze the pointed tip between his skin and the white strands. She saws lightly and with a snap, the strands break. One by one she cuts them, threading them back through his skin. There's no bleeding. The operation is very smooth.

When all the strands are cut, she drags them off his cheeks and bundles into a clammy ball in her lap. The knife, she notices, stays clean. Nothing sticks to it. It's warm against her skin, almost like a handshake.

Matt sighs deeply but doesn't wake up, not even when she's finished. She bends close to him and checks his face, all baby fat and innocence. There are no more signs of the threads or the holes in his cheeks. She smooths his forehead with the back of her knuckles and he frowns in his sleep.

On Karl's face she finds only some small white tufts like mushrooms sprouting from his pores. They haven't grown into a web yet. She rubs them away with her thumb. Karl opens his eyes groggily and smiles. She grins and ruffles his hair, like she did when he was little.

"Still little," she whispers, but Karl is asleep again and doesn't hear.

Ellen's legs have stiffened up, and she limps to her room with the bundle of thread in her hands, the knife hanging between her fingers. Behind her, Chess whines. He wants to keep her company, but won't be parted from the boys. Ellen shuts her door and sits cross-legged on the floor. She lays the sticky bundle down and slices it like an onion. The knife rocks against the floorboards as she mushes the thread into paste.

By breakfast time, it's pooled across the centre of her room. It's harmless now, not sticky anymore, and it falls through her fingers like dust. She's not sure whether to fetch the mop or the vacuum, but decides on the latter. The house is too quiet, and the mechanical clatter of the vacuum's motor will do her good.

"There," she says when's she's finished. It's done.

She wraps the knife in a cardigan then unwraps it again to make sure it hasn't sliced the thick wool. It hasn't. She hesitates about where to put it, but it's not the kind of thing you put in a drawer, and so she places it carefully in the top of her closet. Like a rifle, she thinks, you have to keep it out of the reach of children. She practices for a while pulling it out and putting it away again. She might need it in a hurry next time.

With the room cleaned and the knife put away, there is a moment where she feels … something. Different. She feels — she realises — comforted.

The sun is warming her windows and she hasn't even called in sick today. Someone has to be here for the boys when they wake. She takes a breath. Perhaps she should use this day to make ready for the rest of the week. Fix lunches, iron shirts, straighten shoes. But instead, she goes back to Karl's room and steps over the sprawled Chess. He growls softly in his sleep.

The boys have both crawled onto Karl's bed and lie in a diamond shape, heads apart but toes together. They're sleeping normally, and their eyelids twitch as they wrestle with dreams. Squares of bright sunlight keep brushing their faces from where the curtain flaps. Ellen goes to shut the window. She's never really looked out this window before. From here, she can see nearly half the street. Her neighbours' houses are shut up tight. It's a school day, after all.

The razor salesman has returned. Ellen takes a breath, but he isn't coming to her door. He's across the street at Mrs Reid's house. She didn't realise Mrs Reid had children, but perhaps there is a new baby. Ellen, after all, hasn't been keeping up.

Mrs Reid is young and tired looking. She seems almost frightened, but she's looking at the knives. *Go on*, thinks Ellen. *Go on.* But Mrs Reid shakes her head. She shuts the door and the salesman turns away. There is no change in his expression as he carries the two briefcases back along the path to the street.

Poor — what's her name? — Laura? Poor Laura's going to need some help, Ellen realises. She settles beside Karl on the edge of the mattress. In a moment, when the boys wake up, she'll take them across the street. Perhaps she'll bring some biscuits and also some tea for the grown-ups. Then she and Laura Reid will sit in her lounge room. They'll talk about babies and pick-me-ups and all the household things. And then Ellen can tell her just what to do when the razor salesman calls around again.

The Dying Light

Anu fell, twisted his ankle, fell again and kept falling. He rolled, grabbed at the ground and came away with handfuls of dirt. The mountain known as Old Man was steepest here. His face slammed against rocks and he swallowed gravel trying to scream. Earth and sky were both black and impossible to keep apart in his mind.

His ankle snagged a sapling and he roared, spinning so that he fell head-first over a precipice into deeper night. One hand shot out for the sapling and found it in the dark, gripped it hard so that he swung in space.

The grit in his mouth tasted of blood. He tried to spit it out, dribbling it onto his chin instead. Carefully he took a breath, afraid the air in his lungs would make him too heavy for the sapling. His heart beat in his ears, and his face was hot and numb though the air on his bare skin was cold. His arms had hollowed out from shoulder to fingertip and his fingers had grown fat. Too fat, he was sure, to hold on.

His mother would be angry. She would say he was careless, that just because he hadn't found the story of his dying in the stars yet, still it didn't mean his dying couldn't find him. She would call him foolhardy.

"Until you have the foretelling," she would say, "and can see what is held for you by the constellations above your foolish head, you should be careful."

What would she know? Anu had grown old enough for doubts but not for certainties. Just old enough to distrust his mother's advice. Not old enough, so he'd thought, for death.

"Help me! Please. *Please.*"

He was crying, and embarrassed by it. The emptiness in his limbs had been replaced by an ache. Above him, the constellation known as the Sickle gleamed, its five points as familiar to him as his own skin. He counted its stars over and over, trying to ignore the trembling in his elbows, trying to hold on until help arrived.

"Onetwothreefourfive, onetwo…"

Something had changed. There was a sixth star now, its light strengthening as he watched. And then he realised something. His entire life, he'd been looking at the Sickle wrong, because surely that sixth star told a different story. He knew what it was. He knew what he had found.

The foretelling.

This was it, this was the thing he'd searched for before he'd even known to search. Everything in the sky and under it began to make a new sense.

The Sickle blurred and danced and between it and him appeared the face of the Messenger. Just like his mother had promised. He almost laughed in recognition. He let this new knowledge fill him up and it was like he took those stars and put them inside himself and he was warm. He was whole. He had found it. He had found his dying.

He let go of the branch and fell.

Do you think that Father's really blind?
I heard he went blind from grief.
I heard he's faking.

"Today in class, Nisi found her dying at last. Everyone was pleased for her because her foretelling showed that she would have a long life. Time enough for children and for grandchildren, they said. Maybe even great-grandchildren."

"Her family must be pleased." The old man beat out a soft rhythm on the ground with his palm, his sightless eyes fixed on the empty air.

They sat in the shade of an outcrop in front of a cave, on the side of the Old Man. He was sprawled so his feet alone were in the sun, and now and then he'd rub his toes against each other, or along his insteps. He was bare except for a cloth wrapped around the tops of his legs. The girl was bare too, since she was young, and she sat beside his knee with her legs drawn up beneath her, careful not to touch him.

"Yes, everyone is happy," she said. "Nisi says it makes her very marriageable."

The old man laughed deep in his throat. He rubbed brown dirt across his shinbone and nodded, his toothless smile swinging this way and that.

"Very marriageable, yes. Nisi must be eight now, yes? Time enough for marriage and children, I should think."

His cackle turned to silence and after a while, Shobe asked, "Did you ever find your dying, Father?"

He wasn't her father, but the term was one of respect and he nodded acceptance. Shobe edged closer in return, and looked to where his fingers folded over one knee. Father was very old, and his skin was soft and thin. Even his hands were soft. Blindness had saved him from hard work. The rest of the tribe didn't particularly resent him for that, but nor did they love him, and perhaps it was this that had driven him to move to the far side of the mountain and out of their sight.

"Never did, no, never saw it. Not even when I had eyes that worked. But," he sighed, scratched at his neck, leaving ochre streaks, "I was young when I was blinded. Same sickness that took my sight took my mother's life, did you know? They say when she saw her dying at last — because she was very old, and already with another child in her womb — that she went to the valley and wept tears enough for a lake, and her tears were pure, not made of salt. That valley is where Lake Begoan sits now." He nodded, his head loose on his neck. "Imagine their surprise, when they went to look for her and found an entire lake! Now the lake has fish. Animals come to drink. Her grief feeds the whole tribe."

Shobe hesitated. This story opened many questions in her mind, but she was careful not to irritate the Father, so she tried to ask just one.

"Do you remember what it's like? I mean, to see? To see anything; not just your death, but anything. Do you…"

Her voice dried up. She wanted to ask if he remembered colours and trees and whether he knew the kinds of animals that came to the lake. She wanted to know whether he understood any of these things himself, or whether all his knowledge had become only words given him by others. She imagined him asking, "what is a devil?" and someone explaining it, describing the thick neck and heavy teeth, and describing the colour grey. Recounting how it would slurp water under its whiskers. She wondered how the devil would look when the storyteller was done, whether it held together in the Father's mind. Or whether there would always be gaps when he thought about a devil, like gaps between symbols marked on the walls of a cave, the devil no weightier than the marking that meant it.

But she resisted asking, because this Father was called Frail, and his bones were thin like reeds beneath skin that sagged and hung loose. His belly protruded like a fat thumb, and his chest, almost concave, rested on top.

His hands lay at his groin like abandoned cups now, the skin partly translucent as if he were made of muddy water. She almost wanted to check his neck for a pulse, but couldn't bring herself to touch him. She feared the coolness of his skin and the sourness of his old man's breath. He stirred then, straightening his back and sighing.

"I remember…" he began, as if no time had passed at all. "I remember the moon and my mother. I remember someone — her, perhaps — teaching me the constellations that lie in the darkness over our heads." He raised his hand and made the shape of an arrow with his fingers, pointing to the sky. "She taught me the Sickle and the Horned Bull. She taught me winged Oberon and the Nascent Triplets, their hands reaching across the horizon. She tried to help me find my foretelling, but I never saw my dying, not once. It wasn't my time, and then the virus caught me up. No one could see that coming for me. My mother saw her dying and she understood how the loss of a mother would affect a child. In the end, I'm not sure which loss she felt worse, hers or mine."

His hand fell back to the ground, slack skin by his armpit trembling. "I kept my blindness from her. I was young, but already I knew that without the use of my eyes I could never follow the lessons. Still she asked whether I'd found my foretelling. And because she wanted that so much, I told her yes, I'd seen my dying. She asked me to tell her the story of it and I lied and said I would have a long life. Or, I thought I lied. In the end it has turned out to be true."

Shobe was still, because it seemed there was more to be told.

"In the mind's eye she is no more than a shadow," he said. "But bright like light. I try to catch her face and there is only white. Like the moon."

Shobe watched the afternoon light stretch the shadows of Father's feet. Soon it was evening. Father couldn't see the world with his eyes, but he must have sensed it with his skin. When the time was right he said, "Off you go to class," and she went.

I guess the telling helps.
I guess. Maybe it helps you feel like you own it.
Why would you want to own it?

Nisi was there, and Teka, Gef, all the others. Mama Teacher had already started the lesson and didn't acknowledge Shobe's tardiness, not with a glance or a movement. She did the same when Fe arrived even later. Fe made a point of going to the front and sitting at Mama's feet, staring up at her, almost daring Mama to say something. Fe's long hair (nut brown by daylight, but now dark like deep waters) hung to her waist, and when she bent herself almost into a ball her hair brushed the ground.

Shobe sat at the back. She was restless, like always, and couldn't focus on the lessons.

"Now," said Mama Teacher. "There are two ways to eat. The found way, like ours: what is hunted, what is discovered on land, in water or air, that is ours to eat. But there is also the made way: what is grown and kept and built and counted. Those that follow this way say it is earned or owned."

"Kept on purpose?" asked Gef.

Mama nodded. She was sitting in what they called the beehive, though it had never held bees. It was a dirty brown bubble big enough for half a dozen grown-ups to climb inside. It had twin holes like staring eyes, and Mama was sitting in the one on the right, her feet dangling just above the ground. The eyes went all the way through the beehive and out the other side, and inside were soft, rotten shapes that looked almost a little human. Mama called these "seats", but she didn't sit on them because sharp coils stood out like twisted teeth.

"But how can both those ways be equal?" Nisi asked. She leant back on her hands and stuck her feet out in front of her, crossing her ankles and rolling them from side to side. She tossed her hair off her shoulders — though it was nowhere near as beautiful as Fe's — and smiled conspiratorially around her, meeting the gaze of no one in particular. She at once commanded attention and despised it.

Yesterday, Nisi had been merely vain. But now she'd found her foretelling, she was also smug. Shobe wrapped her arms around her knees and hid her sneer behind her legs. She felt bad for her negative thoughts, but also right. She tried to tell herself that Nisi deserved to know her story, that perhaps she'd been studying the stars for hours every night, but she didn't believe it. Nisi wasn't patient and meditative the way the children were schooled to be when searching the constellations. The foretelling had come to her unearned.

"Why must they be equal?" Mama asked.

This was her way of teaching, this questioning and reflecting. It was said that when Mama Teacher was little, her parents had called her a nag. She had found her place, though. Surely everyone did eventually.

Nisi had shrugged as if the question were beneath her and trained her gaze on her toes, ignoring Mama.

Fe said, "Because both are ownership. Finding and making."

Mama Teacher nodded thoughtfully. "Perhaps, yes," she said, still not looking at Fe. "Our way is to exist side by side with things. The plant or animal gives what it is able, and so we have. We take what is available. The animal or plant is not beneath us." (Here Shobe noticed a meaningful glance at Nisi.) "But to some people and in some ages, things had to bend to your will. They had to be controllable. A thing was *made* to give. That is what ownership meant. In some ages, even people could be owned."

"By who?" This from Gef.

"Other people."

Mama Teacher didn't correct him and tell him to say, "by whom", but Shobe was sure she thought it, just as Shobe herself did. Gef would learn in time, if he listened hard enough to what others said, and no doubt Mama Teacher trusted this tradition of learning to correct him on such a minor point.

Still, Shobe was pleased she knew better. At the same time, she wondered what worlds of knowledge were still out there for her, what she didn't know and hadn't thought to guess. Sometimes this way of learning frightened her for all it must be leaving out. It made her afraid to open her mouth, in case others found what she didn't yet hold in her mind.

"Why would people want to own people?" Gef again. In the moonlight his skin was oil-blue and he sat on ground only a little darker than himself. He had a body wrap that went from his neck to the tops of his thighs and seemed almost fluid. Only the outline of his arm beside his waist gave him shape.

Fe turned to Gef and said, "So you can make other people do your work, so you can rest and they can bring you food as if you were a baby and they were your mother."

"Very good, Fe," Mama Teacher said, and smiled, the blue-whites of her eyes squeezing up.

Shobe couldn't see Fe's face, but no doubt she smiled, too, at this blessing from Mama.

Teka, who was the youngest though not the smallest, said then, "The days and nights when they owned people, were they the same as the age of machinery?"

"They overlap, yes, and perhaps one fed the other," said Mama. "Once the idea of owning machinery was born, perhaps they concluded plants, animals and also people could be owned. Or perhaps it was their attempts at owning people that made them build machinery."

"Perhaps people can't be owned very well, and so machines were made because they could be better owned," Gef offered.

"Machines would be more compliant," Nisi said.

The others looked about in confusion, and waited for Mama to add to this.

"Yes, machines were probably more compliant than people. If machines worked now, perhaps we would know this, but as we see..."

Here, Mama gestured around her at the beehive.

"The car," said Teka.

"Good, the car. It's said it moved, though it has no legs with which to do so. See?" Mama leaned forward and looked between her feet, brushing the long grass aside so the children could see there were indeed no legs.

Deborah Biancotti

Under the eyes of the car were two long shapes, hard, like pared branches. The branches were dark red-brown in the daylight, and left flakes and smears of colour on the children's hands if they touched them. They rested on square piles of sand-coloured blocks, which crumbled and left no colour. They had discussed the possibilities of the car many times, and none had come up with an answer as to how the car could move on those branches and blocks. Perhaps one day someone would be born with sight enough to discover the secrets of the car.

Shobe leant back and rested on her straight arms. She looked up at the stars, at their blinking, shrugging indifference, and wanted, almost, to plead with them to show her what kind of dying to expect so she could begin to prepare herself. It was said by some that when the stars told stories it was like music, sweet sounds like streams made of amber; and some stars had voices like birds, except richer. Shobe wasn't sure she believed these stories, though Nisi tried to make out that she'd heard every one herself. For Shobe, as always, the stars were silent.

Teka broke the quiet when she said, "What's 'compliant'?"

What do you see?
Nothing. Darkness.
Darkness isn't nothing.

The discussion wound through many subjects that night. Mama told them about agriculture, and how it was possible to own water (though how could you control water? Shobe couldn't understand that; water would go where it wanted). She talked about art that was made and kept and some people said what could be art and what couldn't, and where it could be kept and who could keep it. Shobe grew bored of such fanciful stuff and anyway, why was it important? What did those ages have to do with anything now?

When finally Mama called for quiet time a few hours before dawn, all the children were grateful to lie back and study the constellations. Shobe focussed on Wind Caller, which seemed to hang over just her, accusing her with its long pointed beak. She glared back, almost daring it to come down and take her. Frail Father had told her one day a particular constellation might call to her, and that it might be this very one that would eventually reveal the secrets of her dying, but the sky was so busy with constellations that all any of it did was confuse her.

Closer to dawn, Mama said, "Perhaps we have time for one story. Who would like to tell?"

Nisi was cross-legged and leaning forward, but when Mama finished speaking, she straightened up with a sly smile and said, "I could tell you about the night I found my dying."

Some of Shobe's classmates rolled their eyes, the whites flashing like falling stars. Mama laughed. They were all good-humoured though, and Shobe had to hide her face so they wouldn't see the scowl there.

"Nisi," said Mama. "That was only yesterday. Are you sure it is a story worth telling already?"

But Nisi nodded and got to her knees. "It is a story now, and my mother says it will be a better story with each telling."

Mama Teacher grinned and nodded. "She's very smart, your mother. Perhaps it is never too soon to tell your story."

"It would be better with fire," said Teka.

"Next time, when we have a fire, Nisi will tell it then, too, and it will be better," Mama agreed. "But tonight we will also listen to the story as it is. Begin when you're ready, Nisi."

Nisi cleared her throat, the way a real grown-up might, and began.

They say knowing your death means you can quit worrying and settle into having a good life.

But what if it's not a good death?

Nisi's Story

It was a day and a night like any other. My mother, Mama Home, had been gathering corn and wildseeds. We were coming along the track that goes to and from the river and, as we came along the top of the mountain, I saw Frail Father's feet sticking out into the sun. His feet are darker than the rest of him, so I always know it's him when I see his dark feet and his paler legs. And also he is the only one to ever sit there, of course.

Seeing Frail Father, so old, always makes me wonder at his dying. So I asked Mama to tell the story of the first time she'd found her dying. So she told me again, though I've heard it many times. And though I was behind her and the wind whipped away some of her words and left gaps in her telling, I knew the story well enough that I could fit the gaps with words from my own memory.

She said it was a day and night like any other for her, too, and she was a young woman, older than me, when she first saw it. She looked to the constellation of Small Bears like she did each night, and there it was: a new star between the paws of the third and fifth bears, paler than all the rest. And above the ears of the fourth bear was a star that had been there forever, but had always seemed wrong. Like it was lost. Suddenly it made sense.

Mama Home said, "I realised why it had felt wrong, why I had wanted to erase it from the sky for messing up the Small Bears. It was because that pattern was my dying, and it told me my death would be painful and long. I didn't like the message. Perhaps that's why it took so many years to see it."

Mama Home cautioned me that I may take a long time to find my own dying, too, and that I mustn't fret that the constellations were not always compliant.

"Is it better not to know, Mama?" I asked her.

"No, it is always better to know, because then you don't waste time trying to find out. You don't bother trying to rush your death, or to avoid it. You're able to move towards acceptance. It's just that sometimes knowing isn't good, either, and acceptance is difficult."

I asked if her death was at least a long way off, and though she always said yes, this time the wind pulled her answer away from me, and I saw her bow her head towards the wildseeds in her hands. Her shoulders slumped and I didn't ask again.

That very night we had fresh water and corn cooked on coals in the ground and while we ate I looked up at the Silver Gryphon and saw it. I understood that pattern was just for me and I had found my story at last, as it appears in the stars. It was my foretelling. It said my death was many, many years away and it was a good death and perhaps it was so far away that my children and children's children would live long enough to see it.

I rushed to tell my parents. Papa Home was pleased for me and told me I could choose any husband I wanted with a story like that, it was such a happy future. Mama hugged me and when she thought I wasn't looking, she wiped away tears.

My home parents are very happy to be bonded, though I wonder sometimes what it took for my father to choose my mother when her death is known to be such a difficult one.

So, when you're older, do you become more afraid of death, or less?

"Did you see the Messenger?" Teka asked.

"Stupid," said Gef. "You only see the Messenger when you're really dying."

Mama Teacher broke in, "Thankyou, Nisi. That is an accomplished story."

"Mama," said Fe. "Has anyone ever lied about their death?"

"Of course some have tried. One, Falla, tried to conceal her early death and choose a man with a good foretelling, but in the end her guilt drove her to grief and she drowned herself in Lake Begoan rather than face him again."

"Did she see her drowning in the stars? Why couldn't she avoid it?"

"Avoidance won't take it away," Mama said quietly. "When she was ready, Falla followed her constellation to the lake. No one thought to go after her, because they believed her death was a long way off. It was only when she didn't return that night they realised her falsity and they were very angry she'd lied."

The children were quiet.

"So you see," said Mama. "No matter what choices you make or what plans you think you can control, there is one story in the sky for each of us. It is why we use the found way. Because we accept we can't control what's most important in life. We can't control our dying."

Shobe pressed her lips together and rocked on her heels, avoiding

Mama's eye. She hated this passivity. She wanted to know why nobody raged against their deaths, why they didn't fight and scream out at the inevitability, hanging like a precipice in front of each one of them. But she said nothing. Once before she'd asked Mama Teacher these questions, but Mama had merely replied that it was only those who had not yet found their dying who could feel such fear and make such arguments.

"Once recognition is reached, acceptance is the only possible course," Mama had said then. Just like she was saying now. "It is the found way."

Nisi was asking, "What do you think will happen to Father Frail?"

Mama paused. Nobody had said it out loud, but Shobe knew they were all wondering if, being sightless, somehow he would avoid death altogether. He had lived a long time, longer than anyone else in the tribe. Perhaps it was possible that he would go on living, forgotten by the stars, his death lying unseen and unused somewhere in the sky.

"Some say," Mama began carefully, "that the real story of dying lies not in the constellations, but in our selves, and it is just that the stars release this inner sight. If this is the case, then perhaps Father Frail knows more than we realise."

Some of the children sniggered at this, since many people believed that if Father Frail was a burden, he must also be a fool. Mama cut them off, saying, "If you can't see the purpose in another, it may be because you lack purpose yourself. Each of us has the power to help others. But I think that's a story for another time. Good night, children."

Shobe ran from the class back towards the mountain. On the way, she realised what it was that had been nagging at her during the entire lesson.

Anu.

He hadn't been in class for two nights.

Why lie? Everyone will know eventually. There is nothing more honest than death.

Desperation. Arrogance, maybe.

Don't those words both mean "fear"?

The next day, Frail Father was in his place, his toes curled around each other in the sun. He seemed to be staring out at where the boys were playing catch at the foot of the mountain, but of course he couldn't see that far, and it is only because Shobe's eyesight was so young that she could make out the children with any level of detail. She looked back at the father and wondered what went on behind the grey-whites of his eyes.

He turned at the sound of her light steps on the path.

"Did your mother give you any food to bring?" he asked.

Shobe shook her head. "Sorry."

"Ah, it's you. Never mind," his eyes crinkled good-naturedly, but Shobe was ashamed. It was true, she never brought anything with her.

She took a seat silently at his knees and watched the children's game. Some of the girls had joined in now, and they were all intent on throwing a small, white object to each other. From this distance it was difficult to make out what the object was, but its size and colour suggested the skull of a small animal. They were covered in dirt and scratches, but they had broad grins across their faces and each one of them squealed in terror and delight when the skull was nearly dropped.

Beside her, Father Frail appeared to be dozing, listing sideways on one arm, mouth slack against his shoulder. She wasn't sure why she chose to be here instead of with the other children, except that she felt sorry for him. No one else was interested in his stories any more and he received little company.

When he stirred at last, bending his elbow as if in pain and shaking the sleep from his opaque eyes, Shobe asked, "Do you stay awake nights and sleep days, like the rest of us?"

Father chuckled. "I wake and sleep when I want," he said. "Night, day is nothing to me. Hardly any difference, except night is cooler. But what I see and think is the same at any time."

It was a strange idea, that night and day could be so similar, when at night all the world of stories lay in the sky above their heads, to be blotted out by the dawn. Father rubbed at his elbow, wincing. His breath rattled while he did it and he sought to correct it by coughing. He wiped his mouth and sighed, leaning back against the rock of the Old Man.

Shobe found herself wondering again whether he really had outlived his death. She didn't like to watch his labour with life. She wanted to pass on Mama Teacher's lesson, that he could look inside himself for the sight denied him in life, but somehow it seemed disrespectful to play teacher to a man so old.

She'd grown protective of him. The other children mocked him and called him a skinny good-for-nothing. He was only skinny because he couldn't fetch for himself. They should see it as a sign of their own shame that they didn't feed and keep him better. But many adults said this was not the found way, to fetch and carry for someone else. You were meant to rely on yourself, what you could find and bring.

Shobe's thoughts went around and around in her head. Father startled her when he asked, "How are your lessons?"

"Last night," she began, speaking quickly to cover her embarrassment, "we discussed ownership and agriculture, and Nisi told the story of her foretelling."

Father cackled. "Already? She's keen. She'll be a good storyteller."

"Why did you never become a teacher, Father? You know many stories, and then people…"

She trailed off. She'd been about to say people wouldn't dislike him so much if he could give something back, but she knew there was something wrong with the thought.

"People…?" Father asked, but didn't press her for an answer. "People learn when they are ready, and it is easier to be ready when you find a teacher you respect. Many people are not ready to respect a blind man. Which is your teacher now, Mother or Father?"

"Mama. Mother, I mean."

Father Frail nodded. "That's fine." He was silent again, his dry feet rasping against each other.

The children playing catch had wandered close to the precipice and were looking down. Shobe knew they felt safe, because these ones had all already found their foretellings. They thought they were invincible.

"Their parents should teach them about injury," Shobe murmured, not meaning to say it out loud.

"I'm sure they do," Father said, though he couldn't know what she meant. "And about responsibility. To the group, to the families. They should know not to cause grief, and that grief can come from hurt as well as death."

Father Frail must be speaking generally, she decided, but her attention was on the children below. They were pointing down the mountain, and a nervous energy worked through them. She wished they would move back from the edge, but the biggest boy leaned out even further. He rested on a bent sapling, tipping over the precipice until a friend grabbed his shoulder and pulled him back. One of the girls raced away toward the gathering plain, leaving the others holding onto each other and staring down the mountain.

"Not long now, then," Father Frail said.

Shobe tensed. "For what?"

"For Weki," Father said, and was silent again. Eventually he began to snore.

Shobe didn't ask who Weki was.

The girl had brought Papa Gorge back with her. He looked over the edge just once, then he too turned and ran, seeking more help. Anxiety prickled Shobe's skin, pulling her ribs in tight. She stayed in the cave, waiting for Papa Gorge, waiting out the sun.

Gorge returned with two others. Mama Temple had brought reeds tied into rope. They walked a way around the precipice, then tied the reeds to Gorge and lowered him slowly down the mountain. Papa Able and Mama Temple held the ropes and shouted at the children to stay away from the edge if they knew what was good for them.

When Gorge returned he had a long, dark bundle with him. Mama Temple reached out and, as they transferred the bundle between them, Shobe realised what it was.

Anu. His skin blackened, his head lolling. He looked as though he'd been burned. Dark sooty smudges covered his skin. Even from here she could see his mouth hung open and his eyes were closed. Mama Temple gathered his body to her, pulling his head against her neck as if comforting him.

Shobe leaned against the smooth wall of the cave, unable to look away from the small procession below. They walked slowly. Next they would have to return the boy to his family, and clearly they didn't want to meet that moment. The tribe would be gathering for evening meal by now, but there would be little eating done that night. All deaths were determined, but not all deaths were easy to accept.

Papa Able ushered the children before him, allowing them to cling to his arms. They kept their eyes on Mama Temple, on Anu, his face buried against her neck. Mama kept one hand on the back of Anu's head and she seemed to be consoling him.

Shobe watched the figures retreating, taking their time. When they were nearly out of sight, she stood and silently left the cave, following them. She didn't want to be part of what would happen next, but to avoid it would be selfish. She should be there to bear witness with the others.

As she picked her way down the slope, she reflected that she'd known nothing much about Anu except his name. He was like many of the younger children, always throwing themselves at the edge of things, thinking their deaths were lifetimes away. She wondered if Anu had been lucky enough to find his dying before the end. She wondered if Father Frail had known about him, whether he'd been able to hear the boy cry out and if he had, whether he'd gone to help, or had wanted to help but hadn't been able to reach over the edge of that precipice, being blind.

Just before she reached the gathering place she remembered who Weki was. Home Mother to Nisi. And Anu.

Do you really think that, for all their searching, some people simply never find their stories?

No. No, I don't think that. Do you?

Weki was feeding kindling to the cooking fire when they reached her, but even the crackle of the flames seemed to dim when she looked up and saw what they carried.

"My son," she said into the silence, and her voice held the kind of certainty that comes from waiting just one moment too long. "My son."

The tinder fell from her lap as she rose and stepped forward. Straight into the fire.

Those gathered nearby were slow to react, their gazes fixed on the returning group. Possibly it was the smell of burning skin that woke them. Only Father Lakeside had presence of mind enough to turn to

Weki and, seeing her already within the circle of fire, to reach for her arm. Weki twisted away from him and tipped forward, falling further into the flames. Kindling snapped beneath her as she hit the ground, but her eyes never left her son's body.

At first she seemed to feel nothing. She got to her knees and the flames licked along her back to her hair, lifting and curling it as if she would be carried away on its fiery strands. She tried to shake the flames off, reaching a hand to her forehead absently. She seemed lost. Then her eyes locked with Shobe's, standing apart from the rest of the group. Her vision cleared and she began to scream.

Shobe stepped back involuntarily, stuffing her hands against her own mouth to stifle a cry.

Weki strove to stand, but the logs beneath her rolled. She stumbled and this time when she fell she snapped her forearm on the rocks bordering the fire.

The others were immobile, even Father Lakeside. Fire was a power they had stolen from the sky. They were afraid and ashamed of it. The only one to move at last was Weki's husband, Lito. He picked up a log and hit her so that she was pushed beyond the edge of the flames and as he did so, he shouted to match her screams, tears spilling from his eyes.

Weki rolled, clutching at her arm, screaming and burning still. No one helped her. No one knew how. When she stopped moving she was burned from head to toe and her long hair was ash around her. Her voice had fallen to a croak.

They took her home and lay her on a mat, where her skin swelled and oozed and stuck to the floor. She spoke no more words after that, and they weren't sure whether it was the fire or grief that closed her throat.

Nisi crouched by, wrapped in her father's arms, tears dripping from her chin. Her crying drowned out the condolences of the neighbours. Mama Teacher stood at the opening to the cave, some of the students pressed against her. No effort was made to protect them from the knowledge that this was one of Death's many faces. It was believed that no child was too young for this lesson.

Weki hadn't even died yet, but Shobe could hear people discussing the funeral. She didn't like this too-public dying. She wanted to scream at everyone to get out of the way and leave the grief to the family, but she was always silent in crowds. The habit had become as strong as stone.

Most people had left by the time Nisi's sobs gave way and she whispered, "Mama never told me it was to happen already."

Already.

Living with all this dying, thought Shobe, was like dying already.

And then she knew.

The knowledge drilled into her spine and into her knees. She ran all the way back to Father Frail's place on the side of the Old Man and there was a hollowness in her ears and forehead. Frail's blank eyes were focused keenly on the space by the front of the cave where she came to rest. He'd been waiting.

She was sobbing, furious, wiping fiercely at the tears on her face.

"I thought I couldn't live with not knowing, but Father, I can't live with knowing," she shouted.

Father Frail said gently, "What is it you know, child?"

"I know why I have never found my dying in the stars, why the sky seemed so busy with so very many stories, and none of them made any sense. It is because my death is everywhere *already*. There is nothing in the world for me but my dying."

With no death to find outside herself, Shobe had looked within and seen that this was the only answer, the only possible way forward.

Unthinkingly, she edged closer to Father Frail and put a hand to his arm. She was surprised to touch him at last. His skin was dry and cool and she could feel it just as if she were alive. Father patted her hand and smiled, his eyes not quite meeting hers.

"Father," she said. "I have already started my dying."

She glared, willing him to prove her wrong, to give her some other explanation for this, this *thing*, this terrible, awful injustice she'd found.

He was still stroking her hand, tracing patterns on the back of her palm.

"Give me your telling, child."

Shobe was self-conscious. Her story was grotesque and unfair and speaking it would only confirm that. She wanted to resist, but the words came out of her like heat.

"It was a day and a night like any other. My own Mama Home said I was too young yet, much too young to find my dying in the stars. She said, when you're ready, you'll be able to see. She said there was no point staring, that the stars weren't even out yet and if I stared too much in the sun I'd go blind like that boy with the virus. That boy…" here she paused and looked at Father Frail and saw, for the first time, something other than his age. Saw the story of his life in the pores of his skin.

Father Frail chuckled, a dry, rasping sound.

"Are you only as young as all that, child?"

Shobe continued. "Mama said it wasn't a virus that blinded him — you, Father — it was all the searching he did, hunting for his foretelling amongst the constellations when he was much too young. This is the found way, she said, to learn patience and to wait until a thing is given. She said all that seeking and not finding had sent him mad, and all he could do was sit and talk to ghosts, and that's why people were afraid of him. Why he spent much of his time alone on the far side of the Old Man."

"Did you stop searching?"

"No."

"Of course."

"I didn't stop; I wanted to know. Mama Teacher — I mean, the Mama Teacher I had before my dying, because it was a Mama Teacher then, too — said it is given to some to always seek. I was proud she thought that of me, that I had a place, and I wanted to prove I was ready, that I was grown-up enough. I was bored with children's things. So I was staring at the sky as the evening star appeared. And I knew, that day, that this was my star. That my death was clean and immediate. Not even a pattern. Just one star. It was so bright and big I thought it would eat up the whole world. It seemed to explode and I thought at first the forest had turned to fire. I stood up so I could run and warn the others, because I was afraid the evening star would kill all of them that day, every one. But when I tried to take a step, my legs buckled and I realised that the fire was in my heart. I knew what the star was saying, that my heart had burst already."

Shobe took a breath to steady herself, "Somehow it feels as though it was the very act of seeing my death that caused it, Father. It's so strange, to see it and feel it at once."

Tears were still rolling down her cheeks and she found that strange, too, that she could cry yet.

"Dying is hard work, child, but we all find our way eventually."

Father Frail lay back against the rocks and rested his head, his chin pointing to the ceiling of the cave. He sighed.

"Father, if I've been passing through my dying all this time, does it mean that you are the Messenger? The one sent to guide us at the moment of death?"

Father's voice was whisper-thin. "Have I been your guide, child? Strange to think that, when all this time you have been mine. I suppose…"

But he was silent. Shobe found the truth inside herself. She said to him, closing his lids against his bare eyes, "I suppose," she continued, "we all guide each other, Father. The Messenger is not one of us; it is all of us."

Do the stars ever lie?

Does it matter, once the story is told?

This Time, Longing

Belle wasn't prepared for brave strong daughters. When they arrived — solemn-eyed and hair the colour of dark earth — she looked about for a gift for each of them. She gave them everything.

She named them Hero, Spirit, and Dare.

"Mamma, are you ready?"

It was Dare, her proud face tilted to the side, glancing from under long eyelashes. Belle thought Dare had the strongest jaw, the easiest laugh of them all.

"Ready for what?"

"Mamma…" she scolded. "For the funeral, Mamma."

"Oh yes, oh yes," said Belle. "Whose funeral, darling?"

"Mamma…"

It came out like a moan. Dare, her mother realised, looked almost pale except for the circles under her eyes. Her shoulders hunched, her chest was concave, her hands hung limply by her side.

"Spirit's funeral," Dare said, her voice an echo of what it used to be.

Oh.

Belle cried as she stood up and she cried as they led her to the car and she cried all the way through the service. So much so she couldn't remember it later and had to ask, "did they play the song Spirit asked for?" and "were the flowers yellow?"

There was no earth left to lay Spirit in. The pockmarked world, bristling with its human dead, had run out of room.

So Spirit was cremated and her ashes given to her sisters for safe-keeping.

"What shall we do with them, Mamma?" Hero asked.

Hero's hair had darkened over the years, then lightened again as it faded to grey. Belle reached out and smoothed a strand of it behind her firstborn's ear.

"We could spread them across the community garden," said Hero.

"No," soothed Belle.

"The public garden—"

"No," Belle said.

It wasn't enough. Not some market garden where peas and dry tomatoes ran higgledy piggledy across stakes in the ground. It wasn't the right thing to do for the unbreakable resolve that had been her daughter's trademark.

"What about the ocean?" Dare asked.

"The ocean is a long way away," Hero argued.

She wrapped her hair around her fist and pinned it to the back of her head, then fanned herself with both hands.

"It will take two weeks there and back."

There wasn't much that took them outside into the desert heat, but funerals were one of them.

"You think it's too far to go for Spirit?" Belle asked.

Hero was quiet. Her reddened eyes matched the red funeral shirt she wore.

"Of course not," Hero said, "not for me, Mamma. But for you?"

Belle knew she was old and her brain was turning to honeycomb. Sometimes she thought the gaps and losses outweighed the substance holding her together.

Hero's question hadn't been cruel, it had been careful. Belle wasn't sure she could make the journey. She only knew she had to try, drag her old bones all the way to the ocean and back, if she could.

It was Thurs, the day of departure. She'd written reminder notes and left them in each room of the house. Thurs. She couldn't afford to forget. She packed a small fraction of her belongings in a bag, ordered and secured her home.

Then she picked up the plain brown box that managed to enclose everything left of Spirit. And she waited.

Dare had paid the eldest teenager in the building, Seen, to carry Belle's small bag of belongings twenty storeys to the ground.

But Seen had done better than that. He'd swapped out her impractical suitcase for a backpack, and after lifting it over his shoulder and loping down the stairs, he stood waiting at the bottom to tie it onto her old-woman's frame.

Belle tried to thank him, but his desert-brown face merely nodded and he was gone back into the shade of the building before the morning sun could burn him. It was just past dawn.

There was no easy way to get to the ocean. They would have to walk. They would use the underground tunnels that used to supply water. When there used to be water.

"Are you ready, Mamma?"

"Yes."

Belle allowed Dare to take her arm.

The tunnel entrance was a rough-hewn spout, its cover awkwardly affixed with two lengths of wood, hammered over the top like handlebars.

"Where's Hero?" Belle asked. "She remembered it was Thurs, didn't she?"

"Of course, Mamma! She's on her way," Dare assured her.

She was right. Hero was there not long after. The two tall sisters — the two remaining sisters — took up position either side of their mother. *Bookends*, Belle thought. *Sentinels*.

Belle looked back like she was leaving something important behind. Neither of her daughters did the same, though they had family and work and other engagements waiting for them. Perhaps because they were sure they were coming home again.

"You first, Mamma."

They descended into the dark, into the spout via a ladder that rocked under their weight.

In the gloom Belle could just make out the human traffic that flowed in two directions. She could smell the human life, the familiar mustiness of unwashed clothes and hair.

She stepped over people lying across the curve of the pipe floor. Sleeping, she assumed, though she couldn't be sure. Their bodies lay as if abandoned, arms flung either side or hooked almost carelessly under their heads.

"They must be travelling a long way," Belle observed.

"They live here, Mamma," said Hero.

"Here?"

Here was surely an impossible place to live, even for the desperate, what with the throng of people coming and going.

"They have to be somewhere, out of the heat," Hero said.

She was the practical one.

The pipe was cool except for the times they passed under more spouts. They could feel the heat even metres away, pressing on their fronts as they neared and pushing on their backs as they passed.

Hardly any of their fellow travellers looked up as they walked. They focussed on their feet or the passage they were making, on the sleeping bodies beneath them. Some carried walking sticks, but the pipe allowed little room for elbows and so it was best to walk with your hands wrapped in the straps of your backpack, or your arms pinned to your sides. Belle learned this quickly. She thought she might remember more from her first journey — how to cope with the relentless movement forward, how to relax into her stride — but this time all of that was lost.

When the heat of the day made even the deepest parts of the pipe difficult, they stopped for their siesta, making a space amongst the bodies of their fellow travellers. Belle's two long daughters lay so their shoulders and legs followed the circumference of the pipe, heads slightly higher than their feet. They opened a tin of floury root vegetables and shared it between themselves while other travellers stepped over and between them.

Belle curled between her daughters and affected sleep. She was too exhausted to join in their conversation. She was too exhausted even for sleep. Her body ached in complaint.

She tried equally to remember and not remember pieces of her past. Mostly, she tried not to remember Spirit. Instead she challenged herself to remember all the names of her wedding guests and what they'd worn and what they'd brought to eat. What they'd carried along this pipe on that other journey to the ocean. And she remembered Guess, her husband, tall like their daughters would be, quiet and affable like them, too.

"I think I'm losing my mind," said Hero.

"Why?" Dare asked.

In the tunnel their voices were hollow, a whispered rush above the buzz of conversations from other travellers.

"I can't remember things the way I used to."

Dare said, "So? Do you need to remember things?"

"I used to be able to remember every birthday present I'd ever received, and every trip to the market—"

"You mean, when you were a kid you could remember that," said Dare. "There's been a lot more market trips and birthdays since then. A lot more to remember."

"I can't even remember the last one," Hero hesitated. "Do you think I'm getting old?"

Dare shifted her weight against Belle's side.

"I think it's been a bad year," Dare sighed. "Since Spirit became sick, I can't remember anything else either. Don't be hard on yourself."

Dare, the compassionate one.

"Ready to keep going, Mamma?"

"Of course."

Belle scrunched over to one side, out of the way of the human traffic, and rubbed the sweat off her neck and face with the hem of her dress. It was harder getting her pack back on, though, even with her daughters' help. It felt heavier, and Belle's bones felt softer, and though she refused to let anyone else carry it, she wished she didn't have to carry it herself.

She tried to keep the pain out of her face, but tears still sprang to her eyes.

They walked for three more days before they ran out of food, then rested in the pipe until after nightfall. Several strangers waited with them, making conversation about their own journeys. Where they had come from, where they hoped they were going, how the day had been for their feet and bones.

When they ascended from the spout they found themselves in the middle of a carnival. The streets either side were lined with stalls. Vendors sold clay pots of aromatic food and rolls of cloth in bright colours like desert flowers. Dancers moved in clockwork lines and the air stank of humanity.

Belle shrunk back from the noise.

"Come on!" said Dare.

Belle thought she might lose herself in the crush and never find her way back, never be able to move either backward or forward. Always stuck in this foreign place with her dead daughter on her back.

But Hero stayed protectively at her mother's side.

Dare was at the stall with the brightest cloth, wrapping a piece of magenta around her chest, spinning into the colour with a smile.

"Take that off!" Hero shouted. "Take that off or we'll never find you."

Heeding Hero, Dare unrolled herself and let the merchant fold it back onto his table.

It was true. In their mundane desert-white the sisters were impossible to miss in the crowd. But dancing in local multi-coloured cloth, Dare was almost lost to them.

Belle felt a stitch in her heart like braided grief and guilt. How could she stop one daughter from dancing? How could she lose a daughter and live?

Dare paused fell into step on the other side of her mother without question. She wound strips of turquoise cloth around her brown forearms.

"What did that cost?" Hero asked.

"Never you mind!"

When they'd found some food they recognised and a comfortable place to sit, Belle stayed put. She rubbed her gnarled hands over the aches in her knees and thighs.

Belle's elbow was snagged by an errant hand.

"Read your palm, Lady?"

Belle looked from the hand to its owner, a small, lean gypsy figure. She couldn't tell if it was a man or a woman. Age had wiped that evidence from its voice and from its face. Black tattoos swirled along its cheeks. On the chin, an image like a layered tongue.

Belle tried to shrug off its advance.

"Grief in how you lean," said the figure, pointing. "Like you've lost something important. Someone."

Belle hesitated, until the figure said, "No cost to you tonight, sister."

She held out her hand, palm up. The gypsy traced the line of Belle's life backwards.

"Here, you have said goodbye. And here," the figure pointed. "When you first made this trip, it was with joy. A marriage? This time—"

"How many more?" Belle cut in.

Meaning, how many more goodbyes, how many more losses did she have, how many more times was she meant to endure?

The gypsy said, "Just enough."

"For what?"

She could feel a prickling sensation like her insides were peach skin.

"Enough to know how much you've gained."

"That's not good enough," she said.

The gypsy just shrugged. "Some make their peace with it."

It's a shame, Belle reflected, that when the taking happens the giving is most-ways done.

They were in the pipe for three more days and then up again, into a much quieter place where food was harder to find. Belle's belly growled, but it wasn't the worst of her pain. She had a limp in her left leg and bruises along her ribs and hips where the pack hit.

Two more days and they could hear the whisper-pulse of a heartbeat.

"It's the waves," said Hero, and she was right.

The crowd of travellers they had moved in was near gone, very few choosing to come this close to the edge of the world.

The pipe ran straight for the last eight miles and a hot wind pushed at them. Hero abandoned her place in back to act as wind block for her mother.

Belle peered around her daughters to spy the tunnel's end. Not a spout, but an open mouth pointing at the roar and rush of the inhospitable ocean.

When they reached the end, they clung to the pipe's rim to avoid being blown away. Like madwomen, Belle reflected, the three of them, the remaining three, skirts flapping behind them and hair streaming out in all directions.

She pulled herself out and jumped from the pipe's mouth onto sand that was hard and flat, compressed by centuries of wind. She fell and twisted her ankle. Then Dare and Hero were beside her, hauling her up and trying to protect her from the sting of wind-blown sand.

"I'm fine," she said. "No harm done."

They turned their backs on the ocean first, dwarfed by its noise. When they had the courage to look over their shoulders, the wind was so strong they were forced to cover their faces with their hands and peer between their fingers.

The ocean was still a mile away.

Even this water, Belle thought, this salty, useless, groaning water, was smaller than it used to be.

"How are we going to scatter her ashes here?" Hero asked.

Belle shed bitter tears that trailed down her cheeks. The wind fought her for them while she wiped her face and pushed the salty water back into her mouth so she didn't lose it.

Belle hurt all over, and it wasn't just from the two weeks in the tunnel. It was a pain that went through and through.

The first time, the first trip, the ocean hadn't been as grey and the wind not as fierce. That time there was yearning and hope, a young couple, a whole life ahead of them. This time yearning and loss, a lifetime of it, and the two of them had been lost, and she didn't recognize herself most days.

Hero had her arms around her mother. She said, "We'll go to the edge of the water, Mamma, and we'll stand with our backs to the wind."

It was so brief a time, Belle thought. You're born and you're dumb about everything, the world, how to live in it. Then you grow and get smart and raise children and watch them get smart. And then it's all backwards again, to feeling small and stupid.

They walked side-on to the ocean, sand stinging every exposed piece of skin and pummelling their skirts. Their hands were to their faces, their packs were left behind them, and just the small wooden box, wedged under Belle's arm, signified the missing woman.

Spirit had been the tallest of them, the most naive, the centrifuge of their family.

Belle wasn't sure how long it took them to reach the water, where it rocked on the edge of the world. The waves rolled and slapped, rolled and slapped, drawing back like a serpent and snaking suddenly forward, fangs slicing down into the hard sand.

Up and back, then *whoosh*, *smash*, *hiss* into the beach.

"Now, Mamma?" asked Dare.

All this time, Belle thought. All this time and no time at all.

She looked at Dare, whose lips were pressed together and cheeks puffed out. Like a little girl, Belle thought, and saw Dare suddenly at her fifth birthday party, suffering her older sisters to count the candles and make sure the numbers were okay. "Asking "now" and "now"," waiting for Belle to give permission to blow out the candles.

"Now," Belle confirmed.

With their backs to the ocean, Belle slid open the top of the wooden box.

"Shouldn't we say something?" Hero asked.

"Say something, if you want," Belle said.

But the wind was already rushing into the space under the lid, pulled out a trail of ash and whipping it out in front of them in a cloud that rose above the tunnel and disappeared into the metal sky.

Spirit was away.

The wind pulled and pulled at her missing daughter, spreading her soul, her body, her substance into the world, filling the world with her.

"Goodbye," Belle whispered. She said it again, "Goodbye, goodbye, goodbye."

Trying to get them all out of the way.

She wanted to tell her daughters not to take it on, not to try to live. It was too heartbreaking. But it was too late. It had always been too late. Hero was pregnant with the first of the next generation, and Dare was soon to be married.

When the wind slowed down she pulled the lid right off the wooden box and held it out and up, willing her daughter to rest in the sky of the restless world.

And when nothing more would come out at all, she sat on the hard sand with the waves at her back. She watched the world from the edges, and her daughters sat with her.

The sun rose behind the cloud. Dulled, it was a cataract, a blind unrecognizable glare. Belle scooped fistfuls of grey-white sand into the box. Then she waded into the ocean through the rocky waves and cupped salty water into the box, too. Not enough to wash away the sand that had replaced her daughter. Not enough for that, but enough to damp it down into the edges. Ocean water, salty and strong, with no other use but this.

"Think you can make the journey home, Mamma?"

Belle smiled. "Always."

It was the journey home that made the rest of life worthwhile, Belle thought. She could drag her old woman's body in that direction as many times as she had to. Though this time she carried the weight of memories, the bittersweet knowledge of the ones that wouldn't ever make the journey home again.

Afterword

Humanity had resolved the plague of mortality almost unintentionally.
Whole families survived genetic death sentences. Births were
uncontrollable. The population grew without restraint.
Life was abundant.
Life was cheap.

I started writing a post-apocalyptic story for *A Book of Endings*. It seemed the logical conclusion to the premise I'd built by choosing the title. But it became clear that the end-of-the-world story I had in mind was too large for a book of short stories. So I went back to the personal apocalypse of stories like "This Time, Longing" and "Diamond Shell" — fitting partners for previous stories such as "Number Three Raw Place" and "The Dying Light".

Originally I went for a more generic, less ambitious title than *A Book of Endings*. Something with personal resonance, like *Not a Novel*. Or something reflective and frankly awkward like *Trajectories of Time and Light*.

But *A Book of Endings* received the most reaction from my test audience, so I stuck with it — ultimately wondering just how much I'd backed myself into a corner. *A Book of Endings* started off as an ironic play on the history of criticism for my story endings — some too understated or confusing for audiences to feel comfortable with, some too slight. This ruled out a couple of personal favourites (though I won't tell you which ones), but did make relevant a few stories that hadn't made it onto award or favourite lists so far. "Life's Work", written after my grandmother's death, joined the collection. "The Razor Salesman", a survival story, made the cut. And in fact these two stories probably underpin the themes that most obsess me: death and work, physical death and soul-death, loss and determination. And rage.

I heard once that three out of four readers are or want to be writers, so I'm going to assume that when I say "work" you already know I don't just mean the work you do in your day job. That's only part of the equation. There's also writing work (frequently underpaid or unpaid), housework, family work (working on relationships), self-work (called Self Help in bookshops), volunteer work. And then the work that means "success". Edison said, "I have not failed. I've just found 10,000 ways that don't work."

"I work," we say when talking about how we spend most of our days. "It works," we announce about our processes, our lawnmowers, our ideas.

Work is that contradictory state that appears to underpin all of human life. "Find a job you love and you'll never work a day in your life," goes the quote (apparently from Confucious). Yet if you asked someone to tell you the opposite of the word "play", what would they come up with?

"Work is the curse of the drinking classes," observed Oscar Wilde.

Work — any work — will still consume hours of your day even as it's feeding your soul (and hopefully your bank account). This is life: trying to balance the practical needs for things like shelter and food (via that most practical medium of all — money) with the needs to rise above those things through beauty, faith, meaning, belief, achievement, effectiveness.

"The work-life battle" one recent tourism campaign called it. And of course, today's media carries messages about the impossibility of that balance, the insane modern misapprehension that we can "have it all".

This is the schism underpinning stories like "King of All and the Metal Sentinel", "The Tailor of Time" and even "Coming up for Air": work and self, duty and self-actualisation. Whereas stories such as "Silicon Cast", "Hush" and "The First and Final Game" examine the monstrous in our work.

Life versus work is the theme of 'Stealing Free", "Watertight Lies" and "Problems of Light and Dark". And life itself is the subject of

"Summa Seltzer Missive", "Six Suicides", "The Dying Light", "Stone by Stone" and "Seven Ages of the Protagonist".

I've been called a horror writer, dark fantasy writer, urban fantasy writer, steampunk writer, young adult writer, though in describing myself I've often fallen short. Nowadays I usually refer to the format — "short story writer" — than the content. I'm hoping one day to drop the prefix entirely and just be a writer. But since most writers I know have this aim, and most of us never achieve it, I'm not betting the silverware on it. I figure I'll continue simply to look for work worth doing, and doing it, and making that into a sustaining lifestyle.

Flaubert said, "Be regular and orderly in your life so that you may be violent and original in your work."

Here's hoping you get those words the right way round in your own life — and work.

Bibliography

Diamond Shell
A Book of Endings, Twelfth Planet Press, Alisa Krasnostein and Ben Payne eds., 2009

Hush
A Book of Endings, Twelfth Planet Press, Alisa Krasnostein and Ben Payne eds., 2009

Coming up for Air
A Book of Endings, Twelfth Planet Press, Alisa Krasnostein and Ben Payne eds., 2009

Six Suicides
A Book of Endings, Twelfth Planet Press, Alisa Krasnostein and Ben Payne eds., 2009

Problems of Light and Dark
A Book of Endings, Twelfth Planet Press, Alisa Krasnostein and Ben Payne eds., 2009

This Time, Longing
A Book of Endings, Twelfth Planet Press, Alisa Krasnostein and Ben Payne eds., 2009

Seven Ages of the Protagonist
Scary Food, Agog! Press, Cat Sparks ed., 2008

Pale Dark Soldier
Midnight Echo, AHWA, Kirstyn McDermitt and Ian Mond eds., 2008
Aurealis Award shortlist Best Horror Short Story 2008

The Tailor of Time
Clockwork Phoenix, Norilana Books, Mike Allen ed., 2008
Reprinted at *Steampunk Workshop*
Aurealis Award shortlist Best Young Adult Short Story 2008

Watertight Lies
2012, Twelfth Planet Press, Alisa Krasnostein and Ben Payne eds., 2008
Honourable Mention, The Year's Best Science Fiction Twenty-Sixth Annual
Collection, Gardner Dozois (ed.), 2009

The Dying Light
Eidolon 1, Eidolon Books, Jeremy Byrne and Jonathan Strahan eds., 2006
Aurealis Award shortlist Best Young Adult Short Story 2006
Australian Shadows Awards shortlist

Stealing Free
Agog! Ripping Reads, Agog! Press, Cat Sparks ed., 2006
Podcast coodest blog
Honourable Mention, The Year's Best Fantasy and Horror, Ellen Datlow and
Kelly Link and Gavin Grant eds., 2007

Summa Seltzer Missive
Ticonderoga Online #6, Dec-05, Russell B. Farr, Liz Grzyb and Lyn Battersby
eds., 2005
Ditmar Award shortlist Best Short Story 2005

Number 3 Raw Place
Agog! Smashing Stories, Agog! Press, Cat Sparks ed., 2004
Published The Year's Best Australian SF and Fantasy #1(September 2005), Bill
Congreve and Michelle Marquardt eds., 2005
Ditmar Award shortlist Best Short Story 2004
Honourable Mention Years Best Fantasy and Horror 18, ed. Ellen Datlow et al.,
2005

Stone by Stone
Southern Blood, Sandglass Enterprises, Bill Congreve, ed., 2003
shades Theatre production, Shadowmuse, producer Anita Whelan, performed
2009
Radio National Short Story Programme rights procured

The Distance Keeper
Borderlands #1, Borderlands Press, Borderlands Committee eds., 2003
Reprinted online at infinity plus
Honourable Mention Years Best Fantasy and Horror 17, Ellen Datlow, Kelly
Link, Gavin Grant, eds., 2004

The Razor Salesman
Ideomancer Unbound, Ideomancer, Chris Clarke and Mikal Trimm eds., 2002

Life's Work
Passing Strange, MirrorDanse Books, Bill Congreve ed., 2002

King of All and the Metal Sentinel
Agog! Fantastic Fiction, Agog! Press, Cat Sparks ed., 2002
Reprinted online at infinity plus
Ditmar Award winner Best Short Story 2002

Silicon Cast
Redsine 7, Garry Nurrish and Trent Jamieson eds., 2002
Honourable Mention Aurealis Award Best Horror Short Story 2002
Honourable Mention Years Best Fantasy and Horror 16, ed. Ellen Datlow and Terry Windling, 2003

The First and Final Game
Altair online, Robert Stephenson ed., 2000
Altair 6/7, Altair Press, Robert Stephenson ed., 2000
Aurealis Award winner Best Horror Short Story 2000
Ditmar Award shortlist Best Short Story 2000

ALSO FROM TWELFTH PLANET PRESS

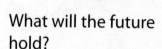

What will the future hold?

Eleven stories.

Eleven glimpses into possibility...

Where will the world be in four years time?

These Australian authors imagine the world as it might be, presenting unique possibilities for the very near future. Each story presents an original take on the imminent future of humanity. Each has something to say about who we are and who we might want to be. *2012* is both a call to imagine the future of the world, and a call to create it.

"Watertight Lies" by Deborah Biancotti
"Fleshy" by Tansy Rayner Roberts
"Oh, Russia" by Simon Brown
"Soft Viscosity" by David Conyers
"Apocalypse Now" by Lucy Sussex
"The Last Word" by Dirk Flinthart
"Ghost Jail" by Kaaron Warren
"Love You Like Water" by Angela Slatter
"Skinsongs" by Martin Livings
"David Bowie" by Ben Peek
"Oblivion" by Sean McMullen

Coming soon from the Twelfth Planet Press Novella series...

Horn

by Peter M. Ball

There's a dead girl in a dumpster and a unicorn on the loose – and no-one knows how bad that combination can get better than Miriam Aster. What starts as a consulting job for City Homicide quickly becomes a tangled knot of unexpected questions, and working out the link between the dead girl and the unicorn will draw Aster back into the world of the exiled fey she thought she'd left behind ten years ago. All in all, Miriam Aster isn't happy. The last time she worked a case like this it cost her a badge, a partner, and her life.

This time things are going to get much, much worse.

www.twelfthplanetpress.com